THE ORDER OF THE LUCIFUGE

BOOK ONE:

ANTILLIA

PETER HAMMARBERG

Cover design: Robert Paul Nixon
robertpaulnixon.com

DEDICATION

This book is dedicated to:

_____

(Your name)

ACKNOWLEDGEMENTS

Thanks and bourbon-soaked apologies go to the following in no particular order:

Christina Hammarberg, for everything. Literally, EVERYTHING. Robert Hammarberg, Mom and Dad, for giving me the tools of imagination and story telling, Mom and Dad D'Airo for their love and support; housing and feeding me, and putting up with my crap. Robert Paul Nixon for his support, and for making this thing look badass, Angel Larcom, for her expertise, Eli Grimstead for allowing to use the coolest last name I've ever heard, and for her first-draft editing input. Tim Mucci, Dom Kreep, Shannon Cox, Justin Blaser, Myla Strange Nixon and MORBO for taking time to test-read and pelt me your honest input and encouragement. Emily Cappiello Dowalo for her undefeatable PR kung-fu, and to all my friends and family.

Rock over London
Rock on Antillia.

PER UMBRAS VENIUNT ILLUMINANDO.
(THROUGH SHADOWS COME ILLUMINATION.)

WITHOUT LIGHT, WE WOULD BE BLIND.
SO, TOO, IS SAID OF DARKNESS.

BALANCE.

ONE

BOSTON, MASSACHUSETTS
UNITED STATES
1897

"THE ORDER OF The Lucifuge," the man known only as Hargraves rattled through the fanged mask that covered the lower half of his face and neck like a *mengu*, "is a commitment that is total and never ending."

As he spoke, the light in The Order's North Atlantic headquarters dimmed and the goggle's red lenses seemed to flare.

No one knew what Hargraves looked like behind the red goggles over his eyes and the strange mask that obscured the lower portion of his face. Hargraves always dressed in a charcoal gray fedora and trench coat, underneath he wore a dark crimson leather *lorica plumata*. His wool slacks and leather shoes matched the coat impeccably. He truly held the appearance of a man out of his time. Whether regarded as folklore or bogeyman, Hargraves was a man of reputation. Many had trembled at his name and the calamity it invoked. His dominion over The Order of the Lucifuge was as absolute as it seemed timeless. Only one man had cause to question the administration:

Professor Alexander Copernicus Grimstead.

"My only cause to draw breath has been ripped from this world!" Grimstead roared. His words echoed in the vast meeting room, bouncing off the various artifacts and specimens collected from places—and ages—unknown to the common man. Creatures and creations lost in the currents of time and perception. He glared at Hargraves across the large round table where they stood. Hargraves bowed his head ever so slightly.

"The... loss... of Lilly Chambers-Grimstead has indeed been felt by us all," Hargraves grimly replied. "There are things in this world that must transpire, or else things far greater will never come to pass."

Grimstead slammed his fist on the table before advancing on his ominous leader, eyes stricken with rage. "Straighten your tongue, damn you! I'll have the truth even if I have to pry it from you with my own hands!"

It did not occur to Grimstead that he had been struck until he felt the impact of his body smashing into the vitrine used to store a large cyclops skull at the far end of the room. He quickly scrambled to his feet and immediately noted that his wire-rimmed spectacles had been displaced to his forehead. He secured them to their proper place, and discovered that the right lens was now cracked in several places. As Grimstead squinted, he saw that Hargraves remained standing at the head of the table. A slow throb started in his temples. As he steadied himself against the toppled vitrine, the shadows surrounding Hargraves appeared to deepen and swirl. *Devil*, he thought.

"You both disobeyed orders. Pity that your *wife* was the one killed. She had so much to offer The Order."

Grimstead dusted off his vest and slacks before approaching the meeting room door. His head throbbed harder now, but more with rage than with pain. He took his overcoat and flat cap from the wooden replica of Venus de Milo that served as a coat rack and paused at the threshold, shaking his head.

"There we have it. Truth from the mouth of the serpent. Curious, though... that the last words I hope to ever hear from your lips are those I share in equal regard." He pursed his own lips in a mock smile and slipped through the door, leaving Hargraves alone among the relics and shadows.

TWO

GREENPOINT, BROOKLYN
NEW YORK, UNITED STATES
1872

"AWEXANDER! SWOW DOWN!" Five-year-old Catherine Grimstead begged her older brother. He burst through the front door of their row house and vaulted down the flight of steps in a single leap. For the intrepid nine-and-a-half year old this was nothing courageous, but for little Catherine it was a wonder to behold.

"Awexander!" Catherine exclaimed as she slowly negotiated each steep step. Her brother spun on his heels with consternation.

"Catty! *Shhhhh!*" He put a finger to his lips. "You'll give us away and I cannot afford to get into trouble. *Again.*"

"Sowee." The girl lowered her head in shame. A mass of brown curls cascaded over her face and shoulders like a veil, obscuring her tiny round cheeks and quivering frown. Alexander sighed then bounded back up the steps to take her hand.

"Don't cry, Catty! Adventurers don't cry, do they?"

"No," she sniffled.

"And aren't we on a secret mission for the Adventure Guild?" Alexander puffed out his chest. Catherine's eyes widened as she mimicked her brother's pose.

"Yes! We're on an adventwer!"

Alexander picked her up around her waist and precariously wobbled down the steps. When they reached the bottom, he set her on her feet and they took off, running hand-in-hand down Kent Street, toward the East River. They ran past the newspaper boy, at his usual post, shouting about the death of Samuel F.B. Morse, the start of the Third Carlist War, and a young scientist named McParland who believed his dreams were actually messages from celestial beings. They paused briefly at the window of Mr. Lastovich's bakery, enticed by the scents wafting from the open doorway, and watched as he rolled and kneaded a mass of dough over and over in a methodical rhythm. Mr. Lastovich took notice of the faces pressed against his window and waved. Catherine exuberantly returned the gesture. Alexander tugged her away and they were on the run once more.

Over the last forty years, the waterside neighborhood of Greenpoint—the northernmost point in the borough—had steadily transformed from humble farmland into a bustling industrial center known for its oil refineries, shipbuilding and waterborne commerce. European immigrants flocked to the area, eager to gain a foothold in one of the biggest cities in America. These roads weren't paved with gold as the stories suggested, but they certainly held a dream or two.

Greenpoint was indeed a starting point for many, but to Alexander and Catherine, it was far more than that; Greenpoint was home. Generations of Grimsteads had lived there long before them. Greenpoint held the stories of their knight-errant grandfather, Benjamin Grimstead, who had famously answered the call to adventure since he was a boy. Be it exploring hidden temples, soldiering through secret wars, or tracking pesky ghost pirates looking for their lost treasure, he had done it all and lived to tell the tale. Grandfather's stories were colorful and fantastic, an integral part of the Grimstead family's oral history. To all but Benjamin's only son, Richard, anyhow. Richard Grimstead was a distinguished and sensible banker who believed that the past was exactly that: *the past.* There was nothing respectable, or profitable, about adventuring. Richard's eldest son, Otto, shared his views. The twelve-year-old chose to spend most of his waking hours holed up in a corner of the house reading about the great industrialists of the early nineteenth century. The last thing this young boy wanted to do was waste time being a young boy. His siblings, on the other hand, saw the world for its limitless possibilities. Life is magic when you cannot see the strings of burden.

Each step that brought Alexander and Catherine closer to the waterfront sent nervous excitement to their young hearts.

"There it is!" Alexander exclaimed.

At the water's edge stood Thomas Ratajczyk's shipyard, the official port of the Adventure Guild's New York chapter. Schooners of various shapes and sizes bobbed and tugged at their moorings along the dock. Colorful flags swayed and danced. Dock hands and crew members swapped hand-rolled cigarettes and stories in the mild April air. Across the road stood the chapter house, a renovated Masonic temple. Three stories of stoic gray stone and red brick. Over the large wooden door was the guild's official crest: two heraldic lions holding a flourished letter *A*.

The children were only a few paces from the chapter house, but the sight of a muscular, dark-skinned man caused them to freeze in their tracks. At the top of the wide marble steps leading up to the door stood Kunal, the Iron Indian of Bombay. He had once been a champion at bare-knuckle boxing, but chose to give that up for the fortune and glory of an adventurer's life. Until he took a bullet to the knee. Kunal never fully recovered from the wound and now acted as the

Guild's watchman. He was still extremely formidable, despite his limp, and few could match his penchant for pugilism. Kunal shifted his weight on his cane and patted his vest pockets. He produced a slim cigar and held a match to it. Swirls of smoke lifted past his coal eyes and danced toward the sky. Alexander quickly tugged Catherine into the alley that lay between the lodge and a fishing supply shop and prayed that they weren't spotted. He cautiously peeked around the corner. Kunal was still smoking and humming a tune that Alexander had never heard before.

"Looks like the front door is out of the question," he whispered, gesturing toward the back of the building. Carefully, they made their way down the alley, testing each of the small, rectangular basement windows until finding one near the rear of the building that wasn't locked. Alexander pushed against the top of the pane and it slowly creaked inward. The opening wasn't large enough for either of them to slip through, so Alexander set his body entirely against the window. It only budged another inch. Eager, Catherine jumped onto her brother's back, adding her own bit of weight such as it was, and the rusty window hinge broke, sending the two tumbling into a dark storage room. Catherine landed on top of a dress form which displayed an animal skin frock and a brightly painted jaguar skull. She grabbed the dress form and held tight as she rode it to the floor. On impact, she rolled—just like grandfather had taught her. When she rose to her feet, the skull was on her head. It covered her face completely. Catherine dusted off her navy blue dress and looked through the skull's eye sockets for her brother. The light from the window only illuminated a portion of the small room, it mingled with the dancing motes of dust they'd kicked up.

"Awexander?" A reply came in the form of tiny grumble that seemed to originate from beneath the window. Catherine carefully weaved through the discarded relics and bric-a-brac until she saw her brother in a tangle of elk horns. His jacket was punctured and shredded. She let out a sharp gasp and rushed to his side.

"Did I... die?" his little voice quivered. "I think I may have." Catherine patted his body for wounds, but quickly discovered that his outer-garment was the only victim.

"You're alright," she exhaled in relief. Catherine grabbed her brother's hands and pulled until he was freed from the antlers. Then she struck a pose. "What do you think?" She gestured to her skull helmet. Alexander was too busy checking his body for holes to fully notice. When he finally looked up, he failed to hold back a gasp. Catherine giggled and swiped imaginary claws with a roar.

"*Shh!* Quiet, Catty!" She spun on her heels with a *harrumph*.

Alexander glanced around the room, located the door and cautiously made his way over to it. Despite his best efforts, the door creaked loudly when he turned the handle. He took a quick peek into the hallway and determined that the basement was unoccupied, lit by a single oil lamp at the bend to the right of the doorway. Cobwebs hung like macabre banners swaying ever-so-slightly in the musky corridor. Alexander caught the sound of voices coming from around the bend and tip-toed out from doorway and into the hallway corner. Catherine followed close behind him, prowling like a jungle cat with her fingers splayed like claws. He peeked around the bend and saw an identical hallway, dimly lit, that ended in a set of stairs. There were four doors along that hallway, all closed except for one. The third on the right from the stairwell was ajar, a soft light from within cut a wedge in the darkness.

"The voices are coming from in there," he whispered. Catherine nodded, the skull sliding up and down as she did. "Take that off, will you?"

"Nuh-uh! I'm Catty the jungle cat!" She swiped the air with her claws. Alexander sighed.

"Alright, jungle cat, let's see how quiet you can be." They

crept to the open door and stole a peek. Three men loomed over a small square table and appeared to be very interested in whatever was on it. The man closest to the door was short and rather portly and wore an ill-fitting black suit. He alternated between dabbing at his sweaty brow with a stained handkerchief and fanning himself with his tattered top hat. The second man was, by far, more interesting than his rotund counterpart. Alexander silently determined that he must be an adventurer. The man was ruggedly handsome, with a square jaw and sun-bleached hair that cascaded behind his ears and across his muscular shoulders. His white cotton shirt was completely unbuttoned, revealing a large tattoo on his chest of a kraken grasping what appeared to be a variety of weapons in each tentacle. On the man's left forearm was a tattoo of a mermaid with a skull for a head clinging to an anchor. His gray pants had a faded red stripe down each side, Alexander thought they might have once belonged to a British admiral. He had a pistol and a cutlass stuffed into a black sash around his waist. The man thoughtfully rubbed the stubble on his chin as he considered whatever it was in front of him on the table. Alexander turned his attention to the third man, whom he found to be the most intriguing of the group. He stood furthest from the door, his form fading in and out of the shadows despite the glow of the lamp on the table. His shape was difficult for the young boy to process, as if he could barely be perceived by the naked eye. The man wore a long trench coat and red-lensed goggles that reflected—and amplified—the lamp light. A wide-brimmed hat shrouded the rest of his face in shadow, save for his mouth. His oversized mouth was crimson red and had fangs that curved down and up like a monster. *No, that couldn't be correct*, Alexander thought. The mouth did not move as he spoke. A mask perhaps? Grandfather had told them many stories about the Samurai of Japan and their intimidating armor. That must be it. Then again, grandfather also spoke of ruthless monsters that lumbered in the darkness and tore tender flesh with their horrible maws. Catherine started to gasp aloud but Alexander clamped his hand across her mouth before she was heard. They both froze in fear.

"Hold on, hold on. One more bloody time," the plump man patted his scalp. "Explain to me—using small words— what the bloody hell that is?" The shadow man plucked a glowing amber crystal from a velvet pouch and held it up with his gloved right index and thumb.

"In a word... energy." His voice was deep and rumbling like thunder over the hills, impending disaster. It shook the children to their core. They grasped hands instinctively.

"Bolivar has discovered a hidden civilization in the bowels of the Congo that is technologically superior to the rest of the world. He found them by happenstance. According to Bolivar they are quite xenophobic, and go to great lengths to ensure their isolation."

"Well, if a tit like Bolivar could find them, they're doin' a bang-up job of it," the sweaty man scoffed. His voice seemed too high-pitched for such a large fellow. The tattooed man held out his hand and the gem was placed in his palm. He rolled it around his fingers as he studied it. He smiled wide, showing off a set of perfectly white and straight teeth, far nicer than those of any sailor Alexander had ever seen.

"It doesn't matter how old Bolly came across those lads." The tattooed man's voice was surprisingly smooth and comforting. "What *does* matter is that he saw fit to send you a bag of these beauties. I wonder what they're worth?"

"A price cannot be set upon an item never before seen, Captain Drake," Monstermouth rumbled. Though he wasn't speaking loudly, each word was a punch to the chest. The Captain's smile grew wider.

"Everything has a price, my friend. Everything has worth. Well, perhaps not Mr. Williams here."

"Very nice, Drake." Mr. Williams shook his head. "Not all

are chiseled from granite as yourself, sir. Though, where I lack in physical... appeal... I more than excel in the realm of strategy."

"Allow me to illustrate the importance of these precious stones," Monstermouth interjected. "A single gem would not only power Captain Drake's submersible for a year at a time, but it would also keep the vessel at peak performance so long as it was sound." His goggle lenses shimmered. Captain Drake squeezed the gem in his fist.

"You're saying my submersible, *The Tiberón*, could outdo that damnable Prince Dakkar's *Nautilus*?"

"Perhaps it would put you on-par with him."

"You flatter me, sir," Drake grunted and returned the gem to its pouch.

"What's your game this time?" Williams asked. "I can appreciate a secret unveiling of a brand new power source, but I'm somewhat at a loss as to why this couldn't wait until the rest of the Order had arrived." Monstermouth swept the pouch from the table and into his coat.

"There is no time to wait on the others, I'm afraid. Bolivar has been abducted. His wife Abigail contacted me and stated that merely a week after his return, his home was invaded and he was taken."

"By whom?" Mr. Williams set his hat down on the table and sat in a dusty chair that creaked under his weight.

"It is undetermined as of now, though I have my suspicions."

"How could they have known about Bolly's little... vacation spot?" Captain Drake inquired.

"You know how he is when he's in his cups," Williams stated. "He'd boast about near anything. *Especially* if they were buying!"

"What will you have us do?" Drake pressed his knuckles into the table.

"I am confident his abductors desire Bolivar's knowledge

of the hidden city and its many secrets. He is undoubtedly being forced to guide the antagonists to the Congo. We will place one of these gems into *The Tiberón* and see if we cannot catch them before they reach their goal. We only wait for one more member of the Order to arrive."

"Who?" both men asked in unison.

"Our newest recruit, Master Ng."

"The Chinese poofter?" Williams chuffed.

"The Shaolin monk, yes," corrected Monstermouth. "His abilities in battle and subterfuge are quite a boon to the Order, wouldn't you agree, Williams?"

"I, er..."

"Your gift for stratagem could not calculate otherwise, I am sure."

"True. The man is quite gifted and—"

"And you'd *also* agree that his personal proclivities are of no concern, correct?"

"Of course." Mr. Williams dabbed his forehead and allowed the cloth hang in front of his embarrassed eyes.

"He spoke to me of once having a wife." Drake scratched his chin. "He's a bit of an enigma, that one." Alexander and Catherine tried their best to process the words these mysterious men shared. Several times it seemed as though the masked man in the shadows knew that they were there. A tilt of the head, an inflection of speech, a scratching in the back of their minds. But he never once acknowledged them, so as far as the two junior adventurers were concerned, they were in the clear. They each felt a heavy hand on their tiny shoulders.

"Well, well, what have we here?" Kunal's deep voice sent an icicle of fear down their spines. "You two are in deep dung, yes you are." His hands clamped tighter. Escape was no longer an option, if ever it was. The three men in the room paused their conversation and looked intently upon the intruders. Captain Drake walked over to the door and pulled it all the way open.

"Is that little girl wearing a skull?" Drake laughed. Catherine growled and swiped her imaginary claws. Drakes laugh danced in her ears. She was too young to know of love, but something in her psyche latched onto the melodic mirth of the sea captain. She blushed beneath the skull. "She's got heart, she does," the Captain smiled. Kunal bowed deeply in apology.

"A thousand pardons, lords. I'll see to it that these scamps get what they deserve." He tugged the children from the door and bowed again. "You've won yourselves an audience with The Commodore," he informed the pair, guiding them by the shoulders down the hallway toward the staircase. Drake chuckled as he closed the door.

"Youth, eh lads? Wasted on the young." He took a seat and pulled the cork out of a bottle of rum with his teeth. "Let's get back to the task at hand. You were saying, Hargraves?"

THE IRON INDIAN guided the children to the main floor of the chapter house, where the Central Hall was located. Once the main chapel for Masonic gatherings, the Guild had transformed the large Hall into a lounge; the stiff benches and draped alters had been replaced by plush couches, massive leather chairs, heavy bookshelves, wooden tables marred by scotch glasses and cigar ash, and, of course, a wet bar. Above it all hung a chandelier made entirely out of candle-impaled elk horns. This was the bragging hall. The air was thick with the stink of leather, smoke and bullshit. Young members darted this way and that, carrying drinks and empty ash trays, hanging on every word the old timers uttered through their thick beards and handlebar mustaches. Each syllable carefully sculpted around fat cigars or pipe stems. The walls were adorned with decommissioned rifles, paintings of deceased members and errant slogans burned into wooden plaques:

'KEEP YOUR POWDER DRY AND YOUR WOMEN WET.'

'THE MEEK SHALL *NOT* INHERIT THE EARTH.'

'HOMINES HOMINIBUS OPUS SUBSTANTIAE.
ET NON EX DICTIS.
('The world needs men of substance. Not men of promises.')

    At the far side of the room, two men were seated in high-back leather chairs near the fireplace. The older man sat with his eyes fixed to the fire, puffing at his cigar while his younger compatriot spoke. He wore a fine suit in the darkest hue of brown he could find. His shirt was open three buttons from the collar, revealing a wide chest. His square jaw flexed as he puffed. He was pushing sixty and in better shape than most people half his age. Then again, most people were not carved from volcanic rock, as many mused he was. He listened, halfheartedly, as the younger man prattled on about his adventures. Nothing of note, the older man concluded, but it would be bad form not to let the novice finish his tale.

    "And then, suddenly, there were *three* twin sisters!"

    "Triplets," the elder corrected.

    "Yes, triplets! These triplets were witches and focused on nothing but using me to impregnate them. What could I do, Commodore? I was under their evil spell."

    "Naturally."

    "It was as magnificent as it was horrifying, I can assure you."

    "Yes, I am quite sure your bedding of three whores in a tavern you've frequented many a time is the stuff of paranormal tomfoolery. How much money did you say you lost?"

    "All of it, sir." The young man hung his head. "Their powers were quite formidable."

    "Is that what you tell your wife? That you were *bedazzled* by three witches who used you for little more than a breeding stud and *not* that you drank yourself into a frenzy and plunged your penis into whomever was willing?" The younger man rose from the chair and straightened his bow tie.

"I-I believe I should go, Commodore," he stammered. The Commodore tapped his cigar ash into the ash tray on the small table to his right next to his tumbler of rum.

"Yes, a capitol idea, Raymond. Oh, and should you see Raul on your way out, do be a lamb and tell him I'll need a refill before long." Raymond nodded and shuffled off as Kunal approached with the squirming imps in each hand.

"Commodore, we have intruders!" The old adventurer turned slowly in his chair and growled.

"Is that so, Kunal? Well, bring them here! I would like a snack!"

"Of course! But there isn't much meat on these two." Kunal shoved the children to the growling man as they squealed. With amazing speed, the Commodore grabbed Alexander and Catherine and pulled them onto his lap where he pretended to gnaw at their necks.

"A light snack, then!" The children's squeals became howls of delight as the Commodore tickled them.

"Alexander and my little Kitty Cat! What brings the two of you to see your old grandfather? And Catty, girl! Why have you a skull on your head?"

"Sowee, Gwampa. I tooked it from the basement." Catherine began to remove her new helmet, but the Commodore pushed it back down with his index finger.

"Nonsense, child. It suits you!"

Alexander noticed an old fellow with bright white mutton chops was hobbling his way over to them. The man had only his left leg, and used an ivory-colored crutch to aid him. The boy couldn't help but stare.

"Well, now I've seen everything!" The man chuckled. "Benjamin Eben Grimstead with a smile across his stony face? These little rapscallions must be Richard's progeny, no?"

"Indeed they are! Augustus Ammons, these are my

grandchildren, Catherine and Alexander. Children, this is Mr. Ammons. Auggy, please join us." Benjamin nodded to the chair Raymond had recently warmed. Ammons slowly sat and shifted several times until he was settled.

"Catherine and Alexander," Ammons said as though pondering. "Named after the *greats*, eh?"

"There is also Otto, my eldest grandson. Also, as you say, a *great*. It is a jab, no doubt, from Richard."

"How so?"

"Richard despises adventuring. He took after his mother in that fashion, may the gods rest her soul. I suppose taking him on perilous journeys as a child may have... scarred him a bit. He believes that industry is the future, not discovery. I think naming his children after the greats is his way of telling me that their names are the closest his children will get to my way of life." Benjamin finished his rum and set the glass down harder than he intended.

"I wanna be an adventwerer!" Catherine professed.

"Me too!" Alexander concurred. He turned his attention to Ammons. "Mister, what happened to your leg?" If Alexander's father were there, he would have chastised the child for such a rude inquiry, however, at the Adventure Guild, it would be considered rude *not* to ask. Ammons smiled.

"I was shipwrecked in the Pacific and drifted on a raft I fashioned out of rope and dead sailors. Once marooned on an island, I succumbed to dehydration and passed out for quite some time. When I awoke, I found myself on a bed of palm leaves near the center of a small village of twig huts, with the most delectable scent dancing in the air. Thirty naked natives stood reverently around a fire pit. Men and women with their squishy bits exposed to the elements. Some danced, some chanted, though most licked their lips at the sizzling meat on the spit. I must confess it was quite intoxicating." He closed his eyes in reverie. "Then I saw just *what* it was they were cooking. Those devils took my damned leg! They cut it off just below the hip and cauterized the stump to avoid my bleeding out. Dead meat spoils so much faster. They knew to keep me alive as long as possible in order to keep me fresh, as it were."

"Why did they start with your leg, Mr. Ammons?"

"Think on it, Alexander. Take a man's arm, he may yet run away. Take a man's leg and well..." Alexander nodded that he understood. Catherine shifted her skull helmet so that it only covered the back and top of her head. Her brown curls bounced out like springs.

"How did you suwvive?" she whispered in astonishment.

"Well, my dear, I must admit that my luck was tri-fold that evening. In the savages' excitement at fresh meat, they left their carving dagger where my missing leg once was. They also weren't adept at telling when a man was only *pretending* to be unconscious. I was very cross, you understand, but I knew patience would allow me an opportunity to strike. And strike I did. That night, as the savages slept with me inside their bellies, I took that carving dagger and stalked from hut to hut, cutting throat after throat. They were intoxicated by a strong root drink that had immense hallucinatory properties, as I later found, which allowed me to take my time as I hobbled to and fro. Come morning, my dark work was finished, and I ate my weight in the fruit that they had gathered. They weren't just cannibals, you see. Opportunists, more accurately. The island teemed with various wildlife and fruit. The occasional cast away was seen as a gift from their gods. I spent months on that island. I found a mass grave full of human bones and fashioned this out of femurs. I thought it not only ironic, but somewhat a way to honor the victims of misfortune." The children stared at the crutch with wide eyes, and studied its contours. "If it weren't for a Spanish trading ship stopping to hunt and replenish their drinking water, I'd still be on that blasted island. Fortunately, I've never had to resort to that level of violence since that night."

"Father says we should abooor violence." Benjamin

caressed the back of his grandson's head and smiled.

"Indeed it is good to *abhor* violence, my boy. But it is also good to be *good* at it."

"Agreed!" Mr. Ammons clapped his hands once. "This world is a dangerous place regardless of your philosophy. Better to be prepared! Take your grandfather for instance. There sits a man who has faced extraordinarily poor odds, extraordinarily powerful foes and extraordinarily extreme circumstances, and kicked each one right in their bottoms!" The children laughed and felt a swell of pride. "Your grandfather is an inspiration. A living legend. A—"

"There you two are! I should have known!" Richard Grimstead stormed across the great room, ignoring the greetings from several senior members. He was a slim, handsome man, an echo of his father's features. He wore a thin mustache and pomaded dark brown hair that was parted on the right of his scalp. Richard had grown up with the potential to be anything he set his mind to: a prince of some faraway land, a sea captain of great repute, a king even. But a banker? Benjamin shook his head at the children.

"Uh-oh. Looks like we've been nabbed." He winked.

"What were the two of you thinking, sneaking out of the house? Your mother is worried sick!" Richard aimed his left index finger at Alexander like a spear point. "How did I know I would find you here? And would someone tell me just *what* is on Catherine's head?!"

"Issa skuw, poppa!" Catherine beamed. "I'm a jungle cat!" Richard scowled and plucked her from Benjamin's lap, tossing the skull to the wood floor. It skid across the polished planks toward the fireplace where it skittered to a halt and settled facing them.

"Ladies do not wear skulls, my love."

"Then I don't wanna be a wady!" Catherine pushed against her father's chest, but he did not set her down.

"I'll not allow my children to be subjected to your absurd

and irrational influences, old man." Richard growled. "That life is not suitable. My children will not succumb to the horrors you've heaped upon me. They will be punished for their actions." Benjamin held his hands up in surrender.

"My boy, Alexander came here not for the tales of old men. He came to ask for employment. He said it himself that he would like to earn money so he may contribute to the family. I've agreed to have him tidy up the place a bit. Empty ash trays, wipe the tables down, that sort of thing. Provided that it is after school, and with your blessing, of course."

"Is this true, Alexander?" Richard studied the boy's face for hesitation. If he caught him in a lie, it would be more than enough reason to give him a whipping.

"Yes, papa." He smiled brightly. "May I?"

"I... suppose." Richard said with great hesitation. "But only after school, agreed?" Alexander nodded. Benjamin set the boy on his feet and they shook hands.

"Then it is settled," He smiled, broadly. "Thank you both for visiting your old grandpa." He turned to Richard, the smile faltering slightly. "Thank you for stopping by. Son." Richard took Alexander by the hand and left without another word. Benjamin retrieved his cigar from the tray and lit it back up. His face once again turned to stone.

"Where the devil is Raul with my bloody rum?"

"RAR!" CATTY SWIPED imaginary claws at Wade Duggan as he swept the walkway in front of his home, which was two doors down from the Grimsteads'. Richard sighed and tugged her by the arm. Wade Duggan chuckled.

"Come along, Catherine," her father muttered with a half-apologetic smile. "Up the stairs, monster."

"I'm not a *monstuh*, I'm a jungle cat!" She bounded up to the door then spun, gnashing her teeth and wiggling her fingers. "RAR-RAR-RAR!"

"Inside, beast! You too, boy."

Rachel Grimstead—Mother—stood in the kitchen in her patented scowl-pose: arms folded, head slightly lowered to increase glaring intensity and one foot tapping the wooden floor under her slate gray skirt. The cadence signified trouble. Otto, pudgy mother's boy, sat at the table delicately spreading butter on a surgically-bisected scone. His smile was patented too, of course. *Nyah nyah, you're in trouble and I'm not!*

"SCONES!" Catty shrieked as she ran to her chair at the table. She snatched up the scone that was waiting on her plate and glommed half of it in one bite.

"Catherine, small bites!" Rachel instructed. Her gaze turned to Richard. "Let me guess where you found our missing children, children who made their mother and father absolutely *sick* with worry. Children who will be *punished* for *sneaking* out to *visit* their grandfather *without* permission!" Her voice increased in volume with each word. "I should say *child*, as your sister is too young to have known better. But you, Alexander... I am disappointed in your recklessness! You and your sister could have been hurt! Look at your clothes! It's like you were attacked by an animal!"

"Alexander went to ask old Ben Grimstead for a job." Richard placed a hand on Alexander's shoulder and jostled him a bit. "Isn't that right, son?"

"Y-yes, sir."

"Really?" Rachel cocked an eyebrow. She expected hijinks, or a tale of ridiculous proportions.

"He said he wanted to help the family."

"Is that true, Alex? You asked him for a job?"

"Yes ma'am."

"We—*mmf*—hearded about—*mmff*—Mr. Mammo's weg!" Catherine exclaimed as crumbs shot from her lips.

"What have I told you about speaking with food in your mouth, young lady?" Rachel's nostrils flared. She was a beautiful woman, even when angered. Dark brown hair pulled tight in a bun with two free strands that framed her face. Her lips were thin and elegant. Richard often mused that she could have been the subject of Renaissance paintings. That usually brought color to her otherwise milk-white cheeks.

"Sowee." Catherine tilted her head left then right with each syllable.

"As for you, young man! March straight to your room. No lunch, no dinner. I do not want to see you until the morning, you understand?"

"But..."

"Your mother is right. You may have had good intentions, but you did sneak out and put your sister in danger." The scent of the warm scones and tea sent Alexander's stomach into a rumbling frenzy. "I'll see you to your room and I want you to think about *what* the rules of the house are and *why* we have them. Understood?"

"Yes, sir." Alexander hung his head and the two walked up the wooden staircase to the children's room. A small bed was tucked into the corner closest to the door. Catherine's. The boys shared a bunk bed in the opposite corner. A dresser flush against the wall between the beds acted as the neutral zone when the three young nations were at war, which was often. Alexander hoisted himself up the wooden ladder to the top bunk, then swung his legs over the side and let them dangle. Richard folded his arms on the mattress and looked upon his son with an emotion unfamiliar to the boy. Not frustration. Not even anger or disappointment. Those Alexander had seen before. So what was it in his father's eyes and written across his furrowed brow?

Remorse.

"I know you lied about the job." Alexander's heart jumped. He was doomed. "I'm not angry," Richard sighed. "I was no different than you when I was your age. My father was a world renown adventurer and explorer. He's fought in wars you would never learn about in school. He took me on several of his grand escapades and I remember thinking, *Oh, how exciting! What fun!* but that ended soon enough. When hunger sets in while you're out to sea without sufficient provisions, when the violence starts in faraway lands, and you watch those around you die wretched deaths, or reveal their true devilish nature, when the lusty facade of adventure soon fades, leaving little but the hideous truth of it all." Richard's gaze drifted to that long ago place in his memory. Alexander placed his hand on his father's arm. This was a side Alexander never saw before. His father was fire and brimstone about leaving the Grimstead legacy behind, but never explained why. He avoided the past and what those thoughts would provoke. What changed his mind? Seeing his father? Being in that place of old men, strong drinks and tall tales? Perhaps he wanted to finally connect with Alexander and tell him, *show him,* that the ways of Benjamin Grimstead are obsolete at best. Damning at worst. Richard unbuttoned his shirt and revealed a tapestry of scars. Alexander sat silent, mouth agape.

"No child should see what I have seen. Done what I have done. Hurt the way I have hurt." Alexander's eyes traced each scar like the details of a treasure map.

"What are those?" he asked, pointing to four vertical divots in his father's breastbone. Richard ran a finger down each one.

"This is where a maniacal Indian death cult priest attempted to dig his fingers into my chest and remove my heart for the goddess Kali. I was sixteen when that happened. These curved marks here on my right shoulder blade are from the claws of a jaguar. Honestly, I cannot tell you how the devil I survived any of that. I understand the allure, Alex, I truly do. But this is no life worth living. It is usually a short, brutal existence leading to a quick, brutal death. Your grandfather somehow beat the odds. I suppose every rule must have an exception from time to time. I want my children to live for the new world we live in. The age of industry and science. I want you all to live long, happy lives. Your brother Otto understands."

"Otto is a coward!" Alexander heard the words before he felt them pass his lips. Too late to take them back.

"I do not think that is the case." Richard buttoned his shirt and tucked it in. "Your brother is a bit older than you and your sister, and therefore has a better grasp on where the future of America is headed. If you work hard, study hard, you can achieve great things. One day, you will all be successful, with a family all your own. That is the American dream, my son."

"I'm not dreaming for America, I'm dreaming for me," Alex mumbled. Richard took his son's face in his hands and looked pleadingly into his eyes.

"Promise me you'll give up on this foolishness. Promise me you'll make something of yourself other than a washed-up relic. Promise me."

"I... promise..." Alexander whispered a solemn vow.

"Good!" Richard playfully shook his son's leg. Now, give me that jacket so your mother can mend the holes. Honestly, it looks like you've been bored by antlers!" He took the coat and walked to the bedroom door. "By morning your punishment will be lifted and we can talk further about this... job. Could be good to earn a bit of money."

"Poppa?"

"Yes, Alexander?"

"Was... was it always bad?"

"Adventuring?"

"Yes."

Richard opened the door and stared into the hallway. He could lie to the boy, *should* lie to the boy. The last thing he wanted to do was rekindle the fire of wonder and intrigue. He thought about the places and people he'd seen: royalty with mountains of gold, inventors and artists and sorcerers, sights that were unbelievable even to those witnessing them. He also remembered the princesses. "Not always," he whispered, then closed the door behind him. Alexander counted the twelve creaks in the floorboards that trumpeted his father's footsteps to the stairs. Believing the coast was clear, the boy dropped to the floor and slid under the bottom bunk on his stomach. With practiced precision, Alexander pressed down on a floorboard, causing it to rise on the opposite end. He lifted it and set it aside. He pulled a cigar box from the opening between the support beams and ran his fingers over the letters on the cover. *El Rey Del Mundo*. He smiled at the man being pulled on a carriage by a horse, elephant, donkey and a ram.

"King of the World." Alexander opened the lid like a sacred tome and reverently removed the items therein:

One Spanish gold doubloon from 1798.

One onyx American Indian arrowhead.

One tooth from a great white shark.

One flat rock from Denmark intricately carved with the image of an antlered god sitting cross-legged, and surrounded by a snake, a raven, and a great hound.

Grandfather called him a *Cernunnos*, a primitive and powerful entity of the forest. This held the most magic of all the cigar box treasures and Alexander felt it pulsing. Not even sweet Catty knew of these possessions. Alexander couldn't risk her accidentally telling mother or father. They wouldn't see the value. They would confiscate the treasures, or worse, discard them. No, these artifacts are Alexander and grandfather's secret for now.

Alexander caressed the carving and felt a soft wave of dizziness. The hair on his arms stood on-end and he swore he could hear whispers. Laughter. A power beckoning him from across epochs. Then the beating of wings, and the weight of a coiled snake in his stomach. A warm breeze carried the scent of a fresh kill on the breath of a hound. Brooklyn peeled away like flecks of paint and gave way to a twilight realm of dirt, moss, and deep, wooded isolation.

A sacred grove.

There, in the center, sat a naked man with great antlers that stabbed the evening light like the boughs of an acacia. His pointed ears pricked and twitched, as luminescent pixies floated on the syrup-thick air like dandelion seeds. Eyes green as emeralds, pierced the deep-set shadow of his brow. His chest was broad and mud-dappled. His muscles were lean and ever ready for the hunt. He sat in the lotus position in a mossy patch of mud and blood—a filthy, mockery of the Buddha. A black and yellow snake slithered over Alexander's foot and coiled in the lap of the horned god. A stout raven, ruby-eyed and black as pitch, landed on the god's antlers and jumped to and fro until it settled. It looked upon the boy and let out a judgmental caw. Finally, a large, gray hound padded from the growth with a bloody maw and laid next to his master. Alexander felt at peace. This, after all, wasn't his first visit.

"Long since last you came, O'Child," the horned god spoke with a voice like creaking trees, wind through leaves, the screams of spreading petals. "Come now at last to stay?" He held a hand out toward Alexander. A pixie landed on his upturned palm and danced betwixt his fingers. Its giggle was like the twinkling of stars. Alexander felt the pull of the magic. He felt safe there among the beasts. Secure midst the wooden sentry forest. Any other child would have been scared out of their minds. And rightfully so, but Alexander felt strangely at peace. The horned god beckoned with curling fingers and the raven hopped to the other antler. The hound simply yawed and rested his big head on his crossed paws. The snake, however, moved up the horned god's torso in a spiral and draped across his neck and bit his own tail like the clasp of a necklace.

"O'Child... O'Child..."

"WHAT'CHA GOT?!"

Alexander's head shot straight up into the bottom bunk with a sharp crack. Pain exploded like fireworks. Catherine was laying on her stomach mere inches away from her brother. Alexander scrambled to secure the items in the box. It was then he saw the strand of drool that connected his lip with his right forearm.

"Secwets, Awexander? I thought we pwomised no secwets!" Catherine pouted.

"I'm sorry, Catty. You-you scared me, is all."

"So-weeeee." She tilted her head left then right. Alexander couldn't help but smile. "Oh! Wook!" She produced a napkin with a lump. She shoved it at her brother with a broad smile

"A scone! You snuck me a scone!" Alexander shoved as much as could into his mouth. "*Mmff, mmff!*" Crumbs flew and Catherine giggled. "You're right, Catty. No secrets." Alexander spread the contents once more and described each as it had been described to him.

"A sakwed gwove?" Catherine wrinkled her nose. "Wid a nakkee man?"

"Yes. I dreamed that I was there again. I've had that dream before, but this time it was as if they were waiting for me."

"Awexander?"

"Yes?"

"If it was a dweam... why are your shwoes covewed with mud?"

COLLEGE OF ST. JOHN THE BAPTIST BEDFORD-STUYVESANT, BROOKLYN 1892

The rain crashed onto Professor Alexander Grimstead's office window like the spray from a Gatling gun. He sat hunched over his rickety wooden desk, which he had pushed flat to the wall to make room for column after column of stacked books and artifacts. His finger traced lines of text in a thin pamphlet that contained eyewitness accounts of a demon-like entity known as Spring-heeled Jack. Allegedly, this red-eyed, black-cloaked gentleman capable of leaping extraordinarily high, had made his first appearance in Great Britain in the late 1830s. Some considered him a hoax, or mass delusion, but there were several similar eyewitness accounts, spread far and wide across the country, that led Grimstead to believe that this demon-man was real. Whatever the case, Grimstead had attempted—several times—to convince the Board of Deans to send him overseas to investigate. Each proposal met with equal disdain.

You are a professor who'd rather spend his time out *of the classroom? Occult studies and mythological nonsense is barely a subject to begin with. Surely, you would be more successful teaching underwater basket weaving!*

He was not well liked by his contemporaries, either. Professor Crackpot was just one of the monikers he had been bestowed, the one they chose to snicker aloud when he passed them in the hall.

Bang-bang-bang, the window rattled. *That wasn't rain,* thought Grimstead. A figure stood on the other side of the pane of glass, wet and shivering. Grimstead turned the latch and the window slowly opened.

Catherine.

"Catty! What are you doing here?!"

"I must tell you something!" Streams of water cascaded from her lips as she spoke. Her curled locks did not bounce, but instead hung like a shroud. She wore a black skirt and a navy blue pea coat. Her shoes resembled mounds of mud.

"Come in! You're soaked!" He motioned to the small office behind him. Catherine waved him off.

"No time! My ship leaves in—" The thunder drowned her words.

"Your what? *Ship?*"

"I'm leaving, Alexander," she shouted over the noise of the rain "I'm getting as far away from Father as I can."

"But... *why?*"

27

"Because I want to live my life the way I see fit! I refuse to be a housewife, and have no interest in becoming a mother. Father would have had me married years ago if I didn't manage to scare the suitors off. I want to see the *world*, brother! Like grandfather did so long ago. And I want you to come with me." The words sent a jolt through Grimstead, as if he'd been struck by lightning.

"With... you? To where?"

"The Orient! The Guild's own Captain Stout is setting out tonight! There's talk of adventure, and I should be part of the conversation."

"Stout?"

"Old Kunal vouched for him, so he's bona fide to me. Gave me his pea coat!" She popped the collar, unintentionally splashing water in her brother's face. "Come with me, *please!* Come away from this... lie."

"I—I'm... Catherine, I..." He turned and looked around the room, at his work. He was a grown man now, and as such , he couldn't afford to waste time in flights of fancy. "...cannot."

"*Will* not, you mean." She bit her lip. "Father has his hooks so deep inside you. What happened?"

"I grew up." He regretted those words as soon as they were released. Catherine nodded slowly.

"Bully for you, then. See you when I return, Alexander the Great." She pulled something colorful from her coat and tossed it to him. She turned and ran, deaf from the thunder, never hearing her brother's pleas as he clutched the jungle cat's skull to his chest.

GREENPOINT, BROOKLYN
1893

"Well, well, look who it is!" Kunal waved to Alexander

Grimstead as he approached the old Guild hall. Kunal's hair was white as snow now, his cigars replaced by a curved pipe. Despite his advanced age, the Iron Indian was still formidable.

"Hello, Kunal. How have you been?"

"Oh, I could complain, but who would listen?" He chuckled and slapped his large right hand against Grimstead's shoulder. Grimstead felt it in his teeth. "Still no word from your sister?" Grimstead shook his head. "None from our end either, I'm afraid. Come in, he's waiting in the great hall." Kunal opened the door and they entered the aged building.

"These rooms and passageways used to be brimming with people." Grimstead recalled the stories and voices and colors that brought life to each corner of the old hall.

"Now full of memories," Kunal sighed. Several older members waved at Grimstead as he passed. *Relics,* he thought, *as dusty as the counter tops.*

"We need new blood like you," Kunal said, as if he had been reading Alexander's mind. "Get the color back into our cheeks." Grimstead smiled.

"Kunal... have you ever regretted becoming an adventurer?"

"No one ever lives to regret it," the old man winked. As they entered the main hall, Grimstead's eyes immediately flew to the far end of the room, where grandfather's empty chair still sat, untouched, by the fireplace. He imagined he could still see the swirls of smoke rising to the ceiling. Hear the clink of ice in a glass. And the stories. He was surprised to see a familiar figure standing by the fireplace, one that Grimstead had not seen since he was a boy. Kunal cleared his throat.

"Alexander Grimstead, I am sure you remember Mr. Hargraves." The tall man turned to face the Professor. His red-lensed goggles flared.

Monstermouth.

Hargraves extended his right hand in greeting. Grimstead tried not to wince under the grip. Hargraves sat in Mr.

Ammons' old chair and motioned that Grimstead take his grandfather's.

"No, thank you, sir," Grimstead said solemnly. "That seat is not meant for me."

"Such reverence. It is... admirable. Benjamin Grimstead was a great man." Hargrave's voice gave Grimstead goosebumps. *Like a death rattle.* "Have you considered my offer, Professor?" Grimstead's eyes drifted across the Guild hall and then to his grandfather's chair. He thought of Catherine and her overture. *Come with me,* please. *Come away from this... lie.*

"I accept."

"The Order of The Lucifuge welcomes you, Professor." The fanged mask never moved from its grimace. "You will not regret this."

THREE

LIMEHOUSE, LONDON
ENGLAND
1898

THICK, ACRID SMOKE snaked through the back room of The Jade Gate, each swirl a memory, a fantasy, or phantom given life by the withering self-condemned patrons languishing on large stained pillows behind silky curtains. A sickly lime-colored light, barely capable of wading through the murky darkness, emitted from a single strand of decrepit green paper lanterns hung precariously from the ceiling.

The Jade Gate was infamous as an establishment of ill repute; its primary commodities being prostitution, opium, and fine tea. On this night, Alexander Grimstead was among the lost souls. He lay curled in a fetal position, shirtless, on a tattered oversize pillow, drenched with sweat and abdication. A long pipe dangled precariously from his thin lips, barely visible through the thicket of coarse facial hair. His gaunt cheeks barely moved to draw the poisonous smoke through the pipe stem and into his lungs. He had often been a man who defied death, but now he longed for its cold embrace. He looked far older than thirty six. Only a year had passed since he last laid eyes upon his wife's beauty, but his poor decisions had ravaged him quickly. Not as swiftly as he had hoped, however. His dark brown hair, once slicked-back and neat, was now long and matted with sweat and filth. His six-foot frame wilted from neglect. His mind, addled and thickened from the opium, now floated idly, but always to the same thoughts...

Would that he could turn back the clock. Shore up the sands of the hourglass and regain the happiness he once held dear. Beloved Lilly. Chestnut hair caressing her shoulders, encompassing a face so lovely none could find comparison. She was beauty incarnate. Grimstead's True North. Alas, the hands of time tarried on without reprieve, Grimstead understood that all too well. Especially here, in this hell he had built, where he was both tormented and tormentor.

He gazed absently into the green, smoky nothingness. A dark figure materialized from the shadows.

"This is how you mourn me?" an ethereal voice pierced his opium stupor. Grimstead rolled his eyes toward all four corners of the room, but could not discern anything from the deep, swirling shadows. *"I expected more from you, Alexander."*

The pipe slid slowly from his mouth. "What... would you... have of me?" The curtains flapped as if a strong breeze had passed through.

"I would have you live in my memory, not languish from it!"

Grimstead slowly rolled onto his back. His hazel eyes tried in vain to trace the shape of his lost love in the shadows. He could feel her presence with him in the room. "Is that why... you've never appeared to me before?"

"I have never left you," the voice continued. *"Though, you weren't ready to see—or hear—me."*

"Why now?" he pleaded. "Why reveal yourself to me now? Am I ready? Do you deem me worthy?" He extended a weak hand into the empty dark. The curtains calmed as the shadow began to dissipate. "Have you finally come to free me?"

"No, my love. You've much more left to do."

At that moment, three Chinese henchmen rushed into Grimstead's little slice of hell, yanking him from the pillows. He wrestled against their grip, trying to scramble back to his bar-less prison, but to no avail. A fourth man approached, twirling a wisp of long, black chin hair in his right hand. His smile was wicked and thin, and his eyes were like those of a reptile. The fourth man was called Mr. Chen, his reputation for being a sadist was legendary. He grabbed Grimstead's face with the bony fingers of his left hand and looked upon the American with both amusement and disgust. His long and pointed fingernails dug into Grimstead's flesh. He tried to pull his face away, but Mr. Chen held it tight.

"Stop fighting, white ghost. Your time here finish."

"No!"

The eyes of the men around him began to resemble those of dragons, flaring yellow against the dull, green light. *The opium must be playing with my sight,* Grimstead though. Mr. Chen smiled and pushed a laugh that sounded like a hiss through crooked teeth.

"Yesss."

Grimstead braced himself against the two men holding him and kicked the hissing man in the groin and smashed the back of his head into the nose of the man holding his left arm. Then, like a wild animal caught, Grimstead flailed against his captors. One of the men drew a dagger from the red sash tied around his waist and thrust it toward Grimstead's exposed stomach. Grimstead shifted his body backwards with precision timing, missing the blade with only millimeters to spare between the blade and his flesh. He grabbed and twisted the attacker's wrist, sending him spiraling to the floor with a sharp popping sound. Grimstead clutched the knife as if it were the only source of light in a bottomless pit. The other two henchmen pulled the daggers from their sashes and began to stalk closer.

"No!" Chen raised his hand. "He live, or no money!"

The man with the broken wrist ignored his leader's order and lunged at Grimstead once more. With a roar, Grimstead buried the curved blade into the man's sternum. Chen shouted in Chinese and two men, so large and burly that their frames cut massive holes through the thick opium clouds, entered through the round wooden doors at the front of the room. Grimstead adopted a fighting stance, his body trembling from the weakness in his legs. He executed a front-thrust kick that bounced off the stomach of one of the large men. The other punched Grimstead in the head, sending him to the floor. The men each took hold of an arm, hoisted him off the ground and held him aloft. Chen stepped in close and scowled.

"You kill one of us, your price just go up!"

OUTSIDE, GENTLEMAN MASK, Britain's premier vigilante—self-proclaimed—leaned against the side of the building and anxiously tapped his brass pommel walking stick against the cobblestone alley floor. He twitched his pencil thin mustache, pulled his pocket watch from his tuxedo jacket and sighed. He hated to be kept waiting. He returned the watch and pressed the dark mask that covered his eyes a bit tighter to his face. He flexed and released his hands inside their leather coverings and stretched his neck. The alley door opened with a slow creak. Gentleman Mask immediately pushed himself up from the wall.

"You must certainly best have a bloody brilliant reason as to why I've been kept—" Mask was halted by the grim visage of his long-time friend being carried out by Mr. Chen's bouncers. The two large men held Grimstead so high that his toes barely touched the ground. One of the henchmen held a dagger to Grimstead's throat and another followed close behind.

"What is the meaning of this, Chen?" shouted Mask. Mr. Chen folded his arms and smiled.

"The white ghost kill my man. You pay double now."

Mask threw his head back in a hearty laugh and Chen's smile faded in confusion.

"Double isn't *nearly* enough for the good Professor, there." He jerked his chin in Grimstead's direction. "I'll give you four times the bargained price! What do you say?" A thin smile crept onto Mr. Chen's face. He bared his teeth and laughed.

"You make terrible business man!"

Mask twitched his mustache again and pointed the bottom of his walking stick at Chen.

"Not at all, you daft tit." He smiled. "I would have promised you anything your greedy little heart desired. I would have promised the Queen's knickers if you were so inclined! I never had any inclination to make good on our so-called *bargain*. You lot are filthy criminals. A dragon cult no less! And I am Gentleman Mask, Britain's premier vigilante! I've terrorized London's underworld with savage elegance and brutal..."

A loud *thunk* echoed off the alley walls. Chen spun in time to see his burly henchmen fall to the floor like sacks of offal. A very large man stood just behind Chen cracking his leather-clad knuckles and chomping a fat cigar. He was curiously decked in a bowler hat and frock coat which came down only midway on his pinstripe trousers. He wore a black mask around his eyes that matched his cohort's.

"...panache!" Mask winked. Chen's lips fluttered in shock. Mask jabbed the tip of his walking stick into Chen's sternum, causing him to falter backwards. "It seems that my mate The Basher and I have things well in hand, my boy. Do be a dear and piss off back into your little rats nest? There's a good lad!"

Chen cursed and spat. He knew he'd just been outclassed. He walked backwards to the door and slid in without taking a sinister eye off the vigilantes. Mask moved quickly to his fallen friend.

"Up you come, old chap." Mask lifted Grimstead's head

off the ground. One of the bulky goons stirred and sat up. The Basher landed a devastating punch to the back of the henchman's skull, sending his head forward in a snap and knocking him out cold.

"These gobshites are barely worth the knuckle-wear on me gloves!"

The back door of The Jade Gate suddenly sprang open. Chen was at the thresh hold, a group of sour-faced men stood poised eagerly behind him, waiting for his signal to come tearing into the alley. Mask wiggled his fingers in a mock farewell. The fifteen irate henchmen burst into the alley and gave chase. The Basher draped Grimstead over his shoulder and the vigilantes ran toward the alley's mouth.

"To the carriage!" Mask shouted. The Basher tossed Grimstead with ease into the cabin of the ebony Berlin carriage waiting just around the corner, then jumped up onto the perch and took the reigns. Mask jumped up onto the footplate before turning to address the advancing mob. He bowed deeply and called out to them. "Tell your wives that you've been bested by the—" a meat cleaver whizzed by his head, narrowly missing his slick blond hair and embedded itself into the cabin body.

"Oi! Whataya doin'?!" shouted The Basher.

Mask barely closed the cabin door before a barrage of pointy objects peppered it. The Basher cracked the whip and two massive black horses pulled them away from the curb in a torrent of clacking. The carriage sped through the cobblestone streets of the Lime House District at an alarming rate. The colors from storefront lanterns danced across the lacquered chassis in a kaleidoscope of red, blue, and yellow. Merchants, sailors, prostitutes and assorted malcontents scattered like roaches.

Inside the cabin, Grimstead stirred.

The violent sway of the speeding carriage had rocked Alexander into awareness. His head throbbed. The events of the last hour visited in muggy snippets. He stretched his thin neck upwards to peer through the window and concluded two things: it was night and the people about in the streets looked like ghouls. Garish and gaunt with dark, sunken eyes and blood-rimmed mouths. They stared at him. He wanted to look away, but he couldn't. The sound of the hooves echoed unbearably loud in his ears. Gathering up what strength he could, Grimstead turned his head away from the grotesque display and toward his old friend.

"Wh-where are we going?" His voice hissed and crackled.

"To the docks," Mask coldly replied.

"Wh-why? What's at... the docks?"

"Destiny, old friend. Or some such nonsense."

Grimstead turned his head back to the window. The buildings warped into jagged spires that punctured the night sky. Steam-powered dirigibles hung waiting in mid-air like fat coffins. The stars became droplets of blood trickling from throbbing wounds. Mask studied the young scientist for several minutes. He felt a swell of pity and loathing for this husk of a man whom was once held in the highest regard by many across the globe.

"Why did you do this to yourself?" Mask whispered. Grimstead's eyes were transfixed on the passing horrors.

"Lilly..."

Mask curled his lip in disgust. "And you think this is the way to honor your lost wife?" He strained to keep his voice even. "Do you think Lilly would be satisfied to know that her beloved chose to wither away in a heap of bones and shit in lieu of seeking vengeance... or even peace?!" Mask shook himself into composure. "I love you, my dear friend, but I am simply appalled." He turned to face the window. "Do you remember when we defeated King Shadow in the sewers leading to the Thames? Do you recall how I wanted so desperately to give up, to let that mad bastard go on terrorizing the populace, because it seemed impossible to defeat a man in his own element? We were clearly in over our heads, but you wouldn't let us quit.

You said, and I quote, *'If we give up and allow this fiend to continue, how many will suffer due to our lack of resolve? We sacrifice so others won't have to'.*" A thin smile crossed his lips. "Where did that stoic Yankee madman I'd grown to care about go?"

Grimstead gave no answer. His consciousness ebbed and flowed between reality and the opiate abyss. Clarity touched him for a moment.

"Hargraves... is behind this?"

"Who else?"

"If... you truly care for me... you would let me out here." Grimstead's voice gained strength. Mask shook his head, grimly. "Why did he choose you? Did he threaten you?"

"He chose me because of my vast knowledge of London's crime world, and no, he didn't threaten me. He simply gave me an opportunity to do right by an old friend."

Grimstead groaned. "You've condemned me."

"You've condemned yourself."

The carriage approached the docks and came to a clattering halt in front of a massive steam-ship. Dock hands darted to and fro, transporting crates of supplies onto the ship. Mask moved close to Grimstead, placing his hand gently on his friend's cheek. "Resurrect yourself, Alex. This world needs you whether or not you need it in return. Live for her...or so help me I'll kill you." Mask winked and exited the carriage. A voice rumbled though the salty air.

"Do you have him?"

Grimstead looked out the window and saw the shadowy, menacing outline of his former mentor. The darkness always seemed to obscure his features, it was as if they were made to complement each other.

"Yes, I have him. Though, I'm not entirely sure you would *want* him. The poor sod has gone quite astray, I fear."

Grimstead thought he witnessed Hargraves' goggle lenses flare, or perhaps the opium was still burning through his psyche. Hargraves gestured toward the carriage and three men in bright red tunics rushed over to it. They opened the door and pulled Grimstead down from the cabin and out into the night air. Gentleman Mask tilted his head in curiosity.

"Are those the fabled Crimson Crewmen of the SS *Skidbladnir*?" he wondered aloud. "I've heard that Captain Rogerson insists that his officers wear blue while the cannon fodder all wear red. To distinguish the ranks, *of course*. The captain himself dresses in gold." One of the men in red frowned at Mask and shook his head as they dragged Grimstead to Hargraves.

"Don't you believe those stories." The Crimson Crewman —commonly known as a CC—proudly puffed out his chest. "We aren't cannon fodder. We keep the *Skidbladnir* sailing true!"

"Enough!" growled Hargraves as he produced a large syringe filled with a sepia-colored liquid that seemed to glow in his gloved hand. Without hesitation, he pushed the needle into Grimstead's neck and pressed the plunger. The shadows beneath the brim of Hargraves' fedora undulated. Gentleman Mask looked away as his friend drifted into the darkness once more.

"Lock him in his quarters," Hargraves boomed, "until the screaming stops."

FOUR

CONSCIOUSNESS DANCED ACROSS Alexander Grimstead's eyes like an inebriated ballerina. He found himself chained to a wall in what appeared to be a subterranean chamber. The wall overlooked a rectangular stone altar, encircled by figures clothed in hooded, red velvet cloaks. The cloaked figures were kneeling and swaying in unison, chanting in a language unknown to modern man. A shout drew Grimstead's attention to the altar and his blood went cold. His beloved wife Lilly was sprawled across the altar, writhing against the straps that bound her to the stone slab.

"Alexander!"

"No!" he bellowed, struggling against the ancient chains to no avail.

A tall, hooded figure appeared before him and bowed. Grimstead knew instantly that the figure was Kristian Fowler, High Priest and Red Right Hand of the Moonshield Society. Grimstead's panic surged. Fowler was also a former member of The Order of The Lucifuge, having parted ways with his brethren on unfavorable terms. In his time away from the Order, he further solidified his reputation as a marked scoundrel and renown megalomaniac, quickly assimilating to the Moonshield's charters and ascended the echelons of the cult's aristocracy. Fowler had reliably proven that he would stop at nothing to propel himself into the highest rank of power that existed. If he could not become a god, then he would do whatever it took to *control* one.

Thus, the trembling beauty on the altar.

Hargraves had known for some time that his former colleague and pupil had been planning something big. Just how big needed to be uncovered and put to a violent, bludgeoned halt. He sent Alexander and Lilly to Scotland on strict orders to detect and observe any activity related to the Society, but by no means were they to get involved. Things rarely went as planned for the two adventurers, however. Fowler not only knew of their meddling, subtle as they were, but their presence had been essential to his grand design.

"Alexander, old man, good to see you're awake!" Fowler smiled as he pulled the hood from his head. His dirty-blond hair, perfectly parted on the left side, did not move. He was dashing, alright. Stormy blue eyes, knowing smile and a German accent so soft and seductive, many fell to his charm. "I would truly be heartbroken if you missed my crowning achievement."

"Fowler!" Grimstead railed against his bindings. "Let her go! Let Lilly go!"

"Tsk, you sound so concerned. Could it be that the incorruptible Alexander Grimstead is jealous that his wife is on that altar and not him? *Ach*, for this I cannot blame you."

"Why are you doing this?"

"You stand—well—*hang* there and honestly tell me you wouldn't want to summon a god from the deep eternal? Imagine what secrets will be revealed once Goy Gothog is inside our lovely Lilly?"

"You have lost all reason, Kristian!" Grimstead spat. "You seek nothing but madness and the ruination of mankind!"

"I knew you'd understand." Fowler winked.

"Let us go. You of all people know the foolishness in this. Even if it were possible to summon that primitive deity, you would need the Eye of—"

Fowler unfolded his arms and pulled a large talisman from the sleeve of his robe. Grimstead recognized it immediately as the Eye of Goy Gothog, Arch Duke of the Seventh Abyss, Scavenger of Souls, Plunderer of Bodies and Minds. The talisman was made up of pure silver tentacles which wrapped over and around an onyx gem the size of a man's fist.

"You were saying?" Fowler laughed and descended the stairs toward the altar. Lilly resumed screaming and struggled against her leather restraints. She looked to her husband with pleading eyes.

"Alexander! Please!"

Fowler entered the circle of cultists and loomed at the head of the altar.

"Lilly, I would like you to know that this is truly an honor for you."

"Rot in hell!" Lilly spat onto Fowler's cheek. He smiled and let it slide to his lips.

"This is why you should have chosen me instead of that insufferable book worm up there. Imagine what we could have accomplished together."

Fowler pulled the hood over his head and held the Eye of Goy Gothog aloft as he chanted in ancient Sumerian. Grimstead raged against the chains.

"Take me! Take me instead!"

Fowler continued without flinching. The gem in the talisman began to glow with a brackish amber light. Two of the Society members stood and approached the altar to either side of Lilly. They began removing her shirt.

"Alexander! Help me!"

Grimstead twisted and fought the chains, but could do nothing except watch in horror as Fowler took hold of a curved knife in his left hand and began to carve a thin line between Lilly's breasts. Rivulets of blood spread like veins across her bare chest. Fowler placed the talisman on her sternum and its silver tentacles immediately sprang to life, writhing and sprawling outward and down, burrowing deep into her skin. Her screams pierced the chanting that echoed in the chamber. The gem's light grew brighter and the altar began to rumble. Fowler raised his hands. The sleeves of his robe slid down to his elbows, revealing his heavily tattooed arms. Each was a sigil or mark that represented various religions, in particular, the Lesser Key of King Solomon. Lilly's body convulsed and trembled as if in a seizure.

"Goy! Gothog! Goy! Gothog!" Fowler bellowed. "Rise!"

Lilly's back arched and her screams became gurgled. Her desperate eyes swelled into solid pools of black. Suddenly, her jaw exploded in an amalgamation of thick crimson mist and undulating tentacles.

FIVE

THE SS SKIDBLADNIR
MID-ATLANTIC OCEAN
1898

"HOW MUCH LONGER must I listen to that insufferable man scream?!" Emma McParland burst through the polished wood door of her cabin in a rage. She stormed down the hallway and stopped in front of a door identical to her own. "I haven't slept a wink since we left Great Britain," she muttered. Emma wrapped thunderously on the door. An elderly red-shirted guard slumped over, fast asleep in a chair next to the door woke with a start to Emma's hammering.

"Miss, please do not disturb the—"

"You shall not *Miss, please* me this time, plebe!" She eyed the key he was wearing around his neck on a thin piece of twine. "Hand over the cabin key and toddle off, will you?"

"I can't, Miss Emma," the CC said, straightening his posture. "Captain's orders." Emma snatched the key, ripping the twine in half and inserted it into the lock before the guard could protest.

"Ha!" she shouted, triumphant and immediately fell silent as the door opened with a slow creak. Emma took a cautious step into the unlit cabin, the indignant guard at her heels.

The room was in utter disarray. Amid the rubble of overturned and splintered furniture, Alexander Grimstead stood naked and distraught. His eyes, sensitive to even the weak light from the hallway lanterns, squinted involuntarily. Emma's figure in the doorway was a beacon to him, her profile shining ethereally against the room's heavy-hanging shadows. He fought the urge to reach out for her. After several long moments, his eyes began adjusting to the light. Emma's rage quickly returned.

"You, sir, have been a nuisance for the past fortnight!"

Grimstead's eyes were suddenly fully-focused. The objects in the room sharpened and he could see Emma's true form: A roundish face, blond hair cascading across her shoulders, over her small frame was a pale blue silk nightgown, ending just above her milky-white ankles. Her baby blue eyes flared with anger.

"It is five in the morning. The Sun has barely begun to rise. Your nonsensical blathering of monsters and oddities have vexed me for the," she gasped, suddenly realizing that she could see Grimstead's nether regions. "Oh! Cover yourself!" She quickly turned back toward the doorway.

Realizing that he was, in fact, in the buff, Grimstead hastily grabbed the first thing he could—a sheet from the overturned bed—and covered himself. It was then that he noticed his body had been restored to its pre-Jade Gate form. An image of the sepia-tinted liquid being pressed into his neck flashed through his mind. *Hargraves.* He touched a hand to his chin and found that his scruffy beard had grown rather lush over the fortnight and his hair seemed to be standing in wild tufts about his head. He suddenly felt rather feral—and ashamed. He noticed Emma was still facing the doorway, a hand on either side of her face to prevent her from glimpsing any further instances of random nudity. He also noticed the elderly guard peering inquisitively from out in the hall.

"I... do apologize, miss," Grimstead stammered. "May I ask... where... I am?"

He scanned the cabin for some familiar clothing, but they were buried in the mess. Several men dressed in crimson rushed into the room and began to straighten up. A tall, muscular dark-skinned man entered the room followed by a much shorter, older man. The older man was carrying a stack of clothes under his right arm and balancing a set of barber's tools on a silver tray in his left. Both men wore uniforms identical to the other crew members, but their shirts were blue instead of red. The taller man coolly held his massive hand out to Grimstead in greeting, but did not smile.

"Welcome aboard the SS *Skidbladnir*," the taller man spoke with a Jamaican accent. "I am Mr. Bonitto, the First Mate. This is Mr. Laveglia." He made a sweeping gesture to the smaller man. "He will see to it that you are made presentable. Once you are cleaned up, you will report to the navigation room and see the Captain."

Mr. Bonitto bowed his head stiffly before exiting the room. As he passed Emma, he paused to look her directly in the eyes.

"You as well, Miss McParland," he said sternly. "Your father requests that *all* should be present to welcome Professor Grimstead."

"You do not command me. Sir." She thrust her pert nose into the air defiantly.

Mr. Bonitto ignored her and proceeded down the hallway. Emma glanced back into the room, now buzzing with activity, and realizing that she was little more than a phantom in the doorway, huffed off to her room to get dressed.

LOCATED JUST BELOW the bridge, the navigation room was a vast two-level marvel. At the center of the first level was a massive oval-shaped mahogany table that took up a good portion of the room. The table's centerpiece was a large, topographical globe made of copper that appeared to be floating several inches above the table's surface. The copper sphere was affixed to the table by a sturdy rod, a series of internal gears could move the globe up or down the rod or make it rotate. The globe also featured tiny three-dimensional ships which floated over the oceans, courtesy of a series of thin, but sturdy, wires and powered by small gears. There were also tiny men that stood on land, and the slightly larger cryptids that stalked them. A perfect replica of the *Skidbladnir* was included, as well, slowly moving across the Atlantic Ocean. The gears and wires kept a perfect scale of the steamship's course, always keeping track of its position on Earth. An extensive library occupied the entire upper level, its shelves were crafted from the same dark wood as the navigation table and filled entirely with texts, thick and thin, on topics ranging from ancient history to modern philosophy.

Emma McParland sat on one of the library's big leather chairs, casually thumbing through Pliny the Elder's *Naturalis Historia*. Her father, Dr. Douglas McParland, PhD, entered the room on the lower level, clutching several documents and rolled-up maps to his chest. He was a short fellow with wild, white hair and ingenious—or, perhaps, mad—brown eyes staring through round spectacles. He dumped the papers across the navigation table and spread them with exaggerated circular motions.

A longtime associate of the Adventure Guild, Dr. McParland had spent many years traveling the globe, quite often with his young daughter at his side. At her insistence, of course. Emma thoroughly enjoyed these exploratory romps, much to the chagrin of her mother, Angelica. Mrs. McParland was never much for traveling, let alone adventuring, and quite preferred her tea, embroidery and general solitude of their mansion and laboratory in coastal Maine. An only child, Emma had grown up with an unusual personal dichotomy; she was a vibrant, intelligent young woman in a society built for men. She could scrap with the best of them, yet she didn't shy away from exercising her feminine wiles, when the mood struck. The good Doctor always mused that his beloved daughter had inherited his thirst for adventure and her mother's disdain for most living things. She welcomed modern ideals in a world that still clung desperately to old ones. Her father, on the other hand, was a brilliant man clinging to sanity.

"Emma! Emma, my darling dearest! Come help me prepare the documents for the good Professor!" the Doctor shrieked. His daughter replied with an aggressive exhale, tossing the book aside. She sprang up from the chair and leaned over the railing by the winding metal staircase.

"Father," she began, her voice cool and even. "I am not a child. I am twenty-four-years old. You needn't summon me as if I were an impudent whelp."

The large wooden door swung open and Captain Robert Rogerson entered. He was a tall, stoic-looking fellow with a strong jaw line and dark brown hair that parted on the right side and fell casually across his forehead. He wore the same uniform as the rest of ship's crew, but his tunic was tan with gold-colored trim on the cuffs and collar. He sauntered over to the table and winked up at Emma, who was leaning over the balcony. She glared back.

"At twenty four, I'd say you qualify as an impudent spinster," he laughed. "Good morning, Doctor. Sleep well?"

"Ha! I've barely closed my eyes since we left London! Quite captivated with my latest creation, you know. Tucked away in that cargo hold of yours."

"Yes, yes. I'm glad you've slept well. Cargo," Rogerson replied, distracted by the sight of Emma's cleavage.

The door opened once again. Mr. Laveglia slid into the room then clicked his heels together as he stood at attention.

"Captain! Doctor! Spinster! I present to you, one Professor

Alexander Copernicus—"

Grimstead stormed into the chamber, ahead of cue. He was immediately awestruck by the impressive room despite his anger at being abducted.

"...Grimstead." Mr. Laveglia waved his right hand in a pseudo-blessing before swiftly exiting the room, slamming the door behind him.

"Come in, Professor! No need to be antisocial." Captain Rogerson offered an open hand and a broad smile. "I trust you're feeling better?"

Grimstead swiftly approached the Captain and batted his hand away. Rogerson chose to ignore the insult; the Professor has had a stressful journey thus far.

"Do the clothes fit to your liking? Mr. Laveglia is a skilled tailor, among many other things. Forgive me, where are my manners? Welcome aboard the SS *Skidbladnir*. I am Captain —"

"I know who you are," Grimstead snarled, his eyes narrowing. "Captain Robert Rogerson, Scourge of Rondisle, the Bear Island Butcher, the—"

"Scourge of Rondisle?!" Rogerson interjected. "I take umbrage at the very notion that those savages didn't deserve what came to them! No sooner did my boots touch the soil, were they poking me in the ears and spitting in my face!"

"That is their custom!" Grimstead barked. "That is how they greet new friends! You simply began beating them all to a pulp! And what about Bear Island?"

"What about it? That Island was a madhouse of human slaves with bears dressed like men as their masters. I was merely seeking to free those poor souls."

"You slaughtered an entire village," Grimstead said, wearily. "Your reputation precedes you, you do realize. You never take time to research the creatures you destroy. Never learn their ways or habits, just drop anchor and begin the mayhem. Not to mention that the number of deaths in your crew is nothing short of staggering. I am surprised there's anyone left to steer the ship!" Rogerson slammed his hand onto the table.

"My men are loyal! I would die a thousand times over for each of them! No matter how dire the situation, my men always seem to keep me alive despite my desire for the opposite. And what of you, Professor? You've a reputation for getting your hands dirty, as well!"

"Only when there is no other choice," Grimstead growled. "You said something just now about wanting to die? What do you mean by that?"

"I, well, that is..." Rogerson suddenly shifted his eyes toward the floor. Dr. McParland cleared his throat obnoxiously loud.

"Now, now, settle down everyone. We can talk about suicide, genocide and bears with hats later on. Now, it's time to discuss the matter that has brought us to the middle of the Atlantic Ocean!" He tapped the maps spread across the navigation table.

"Yes, I would very much like to know why I've been abducted. Where is Hargraves?" Grimstead balled his fists so tight his knuckles popped. "Where is that *scoundrel* Hargraves?"

Rogerson, too, had his fists ready to go.

"Hargraves is wherever Hargraves is—but that is not here. And I'll encourage you to mind your tone while on my ship."

"*Pshhh*, men." Emma scoffed.

"I'll have you know, Grimstead, I wasn't particularly keen on having an opium sot join our expedition, but McParland *insisted* that a member of your precious Order join us. As if it would make a damned difference. Hargraves said you had to be the one. He gave no further information as to why. So, buck up, chum! I don't want you here either!"

"Well, good! I'm glad we've had an opportunity to beat our chests like jungle beasts," the Doctor said. "Now if I could have your attention, there are certain matters that I would attend to. Gather round, gather round." The men joined him at the head of the table. Grimstead's heart still pounded in his ears. Once his eyes met the maps, however, his analytical mind put everything else aside.

"There is an island of varying validity off the eastern coast of South America called Antillia. I have been fascinated with this location since I was but a pup! I remember listening to the Portuguese sailors at the wharf speak in harsh whispers about this place and its myriad of wonders. My dreams were rife with imagery of lush forests, exotic birds and even the key to eternal life! There are many, many legends surrounding Antillia and yet there are none that can be truly authenticated! Some have heard of it, most have not... and some chose ardently to ignore me as I pelted them with questions and small rocks! Why, there was this one time where I—"

"Father, you're rambling again," Emma sighed from above.

"Don't you think I know that? As I was saying, I scoured library after library, Adventure Guild Chapter house after Chapter House, to no avail. But one day, in the New Orleans Chapter House, I came across an elderly anthropologist named Dr. Ving Irving. Dr. Irving explained that not only has he *heard* of Antillia, he had spoken to someone who had *been* there! Can you imagine?! He then went on to explain that the person only came to him in his dreams, but Irving was convinced of the validity. We shared the same dreams, he and I. How could I not take advantage of the serendipitous algorithms? *'Look to the University of Cambridge,'* Dr. Irving said. There I would find several maps that would shed light on my quest. Also in the New Orleans Chapter House was our good Captain Rogerson here. I took that as another sign from the science gods, chartered his ship and made haste to England. And what did we find once we threatened—nay, *coerced*—the scholars there? That's correct! The maps containing the

Phantom Island of Antillia."

"The Phantom Island of Antillia," Grimstead repeated. "I don't recall ever hearing of such a place."

"Of course not!" It's been lost for quite some time. *phantom* island and all that. Come, look at the maps." He reached for the map spread furtherest from him and pulled it to the edge of the table. "This first map, well actually each of these maps, I've stolen from the library. Be that as it may, the first map that mentions Antillia was made by a fellow named Ragnar The Mad Varangian. Ragnar and his merry band of murderous vikings were headed to The Holy Land from Scandinavia about 980 AD. In those days, vikings would hire themselves out as bodyguards to mighty sultans and the Arabian elite, gaining riches and status along the way. Ragnar set out with his son, Vargas, and twelve other massive men. But, according to the scripture written around the borders of the map, Ragnar was the only one to make it to Constantinople! For some such reason, his ship traveled *east* of South America and encountered a strange island. Running low on supplies, Ragnar and the crew decided to investigate. Needless to say, none but Ragnar escaped. There appears to be more detailed text on this map, but I do not read runes. Perhaps the good Captain would do us the honor?"

Rogerson peered over the map. "Thus is the saga of Ragnar, sole survivor of Nightmare Island. Fourteen strong were we, when we left the coast of Gamla Uppsala. Strong currents and magic took our ship astray. We sought refuge on an island full of dangers. My son Vargas mistook this place for Jotunheim, as the fighting rarely stopped. Most of the men died in the first few hours. Massive insects and ravenous vegetation claimed the lives of Gunnar, Sven, Inar, Grun, Albin and Magnus. Eight of us remained. Then came the Stalkers of the Night. Bodies like men, though dark and bloody. Faces painted white. Giant eyes reflected the pale Moon with shimmering fierceness. Heed my words, traveler. Fear the Night

Stalkers."

The room fell silent.

Dr. McParland cleared his throat. "This second map here is from a chap named Piri Ibn Haji Memmed, also known as Piri Re'is. It was signed in 1513, and the scholars from Cambridge have said that the western section of this map is based on the lost map of Columbus himself! The island resides in the Antilles Archipelago off the South American coast; in fact, the archipelago's name is derived from Antillia. Over the centuries, there have been many stories of this island. Some have called it *The Island of Seven Cities*, though most have claimed that it has vanished as they approached."

Grimstead and Rogerson loomed over the maps in silence. The Doctor continued. "The island visually appears in approximately twenty three of the ancient maps and is made mention of in several others, notably in accounts by Zuane Pizzigano, Battista Beccario, Martin Behaim, as well as several anonymous accounts. There are also a lot of goings-on about a certain *Isle of Demons* just north of Antillia. The majority of these maps here were made in the 1400s. Apparently those were busy times indeed! Many other maps of the same area do not depict the island as being there at all." The Doctor reached across the table to retrieve two additional sheafs of parchment and placed them on top of the pile. "However, here are two more accounts, drawn centuries apart, of the same shaped island in the exact same coordinates. Even Ponce De Leone makes mention of the key to eternal youth springing from the *ground of sacred illusion*. I believe he had traveled to, or at least peered at, this ghost-like landmass. Though, he didn't bother to draw a map... which is quite unprofessional if you ask me. Mercifully, in 1548, a man named Pedro de Medina stated that the island was on the same latitude as the Straits of Gibraltar, and was *'twenty eight leagues in width, and eighty seven in length.'* Each reference seems to omit exact coordinates—mostly due to the blasted thing disappearing as they approached—but they *do* seem to keep it in the general area off the eastern coast of South America. I for one am currently disenchanted at the un-thoroughness-ness of our seafaring forefathers. I suppose I would be wary too, had I not a big metal ship."

Emma sighed heavily. "Do get to the point, father dear."

"Fine, fine. The point, as it were, is that every few hundred years an island, whom several renown explorers, historians and occult theorists believe to hold the key to immortality and strange magic, appears and then vanishes with only horror stories in its wake. Some have said that the Christian Bishops of Visigoth Hispania fled from the Muslim conquest and founded Antillia. Other reports state that the Portuguese were the occupants of the Seven Cities. Though this is all hearsay, it seems that there is but one way to put to rest all the legends of monsters, eternal life and Christian runaways. We, my dear friends, are going to the Lost Island of Antillia to find the fountain of youth!"

The room remained silent. Dr. McParland pushed his glasses up the bridge of his nose. "I... had anticipated more... excitement."

"Well, then. I understand why you would need Rogerson and his boat."

"Ship," Rogerson retorted.

"But, where do I come in to all of this? Why extricate me from London on a fool's errand?" The Doctor shook his head.

"We needed someone with experience in the... er... stranger side of existence. Someone who's vast knowledge in the unknown could give us an edge no matter what we run into. I put out the word and only days later I was contacted by that Hargraves fellow. He gave us your name. Funny, how things work out, no? When I first saw you, I thought Mr. Hargraves had played a joke on us. He assured me that you were in fact, the man for the task. Thankfully, you seem to be coming along, eh? In addition, The Order of The Lucifuge couldn't sit idly by and watch one of its most prestigious members sink into such waste. This is redemption, my dear boy! Mr. Hargraves felt that this noble *fool's errand* would give you the opportunity to absolve yourself, so to speak. That, and we need someone with your vast knowledge of the occult, just in case the good Captain's bullets do not do the trick."

Hargraves. Hearing that name never got easier. It assaulted Grimstead's chest like a cannonball. He clenched his jaw, trying to physically stifle the rage building up within him. His mind was an overturned hornet's nest. Hargraves the infallible. Hargraves the manipulator. Hargraves the heartless. Grimstead would not allow himself once again to dangle from the puppet master's strings. Hadn't he made it quite clear that he wanted nothing more to do with the Order or its wretched leader? Yes, technically, he had taken a solemn oath into lifetime membership, but surely those ties were severed after his last encounter with Hargraves. Just how many lifetimes would it take to be rid of that demon? Grimstead forced a long, deep breath through his quivering nostrils and regained composure. He slid his fingers over his goatee and slowly shook his head. The Doctor looked at him expectantly, concerned by his silent smolder.

Captain Rogerson broke the silence. "We've only a few more days till we arrive at this mystery island. I suggest we spend that time preparing supplies, munitions and something resembling a plan."

"Sir! Sir!" Mr. Laveglia came crashing into the room, shouting. The group jumped to attention.

"What the devil happened, Angelo?!"

"Lunch is served in the dining hall," he replied with a bow.

SIX

AFTER LUNCH, GRIMSTEAD took it upon himself to explore the *Skidbladnir*'s lower deck. He soon found himself in the Captain's trophy room and was horrified by the numerous cryptids and other formerly-living oddities that were now little more than extravagant maritime décor. Keenly placed around the room were the typical—almost sophomoric—examples of fine taxidermy: tigers, bears and other exotic fauna. The Captain's true treasures included an extremely rare white bull from the continent of Coradine, several tiny pixies floating in formaldehyde, a mounted mermaid mummy from the South Pacific and—the most impressive—a North American Sasquatch. Swords and rifles were also mounted in close proximity to the creature it was used to slay. *All relics of a mortal obsession with conquering the unknown.* The room's ornate wooden door opened almost silently and Emma entered. Her eyes scanned the room and a look of disgust curled across her face.

"Men and their trophies."

"Miss McParland." Grimstead nodded his head slightly. Emma stood next to him and peered into the eyes of the Sasquatch. Though its face was forever frozen in a shriek of mock rage, its eyes showed fear.

"Emma. You may call me Emma. This is the 19th century, after all. Such pleasantries are banal and impractical. A pitiful creature, is this not?"

"Ah," Grimstead smiled. "The majestic Sasquatch, or Yeti, depending on the region. Some say they are the missing link between apes and modern man."

"Well, I can certainly see a resemblance between this poor fellow here and our fearless leader," she smirked, her blue eyes sparkling. Grimstead couldn't contain a laugh which echoed in the large room.

"Ah, I'm sorry, Miss—*Emma*. You remind me so much of... someone I once knew." He smiled wistfully.

"Your wife, Lilly?"

Grimstead startled. He cocked his head in wonder at the young girl. "No, of someone else, actually. My sister Catherine." His brow furrowed. "But, Lilly... you know of her?"

She nodded. "In a way. You often... spoke of her as you were, er, recovering from the opiates."

His face reddened. "I am ashamed, to be honest. After she died, I lost my bearing. I-I lost my way." He turned his gaze back to the Sasquatch. Emma studied him intently.

"What happened that day?" she boldly inquired. Grimstead drew in a long breath. He kept his eyes on the Sasquatch.

"It was nearly a year ago. Lilly and I were on a reconnaissance mission in Scotland to obtain information on the dealings of The Moonshield Society, an Illuminati of sorts. They managed to take us by surprise. Th... they chained Lilly to an altar and..."

Emma took his hand and squeezed it gently.

"Then, using a talisman of an ancient deity, they... he... summoned a being of immense evil." Grimstead fought to keep his voice steady. "The essence of the creature used Lilly's body as a host. There wasn't any way to save her. I was bound and helpless. If not for Hargraves and The Order of The Lucifuge, the ramifications would have been catastrophic."

He squeezed Emma's hand tighter, his eyes clouding over

with visions of those terrible moments. He could see Hargraves' clockwork pistols with their spinning gears and enhanced velocity bullets tearing into Lilly's back, ripping through her chest and destroying the amulet of Goy Gothog.

"Enough. Enough about that, please." He dropped her hand with a shudder. After a moment's pause, he turned to face her.

"Of course, I'm so sorry." She dropped her eyes in reverence. "I can't begin to imagine what pain your memories must evoke." She bit her lip. "However, I am curious though as to what exactly the Moonshield Society is. And the Order of, what was it?"

Grimstead breathed deeply and slowly. "The Order of The Lucifuge," he began. "Legend has it that King Solomon had been trapping demons and Djinns because he felt that their evil was a blight on the world. Too many evils were wrought against mankind, so Solomon put his understanding of sigils and rites to task and brought even the most formidable of demons to heel. This caused an imbalance. Lucifer's Prime Minister of hell, Lucifuge Rofocale was sent to the King to mediate a truce of sorts. The scales must be level for the world of men to thrive. Solomon agreed and the Pact of Lucifuge was made. Solomon had two disciples—their names lost to antiquity—who were present when the treaty was met. One who followed the teachings of Solomon The King and upheld his fealty to the Pact, and another who felt that the power of these entities could and *should* be exploited for gain. The latter disciple left with a perversion of Solomon's knowledge and formed The Moonshield Society. Their members are cunning, resourceful and will do whatever it takes to gain power and control, be it political or occult. Society members could be any*one* and be any*where*. The former disciple created The Order of The Lucifuge: people dedicated to keeping the balance between darkness and light. Their duties were to uncover and understand the world outside the margins of convention."

"What do you mean?" Emma ran her hand along the mounted harpoon that had been used to slay a mermaid of Fiji.

"Our world, Emma, is but a shadow. There are many things that lurk on the fringes of our comprehension and beyond." He tilted his head toward the Sasquatch and raised his eyebrows.

"Speaking of things on the fringe of comprehension, I had come here to tell you that my father would like to see you in the cargo hold. I fear that he is in dire need of external validation."

He nodded. "I'll take my leave then. Until later, Emma." He bowed before leaving the beauty with the beasts.

THE SS SKIDBLADNIR buzzed with activity. As Professor Grimstead made his way through the outer passageway to the main deck, he encountered dozens of Crimson Crewmen scurrying to and fro on their daily tasks. Once outside, he paused to gaze out at the Atlantic Ocean. The large steamer was cutting through the open waters at an amazing rate of speed. The *Skidbladnir* was a rare and powerful ship for its day. There were hardly any others like it in existence. *Truly a marvel to behold*, he mused before continuing on to the starboard staircase that led to the lower decks.

The cargo hold resembled a warehouse. It was a spacious room and surprisingly well-lit considering its location in the bowels of the ship. Giant wooden crates, some marked 'Explosives,' were stacked ceiling-high along the hold's perimeter. In the center of the room, beside some heavy-looking machinery and several piles of metal slats, was a large gray tarp concealing *something*. Grimstead cautiously descended the stairs, taking in every detail of the room he was about to enter. He quickly spotted the Doctor's arched back hovering over a cluttered workbench, a torrent of sparks flying out from his arc welder. Grimstead's eyes darted from the sparks to the crates then to the sparks again.

"Dr. McParland!"

The sparks continued to soar unabated. Grimstead approached the Doctor and gingerly tapped him on the back. McParland spun around with the arc welder still alight and Grimstead jumped back at least two feet. A pair of oversized goggles with thick black lenses obscured the Doctor's face.

"Who is it?!" McParland shouted, looking around. He suddenly regarded the still-blazing welder and switched it off before pulling the goggles to his forehead. "Ah! Alexander, my boy! Come, let me show you my latest creation. Or, most of it, anyway." He produced a soiled handkerchief from one of his pockets and mopped the sweat from his face. "I've been quite eager to have your trained eyes, and mind, on this little pet project of mine."

"They look like sheets of metal to me."

"Indeed! These are being welded to modified hinges, which will then be attached to... this!" The Doctor pulled the tarp from the large object, revealing a standard-issue Duryea Motor Wagon. McParland motioned to Grimstead and the two began to walk around the vehicle. On closer inspection, Grimstead found a complex-looking array of pipes and support struts that weaved around, under and through the wagon body before ultimately jutting out vertically from the sides. A second bench seat was affixed to the back of the first, which Grimstead thought to be extremely out of place. Until he saw that it was aesthetically concealing a second motor, three-times larger than any automobile motor he'd ever seen, set in the rear of the carriage.

"This will be the future of human conveyance, my boy! Once those metal sheets are properly attached to the support beams here, it will house a large hot air balloon." He gestured toward the tarp, which Grimstead now realized was the balloon material. "It will be half automobile and half dirigible! Need to go to the market? Hop in and enjoy the smooth ride! What's that? The market is on top of some ridiculous mountain? No worries! With a shift of this lever," he gestured to the right of the steering column, "steam from this converted engine will instantly fill the balloon and off you go, you lucky devil!"

"A personal dirigible!" Grimstead let out a kind laugh. "You, sir, are dedicated to your work. Your excitement is contagious, I must say."

"The only problem that I have encountered thus far is the speed in which it can go while in flight. The port-side pipes fill the balloon while the starboard pipes release the steam. This design enables it to ascend and descend with ease. Propulsion, however, still escapes me." The Doctor peered over the machine as if it were a terminal patient. "And to steer it once in the air? Perhaps a turbine of some sort? A giant rudder?"

Grimstead looked at the balloon, a thought forming in his mind. "What if you were to use a series of smaller balloons in conjunction with this larger one? The larger for altitude and the smaller to act as bladders, if you will." His eyes lit up, envisioning the grand dirigible in flight. He gestured enthusiastically in the air. "With more piping you could effectively make the steam fill or escape as needed. If one would need to go left, one would release the port bladders and fill the starboard."

"I could effectively have the pipes work as ventricles would in a heart!" McParland's sense of inspiration was renewed. "Yes! A series of bladders working to pump, or pull, steam as needed. I could add more vents. Even see if I can't fashion the steam mechanism into the auto's steering device!" The petite doctor could barely keep still through his excitement. "Perhaps... perhaps a lever that pulls the steering column from the drive train and into the dirigible controls. Oh, how I love levers! If I fashion it correctly, it would be no different that changing the gear from park to go! And, then, perhaps a tiny, teensy weensy lever that will send the steam up to the bladders as opposed to the engine. Oh, I have so many options now! Thank you, Alexander, thank you! I shall have to name it after you, you know! The Grim-Zeppelin, perhaps? Oh! Perhaps The Grim-Rigible?"

Grimstead bowed, shaking his head. "I am honored to have lent my assistance, but the credit is really not necessary. Anything else I may do for you, Doctor?" His inquiry fell on deaf ears. McParland was muttering to himself now, squeals of delight randomly punctuating his self dialogue. His was certainly a mind that constantly blurred the line between brilliance and madness.

Grimstead's eyes darted once more to the crates with volatile contents, thinking that it would be a good idea to see how the opposite side of the ship was getting along.

GRIMSTEAD LEANED OVER the port-side railing and marveled at the speed which the *Skidbladnir* traveled. "Fast boat," he chuckled to himself. In fact, the SS *Skidbladnir* was the largest—and fastest—steamer of its time. She was a veritable fortress; capable of enduring cannon fire or the sea when it grew angry. She had proved herself to be more than just the boasts of a deranged captain, that much was certain. A pod of dolphins appeared and raced the ship, to Grimstead's delight. His spirits lifted as he watched them leaping and playing. A few minutes later, Mr. Bonitto exited the stairwell hatch and joined the Professor at the railing. The first mate leaned on the railing to the right of the Professor and nodded. He was a big fellow, to be sure. However, he was not quite as large as The Swede, a mountainous crew member that Grimstead had only seen in passing, but enough to make even the most seasoned brawler think twice. His features were stern and noble, his solemn eyes were ever processing the world around him. The ship's first mate was a stoic foil to his captain, and his presence was not to be ignored. Grimstead returned the nod with a smile.

"Mr. Bonitto."

"Professor." His voice was deep and smooth, a Caribbean zest with a worldly neutrality. One had little choice but to listen.

"I must admit, this ship impresses me more and more."

"Indeed!" His face brightened "She's designed for power and speed. Four turbines combined with the finest sails—there's hardly a ship out there than can catch her, let alone know what to do with her if they did." His expression became solemn once more. "There is something I need to say..."

"Is there a problem?" Grimstead suddenly wondered if the dolphins would save him if he were thrown overboard. Mr. Bonitto exhaled in a heavy huff.

"There is no easy way to say it, so I'll just say it. I knew your sister." The words hit Grimstead in the chest like a club. His left hand clamped the rail as if they were suddenly struck by a rogue wave.

"H-how? When?"

"Every so often, when the luxury is granted, Captain Rogerson goes on sabbatical. Takes a long while off. During this time on land, the crew go to their family and whatnot, until summoned. If they choose to come back, they come. Otha-wise they stay gone with no worries. I am no land-lubber, Professor. My soul belongs here on the waves. Every now an' again I go ashore, but soon enough wan come aboard again. Land makes me feel in chains, they do. You look around us now, and you see nothing but freedom. So, I find myself on Captain Stout's ship, *The Avenger*. I signed on for a job in the Orient. They a'ready had a first mate, so I become the quartermaster. You know who the first mate was?"

"Catherine."

"Exact. Catherine Grimstead, or as they call her, *Cunning Catty Cutthroat*. I was told she rose through the ranks like there were none. She was always by the Captain's side. Guess that why she soon became Catherine Stout, no? She proved her salt, alright. At first, Stout saw her like a good luck charm, but learned quickly she was a natural leader. This job I told you about? It was a contract from Chulalonkorn, the great King of Siam himself! We had to escort a ship from Bangkok to Great Britain that carried a British Foreign Minister. A pirate named Pan patrolled those waters and the King knew a British minister would mean big ransom. Captain Stout wanted to flaunt like a peacock behind the British ship and scare Pan away, but your sister, well, she had a better plan. She say, *'Pirate see us, he finds an easier target someplace else. We draw him in, we take him down.'* Stout ask her, *'How we do that?'* She smile and say, *'By giving him exactly what he wants.'*"

"The British ship sailed at full mast, looking to make haste. The Avenger was at half mast, keeping well behind. Just as hoped, that scoundrel Pan spotted the ship and made his move. A warning shot across the bow was a friendly way to get your intentions known. The British ship stopped. Pan and his best scallywags boarded without a fuss. Pan then make his demand for the minister. *'Minister below deck, minister want no trouble',* they tell Pan. Pan say, *'Good'.* This be an easy day's work. Once the hatch was open, Captain Stout and half his crew come bursting out like wild devils, guns and swords and hollering like beasts from hell. Pan didn't know if he should fight, run, or shit himself. By that point, *The Avenger* was well in range and fired a mortar near Pan's ship. I stood next to Stout and laughed when Catherine kicked that dreaded pirate in his balls! Thanks to her plan, not a soul was lost on either side. Pan was taken back to Siam for trial and execution, and his ship was presented as a gift to the king. We got a fat purse that day. Duppy know who fi frighten!"

"Duppy knows who to frighten?"

"Jamaican saying, means people pick on those they know can't defend themselves. But thanks to your sister, a real mean bastard was taken out of the game for good. She was something else, alright. My heart beat heavy when I heard she die. She was a great woman. She thought the world of you, you know."

"She told you that?"

"She told everybody. She was a talker too, hoo-boy!" They shared a laugh and turned to gaze at the endless sea. Grimstead looked at the fat cotton clouds and smiled.

"Thank you for telling me that story. There are so many things about Catherine I wish I knew. Cunning Catty Cutthroat," he laughed. Mr. Bonitto smiled and placed a reassuring hand on Grimstead's shoulder.

"As my granny used to say, *'Every mikkle mek a mukkle'*. Every little bit counts."

GRIMSTEAD ENTERED THE navigation room long after midnight, hoping to do a little late-night reading. A dim light emanated from the library level, where Dr. McParland and Mr. Laveglia sat at a small table, sipping at tumblers of the Captain's rum. Between them lay a chess board that was far larger than the table. As Grimstead plodded up the spiral stairs, he could hear the men arguing as to who's turn it was.

"...and for the last time, get your glass off *my* board! It's not a coaster!" Mr. Laveglia swatted at Dr. McParland's glass, nearly knocking it to floor. The Doctor caught it and noticed Grimstead standing just outside the shadows, smiling at them.

"Alexander, m'boy!" he bleated. "Come, pull up an uncomfortable chair and join our little soirée! The rum is quite good! Though, I must admit that Angelo here is testing my patience. He is a very good chess player."

"We haven't played chess this whole time, Douglas," Laveglia laughed. "We've just pushed the pieces around."

"Eh, that's all chess is to me, my friend." The Doctor raised his glass in salute. "I much prefer conversation and strong drink over trapping queens and toppling knights." Grimstead lifted a narrow chair from the corner of their nook and sat. Mr. Laveglia spun in his chair and plucked a glass tumbler from the serving tray on a small end table and tossed it to Grimstead. McParland topped his own glass off with the brown rum then handed the bottle over."

"I really shouldn't," Grimstead protested.

"All the more reason you *aught*, m'boy!"

"Yes, you can't let us two gaffers drink by ourselves." Mr. Laveglia swished his glass around. "Makes it seem like we have a drinking problem." Grimstead exhaled in defeat and filled his glass.

"To good friends," Grimstead toasted.

"And better rum," added Laveglia.

"Oh, my, yes! And to our adventure! May we go henceforth and whence safely and successfully!" Dr. McParland raised his glass—a few drops of rum crested the rim and landed on his lap. "Oh, now it looks as though I wet myself!" His timid giggle quickly evolved into a full-blown cackle. There was no denying that his grasp of sanity was markedly tenuous. Or perhaps he just didn't give a good god damn what anyone else thought. Grimstead couldn't decide which better suited his odd companion.

"What is the topic at hand, fellows?" Grimstead sipped the rum. Its sweet sting warmed his tongue.

"I was talking about how my emotions are mixed between excitement and terror, now that I may be close to the culmination of my life's work. For decades, I have bounded here and there, chasing this lead or that hunch. Nothing more than a fly flitting across a table to find a morsel of food that may not even exist!"

"Or shit." Laveglia nodded. "Flies also eat shit."

"Or shit." McParland returned the nod.

"You have been searching for Antillia all your life," Grimstead stated more than asked. Dr. McParland shrugged.

"More or less. Since I was a lad, I have been approached in my dreams by an entity of pure light. It told me that I would one day find the key to immortality. *Where do I start?* I always asked, but the entity would send me on a wild goose chase. It was as if it were stalling me. Antillia was more of an impression, something I heard the old sailors speak about until recently, when I realized that it was *always* the answer. It was only hidden, veiled and obscured, but always in my mind."

"I'm curious about this entity, Doc—"

"Douglas, dear boy. Douglas."

"Douglas." Grimstead smiled.

"In the beginning, I thought it was Jesus Christ himself come to guide me. Then, it was Baldr. In my thirties, the entity revealed itself as Enki, the Sumerian god of intelligence and creation. It never showed itself outright. Most thought I was insane... and still do! I even spent some time in a sanitarium, believing my colleagues' accusations that I was indeed *touched*. Those were dark days." McParland swallowed more rum and set the glass onto the uneven chess board, which wobbled.

"As I was saying, those sanitarium days were wrought with anguish and self-loathing. There I was, an accomplished doctor and scientist, or as they once called it—*natural philosopher*—sitting in a room full of babbling, drooling Genhis Khans, Napoleons and Shakespeares! Once, I even found Jesus. He was in the broom closet, feverishly masturbating like a monkey. My visions uncovered truths, only not the one true truth I've searched for. There is no religion in science. No spiritualism. To a certain extent, I agree with the separation, however, there are instances that no amount of scrutiny can totally and infallibly explain. I believe —*truly* believe—that there are natural causes for everything, even if those causes seem unnatural. What is god? Can we discover what that is and what created the creator? Surely everything must have a natural origin of some sort. How can we understand every aspect of nature? What was here before there even was a *here*? I am positive that one day science will find a way to map out our entire existence—to prove the late Charles Darwin's theories as fact. Or perhaps a god—the god—*any* god will show itself and be the teacher everyone claims it to be. I would very much like to be a part of that."

"Hence the search for the fountain of youth." Grimstead nodded. McParland rubbed the tired from his eyes.

"I very well can't contribute when I'm dead, now can I?" he chuckled. "Though, in truth, it is my simple-yet-overwhelming curiosity of science and its undoubted leaps and bounds that drives me to longevity. I want to see where science leads us through the ages. To touch things that would only be —by today's standards—the delusional rantings of fiction writers. Fiction is the precursor to fact, I've always said."

"You sound like a friend of mine." Grimstead took a mouthful of rum.

"I *am* a friend of yours!"

"Apologies. Yes, you are my friend, Douglas! I wanted say that I am reminded of my friend, Nikola Tesla. He speaks as passionately about science as you, and is also quite the quirky fellow."

"He's a friend of yours? I would love to meet him someday! I have followed his work on rotating magnetic fields. I wonder if that greedy twat Edison will try and steal that idea, too?"

"Doctor!" Grimstead was taken aback.

"What? Have you never met Edison?"

"I have."

"Then you'll agree the man is a twat!"

"Yes," Grimstead smiled and shook his head. "Edison is a twat."

"To twats!" Mr. Laveglia raised his glass. The three clinked and drank deeply.

"What about you, Alexander? Do you ever think about your own mortality?" Dr. McParland went to set his glass down and toppled the chessboard. The glass rolled in a circle but did not break. "Oop! My apologies, Angelo."

"I don't care, I'm not cleaning it up!" Mr. Laveglia chuckled. Grimstead picked the glass up and offered it to Dr.

McParland, who shook his head.

"I suspect that I have had enough for tonight."

"Of course." Grimstead finished his rum and set both glasses on the floor. "I do think of mortality. Perhaps more than any man should. I've witnessed and have come so close to it so many times that it has lost all abstruseness."

"Would you partake in immortality if immortality were presented you?" McParland leaned closer, his eyes reddening orbs of under-slept wonderment. Grimstead thought of Lilly. If he were to live forever, he would never touch her face again.

Would I even make it into heaven? Was there even a heaven to enter? Would she still accept me if we were reunited? These were the questions he tortured himself with time and again as he wasted away in opium purgatory. Immortality would rob him of the answers.

"No, Douglas, I would not."

"Me either!" Mr. Laveglia chimed. "What if you drink from the fountain and it gives you immortality but doesn't stop you from aging? Eh? You ever think of that? BOOP! Now you're an immortal, and on your one-hundred-and-eleventeenth birthday, you're sitting inna hospital bed with a rubber tube in your banger because you're too decrepit to get your crusty ass to the water closet and empty your dick like you did back when you *should'a* died. You gonna say, *Gee, I am sure enjoying this living forever thing?* I think not! How bad you gonna smell? What about when your skin rots off but you can't die? You shit your lungs out and maggots chew on your eyes? What happens when the rest of the world dies off, and there you are in a heap of dirt and bird shit—nothing but a dried-out husk that's being used for a home by a family of possums? Possums are assholes! Who you gonna talk to then? Just you in your mind. You'd go *folle come scoiattolo merda*—crazy as squirrel shit. So, no, thank you. I'll just do myself a favor and die when the reaper comes around."

"What did you do before you became quartermaster,

Angelo?" McParland asked. Grimstead was still processing the wealth of imagery from the outburst. Mr. Laveglia finished his glass and smiled at the Doctor.

"I could tell you, but then I'd have to kill you. What good'll your fountain be then, eh?"

SEVEN

FIFTEEN DAYS HAD passed since the SS *Skidbladnir* had left London and tensions were at a peak. With each passing sunset, the occupants of the steam ship knew that the mysterious Island of Antillia—and all of its haunting legends—was another day closer.

Grimstead stood hunched over the large navigation table intently studying several maps that were splayed out before him. A half-eaten egg-and-toast sandwich had grown soggy and cold on the right side of the table. Several empty china cups were stacked in a pyramid pattern beside the sandwich, not a drop of coffee left in any of them. He chose two maps from the pile: one very old and markedly decrepit, the other newer but still yellowed and torn. With extreme care, he placed one over the other before holding both up to the light; the hand-drawn coastlines of the Island of Antillia were identical on each of the two maps. In fact, the Island was the same on *all* of the maps, save for the occasional extra blip or notation. The same as it had been an hour ago. And, apparently, for centuries prior. He placed the maps back on the table and grabbed the bridge of his nose with his thumb and forefinger. *There* has *to be an explanation. There has to be a plan.* He closed his eyes. The Varangian map showed a swarm of tiny islands off Antillia's southern tip, while the map of Piri Re'is displayed a series of crosshatching which seemed to be harbors, but no surrounding islands. Grimstead found this particular inconsistency to be troubling. He knew that time can alter geography, but it left him with a feeling of uncertainty—and perhaps an ounce or so of dread—as to what incarnation of this Island awaited them.

The sounds of running and shouting erupted just outside the navigation room's door. Grimstead's eyes snapped open, his concentration broken. He tapped Piri Re'is map with his right index finger, attempting to regain his focus. The fracas continued, growing louder by the minute. It was not long before curiosity overcame him. He rushed to the door and peered out. Throngs of CCs were stampeding through the hallway at breakneck speed. The Professor grabbed one and pulled him aside.

"What is the commotion?" he demanded, grasping the young man's forearm tightly. The CC struggled to free his arm but Grimstead's grip was too strong. He looked longingly after his comrades.

"The Captain's ordered us to the deck... for a... a match," the young man gasped, struggling to catch his breath.

Grimstead gripped tighter. "Match?"

"Ow! Yes! When the crew gets too... uh, anxious, he holds boxing matches... on the main deck." Satisfied, Grimstead let the lad's arm go and he hurried off. After a moment's consideration, Grimstead decided to follow.

THE FIGHT WAS already under way when Grimstead arrived. Two shirtless men slowly circled one another, fists at the ready. The midday Sun fought to burn through the milky fog that coated the ship. Crew members of all ranks swarmed around the raised cargo hatch at the deck's center, which acted as a makeshift boxing ring. Captain Rogerson, stood on the ship's bridge, overlooking the action. He was flanked by Emma on his left and Mr. Bonitto and Mr. Laveglia to his right. Laveglia held a fiddle under his chin and was feverishly playing a feisty Celtic tune. Emma waved when she noticed Grimstead slowly edging his way through the crowd toward the ring. He returned the wave awkwardly as he tried to keep his footing among the rowdy crewmen.

"Ah, the Professor joins the rabble, eh?" Rogerson bellowed, raising his right hand to his forehead in a mock salute. "Just as I had hoped," he added under his breath.

The two men in the ring began to swing wildly at each other and the crowd sent up a cheer. Grimstead regarded their sloppy technique and scoffed to himself. The older of the combatants caught his attention, though. The fighter looked to be in his early forties with a rough, square face and a large quantity of stubble. He also appeared to be in more solid shape than his younger counterpart. The older fighter threw a wide-arcing right punch which landed against his opponent's left ear, causing him to cover his head with both arms. The older man took the opportunity to bury his left fist directly into the young man's solar plexus. The young man doubled over, gasping for breath. Mr. Laveglia stopped playing as the referee declared the older man as the victor. He shook the pain out of his left hand as a crewman handed him a blue shirt. He took the shirt and wiped the sweat from his face and neck, then exited the circle. The loser was ushered out of the ring by two CCs.

"Bravo, Dr. Marrow, well done!" Rogerson clapped his hands and shouted over the cheers of the men. Marrow raised his eyebrows, halfheartedly acknowledging the Captain. He pulled a flask from his back pocket and took two large gulps before exiting the ring.

"Who was that?" Grimstead asked the deckhand beside him.

"That's Old Joe Marrow, our head medic," the crewman replied.

"I see. Colorful fellow."

"And now, my fellow scoundrels," Rogerson barked, "next

into the ring is our esteemed colleague, Alexander Grimstead!"

The crowd began hooting and stomping the ground like a community of chimpanzees. A twinge of panic sprouted in Grimstead's chest. He looked around in confusion. All eyes were upon him. He turned and craned his neck to make eye contact with the Captain, who was gripping the bridge railing so tightly that his knuckles were stark white against his tan hands. He glimpsed Emma's eyes just beyond the Captain's shoulder, wide with shock.

"I have no interest in fighting, Captain!" he shouted. "I'm here because I merely wanted to see what all this commotion was."

"Everyone has to fight at least once on my ship," Rogerson grimaced. "Particularly *honored guests*."

Grimstead felt hands on him and was immediately ushered toward the ring against his will. He struggled to fend them off, but it was in vain.

"Captain's orders!" Rogerson snarled. Grimstead was thrust into the ring and fell to knees. He could hear the Captain's spiteful laughter rising up over the din.

Grimstead slowly stood, shaking his head. He was stoically calm. He hadn't been a stranger to a good scrap in his youth. Grandfather's words rang in his head: *It is good to abhor violence. It is also good to be good at it*'. Once he joined The Order, Grimstead had been trained in a myriad of martial arts by Master Ng—The Order's Shaolin mystic and martial arts master. Grimstead knew how to handle himself, alright. He just didn't appreciate taking orders from someone he considered a dolt.

"I do not want to fight!" He purposely kept his back to the Captain. The cheers and laughter died down. "We are almost at our destination. If we damage ourselves now, what good are we when the game is afoot?"

"This is *part* of the adventure, Professor," Rogerson retorted. "I recommend that do yourself a service today, and try not to become damaged."

The crew erupted with laughter once again. "This is madness!" Emma cried out, but her voice was lost in the ruckus. "He's not well enough," she worried to herself, gathering up wads of her skirt into her fists to hide her sweaty palms. A wave of anger swelled in Grimstead's stomach, but he remained still. At that moment, he wished for nothing more than to show Rogerson exactly the sort of damage he meant.

"Let us relieve you of belongings, Professor," Rogerson barked. Two CCs approached and grabbed for his vest buttons. Grimstead swatted their hands away and grudgingly began to undress himself. He carefully tucked his spectacles into his copper colored vest pocket before handing that over too. His starched shirt was next, and the moment it left his body, Emma let out an involuntary gasp. She had not seen Grimstead's bare upper body since the night that she barged into his room. The darkness had obscured his form, and she certainly had not spent any time staring. But she even more certainly had not expected the athletic build that she saw now, in the milky daylight. She stepped out from behind the Captain for a better look. Grimstead silently turned to face Rogerson, his bare chest and arms now moist from the fog. With each breath, he could feel the anger spreading out to every muscle fiber in his chest, arms and legs.

"What wonders never cease," Emma thought, then realized that she had said it aloud. Her words confirmed Rogerson's surprise. He hadn't expected the Professor to be equipped with lean muscles. He envisioned him as a bespectacled waif who might snap in twain with a strong wind. He pouted for a moment before calling out to his men.

"Any volunteers to test the mettle of the dear Professor?" None in attendance raised their hand. Rogerson pointed at a particularly burly CC. "You there! Good news, you've just been volunteered!"

Obediently, the man entered the ring and tossed his shirt

into the crowd. He casually cracked his knuckles on each hand and then his neck while he sized Grimstead up. The Professor remained perfectly still. Rogerson raised his right hand. "A jaunty tune, Mr. Laveglia!" he proclaimed before closing his hand into a fist and smashing it down onto the railing. Emma leaned forward, fighting the urge to run down into the crowd. Mr. Laveglia stomped his foot three times then launched into a song.

The burly CC immediately raised his fists to his face and began to duck and weave. Grimstead continued to stand still. The burly crewman threw a straight left punch to the Professor's face. Grimstead waited until the moment just before impact then quickly brought his left hand across his face to tap the man's arm, changing its intended trajectory. The punch breezed by his right ear. Emma gasped out loud and the crowd followed suit. Rogerson leaned out even further on the railing so that he was practically doubled over. No one was quite sure as to what just happened.

"What's your name, son?" Grimstead inquired.

"Johnstone, sir," the burly young gent replied as he swung a left roundhouse punch toward the Professor's face. Grimstead ducked, avoiding the punch with seemingly little effort.

"Mr. Johnstone, I will endeavor to not hurt you too badly in this nonsense."

Johnstone scoffed, and threw a straight right punch, which Grimstead deftly swooped underneath and in the same motion, spun counterclockwise to bury his elbow into the young man's solar plexus. Johnstone collapsed in a heap of wheezing convulsions. The crowd murmured its appreciation, uncertain as to whether or not their cheers would inspire the Captain to volunteer them next. Emma's eyes were fixed to Grimstead. He glared at the gape-mouthed Crewman who was currently holding his clothing. The man thrust the garments into his waiting hands and Grimstead turned to exit the ring. Rogerson quickly made a few agitated hand motions at two nearby subordinates—a short, dark-haired Spaniard and a stocky Irishman of about medium height—and silently mouthed the word *Attack!*

Grimstead saw the two approach and paused, dropping his clothes and kicking them off to the side. The men simultaneously entered the ring and began circling him along the perimeter. The Spaniard was first to attack, lunging for the Professor's throat. Without hesitation, Grimstead grabbed the Spaniard's right arm then spun his own body into him, using leverage and centrifugal force to throw the Spaniard into the crowd. He then leaped toward the Irishman, spinning into a right-footed wheel kick which smashed the poor bastard on the side of his head. Grimstead had lost his patience. The Irishman lost consciousness.

Grimstead stooped to retrieve his clothes and tried, once again, to leave the circle. He ducked through the ropes and into the crowd. This time no one stood in his way. But just as he entered the crowd, he heard Rogerson's voice once more. "The SWEDE! Front and center!" At the back of the crowd, a very large reddish-blond-haired man stood up. He was so tall and muscular that his shadow stretched three men deep. The crowd began to chant. "The Swede! The Swede! The Swede!"

"One more opponent, Professor," Rogerson laughed. "One more and we'll call it a day!"

Mr. Laveglia panted as he continued to fiddle. The crowd parted in half to let The Swede through. As the giant plodded toward the ring, Grimstead kept his eyes on fixed on his opponent and reversed his gait back up into the ring. He set his things down on the ground and made his way to the center and waited.

The Swede entered the ring. Grimstead looked him squarely in the chest and sighed deeply. The Swede threw his arms out wide and roared so loudly that it broke Mr. Laveglia's concentration and his fiddle screeched. Grimstead quickly kicked his opponent in the crotch as hard as he could. The

Swede buckled and Grimstead jumped, grabbing the giant's head with both hands and, with all of his might, rocketed his left knee straight up and into the giant's forehead.

The Swede staggered and muttered, "Not fair!" Grimstead jumped again, this time driving his right elbow into The Swede's neck. It immediately began to spasm. Grimstead quickly shuffled to the opposite side of the ring and pivoted, sprinting forward and executing a running drop kick into the midsection of his stunned opponent. The giant toppled over the ropes and into the crowd, crushing several spectator's underneath. Grimstead hopped down from the ring and landed on The Swede, who lay face-down on the ground. As the Professor walked down the length of the large man, he could hear him—and those beneath him—moaning in protest.

"Life is unfair, my Jotun-esque friend." Grimstead snatched his belongings and strode toward the nearest stairwell doorway, consciously ignoring the clamor and confusion behind him and disappeared below deck.

"Captain!" A disembodied voice bellowed over the din via a series of sleek copper pipes that snaked along the ceilings throughout the ship and ended on the bridge in a flourish of metalwork resembling the mouth of a Helicon.

"Laaaaaand hooooo!"

"WE'LL HAVE TO wait till morning," Captain Rogerson conceded, peering through his binoculars from the bridge at the dark landmass on the horizon. The ship had calmed its pace and was now anchored about a ten-minute-row from the shore. Even at that distance the island was barely visible through the thick, humid air.

"Agreed." Grimstead collapsed his brass spyglass and placed it into his vest pocket. "It would be rash of us to begin exploration in this fog and with most of the day already gone."

Dr. McParland paced along the bridge in an agitated state

while Emma looked on. She attempted to hand him a peppermint candy, but he waved her off. "Most distressing," he muttered. "Who knows what ground we might have covered by then?"

"Douglas, I'll not risk running aground on some unseen sandbar or wreckage," Rogerson called down to the scientist. "And spending a night on an island that we've not even begun to explore? That would be true folly. No, we wait till morning. First light."

"Surely you could wait till then, father," Emma pleaded. Though she was intensely curious about what awaited them on that ominous landmass, she couldn't help but agree with the Captain's reasoning. It fiercely irked her. "Though I must admit, there's a terrible allure to it all."

"I shall not be coming with you. I've no back for expeditions, you know. Not since, well, ever. No. You lot will blaze a trail and when you've reached... whatever there is to reach... I will come forthwith. I'd only get in the way otherwise." The old man stopped pacing for a moment and frowned up at the Captain. He turned to Emma, holding out his hand for a candy. She groaned.

"I've *just* put them away!"

Rogerson rolled his eyes.

"Very well," Grimstead clicked his tongue and placed both hands at his back. "First light tomorrow we take a few of the life boats and row to shore. Set up a waypoint and then enter what looks to be jungle just beyond the beach. I suggest we take this opportunity to head back to the navigation room and get a better grasp of what we're about to embark on." He turned and left the deck without another word.

"Who does he think he is?" Rogerson grumbled.

NIGHT COVERED THE ship in a thick, wet blanket. Grimstead stole himself away from the raucousness of the final pre-adventure dinner and stood at the bow. His eyes strained to find the island's shape through the murk. The sound of Mr. Laveglia's violin, meshed with crass sea shanties brought a smile to his face.

Lilly would have loved this, he mused. *She would have delighted in Emma's confidence, the Doctor's manic brilliance and kept the egotistical Rogerson on his egotistical toes.*

"I would have you live in my memory, not languish from it!"

The words pulled at his heart. The voices and music faded to a muted hum as the fog whirled before his eyes.

"THIS IS A joyous occasion," Hargraves rumbled. He stood on a modest wooden platform in front of three kneeling figures. "Our ranks have thickened with these special few. Their talents and dedication will ensure that balance will continue in this world. Mankind will benefit as a result of the commitment they have pledged here tonight. So, rise, Lilly Chambers! Rise, Alexander Grimstead! Rise, Kristian Fowler! You are now members of the sacred Order of The Lucifuge!" Each stood and looked upon each other. Until that moment, none had ever met. Grimstead and Lilly locked gazes for what seemed an eternity until Fowler shoved his way in to kiss the lady's hand. Before Grimstead could protest, he was pulled away by three veteran members who sought to congratulate him: Algernon Colborne—also known as Black Hercules—a massive and muscular freed slave, Dr. Ng, the enigmatic Chinese master of martial arts and arcane eastern alchemy, and Scott, who had been raised by tigers in the wilds of southern Africa. Scott's tiger companion, Kero, roared in celebration.

Grimstead's eyes were ever upon Lilly.

There was a familiarity between them, like they've known each other for ages. He scarcely knew her name, but it felt as though her face had always been etched in his mind—of that he had no doubt. His life would never be the same, and that thought excited him to no end.

"Each of you have been chosen because of your gifts," Hargraves said. "Miss Chambers for her prowess as a psychic medium, Mr. Fowler for his deep knowledge in summoning and magic, and Mr. Grimstead for his understanding of the occult in all its various forms. I am confidant that each of you will add strength and depth to our Order and bolster our impact upon the world. It will not be easy. In fact, it may be the most difficult undertaking in your lives, but we sacrifice what we must to maintain harmony."

...sacrifice...
...sacrifice...
...sacrifice.

"You've much more left to do."

The mist steadied. The sounds from the mess hall crept back louder and louder, shaking Grimstead from his reverie. He wiped a tear from his cheek and kissed it.

"How much more, my love?" he asked the heavy darkness, but was met with roaring silence.

EIGHT

THE ISLAND OF ANTILLIA
1898

THE SWEDE WAS first to set foot on the island. He jumped from the life boat that also carried twenty CCs, Captain Rogerson, Dr. Marrow, Professor Grimstead and Emma, then pulled it ashore. The air lay thick and heavy on them, though there was no morning fog like they had witnessed the day prior. It was less than an hour after dawn and Emma could already feel beads of sweat collecting on her brow.

"Are you alright, Emma?" Grimstead asked. Emma straightened and waved his concern off like an insult.

"This is nothing. I've had hotter baths," she shrugged. Emma often acted tough, though she was grateful that she heeded her father and chose to wear a pair of his trousers and boots instead of a dress. Her white cotton shirt did little to stave the humidity, but she would never admit discomfort. She was both nervous and excited at the opportunity to participate in such a lofty adventure. She was also quite relieved that no one objected to having a woman present on the expedition, particularly the Captain. Once the boats were empty of crew and supplies, the group began to survey the beach for any remnants of an ancient civilization. An hour passed quickly, and all they had discovered was sand. Rogerson made his way to the tree line then motioned that the party follow.

They gathered at the opening of the island's jungle and regarded one another silently for several moments before Dr. Marrow grunted, "Well? We just gonna stand here and braid each other's hair?" He spat on the ground and glared at Rogerson. "Captain?" The Captain kept his eyes on the Doctor.

"We'll head in from here, but stay single-file. Swede, you'll bring up the rear. Marrow, Grimstead, Miss McParland. you're with me at the front." With a swift motion he unsheathed his machete and stepped across the threshold.

The Captain swiped the brush from his decided path with large, powerful strokes of the machete. Those behind him widened what was left, making the path a little more maneuverable from man to man.

"Hey, Joe," Rogerson called out.

"Yeah?"

"Remember Borneo?"

"Barely."

"This is a lot like Borneo. The thick brush, the humid air and endless noise."

"If you say so, Captain." Marrow trudged along, not using his machete nor engaging in any helpful activity.

"Remember the chieftain who wanted me to bed his wife *and* his daughter at the same time, to ensure he would have large sons?"

"That happened?" Marrow scratched his head.

"Almost."

"What went wrong?"

"*Please* stop this conversation," Emma protested.

"It turned out that he didn't have a wife and daughter— just an effeminate brother and nephew!"

"Oh, no." Marrow stopped the caravan by abruptly standing still. Rogerson looked over his shoulder.

"What?"

"I slept with his niece!" Marrow slapped his forehead. "God's balls! Now it makes total sense why she only wanted me to do it in her—"

"*Enough*!" Emma roared. She shoved Marrow from his stupor. "Good lord, you all disgust me!"

Grimstead held back a snicker. Rogerson began chopping again.

"Hey, Joe."

"Yeah...?"

"Remember Paris?"

"Barely."

"This is nothing like Paris."

THE JUNGLE WAS a vast, thick and damp mass of muted greenery. The group proceeded slowly, finding that it was necessary to use their machetes to remove the tangles of vines and undergrowth with every few steps. The fog seemed to be thickening the further inland they went, so Captain Rogerson ordered a few CCs to run ahead as scouts. The air buzzed with wild and strange noises, most were sounds that Emma had never heard before. She fought the urge to jump out of her boots after nearly every howl or shriek. The group had not made it very far when they encountered a section of particularly treacherous undergrowth. As they hacked away, the sound of hundreds of shrieking voices filled the air. Startled, Emma screamed and instinctively ducked. The rest fell victim to the harassment that ensued: scores of Capuchin monkeys swooped down from the tree-tops and took turns menacing the group. The men jumped to attention, blades at the ready. However, the monkeys did not seem to be on the attack. Instead, they seemed to be enjoying themselves as they continuously swooped down at the group, shrieking and grasping at whatever they could touch.

"Disease-ridden bastards!" Dr. Marrow yelled as he attempted to shoo them with rocks and harsh language. Grimstead couldn't help but chuckle to himself, he had learned from the Captain that Marrow calls everyone a disease-ridden bastard at some point.

Rogerson picked up his pace, hastily hacking at vines and batting away the invaders simultaneously.

"Press on, men!" he called back, "They can't keep this up for long!" Grimstead whirled around, anticipating the next barrage when he saw that Emma was still crouched several yards away, with monkeys relentlessly grabbing at her hair and clothes as they swung past. He hurried over and helped her stand, holding his machete over their heads as a shield as they ran to catch up with the group.

After what seemed like miles, the Capuchins finally let up, their calls and laughter now distant in the dense air. Exhausted from the heightened pace, the explorers took the opportunity to pause and catch their breath. Emma sat down on a fallen tree trunk and took a hearty gulp from her canteen.

"Thank you... Alexander," she said breathlessly. "That was... rather unexpected." He chuckled, reaching for his own canteen.

"I believe it's time for you to reconfigure your expectations, Emma." Without warning, a cluster of vulture-sized dragonflies swooped down between the trees and passed close overhead. Everyone braced themselves, but the giant insects were gone as quickly as they had come, leaving the group to stare after them in shock.

"Well, shit!" Marrow exclaimed. "I'd hate to see what those things eat."

"Or, what eats them." Grimstead raised his eyebrows.

"Captain!" One of the CC scouts came rushing toward the group—pausing a few yards away. "Captain! Captain! You must see this!" He waved his arms wildly before running back into the brush from whence he came. They all got up and rushed after him; moments later they were looking at a small clearing with several well-aged corpses scattered among the undergrowth. The CC silently pointed up to one of the trees, where another was dangling from the branches above, tangled up in what appeared to be a parachute.

"I... I don't know what to make of it, sir," the scout stammered, shaken by his macabre discovery. Rogerson glanced over at Grimstead. They exchanged a nod and advanced into the clearing. "Hang back, men," Rogerson called over his shoulder.

Marrow immediately took it upon himself to join them and Emma was close on his heels, leaving the rest to look on and wait for orders.

Grimstead scanned the ill-fated travelers before crouching next to one. He noted that although their bodies were in an advanced state of decay, their clothing was mostly intact.

"Look here, Professor," the Captain waved Grimstead over to where a few of the corpses were heaped together. "Are you familiar with Old Norse runes?"

"Not as well-versed as yourself, I'm sure."

"These fellows have collar brass that depict the rune *sól*, or sun in Old Norse, twice, like a double *S*. In Old English it's known as *sigel*. Either way, it is regarded as a rune of great power and success. It's likely that they were men of rank in some sort of faction. Interesting. I might add that their leather long coats and boots aren't quite conducive to a jungle expedition."

"Indeed..." Grimstead rubbed his goatee. "And look, their red arm bands bear the angled cross known as the *swastika*—from the Sanskrit *svastika*—which connotes luck or well-being. It has been used by many ancient cultures over the centuries, however I am most familiar with it used as the Japanese Manji. Such an interesting juxtaposition." Nearby, Emma picked up a rusted length of metal. "This looks to me like it's some kind of rifle. I've never seen one quite like this, though. I—" Rogerson plucked it from her hands and inspected it from end to end. Emma glared intently at the back of his head as he attempted to pry the magazine from the weapon.

"Ah!" he exclaimed once it was free, raising his eyebrows in astonishment. "It seems as though this *rifle* is, or was, capable of carrying a large number of bullets in this compartment. I can imagine it could then feed those bullets into the rifle with speed, since there wouldn't be a need for constant reloading. Fascinating!"

Emma turned back to the pile of corpses, this time removing a saber from one's bony grip. She held it up in front of her. "This still looks functional. Don't mind if I do." She hastily slid the saber into the machete sheath on her hip, the long, thin blade tearing a hole through the fabric. The saber's sharp point hovered inches from the ground. As she turned to admire her work, it narrowly missed Grimstead's calf.

"Mind the blade, Emma," he chastised. She shot him a scathing glance.

"I'm not a child, *sir*, nor am I an idiot. I know my way around a blade *and* a pistol." She placed her hands on her hips defensively. Grimstead held up a hand.

"I meant no disrespect, it's only that I feel somewhat responsible for your safety in your father's stead."

"Oh, spare me, Alexander. I am fully capable of taking care of myself." Emma folded her arms across her chest and turned away from him, fully aware of the smirk that crossed his face.

"If we're quite finished comparing penis sizes, I would like to press on before we age like our well- dressed friends here." Rogerson tossed the rusted gun aside and strode into the brush. The scout CCs scrambled to get ahead of him and the others followed shortly after. They were on the move once more.

It took roughly six hours to traverse the thick jungle that had greeted the explorers after leaving the ship. When they finally breached the tree line, the group found themselves at the edge of a large meadow which stretched out as far as they could see on either side. The meadow was populated with extremely tall wild grass and weeds, some so overgrown that they towered over Captain Rogerson's six-foot frame. Among the wild vegetation were hundreds of unusually large, reddish-yellow wildflowers—similar in appearance to daisies—except that their flower heads were bigger than a human's skull.

The Captain quickly spotted a path cutting through the greenery, undoubtedly where his scouts had hiked just a short time before. He knelt momentarily to inspect the impression left by the young men's boot tread, then silently motioned the rest of the group to follow along. They walked in single file.

"Everything is so... *big*!" Emma marveled. "The whole meadow is up to my shoulders, some higher! And such vibrant color compared to that horrible jungle. Wouldn't you agree, Dr. Marrow?" She turned and grinned cheerily at the Doctor.

"Yeah, big goddamned flowers."

Emma rolled her eyes. At twenty yards in, the Captain ordered the precession to halt.

"What's wrong?" Grimstead walked up next to where he had stopped. The Captain squatted down to investigate the ground. He stared intently, without saying a word. "Rogerson?"

"The path ends here. It appears that my scouts went no further than this. Yet... they did not return to the group."

Silence fell among the adventurers, their gaze transfixed onto the spot where the scouts had made their final mark. The flowers and weeds swayed in the gentle breeze.

Three deep clacking sounds broke the tranquility of the meadow. Everyone jumped to attention; rifles held at the ready, pistols cocked. At the far end of the single-file line, The Swede's grip tightened on his bearded axe. A single clack rang out and two CCs from the middle of the line screamed as they disappeared into the tall grass.

"Wagon formation!" Rogerson yelled. The crew members immediately spread out into a circle, with their backs toward the center. Emma, Grimstead and Marrow were left standing in middle. Rogerson pulled out his rifle and peered through its telescopic lens—a feature that had been fashioned for him by Dr. McParland. When collapsed, it acted as a magnifier for the rifle's sights. When extended, it enabled sniper-quality precision. He swept it left to right across the meadow.

"Let me join the circle!" Grimstead implored. He held a revolver in each hand.

"Yeah, don't leave us in here with the ladies," Marrow growled, removing a flask from his satchel. Emma whirled around to face the Doctor. "Must you be so insolent?!"

"Quiet!" Rogerson ordered.

Emma scanned the tall flowers outside of the circle. She noticed a feathery shape jutting up above the weeds, several yards east of where the group stood ready. More of these feathered shapes darted up, each similar in color to the flowers. Emma thought they resembled peacock feathers.

A cacophony of deep clacks pierced the thick air like thunder. Some of the CCs began to shake with fear. The Swede cracked his neck.

"Steady, lads. Don't break form," the Captain kept his voice steady and calm as he squared his rifle's sights just below the exposed plumage.

The clacking ended abruptly. Seconds later, the sound of heavy footfalls rushed toward them. The flora erupted to reveal a horde of enormous birds.

"Thunderbirds!" Grimstead shouted, cocking both hammers into position. The five-foot tall creatures resembled Condors, with razor-sharp beaks and massive talons, but with brilliant red and yellow feathers. Each Thunderbird sported a single extra-large plume that extended up from the tops of its head, part of its camouflage against the wildflowers. The beasts descended on the group, shrieking as they lunged onto the outer circle of CCs. Rounds of gun fire went off in chaotic bursts as the circle collapsed into a mass of human-to-fowl combat.

Without hesitation, Grimstead ran toward the fray. He fired several shots at a bird that was tearing into a defenseless crewman. Its thick, feather-covered chest seemed to absorb the bullets. The creature shrieked and lunged at the Professor, knocking him to the ground so hard that his breath was drawn from his lungs. Helpless, he could only watch as the Thunderbird loomed over him and reared its head back, preparing to strike. As its formidable beak opened and plunged, Emma thrust her newly-acquired sword down the bird's throat. The beast fell forward onto Grimstead and writhed violently as it died. Emma stood frozen in shock over the pair. With a loud grunt, Grimstead pushed the bird off his body and quickly rose to his feet.

"I... owe you," he panted. "You have my sincerest tha—*down!*" He pointed a revolver at Emma's head and shouted. She obliged, dropping to her knees quick enough to miss the gun's barrel by an inch. Grimstead fired into the right eye of another Thunderbird. It fell to the ground, lifeless.

"We're even so soon? Damn." She grinned. Grimstead extended a hand to help her up. She walked over to the first bird and placing a boot on the beast's neck, removed her sword from its convulsing body.

Behind them, The Swede swung his axe in a large arc, cleanly separating three birds from their heads. He buried the ax handle into a fourth bird's skull and with a grunt, picked it up by the talons and sent it careening into the distance. Satisfied with his work, he turned and nodded at Grimstead, who returned the sentiment.

Finally, the attack was over. Grimstead surveyed the scene, and was dismayed by what he saw. Many on both sides had fallen and the wounded called out to their brethren. Emma rushed off to assist a CC who was trying to stand. Dr. Marrow slowly made his way toward the Professor. His face and arms were scratched and bloody, his clothes torn. He pulled a cigar from his pocket, ripped the end off with his teeth and lit it. The two watched in silence as Captain Rogerson slowly walked the perimeter of the battleground. The few surviving Thunderbirds were dragging the bodies of the fallen crewmen off into the brush.

Once he had made his rounds, Rogerson ordered a mandatory head count. Of the twenty Crimson Crewmen that had started off the journey alongside their captain, only twelve had survived. Many of those twelve were wounded, which deeply troubled the Captain.

"Any man's death that results from my order is blood on my hands," he quietly confessed to the group. "It is my fault that those men will never again see their families or those that meant most to them."

Emma immediately thought of her father and how he would have never survived this attack. She fought to hold back her tears. The Captain offered a moment of silence in their honor before ordering The Swede to gather and carry as many of the birds as he could.

"We need to move as quickly as possible to that tree line." He pointed to the dense curtain of greenery about a hundred yards west from where they stood. Without another word, he started toward it.

Upon exiting the meadow, the group found themselves in an environment that was much akin to a North American forest. The landscape varied greatly from the damp and vine-filled jungle they had left behind only hours ago. Large rows of pine and birch trees stood at attention. The ground was harder and far less treacherous than the jungle, save for errant roots and moss covered rocks. As they stepped under the leafy canopy, the air temperature seemed to miraculously drop at least twenty degrees.

Grimstead slowed his pace as he took in the scenery. "Extraordinary. To see temperate flora exist—and thrive—in a tropical climate? I haven't seen trees and plants such as this since I last trekked through the North Atlantic coast."

As they walked, Captain Rogerson spotted a small creek and kept the group close to its path. The Sun was beginning to make its way down the western sky and the edges of the forest were starting to dim. The creek grew gradually, and before long, met its end at a large pond situated at the center of a clearing. At the far edge of the pond was a modest waterfall. Captain Rogerson paused and addressed the group without turning around.

"We'll stop here and set up camp. Night will fall sooner than we think, and in our current state, I think we'll have a better chance of surviving the night with the water at our backs."

No one argued. Weary and hungry, they set to work. Half of the group worked to set up their sleeping quarters—an array of small, canvas tents. The rest built a large fire in the center of the camp where they cooked two of the Thunderbirds that The Swede had been lugging along with them. For those few hours, everyone worked, and ate, in near silence. Twilight was overtaking Antillia, closing in from the edges and slowly snaking its way toward the center of the island. Emma gazed through the smoke curling up from the flickering orange flames at the navy-blue sky. She thought of her father back on the ship, pouring a cup of tea and preparing to settle into one of the vast library chairs with some ancient volume: his nightly routine. She wondered if she would ever see him again.

The Sun had just about disappeared from the horizon when Rogerson pulled a flare gun from his cargo pants pocket and slid a red flare into it. He stared at the gun for almost a full minute before he shot it into the air. The flare burst high above the camp and hung like a bloody tear from heaven. They all followed the flare with their eyes.

"What is that for?" Grimstead asked.

"Reinforcements," the Captain sighed.

NINE

MR. BONITTO STOOD on the bridge of the SS *Skidbladnir* and shook his head solemnly. The flare slowly fell back toward the island.

"So soon?" he whispered. He walked over to the broadcasting array and put his mouth close to the copper receiver. "Attention all crew members! The Captain is requesting reinforcements. I repeat, the Captain is requesting reinforcements. Assemble topside at once!"

Within minutes the remaining CCs, over two hundred strong, had lined up on the deck. Mr. Bonitto stood before them, holding a clipboard. "When I call your name, you will step forward. The Captain is in need, and we will answer the call!" The men cheered. Each chosen crew member advanced from the line, eager to join the fray. After calling fifteen names, Mr. Bonitto lowered the clipboard without another word. A collective, unspoken sigh spread across the others as they turned and sulked back to their duties. All but one. Finnbar Stratton ambitiously approached the first mate. He was a stout, American lad of eighteen, with wispy black hair and a face that teetered on the edge between boy and man. He was as strong and able as he was determined, which, as everyone on board knew, was plenty.

"Uh, Mr. Bonitto, sir. Perhaps there's a mistake on that list? I was certain that I was next to go." Mr. Bonitto shook his head.

"If I didn't call your name, you do not go. Dismissed."

"But, sir!" implored Finnbar, "I've been aboard for more than two years and I've never been summoned to battle. Not once! I can scrap! I can do whatever the Captain needs! Just give me a chance to prove myself, I swear I'll make you proud!"

"Puss and dawg nuh have the same luck."

"I'm not sure that I follow, sir."

"It means one may try something and succeed, but another may try and fail."

"I won't fail! This is all I've ever wanted, sir!"

"Wa sweet you a go sour you. Dis. Missed." Mr. Bonitto secured the clipboard beneath his arm and turned on his heel. Crushed, Finnbar walked slowly toward the lifeboat that was being prepared for the second wave of CCs. A lanky young crewman was attempting to carry several rifles onto the boat and Finnbar could see that he was having some difficulty balancing them. The young man beckoned to Finnbar as he approached."

"Oi! Finn! Give us a hand with these poppers, eh?" Finnbar stepped quickly to his friend's aid.

"Sam," Finn began, solemnly. "How do you feel about being chosen to head to that island to die?" Sam studied his friend's face.

"What makes you think I'm gonna die, Finny?"

"What do you think caused the Captain to shoot that flare? You think those boys ran out of tea?"

"Well, no, I..." Sam suddenly looked concerned. Finnbar patted him on the back reassuringly.

"I've got a sure-fire way to keep you alive, you British bastard! You piss off back to your room—maybe hit yourself on the head or something, and I'll take your place! If you get caught, just say I clobbered you." Sam considered this proposition.

"Why do you want to go so bad, Finn?"

"I bore easily," he laughed. The two shook hands and Finnbar hopped aboard the second boat to shore, confident that his presence on the Island of Antillia would make an impact. Or, at the very least, survive long enough to try.

THE JUNGLE WAS eerily silent. The Sun's last rays had finally faded, plunging Antillia into total darkness. The only light to be seen was the large—and bright—camp fire. It flickered warmly through the trees, occasionally illuminating one of the CCs that had been assigned to sentry duty along the outskirts of the camp. Not an hour before, everyone had found a seat near the fire and dined heartily on Thunderbird. It was a solemnly quiet meal, and the silence continued as those who were not on duty began to settle in for the night. Captain Rogerson sat close to the fire and cleaned his rifle. Grimstead cleaned the lenses of his glasses and gazed across the camp, letting his mind wander. He thought the Captain resembled a samurai polishing his sword.

Dr. Marrow stepped out from the brush fastening his trousers. He sat next to Grimstead and produced his trademark flask. He took a large gulp before passing it to Grimstead, who accepted it warily.

"Nothing like a good hard shit in the woods to make a man feel manly," he said. Rogerson nodded deeply in concurrence with the Doctor, acknowledging the unspoken truth. Emma moaned in disgust. Grimstead chuckled. He took a sip from the flask and his eyes widened.

"This is marvelous whiskey! Who's the distiller?"

"Old Jake Beam. Out of Kentucky. Take another swig then pass it to the good Captain, if you will." Grimstead took a larger gulp from the flask then raised it to toss to Rogerson, who shook his head.

"No thanks. I need to stay focused and alert. I'll not drink while lives hang in the balance."

"That's the best time to drink," Marrow grunted as he snatched the flask from Grimstead's hand. He then shook it toward Emma, sitting by herself, across the fire. "And what about you, girlie? Fancy a night cap?"

"I've a mind to gracefully make my way toward you, sir, stomp your living guts out and take that silly drink from your twitching fingers for calling me such a derogatory name." Marrow grinned and tossed her the flask. Emma caught it and twisted the cap off. She filled her mouth with the drink and tried to gulp it down. To her dismay, she began to choke and had to spit the whiskey out. Laughter erupted.

"Drink some water, Emma," Rogerson instructed. He set his polished rifle across his lap. Emma jumped up to catch her breath and then drank heartily from her canteen. "As for the rest of you, keep your voices low and stay alert. I'll not have some beast tear our assholes out because we were too busy carrying on like buffoons." The men settled down, deflated by the Captain's words.

"You are a conundrum, Captain," Grimstead commented. "At our first meeting, I thought you were a braggart and perhaps something of a deranged playboy. However, I am glad to see that, while in the field, you are a different person altogether."

"A man can be two things, Professor," Rogerson sniffed, looking straight ahead. "I can be both stoic and petty. You can be both brilliant and an opium sot. A person may wear many hats, you know."

Grimstead leaned forward, resting his arms on his knees.

"Perhaps I was too hasty in praising you after all, Rogerson. You are indeed a petty man, hiding behind his large guns and bright red targets."

"Hold, man. I was only joking with you. Despite my often off-color remarks, I do respect you. We all have our own ways of coping with the ordeals we endure. Yours almost consumed you whole, yet, you pulled yourself out. And for that, you have my admiration."

"I was indeed, pulled out," Grimstead agreed. From the corner of his eye, he caught sight of Marrow taking a clandestine swig from the flask. They exchanged raised eyebrows. Marrow tossed the flask to the Professor. "Or, perhaps, *dragged* would be the proper term. Though it wasn't by my own hand. I would have happily rotted away to dust, grasping at phantoms in that accursed place." He took another generous gulp.

"How did you come to such a state?" Rogerson ventured. "How does a man, such as yourself, become an empty husk?" Grimstead gave him a hard look. "Not that I am insinuating that you are now, of course! But, at the time. What drove you to throw yourself into waste?"

Grimstead sighed and took another drink. "I'll make a deal with you, Captain. I'll tell you what drove me to be an *opium sot*, as it were, if you expound on the death wish you uttered on the ship."

"Fair enough. You first."

"Very well. Where to begin? Let me see. I was forced to watch, helpless, as my wife was bound to an altar, infused with an ancient demigod from beyond the stars, and then brutally murdered by my employer. Who showed little remorse, I might add. Being immersed in a world of living horrors and mind-shattering secrets was tolerable, enjoyable, while I had my Lilly by my side. But to witness such an atrocity, to have such a light struck from the world—*my world*—was far too much to bear. I tried to carry on. My heart, my mind, my every fiber was lost to reminiscing and grief. And, deeming myself as a hindrance to The Order, I fled to London. There, I quickly found the nearest opium den and tried desperately to destroy myself." He stared intently at the fire. "I'm not proud of it. As a matter of fact, I'm sure Lilly would be furious with me had she been alive to find me in such a state. Lilly was magic. She was life. Her light was the Sun to my meager candle. I... I miss her terribly."

The group was silent. The crackling of the camp fire struggled against the rush of the nearby waterfall to fill the void. Three weary CCs approached the camp and three others immediately rose to relieve them. Rogerson set his rifle on the ground and stretched. It was his turn.

"*Shee-it*, Captain, that's a hard'n to top." Marrow shook his head an exhaled sharply. Rogerson nodded with due respect for the Professor's painful history. He took a deep, slow breath, then began:

"As some of you know, my family found its fortune early. I can trace my lineage back to the Viking era. The Rogerson Clan was infamous for its plundering skills. We were part of several noted raids, and became quite wealthy at the expense of others. Spring ahead several generations and the Clan has become successful whalers, the best in Sweden. Hell, the best in *all* the Northlands! The Rogerson Whaling Company brought in more money than we could spend. Yet with every fortune acquired, each generation would selflessly throw themselves to the fates, for glory or for ruin. The Rogerson men have a proud legacy of high-risk endeavors, met with high-yield profit at the ultimate sacrifice. Lands, titles, riches... all flowed in like the sweetest mead, yet each who sought it perished in a torrent of glory and blood. My grandfather, Axel, died at sea, battling a massive white whale. The beast escaped, regretfully. I heard it has been tormenting sailors even to this day!

After moving to America, my father died single-handedly fighting off a Confederate raiding party in 1864. I suppose the point I am trying to make is that questing, amassing wealth, then dying in the heat of battle is something of a family tradition. A legacy, if you will. The Rogerson males are destined to hold the heathen hammer high in the lofty halls of Valhalla! All but me, it seems. I've gone on countless adventures, fought creatures fit for gods, discovered treasures that are beyond price. And yet, I linger here. Try as I might, I've yet to find the thing that kills me. I have no sons. I've postponed the legacy. I fear

I've failed my ancestors. If I break the tradition, what calamity could befall my kin?"

The Captain shrugged, suddenly lost in his own thoughts.

"That's all a bit melodramatic, if you ask me," Emma scoffed louder than anticipated. All eyes were upon her. "It's just that those in your family are exquisitely adept at amassing fortunes, as you say. They have engaged in very high-risk situations and didn't survive. To call that a legacy seems quite morbid and inaccurate. And most of all, the simple fact that you have outlived them all is cause for celebration, not notions of failure."

Grimstead nodded. "Agreed and well put. The Rogerson Clan seems no worse for wear. I think you are a greater good alive than dead." He smirked then added, "Perhaps the legacy is only fulfilled when an heir is created. Who knows? Perhaps if you never sire a child, you might live forever!"

The Captain laughed. "Perhaps, Professor, perhaps. There's only one way to find out, eh?" He winked at Emma in an attempt to get her riled. It worked like a charm.

"I would just as soon bed this drunken buffoon next to me, than the likes of you!" Emma chuffed, jutting her thumb at Dr. Marrow.

"I'll drink to THAT!" Marrow hooted and downed another mouthful of whiskey. Those within earshot laughed, their hearts lifted slightly.

"Anybody want to hear my story?" Marrow offered.

"Not particularly," Emma shrugged.

"Heard it. Even though I'm in it, it still bores me," Rogerson fought back a playful smile. Grimstead only shrugged, playing into the gag.

"That's *real* nice," Marrow grunted. "Keep this in mind when you're bleeding and I am sole provider of medical aid."

"Alright, man, tell us your secret origin—for posterity's sake, of course," Grimstead conceded. A wicked smile crept along Marrow's mouth.

"Was gonna anyway." He set the flask down, thought better of it, then picked it back up. "Truth to tell, it ain't that interesting."

"*See?!*" Rogerson turned his palms up.

"When I was eleven, I was a drummer boy for Union Major General William Tecumseh Sherman during his *March to the Sea*. By that point in the war, the Confederates were throwing everything they had at us as we destroyed their bridges, burned their crops and freed their slaves. Didn't do much to slow us down, that much was certain. Those Union boys ruined the railroads and effectively disrupted a great deal of the South's infrastructure."

He took a long gulp from the flask. "As I was saying," Marrow wiped his mouth on his sleeve, "since I couldn't keep a beat to save my life, I was sent to old man Nash, the saw bones of the unit. And that's where it all started."

"Your love of medicine?" Grimstead inquired.

"My love of *booze*!" Marrow corrected. "Years after the war I tried to make a go at honest doctoring and worked like a dog to attend medical school. They kicked me out after the first year. They said things like, *don't cut that!* or, *that's enough laudanum to kill a bull moose!* And my personal favorite, *a cadaver is not a suitable dancing partner, do set the body back upon the table!* So, I found a ship and headed for parts unknown. The unknown turned into a great deal of unknowns and my medical skills flourished in the field. For the most part. Then came that fateful evening in Singapore, where I met my good friend the Captain."

He paused for another drink.

"I was sitting at the bar of a place called The One-Eyed Snake, nursing a bottle of rum (*yo ho*), when two men stormed in carrying a massive bastard of a man. Biggest bastard I've seen to date. This tall, white fellow and even taller black fellow tried their best to drag an even *bigger* fellow over to one of the long tables and set him down atop. Turned out those two blokes were none other than the good Captain here and First Mate Bonitto. Can anyone suss who the gigantic freak was? That's right! The Swede! The Captain and first mate were shore-side gathering supplies, when they came across a traveling circus of oddities and wonders. One of those wonders was our massive friend with the axe. Those sadistic bastards in the circus had him fight a brown bear. A *bear!* With his goddamned hands, no less!"

"You fought a bear?!" Grimstead was shocked.

"He had it coming," The Swede shrugged.

"So there they are, covered in blood. The Captain beat the hell out of the circus owner and stole The Swede away. He may have killed that bear, but he also took his fair share of a whupping! The Captain called out for a doctor, any doctor. I slid over and patched our man here best I could. The Captain was so impressed that he asked me to join the crew as the doctor. I make sure he and his men are in tip-top shape and he keeps me in the booze. I believe that's called a fair trade."

"You *really* fought a bear?" Grimstead pressed The Swede, ignoring that Marrow's narrative had reached its conclusion.

"I was world's strongest man. Someone had world's strongest bear. No one could see past the profit. I mourn taking that bear's life. We could have been friends in another life."

"You keep the most colorful company, Captain." Grimstead smiled.

"Indeed I do. Characters to the last." He looked pensively into the fire then turned to Grimstead. "I'm sorry I sent my men to harm you yesterday in the boxing matches. I wanted to test your mettle. Make sure you were someone I could count on in the heat of battle. As it stands, you are made of true grit. I would like us to start over, with a clean slate, Professor."

"I, too am sorry," Grimstead replied. "Sorry that I damaged your men and spoke so cruelly about you. And your boat."

"*Ship*, damn you!"

"Ship." Grimstead nodded. He tried to stifle a yawn, but it got the better of him.

"The two of you are so very darling, the way you carry on..." Emma turned her nose skyward and fluttered her eyelashes. *Oh, Professor! Ooh, Captain!* She clutched her hands to her chest. "Should we leave you two romantics in private?"

"Hoo HOO, that little lady is a spitfire!" Marrow slapped his knee and chuckled.

"Now, Emma," Rogerson shook his head in a *tsk tsk* fashion.

"No! No more, *'Now Emmas'!* I am *not* a child. Am I not my father's proxy on this trek? Does that not make us equal?"

"Who are you, Elizabeth Cady Stanton?" Marrow guffawed. Rogerson held his hand up to silence the Doctor.

"Have I not fought side-by-side with the lot of you? Risked my life with the lot of you? Stood my ground, pulled my weight, proven my worth?!"

"Of course you have," Grimstead offered, but the consolation was little more than a paper crane in a hurricane.

"All my life I've watched my father's dream of finding this horrible island fall to ruin by the hubris of so-called *men*. These citizens of the world, wagging their egos and stories as if they truly mattered. They took his money. They went through the motions. Some even meant well enough, but every single one of them failed him. And with each failure, a piece of hope chipped away. Imagine for a moment, having a goal—a grand ambition—and resting it in the hands of braggarts! I vowed to stay by my father's side, to give him strength when he needed. To prove to him and the world that gender means *nothing* when it comes down to it. I've studied, trained, tore myself from the yolk of contemporary societal feminine mediocrity. I gave up a comfortable life in Maine with my mother, to trudge through jungle after jungle, tomb after tomb with my father. This is a man's world, they say. And it may very well be true! Just *look* at the state of it."

"Emma. Do not change yourself to prove others wrong," Grimstead said. He thought of Catherine, running away from home on the first ship that would allow. Would that he could say those words to her then. "Your actions define you, yes, but don't deny yourself a modicum of happiness and youth to disprove a score of testosterone-addled imbeciles. To hell with what others think! Be yourself *for* yourself."

Emma wanted to say something in her defense—something witty—but the Professor's words bored through her emotional stockade. She looked into the fire and exhaled gently. He was right, after all. Emma had been too long playing with the big boys. She robbed herself of youth. She and no one else, she realized. As noble a cause it was, she denied herself the opportunity to see the world through youthful eyes.

Grimstead's words resonated with the rest of the group as well. They were as silent as the trees. Rogerson set his rifle down and rubbed his temples.

"Alright, get some rest, everyone," he ordered. "We set out at day break."

Grimstead rolled out his sleeping bag and positioned himself so that his feet were closest to the fire. As he drifted off into sleep, his eyes watched the flames dance, slowly fading as the night drew thin.

TEN

PARIS
FRANCE
1895

LILLY CHAMBERS ROUSED gently in the warm glow of dawn. Her chestnut locks splayed wildly from her pale face, shimmering in the morning light. She rolled her head onto the pillow besides her and saw that Alexander was laying on his side, watching her.

"There are fewer things more unnerving than the realization that someone has been watching you sleep." She smiled. He leaned in to kiss her.

"What else could I do? Your snoring kept me from sleep and it had been too dark to read up until now." She shoved him to his back.

"I do *not* snore!"

"You're right... what you do is far beyond snoring."

"You louse!" She began playfully poking her index fingers into his side. He tried in vain to stem the attack. Giggling, Lilly slid closer so she could straddle him and they kissed passionately. Alexander then grabbed her by the arms and in one swift movement rolled so that he was now on top, gently kissing her bare neck and breasts.

"I think we should marry," he said, looking deeply into her dark eyes. Lilly threw her head back in a hearty laugh.

"Ha! Alexander Copernicus Grimstead, you madman! Give me one good reason why I should tie myself down to you." She squinted and pursed her lips in mock scrutiny.

"Because we were meant to be," he said, his eyes never leaving hers. "And I will love you till the stars go out."

They kissed again, briefly.

"Tell me something my darling. Here we are, in Paris, on another of the Order's transcontinental missions, one that has us routing a coven of subterranean vampires who call themselves *Les Enfants De La Mort*. A mission in which we both nearly died. *Again*. Do you really think this is the basis for a healthy, fulfilling lifetime together?"

"I couldn't think of a better reason. Except, of course, the fact that we are both madly in love and extremely gifted in love making."

"Speak for myself!" Lilly smiled, her face brightening. "I'll be your bride, Alexander. But you need to do one thing for me."

"Name it, my darling."

"Wake up, Alexander. Wake up…"

"Wake up, Alexander." Emma nudged him. The golden Parisian morning faded. A single tear ran down his cheek.

ELEVEN

THE ISLAND WAS again blanketed in a thick, morning fog which seemed to cling to the forest floor and obscure anything more than a few feet away, including the rising Sun. As soon as daylight allowed, the explorers broke down the camp and prepared to forge deeper into the island. Before they paused for breakfast, Captain Rogerson called a briefing.

"If we don't run into trouble, we should be mid-island by tomorrow," he announced. "That is, of course, if the maps our good Dr. McParland demanded—for *some* damn reason—we keep on the ship, were accurate. Though, I am confident that maps crafted by *madmen* are up to the task."

Emma huffed audibly.

"My father simply wishes to see that the maps are returned to the library in Cambridge in the condition they were acquired. The maps may be simple, some are quite crude, but we've *each* studied them enough to have a decent idea as to where we are headed." She crossed her arms and glowered at him.

"Regardless, we begin our march after breakfast." They swiftly ate what remained of last night's Thunderbird carcasses and gathered up the rest of their gear. Grimstead caught sight of Rogerson pulling a long red sash from the Swede's back pack then tying it around a tree. He understood immediately that it was a trail marker for the second wave of Crimson Crewmen.

Rogerson waved past the pond and they began their march downstream.

The Sun continued its steady climb up through the treetops, but its light had yet to penetrate the jungle floor; the remaining fog made it nearly impossible to navigate through the brush and bramble. The group stayed close to the stream, which had rather suddenly begun to increase in size, gathering other smaller streams and rivulets one by one, until it finally matured into a river.

About an hour into their march, the explorers came upon a clearing among the trees where three massive white obelisks had been positioned in a triangular formation. Without a word to the Captain, Grimstead broke rank and jogged down into the clearing to investigate. Emma followed close behind him, her eyes wide as she approached the three peculiar structures. She had never seen anything like them up close: The obelisks were made of a smooth, pure-white stone and had strange images carved into their surface. They reminded her of the ancient Egyptian pyramids. The bases were still bathed in shadow, but as the morning Sun touched the pointed tips, the white stone seemed to glisten.

Grimstead walked over to the first obelisk, nearest to the clearing entrance, and ran his hand over the carved images, studying them intently.

"The obelisks appear to be roughly fifteen feet, or four-and-a-half meters, in height. Their carvings are reminiscent of Mayan hieroglyphs," he told her. "Each side seems to depict a progression of a story. Look, this appears to be a deity with a bat-like face, looming from on top of a temple." He directed Emma's eyes further up the stone. "See here? The people bowing in reverence? This particular obelisk definitely tells of the reign of whomever this imposing figure is."

They approached the second stone on the other side of the triangle's base. Grimstead studied these carvings intently, silently rubbing his fingers through his goatee.

"This shows a fierce battle between the deity and what looks to be some sort of a human. Or humanoid. Hmm, his proportions are quite larger than an average human. He also seems to be depicted in the same reverence as the bat-man. This was a battle of epic proportions. The bat deity was defeated, and the people were engulfed either by a brilliant light or a terrible fire." He moved on toward the apex stone, while Emma took another moment to regard the human-like carving.

"Fascinating," she whispered.

When she caught up to the Professor, he was studying a carving that depicted the lone figure of the humanoid. The rest of the obelisk was untouched.

"Curious," Grimstead said mostly to himself. "The style of the carving is different."

Captain Rogerson approached them and cleared his throat. "If you two are finished looking at pretty rocks, perhaps we could—" he paused and cocked his head as though he heard something in the distance.

"What is it?" Emma asked. Rogerson stepped toward her and pressed his index finger to her lips.

"Shhh."

Emma pulled away, wiping her mouth in disgust.

"Listen... voices." Rogerson motioned to the rest of the crew and told them to stay put. "Marrow, you're in charge here. Professor, you and I will investigate the voices. Emma, you stay with the group."

"*Not* walking? I am your man!"

"Stay *put*?! Why?! I'm fully capable of stealth!"

"Like now?" Rogerson raised an eyebrow. Emma placed her hands on her hips and made a face. Rogerson smirked. "Move slowly and follow me."

As they stalked through the woods, the voices grew louder. Soon, there were five distinct voices: two adult males, two adult females and a male child with a foul disposition. All of them were arguing in a near-frenzied state. The three soon approached a second clearing, another open meadow. They immediately spotted the mystery persons standing near a dark-colored clunky rectangular/almond-shaped vessel. It loomed over the small group. Rogerson motioned for Grimstead and Emma to halt and keep low. He took a few steps forward toward the edge of the brush, raised his rifle to his right shoulder and extended the scope. Through it he spied four figures, all wearing strange dome helmets, and bulky copper-colored suits with tubes and clockwork gadgets set on their chest and arms. One of the figures was particularly tall and stocky. They continued to argue, all five voices could be heard, as clear as day. Rogerson counted again. *Where is the fifth person?* The large figure was attempting to remove its helmet, but the slender figure—a male—shouted.

"We have no idea what we're dealing with! For the last time, leave the helmet on!"

Rogerson turned and silently waved at Grimstead, using a series of exaggerated and complicated hand gestures. Totally confused, Grimstead looked at Emma for help, but she just shrugged at him. He shrugged at the Captain. Rogerson sighed and shook his head.

"Go down there and talk to them," he whispered harshly, pointing to the meadow. "I'll stay here and cover you." He pointed down at the spot where they were standing.

"Why can't you go?"

"Because. My gun is bigger than yours. And well, perhaps they won't hit a man with glasses."

TWELVE

"CONNIE, ARE YOU completely, absolutely, one-hundred-and-fifty percent *positive* that you have *no* idea where we are right now?" Dr. Wesley Adams queried the tiny, blue, holographic female head that was being projected from the device sitting in his palm. Their routine mission had somehow gone awry. "This was only supposed to be a three hour tour. The Department of Super Sciences sent us to investigate a magnetic/vibrational anomaly off the coast of Former South America, and we crash landed on... where?"

"I have a hunch... that we are in the woods," she bleated, sarcastically.

"Damn it, Connie! *B-bitch staples!*"

"Now, now, Wesley. Keep your head." His wife, Dr. Sarah Adams, calmly patted his shoulder with her gloved hand. "Remember, if you get too excited, you lose control over your Tourette's." He turned to look at her and they gazed lovingly at one another through their helmet visors.

"Thank you, darling. I suppose I did the right thing by marrying a doctor of psychiatry and sociology, eh?" They both chuckled and Sarah gave him a quick hug.

"Not to mention her sweet ghetto booty." Connie's shimmering image winked from Wesley's hand.

"Damn it, Connie!"

"I'm just saying that it's not bad for a white girl."

Paul Adams, the couple's ten-year-old son, cleared his throat. "If you three are finished with your superfluous blathering, perhaps we can address the somewhat disconcerting and *rather* inconvenient matter at hand? In case you hadn't noticed, we're all of us stranded without an inkling as to where, and all you two are concerned with is voluptuousness and manners." He yanked his helmet off.

"Paul! P-p-put your helmet back on!"

"Connie already said the atmosphere was safe." The boy said, removing his right glove. "Besides, I've got a boogie in my nose."

Reluctantly, Wesley removed his helmet and the others followed suit. He rubbed the stubble on his gaunt cheeks and ran a hand through his salt-and-pepper hair as he surveyed the surroundings. Sarah fluffed her candy-red-streaked black hair, which bounced down just past her jaw line. Her deep red eyes squinted as they adjusted to the light. The fourth crew member, a burly female named Berta Thompson, grunted as she pulled her helmet off. Her solid, square jaw and dark cropped hair gave her a rather masculine appearance. She, too, rubbed the stubble on her cheeks and stretched her muscular neck until several sharp pops erupted.

"Aah, much better," she cooed in a gruff voice, then picked at her crotch where the formfitting suit had gotten bunched up.

"You are a beast," Paul said, disgusted.

"And you're a dingleberry. Ask me how I know."

Paul opened his mouth to retaliate, but Wesley raised his hand to indicate that they stop. "The only question that needs to be raised is *Where on earth are we?* Connie?!" Her head disappeared into the device then emerged a few moments later.

"I don't have a clue where we are exactly. Our final GPS report before the *Explorer* went down has us just off the coast of the Former South America. I would suggest that you plug me into the *Explorer's* mainframe, but it was fried along with the rest of our systems after we flew into whatever that electromagnetic thingie-ma-jobber was. It's a minor miracle that I survived at all."

"Yes, a downright blessing." Paul rolled his eyes.

"See? What did I say?" Berta laughed. "A dingleberry!"

"If the shim is done grunting, maybe we can get some work done?" Connie scoffed.

"A *shim?*" Berta asked.

"Yes, a little bit she and a bunch him. A shim," the hologram replied.

"If you had a neck, I'd be breaking it about now."

"If I had a neck, I never would have said it!"

"Oh. My. Gods," Sarah whined. "Can we *please* just focus?"

"Yes!" Wesley agreed. "Continue, Connie."

"As I was saying, I can't seem to locate any satellites whatsoever, I—PROXIMITY ALERT! PROXIMITY ALERT!" Connie shouted.

The crew instinctively stepped closer and stared out at the empty meadow. "W-w-where?!"

"Behind you," Connie whispered, tilting her head toward the far end of the clearing where Professor Grimstead now stood. A look of sheer panic crossed Wesley's face.

The four slowly turned around and saw Grimstead's figure from the tree line. He gently waved his right hand. "Greetings! I'm—"

"*Aaah! Ass-badgers!*" Wesley screamed, dropping Connie into the grass as he fumbled to draw his pistol. He fired; the red laser beam shot past Grimstead's left ear and bore a hole completely through a tree trunk several feet behind him. The Professor froze, his mouth hanging open in shock. Emma shrieked. Rogerson hastily fired his rifle from behind. The bullet struck the *Explorer* just above Paul's head.

"GAH!" he shouted, diving to the ground.

The *Skidbladnir* crew waiting by the river bank heard

Emma's shriek followed by the rifle's report and jumped to attention.

"Ah, hell," Dr. Marrow grunted, taking a swig from his flask. He stood, removing his machete from its sheath. "Let's go, boys."

The Professor turned around and realized that he was now able to see the forest behind him through the middle of the steaming tree trunk. Before he could react, Emma charged past him holding her sword above her head.

"*Yaaaaaahhh!*" she cried, heading straight for the Adamses. The startled family huddled closer together as Berta rushed her, grabbing Emma's arms with one hand and her shirt with the other, pinning her to the ground with ease. Emma landed with a thud.

"Shouldn't go around hollering like that, Barbie," Berta chided. "Gives a person all the time they need to prepare."

Rogerson burst forth from the tree line, his barrel aimed at Wesley's forehead. Sarah aimed her pistol at the Captain with a shaky hand. "Let the girl up, sir."

"Suck my left tit, pretty boy!"

Grimstead rushed down to Rogerson's side. "Everyone please calm down! We mean you no harm!" He took a step closer and Sarah immediately pointed her gun at him. He threw both hands into the air and stepped back in line with Rogerson.

"Barbie comes at me with a pig sticker and she didn't mean to harm me? You can suck my other tit!" Berta laughed. Emma struggled under Berta's impressive strength.

"My... name... isn't... Barbie," she muttered, her face pressed into the grass. Dr. Marrow and the band of CCs emerged from the tree line, guns at the ready. The men only needed a moment to assess the scene before springing into action: Marrow and three CCs ran over to shield the Captain and the Professor. The rest fanned out to surround the Adamses and their vessel. Meanwhile, The Swede rushed Berta, knocking her off Emma by several feet. Berta quickly regained her footing and retaliated by striking him with a left hook to the jaw. He staggered, clearly taken aback by the power of the blow. Berta balled her fists and began to circle him, while everyone else looked on in silent awe.

"I'm gonna do some horrible things to you, gorgeous," she cooed. "You goddamn sex mountain!"

The Swede tackled Berta into the brush. Birds and various creatures scattered from the billow of dirt, debris and harsh language in their wake.

No one could quite figure out what to do next. They stood in silence for several long, awkward moments until Grimstead cleared his throat and slowly walked toward the Adams family. He extended his right hand to Wesley once again. "Hello, I am Professor Alexander Grimstead. To my left is Captain Robert Rogerson of the SS *Skidbladnir*. On my right is Dr. Joseph Marrow. The young lady that was, er, detained, is Miss Emma McParland. We are here with our crew on an exploratory expedition. We truly mean you no harm."

Wesley exchanged glances with Sarah before slowly holstering his pistol and shaking Grimstead's hand. "Dr. Wesley Adams. Pleasure to meet you. The beautiful gal to my right is my wife, Dr. Sarah Adams. That's our son, Paul, in the dirt over by the transporter there. And then there's our security officer, Berta. Ah, well, I'm sure you can extrapolate who Berta is. We are field scientists for the Department of Super Science for the United Government of New Atlantis and we were—"

"I'm sorry, but government of new *what*?" Rogerson interrupted.

"New Atlantis. You've... never heard of it?" Wesley was suspicious. Rogerson looked at Grimstead, who shook his head.

"No Dr. Adams, we haven't."

Wesley furrowed his brow. "Out of curiosity, what year do you think this is?"

"1898." Rogerson answered, his own suspicions piqued.

"What year do *you* think it is?"

"2183."

The group fell silent. Only the sounds of Berta and the Swede grappling in the brush seasoned the air.

Grimstead felt a surge of adrenaline, like ice water through his veins. *The physical transcendence of space and time? Could it be possible after all?* He had goosebumps.

"Perhaps you should start at the beginning, Doctor," Grimstead said calmly. He motioned for Rogerson to lower his weapon.

"Men, stand down," the Captain ordered as he slung his own rifle over his right shoulder.

"Actually, before we start at the beginning, what on Earth was that weapon you fired at me?" Grimstead gestured at Wesley's holster.

"Oh, this?" Dr. Adams drew his pistol. "This is the Light Bringer series 20X, a state-of-the-art laser emitter. It'll blast through, or disintegrate, just about anything. I'm... sorry that I fired it at you. You startled me."

"It's quite alright." Grimstead smiled. "You missed."

"How does it work?" Emma inquired, still dusting herself off. Paul sighed heavily.

"Father, if we have to explain to these *cave* people how something even as simple as a laser pistol works, we'll be here till second doomsday!"

"Sounds like the boy might need a good slap," Dr. Marrow sneered.

"And you look like you have a liver that might need transplanting."

"*Second* doomsday, eh?" Grimstead raised an eyebrow. "So, there was a first?" Wesley holstered his Light Bringer and searched for the words to explain.

"Well, uh, yes. You see, back in the mid-2000s, there began something of an age of spiritual enlightenment among the general populace of Earth. Nothing particularly radical, just a heightened awareness of the supernatural that is believed to have stemmed from a few dozen television shows about haunted places, things, people, etcetera. A few dozen more about people who could actually speak to the dead and so forth."

"Tele... vision shows?" Emma asked.

Paul rolled his eyes in disgust. "Ugh. Savages."

Wesley cleared his throat. "Uh, please save any and all questions until the end of the lecture. As I was saying, that era brought about a heightened sense of mass spirituality, which, coupled with the advancements in social media technology that existed at the time, moved human civilization to became *more* connected than ever before. The individual, as it was, began to break down into the beginning stages of a hive-mind society. People couldn't take a dump without informing the entire world about it, which often resulted in hundreds of uneducated people leaving grammatically-incorrect comments in regards."

Grimstead struggled to understand Wesley's explanation. He glanced at Sarah who stared adoringly at her husband.

"Also during that time, we were experiencing a massive socioeconomic struggle, due to job shortages and economic downturn. The rich were still rich. the poor were still poor. But the middle class? They struggled to maintain even the fleeting joys of mediocrity. Hope was just a metaphor. It was a global issue and absolutely everyone suffered. Prosperity and poverty swung like a well-oiled pendulum over the throat of humanity. The world's governments were so in debt, so corrupt in the pockets of big business, that they couldn't help but collapse under the weight of attrition. Then came the riots and rebellions. They started in what was known as the Middle East and soon spread, in a matter of days, if I recall, through to Africa, Europe and Asia. But then, North Korea launched a nuclear attack on some of that era's major cities. It wasn't completely devastating, but it was the catalyst for a series of events that would change history. Civil wars, invasions, occupations, then finally, nuclear- and bio-weapon exchange. Entire countries and civilizations were wiped out as a result, literally overnight. The land was destroyed. The air poisoned. There was nothing but devastation. The fate of life on Earth hung by a thread! Those facts are debatable, though. Many historians hypothesize what happened, as most of the data that was recovered from that time was mostly useless. But, however it happened, it sure screwed things up."

Everyone was dreadfully silent.

"I may have chopped that up a bit, but powerful stuff, no? Around twenty years after the last nuke went off, many who had managed to survive the blast and aftermath were visited by intergalactic missionaries promising them salvation. At that point, people were ready to believe anything that offered them a warm bed and a hot meal."

"Martians? Nonsense!" Rogerson exclaimed.

"Hmph. You sound like my father," Emma said. "Except, his exclamation would have been *'Martians? Huzzah!'*"

"Actually," Wesley added, "they claimed to be from the Pleiades cluster, so they were Pleiadians, I suppose. If you ask me, I think it's a whole conspiracy thing and the missionaries were really just the new government trying to pretend that they were advanced beings, so the general populace would think what they had to say was important and not just another group of madmen with agendas. Either way, these *beings* went on to build several massive megacities all over the globe. The biggest is New Atlantis, which exists just off the coast of New York. There's another megacity off the coast of Los Angeles, as well, and off the coasts of Iceland, New Zealand, the southern tip of South America and one right in the middle of China. These cities are so massive that they, well, let me see if I can phrase this in a way that you may understand. These cities are approximately the size of two New York Cities. That's more than nine hundred thirty six point ninety-six square miles of land mass suspended a mile above sea level by several massive pillars." Adams spread his arms tall and wide to demonstrate. "And that's just the width! In some sections, the buildings are so tall, they count as boroughs." The *Skidbladnir* crew looked on with wide eyes. "Oh, yes indeed! Well, I could easily speak volumes about these places but, another time, perhaps. Though I will say, as a testament to mankind's ignoble characteristics, these metropolises were keenly designed to be utopias. The people of Earth had a plethora of new resources at their fingertips: sciences, philosophy, art, literature. Even potential methods for peace. However, soon after the Pleiadians left, mankind fell back to doing what they've always done best: procreate and degenerate. It was like the previous century all over again. But with cyborgs and ray guns."

"This is absolutely intriguing!" Grimstead uttered.

"If by *intriguing*, you mean terribly confusing and morbid, then I agree," added Emma.

"Ray guns?" Rogerson cocked his head to one side like a curious dog. Wesley pointed to the tree he had shot, and Rogerson understood.

"It isn't all that bad, Wesley," Sarah advocated. "There is a delicate balance, though. The rich tend to stay above the so-called rabble in their deluxe mega-boroughs, while the rest go about their lives free of mutant cannibals trying to tear us to pieces. It has its flaws, yes, but what civilization doesn't?"

"True, true." Wesley nodded. "I suppose you could call it a... a decadent squalor. Yes! And now we get to the five of us, and why we are on this wretched island with you good folks who probably understood only a fifth of what I just said. Well, we are scientists commissioned by The Department of Super Science—a fully-funded exploratory and experimental subsidiary of an organization called Moonshield Incorporated —"

"Moonshield?!" Grimstead interrupted, in disbelief. "The Moonshield Society still exists in 2183?"

"Oh, it isn't a society," Wesley assured him. "Moonshield

is a corporate conglomerate with its logo on practically everything. From military technology to cereal. Moonshield, for all intents and purposes, runs New Atlantis. Its money keeps things moving and its products keep people happy. More or less."

Grimstead pursed his lips in frustration. "I don't understand how..." His voice trailed off. Wesley looked at him quizzically, but continued.

"So, we were selected to investigate a strange electromagnetic anomaly off the coast of the country formerly known as South America. We volunteered to—"

"We?" Paul interrupted from his spot in the dirt. "You have a mouse in your pocket?"

"*We*, as in, *I* volunteered us. *We* couldn't have guessed that the anomaly would have tampered with our systems the way it did. I'm surprised that we made it this far before we completely lost power. Only Connie managed to survive the EMPs, or, electromagnetic pulses."

"Oh, you simply *must* meet my father!" Emma gushed. "You two could rattle nonsense at each other till... what did you call it? Second doomsday!" She beamed a bright smile at Wesley. He blushed until Sarah cleared her throat. Paul sighed in exasperation. He produced a small, rectangular device from his spacesuit and focused his attention on it.

"And just who is this Connie?" Rogerson inquired, rakishly. A look of panic crossed Dr. Adams' face and he began frantically patting down his exploration suit.

"Ugh. I'm still down here, you nitwit," Connie called from the grass near Wesley's feet. He retrieved the small, black square and brushed it off before holding it out to the group. The sphere at the top of the control panel flashed to life and the shimmering image of a young female's head and shoulders appeared about an inch above Wesley's palm. Her hair was pulled neatly into a ponytail, except for a single strand which fell down past her thick-framed glasses.

"Hello," she said. Wesley held the device a little higher so everyone could see.

Grimstead waved his hand meekly. The others simply stared.

"I'll be damned..." Marrow whispered.

"Connie is, essentially, a palm-sized super computer. She is capable of truly amazing things."

"That's what *she* said!" Connie blurted.

"One of which is vicious sarcasm." He raised an eyebrow.

"And while you were waxing loquacious, I have verified that we are no longer in the year 2183." Wesley's face grew stern.

"How so?"

"First of all, there aren't any satellites. I've scanned multiple times without response."

"Perhaps that's because you're just out of range?" Sarah gestured up at the trees.

"Nope. Though I am dealing with some limitations due to my being stuck in the hand-held while the imp fixes the ship, I *should* have at least been able to connect with the Earth-bound Galactic Positioning System. But as I mentioned to Mr. Wonderful before, nothing."

"So, exactly *how* long have you been on the island?" Grimstead spoke cautiously, as if he almost didn't trust the hologram.

"Four hours—thirteen minutes—and a dickload of seconds," Connie stated flatly.

Emma made a face, shaking her head and muttering under her breath.

"Emma, are you alright?" Grimstead asked.

"Only a few hours?! How is that possible?!" Emma began pacing between the groups. "We've been here for... a day and a night! And, and, we've been pursuing it for weeks! In 1898. You set out in 2183, and now it may or may *not* be 1898 still. What if... perhaps... if *all* of the maps are correct? What if the island only appears periodically through time? And we... all of us... have stumbled upon some sort of, well, loophole?" Emma paused and stared up into the trees, then whirled around and looked at everyone with enthusiasm. Everyone stared back at her in utter silence.

Grimstead studied his young friend's face with wonder and concern; it was as though Emma had plucked the very same thoughts from his own mind. *Could time travel really be possible?* A smile crept across his face. "Stranger things have been known to happen. You take after your father more than you care to admit, young lady."

"Please don't tell him."

"Interesting," Wesley said, his voice low. "So you're saying that this island has *periodically* existed in the past?"

"Indeed, Grimstead nodded. "And according to our research, it tends to go missing for hundreds of years at a time."

"I see..." Wesley's mind was already working through the variables. Sarah nudged him with her elbow.

"I know that look. What's running through that brain of yours?"

"Still working on it. Though, I would suggest we go due west from here. Just before we lost power, we were headed toward a ginormous tower-like object, several stories tall, that we spotted in the middle of the island. From the looks of it, the object is entirely smooth and metallic. It's also completely untouched by vegetation. "

"I could have sworn I saw windows," Sarah added. "Maybe it's a military station? It was hard to tell as we were hurtling to the ground."

"That's a sound possibility," Grimstead nodded. "I agree, Wesley. If we are looking for answers, that seems like the place to try and find them."

"Hold a moment." Rogerson held a hand up. "We're combining forces now? How do we know they can be trusted? How do we know they aren't—what the devil did they call them—mutant cannibals?" Sarah and Wesley exchanged a quick glance before unzipping their exploration suits and stepping out of them. Underneath, each wore a form-fitting blue and silver polymer jumpsuit. Sarah's particularly accentuated her figure. Rogerson's eyes darted over her body like hummingbirds.

"I may have ruby-red eyes, but do I look like a big, scary mutant to you, Captain?"

"I, ah... uh... buh. You can. Come along."

Emma rolled her eyes.

"It's settled, then." Wesley smile as he hooked a sleek utility belt and gun holster around his waist. Sarah did the same before collecting the discarded spacesuits and carrying them over to the *Explorer*.

"You seem unprotected in those outfits," Grimstead noted.

"These are bio suits. They're made of an extremely tough fiber that acts as a medium-grade armor. They also control body temperature and other useful things one might need in the wild."

"Great. Wonderful. We're burning daylight, here," Marrow said impatiently.

"Right," Wesley agreed. "Let me just grab our supply packs and we'll be on our way. We've got a job to do!" He sprinted with excitement to their ship and pulled a lever in its midsection. A ladder descended and Wesley scrambled up.

"I'll stay here and fix the *Explorer*," Paul volunteered. "I'm not much of a hiker."

Sarah pouted. "But I can't leave you here alone, sweetie!" She walked over to her son and pulled him into a bear hug. Paul sneered and pushed her away.

"Mom. You know I'm the only one who can fix this thing and we're going to need it to get off this stupid island sooner or later. I would also be a hindrance in a fight without the aide of our vast array of weapons that the transporter here has to offer.

I'll only slow you down. Besides, if things get rough, I'll secure myself in the cockpit. Remember that time in Devil's Landing —or, for you primitive types, New York City—when the ship was covered in a hundred ravenous doornails? Didn't make a dent! It'd take a tank to breach this thing."

"Covered in doornails?" Emma asked.

"Yeah, doornails. Or, walkers, rotters, zombos, the walking dead. Whatever you prefer to call them. The city was teeming with them after the outbreak and—eh. You know what? It's probably too much to get into right now, but trust me when I say this that thing can take a beating." He patted the ship's hull.

"New York is...gone?" Grimstead saddened. Wesley returned with three hard, almond-shaped supply packs and handed one to Sarah. He slid his on like a backpack and grimly shook his head.

"I'm sorry, Professor. Yes, New York City was claimed by the undead. It became what is categorized as a *dead zone*."

"You see this?" Marrow held his hand out and slowly rotated it. "This, in my hand is daylight, and it's still burning away."

"Alright, alright, let's get a move on to appease the good Doctor before he gripes us all to death," Rogerson conceded.

"We'll take a com-link, then," Sarah suggested. "We can use Connie's wireless relay to bounce the transmissions." She kissed her son on the forehead. He lolled his tongue in disgust."Be safe, my cherub!"

"Cherub," Marrow chided. Paul gave him the finger. Captain Rogerson approached the boy and rested a hand on his shoulder.

"Can I at least have one of my crew stay behind to keep you company, son?"

"Those dumb asses would only get me killed!" Paul scoffed. It was then that Berta and The Swede finally emerged from their romp in the brush, a bit disheveled and dusty. They were holding hands. Berta wore a variation of the Adams' jumpsuit. Hers was less form fitting—because Berta did not care for the restrictive nature of the typical style—and came in three pieces: zip up top, bottoms and removable boots. When the pieces were worn together, they worked as one single suit. She slung her uniform top over her shoulder, leaving only a tank top to restrain her massive bosom.

"Well, *that* takes care of *that*!" she exclaimed, with a hint of a giggle. The crowd gaped at them. She looked to Rogerson. "Can I keep him?"

"Eh, I don't think I want him back," Rogerson grimaced, only half-joking. He winked at The Swede who blushed.

"Sorry, Captain."

Rogerson reached out to pat a clump of dirt off his massive crewman's left shoulder, then stepped in closer. "It's alright, my friend," he whispered. "There's a certain... animal magnetism, I'm sure."

"Alright, I hate to interrupt this delightful conversation, but we really *should* be heading out," Connie urged.

"Right!" Wesley quickly agreed. "Shall we?"

He nodded to the Captain who motioned to the CCs that had been wandering along the perimeter. The crewmen immediately fell into line, two-by-two, as they trudged into the wilderness once more. Captain Rogerson and Wesley jockeyed for position at the head of the line, with Grimstead close behind them. Sarah and Emma were next, followed by the remaining CCs. Berta and The Swede were at the end of the procession.

Paul watched them all disappear into the brush then hopped from foot to foot waving his arms wildly.

"*Ooh, I don't want to weave you awone! Ooh, my sweet wittle baby!*" He chuffed. "Last time they left me alone with someone, it was that creepy old Mister Harris and his half-retarded robot, Larry! Ugh. I don't need anyone! I—" A guttural growl came from behind a nearby bush. Paul tripped and almost fell off the ladder as he scrambled up to open the cockpit hatch.

The bush rustled and the growl came again.

"*Muh-muh*-mommie!"

Dr. Marrow peered through the bush with a crooked grin. He almost ruined his cover by laughing aloud. "Have fun, *cherub*!"

THIRTEEN

FINNBAR STRATTON PAUSED to wipe blood from his face. Even though the blood wasn't his own, it still posed the threat of stinging his eyes. He stood alone and silent in a clearing ringed by tall red and yellow flowers. The mud at his feet was spattered with blood. All around him lay the dismembered body parts of his comrades. Some had perished before his eyes, but most had been dragged off, screaming, into the flora.

Finnbar no longer heard them.

Those feathered monsters came in like quicksilver, he thought. *The boys never stood a chance.* He flexed his aching hands. *Strong hands for sure, but what good were they? These hands have failed my brothers in red. They shall* not *fail my Captain.*

He clenched his fists and waited.

The tell-tale clacking sounds began once more. Finnbar smiled. "You're giving yourselves away, idiots." The sounds grew louder. "Come on, then. Come get a piece."

FOURTEEN

"ALL I'M SAYING—*suggesting*—is that you put your uniform top back on," Captain Rogerson pleaded. Berta, who was still sporting her ill-fitting tank top, grunted. "I understand it was hot earlier, but now that it's dusk, you should cover up before you, uh, catch a chill? It won't do you any good tied around your waist."

"Pretty boy, if you want to break a piece off of this salty goodness, all you have to do is say so." She smirked. Rogerson grimaced and quickly returned to the front of the caravan.

"Where did you find *that* one?" he whispered to Wesley.

"She was assigned to us by the Department. Each science team gets their very own security personnel. Most groups have at least six. We have Berta. She's practically part of the family these days. She's also one of the best pilots I've ever met. Not to mention twelve levels of hell in a fight. And, um, by the way your muscle-bound friend is walking, a demon in the sack." He winked. Rogerson shuddered.

"So... Emma is it?" Sarah flashed a bright smile at her marching companion. Emma nodded but didn't make eye contact. "Is something the matter?"

"It's your eyes. They're... like rubies. I mean no offense, but they unnerve me a bit."

"I understand." Sarah smiled. "Where I come from, it isn't uncommon for parents to modify the gene sequences in fetuses to give them certain traits or characteristics. My folks thought it would be novel to have a child with red eyes. Go figure."

"You should probably meet my father. If anyone could understand what you've just said it would be him." Emma smiled uneasily. It struck her how this was the first adventure she'd been on without him by her side. She thought of how truly thrilled he would have been if he were here to meet and speak with the Adamses. Genetic modification? Time travel? Laser pistols? It's all so fantastic that he quite possibly may have soiled himself in delight.

The sunlight was starting to wane, but the group pressed on at the Captain's urging. Night seemed to fall all at once and now the Moon, still low in the sky, was just barely visible through the thick forest canopy. The Adams party each produced a thin, palm-sized flashlight, roughly the size and shape of a silver dollar coin. The tiny devices were capable of carving a remarkably large swath of illumination through the darkness.

"Are those... electric lanterns?" Grimstead asked in astonishment.

"It's called a flashlight," Sarah replied. "This is actually old, old technology compared to the rest of our equipment. But as the saying goes, 'If it ain't broke, then don't fix it till it is.' Would you like to try it? You just press the center to turn it on or off." She handed hers to the Professor, who smiled as he turned it on and off and on again.

"I'd like to have a go!" Emma attempted to grab it from his hands, but Grimstead blocked her advance.

"Wait your turn, Miss. I am testing it in the name of science."

"Ugh! You're impossible."

"Here." Wesley tossed a flashlight into Emma's hand. "We've got a whole pack of them. You can keep that one." Emma smiled and shone the light into Grimstead's eyes.

THE EXPLORERS TRUDGED through the darkness; they had been able to maintain a decent pace up until this point. But now the path was beginning to change: first taking on a slight incline, while gradually becoming rockier, rougher and more overgrown. Eventually, it was a solid tangle of gnarled roots and heavy stones under their feet and they were forced to slow their pace to a near crawl.

"Press on!" Rogerson ordered from the head of the group. "Draw your weapons and light more torches, electric or otherwise! And keep your eyes peeled!" They crept forward, now forced into a single file.

The path itself also seemed to be narrowing; the trees on either side of the path were now much closer together than they had been before.

"It seems as though we're purposely being funneled down this path," Grimstead remarked. "We don't have much choice now of where to go. I do find it interesting that the island has such varying topographical environments in such proximity." He turned and reluctantly handed the flashlight back to Sarah before drawing one of his revolvers.

"Nerds are so sexy," she whispered to herself.

It wasn't long before the trunks of the trees lining each side were so close together that a grown man had barely enough space to pass between them without struggling. Some of the trees were so close, they were growing into and around each other, like puzzle pieces.

"Has anyone else noticed the lack of natural sounds the further we go?" Wesley asked. "I understand that it's night, but no sounds at all? It's not right."

"I don't think this pathway was designed for our benefit," Grimstead stated. "I can't help but think this is what herded sheep must feel like."

Rogerson stopped suddenly and knelt. He raised a fist,

indicating that the others should stay still. He then put a finger to his lips.

"W-what is it?" Wesley asked.

"We aren't alone," Rogerson replied, his voice low. Everyone heard the sound of something rushing up from behind them. It drew closer, breathing heavily. No one dared move. Rogerson stood up and silently gestured for everyone else to kneel. He raised his rifle. As they crouched, something rushed past the last CC in line. He was so startled that he almost dropped his torch.

"Steady..." ordered the Captain.

The group remained low to the ground, barely breathing, eyes darting in every direction. The jungle around them fell silent. Suddenly, two loud pings sounded from Wesley's breast pocket and everyone started. The Doctor removed Connie with a shaky hand and her blue countenance immediately appeared.

"PROXIMITY ALERT! PROXIMITY ALERT!"

"Where?!" Rogerson demanded.

"Do you really want to know?"

"*Where,* Connie?!" Wesley barked.

"Everywhere!"

The trembling CC at the rear of the line suddenly jumped up screaming and began to run back the way they had come.

"Get back here, coward!" Rogerson shouted after him. The crewman's torch stood out like a beacon in the blackened night, swinging wildly as he ran.

And then, it fell.

The young crewman had caught his foot on a root. He scrambled to his feet and stooped to retrieve his fallen torch, his entire body trembling with terror. He didn't see the glint of large, glowing eyes peering at him through the twisted tree trunks. As he brought the torch up to see the path before him, a grayish hand with five long, clawed fingers lashed out from the darkness and split his throat open with one quick swipe.

The group watched in horror as their comrade's torch illuminated the red mist that sprayed out from his throat before smothering the flame. His body was still standing when the torchlight went out, and the path was again plunged into darkness. No one dared to move. Moments later, the sound of the man being dragged echoed down the path.

"Well, shit," Marrow grumbled. He looked to Rogerson, whose face looked pale in his torchlight.

"Grimstead... what the hell was that?" Rogerson whispered sharply.

"I... could barely make it out." He shook his head. The Captain took a moment to regain his composure before gesturing that everyone should be on their feet. They stepped in as close together as they could. Rogerson raised his torch up to the trees in front of them and the rest did the same. Dozens of glimmering eyes could be seen from all sides. Shadows began to appear in the dark spot where they had seen the CC fall, which meant that they were now cut off from any means of retreat.

"PROXIMITY ALERT!"

"Ya think?!" Berta yelled back.

"Dammit Connie, *shhhhhhhhh*!" Wesley sounded as if he was about to vomit.

Rogerson jabbed his torch into the opening between two trees to his left. Several gaunt faces gnashed their teeth. A throaty squeal pierced the silence. Guns and torches clattered to the dirt as several crew members instinctively moved to cover their ears. Berta spun her flashlight to the back of the path and saw a slender figure, crouching as if ready to pounce. Its appearance was very human-like, except its appendages were much longer, rawboned and covered in a very pale, grayish skin. The light reflected off its two large eyes, which were set deep into the creature's gaunt face. It grimaced, revealing a gaping mouth filled with jagged, yellow teeth. Its body was hairless, save for a dark brown pelt resembling a brier patch along its upper back. The creature spread its claw-like hands at Berta, ready to strike. Without hesitation, she aimed her Light Bringer and fired. The laser blasted a hole clean through the beast, killing it instantly. The squealing immediately ceased.

"Pick up your things and move!" Rogerson shouted, taking full advantage of the silence. "Cover each other and follow me!"

They ran as fast as the terrain would allow. The squealing resumed and bony, clawed hands sprang out from in between the trees, slicing and grabbing blindly as the explorers rushed by. The path had become a gauntlet.

Sarah tripped on a root and struck the ground, hard.

"Wesley!" She screamed as two CCs ran to her aid.

"Sarah!" Wesley started back toward her. Berta grabbed his arm and yanked him forward.

"C'mon, doc! Look, those guys got her! We've got to go!"

"N-no! S-Sarah!" He fought Berta's grip, but found he was no match for her strength. He reluctantly complied, looking over his shoulder every few paces and sobbing. Meanwhile, the two CCs stood on either side of Sarah, blocking her from the trees.

"Are you alright, ma'am?" one asked, fighting to keep his voice steady as he stooped and extended a hand to her. Just as she was reaching out for him, she saw clawed hands latch onto his shoulders, torso and limbs, piercing through his uniform and dragging him to the tree line. It took three savage slams to break enough of his bones to pull him through the tangle of trees. She screamed and dropped back to the ground, turning her head away from the scene just in time to see the second CC drop his torch as he was snatched and dragged screaming into the pitch. Sarah pressed herself to the ground in the darkness, paralyzed with fear. The group had ran on without her. Her flashlight, still illuminated, had flown out of her hand and now lay several feet away. Too far to reach even if she could will her limbs to move. Trembling, she squeezed her eyes shut and waited for death. She thought of her son, alone with the ship, and hoped that he was alright. A horrible squealing noise sounded just over her head. She felt something swoop past her head and heard the distinct *thunk* of flesh and bone being severed.

In one swift movement, Sarah found herself being hoisted off the ground and swung over The Swede's shoulder. He was covered in claw wounds and bleeding. He pulled his axe from the twitching gray carcass and hurried to catch up with the others. Sarah saw the beam from her flashlight get stomped out by a flurry of feet and knew that it very well could have been her instead.

All was chaos up ahead. Round after round of gun-and laser-fire exploded into the night, as the explorers struggled to fend off the unseen creatures and find their way through the dark and treacherous path. The rocky slope had given way to small, jagged bits of earth that jutted out from the path, much like steps. The group was again being forced to slow their pace. Grimstead and Emma were now heading up the group, with several CCs just behind them. Rogerson followed his men, while Marrow, Berta and Wesley were last. Berta was practically dragging the distraught doctor along behind her. She fired her laser pistol at random, hoping to fend the creatures off with intensity rather than accuracy. No one had had the time to even consider the absence of The Swede.

"We *were* being herded!" Grimstead shouted as he unloaded his revolver into a tangle of reaching hands. "I hate being right!"

"I somehow doubt that!" Emma grunted as she hacked off a claw that nearly caught her face. She jabbed the flashlight's beam into the creature's eyes, causing it to be slightly stunned, then she swung her blade down hard into its neck. "Ugh! What *are* these things?!"

"They must be the Night Stalkers."

"Wonderful."

As the Captain fired his rifle, he noticed something through the scope. "Grimstead! I... I think I see an opening in the distance! Do you see it?"

Though the darkness, Grimstead could see a round patch of fuzzy-grayness before them, though it was still too far to tell what it was exactly. As they drew closer, the path appeared to level out just before it entered into the grayness of the clearing. The thick trees near it were bowed together, creating an archway at the path's end. Beyond the archway was a dark form that was far too wide to accurately identify.

"Yes, I do! I can also make out some kind of structure just beyond it. If we can make it to that, we might just get out of this!"

As they approached the archway the number of Night Stalker attacks began to wane, while the number of eyes on the path behind them multiplied. As soon as they hit level ground, Grimstead and Emma took off running, and were the first to burst through the forest gauntlet and out into the clearing. They paused just at the entrance and scanned for any sign of the creatures. It was surprisingly quiet and calm. Emma sunk to her knees, relieved and exhausted. Grimstead felt for his canteen and was elated to find it still intact. He drank heavily before offering it to Emma, who graciously accepted.

The clearing was brilliantly illuminated by the full Moon, nearing its apex, a welcome change from the pitch-black of the gauntlet. Grimstead quickly assessed their surroundings. Just a few yards from where they stood, the grass gave way to a cobblestone pathway. The enormous, dark form he had spotted before was revealed as a massive stone structure, one of three in fact. *This had once been, or, perhaps* still is, *the central plaza of a civilization,* he concluded.

Grimstead's attention was temporarily diverted from his discovery as the rest of the group entered the clearing. Rogerson came through first, followed by Marrow and the remaining CCs. Berta, with Wesley in tow, was last. Winded,

Berta released him and the Doctor fell to the ground, tears welling in his eyes.

"Sarah."

No sooner did her name escape his lips, they heard a chorus of high-pitched squeals ring out from the trees. The Swede came running into the clearing with Sarah over his shoulder and two Night Stalkers close behind. Rogerson quickly fired two shots at the creatures, their heads exploding like rotten melons as they fell.

The Swede lowered the wide-eyed Doctor to the ground and nodded to his captain. Wesley ran over to her, sobbing, and they embraced. The horrific squealing began to fade as the creatures retreated back into the forest. Everyone stood in silence, recuperating and just trying to process everything that had just happened.

Rogerson surveyed his crew and noted that there were even fewer of them than before. He silently prayed that the reinforcements would survive to reach them. He reached into his hip satchel and retrieved a handful of rifle rounds. As he reloaded, he took a moment to survey the clearing and study the three structures that towered over the plaza's perimeter.

In appearance, the stone structures were reminiscent of ancient Mayan temples: large slabs of limestone fitted together to create several platforms, each successive platform was built smaller and smaller until it culminated in a terrace with a temple at the summit. The two on the north and south edges of the plaza each had five platforms before the summit. The third, on the western edge of the plaza, had nine. Each structure had a stairway leading up from the plaza to the summit, to an entrance way. The three temples were connected by a network of cobblestone pathways, which appeared to convene at the plaza's center before spreading out like the spokes of a wheel, some paths lead directly to each of the buildings, while some went beyond them and into the wilderness.

As the Moon crept to its highest point, its light shone

directly into the center of the plaza, reflecting brilliantly off the pale, smooth cobblestones.

A flurry of shadows could be seen moving across the terraces and steps of the two smaller temples.

"Professor?"

"I have absolutely no idea, Captain."

Grimstead squinted at the temples, trying to make out exactly what was causing the shadows to stir. He noticed two large torches set on either side of the entrance to the western temple, directly across from where they stood. An inhuman sound, like a guttural growl, drew their attention back to the archway: the creatures were gathered there, stationary, but ensuring that forward was the only viable direction.

"Damn, you guys are severely screwed. Like, no lube or anything," Connie stated. The shrieking started again, quickly growing stronger and louder than before. Night Stalkers began scurrying out and down the sides of the temples like roaches escaping a poisoned nest. They poured out by the hundreds, never entering the plaza, but lining up around the edges in a circle. Within minutes, the plaza glittered with hundreds of orbs reflecting the dimmed moonlight. And then, they began to move in.

"Well, shit." Dr. Marrow grumbled. The group was being corralled to the very center of the plaza by shrieks and swiping claws. They pressed close together and swept their flashlights and torches out at wide angles. The ground began to crunch beneath their feet. Grimstead looked down at the ground and glimpsed what appeared to be a broken rib cage under his boot. The ground was littered with bones.

"Typical," he muttered.

"Well, looks like this is it," Rogerson squared his jaw defiantly and chambered a round. "It was nice knowing... *some* of you." With a sudden, unified shriek, the creatures closed the circle in a rush. Emma panicked and began jabbing her flashlight at the encroaching mob. To her surprise, they recoiled and shrieked in pain. It confirmed her suspicions.

"The light! The light hurts them!"

"Wagon wheel!" Rogerson ordered. "Every torch lit and at the ready, lads!" The CCs moved out into a large circle and began swinging their torches around like wild men. Sarah and Wesley used their flashlights like rapiers, stabbing the Night Stalkers with beams of light. Rogerson, Grimstead, Marrow and The Swede moved inward into an even tighter circle, and stood with their weapons trained. The group moved painfully slow across the bone field toward the large temple.

The closer they drew to the temple, the louder the Night Stalkers shrieked in unison. Hundreds of hungry mouths erupted in an ear-splitting cacophony. Grimstead felt himself growing dizzy from the noise.

"Do not lower the lights!" he shouted, but his voice was lost in the din. A CC stumbled and dropped his torch. Without hesitation, the creatures pounced and he disappeared into the mob. The Night Stalkers tore him up so violently that pieces of the doomed adventurer were cast into the air.

A flash of lightning tinted the clouds a brilliant orange. The subsequent thunder tolled a forthcoming complication: rain. It started softly, patting the ground in fat drops. The explorers picked up their pace a bit, their torches dancing around the large drops as best they could. The bone-laden plaza grew slick and the bones proved nothing more than a tenuous, macabre foothold. Emma stepped into a half-skull and lost her footing, she yelped and she dropped her flashlight as she slid, finally catching herself on Captain Rogerson's back, which in turn, caused him to pitch forward.

"Halt!" he cried, reaching around behind him and inadvertently mushing Emma's left breast. He turned to her with a smirk, as the group came to a stand still. Emma glared indignantly at the Captain as she righted herself. She then moved to the middle of the smallest cluster.

"Take this moment to reload, men. We won't get

another." They were close enough to see the carvings on the temples' walls, yet, countless Night Stalkers still blocked their escape. The drizzle became a steady rain and the torches began to falter. One of the creatures stretched its neck to whiff at Grimstead, its face twisted into what could only pass as a grin.

"Cheeky bastard."

A silhouetted figure appeared at the entrance-way at the apex of the largest temple. It went unnoticed until the creatures began acting as if they had been threatened; they collectively hunched and began to chatter in an strange series of hushed clicks and shrieks.

"Look!" Berta pointed, drawing the group's attention to the temple's entrance-way. The figure stood holding aloft what was clearly a sword.

"Voit taskulamput! Tule taskulamput!" A masculine voice boomed high over the plaza. Rogerson was taken aback, as he understood what the stranger was saying.

"To the torches! He said come to the torches!"

"You understood that?" Marrow asked.

"Yes!" Rogerson grinned. "It's Finnish!"

The figure bellowed a battle-cry to Odin and came bounding from the entrance-way into the plaza, swinging a large sword right to left across his body as he ran. The creatures reacted immediately, clamoring to escape the attack, but they could not scatter fast enough. Within seconds, howls erupted and body parts soared. Rogerson took advantage of the opportunity.

"Rush the temple!" He took off running and the group followed, dashing toward the temple with weapons blazing. The Night Stalkers offered little opposition, and soon the explorers had reached the stone steps leading up to what they hoped was safety. They ascended slowly and carefully, as the limestone steps were steep and slick from the rain. As Grimstead hauled himself up the many, many steps, he realized that he was drenched, sore and weary as hell. He couldn't help but to pause and look back down at the fracas they had so narrowly escaped, as if to convince himself that it had actually happened. He turned just in time to witness a throng of gaunt, yellow-fanged beasts retreating back toward the other temples and into the forest. He also glimpsed their sword-swinging savior as he moved through the creatures like a scythe would move through wheat. Grimstead could have sworn that he heard laughter.

"Inside! Move inside!" Rogerson barked, pausing in the entrance to make sure everyone was accounted for. The explorers found themselves at the mouth of a long and extremely narrow limestone corridor, carved from floor to ceiling with petroglyphs similar to those that adorned the white obelisks they had encountered that morning. These carvings, however, were more intricate and brightly-colored.

"It looks to be well lit." Wesley observed, as he and Sarah hurried ahead of the others down the passage, which led directly into a large, square room that was mercifully lacking carnivorous fiends.

"We've found a place to hunker down and tend to the wounded! Quickly, everyone!" He called back down the passageway.

As Grimstead reached the top of the stairway, he saw that Rogerson was standing there alone, his eyes on the plaza. Grimstead joined him and they gazed down at the bedlam below.

"I can honestly say I didn't think we were making it out of that one."

"Nor did I, nor did I." The Captain shook his head and clapped the Professor on the shoulder. "Who knows how long our Finnish-speaking savior will be able to deter them. I don't know what the other temples are like, but this corridor here is narrow. If those *things* do enter, it will be single file or two by two. We could hold them off easily enough. For a while, anyway."

"I doubt we'll even have to worry about another attack.

They didn't chase us up, and, from what I can tell, wouldn't even lay eyes upon this place. There's something about it that makes it... different." The Professor's voice trailed off. There was something vaguely familiar about these glyphs, but he just couldn't place it. Had he seen them long ago? Read about them? Dreamed them?

"Let's get out of this rain." The Captain shook him from his thoughts. "I don't know about you, but my britches are soaked through and it's starting to chafe."

The two sloshed their way down the narrow hall and into a cavernous chamber constructed entirely of pristine limestone. Like the corridor, the chamber's walls were carved and painted with intricate and colorful images. The walls were lined with scores of limestone sconces—carved from the walls themselves —each bearing a lit torch, which provided just enough light for the large space. The majority of the group was already huddled closely around a large cauldron which was being used as a makeshift fireplace. Rogerson walked over to join them, while Grimstead stood absorbing every detail of the massive room.

A perfectly square opening was cut directly into the center of the chamber's floor and a stream of water poured into it from a matching opening in the ceiling. Grimstead noted that this was an ancient plumbing system of sorts, which allowed the rain to pour in and down to the other levels of the temple —also sunlight, he reckoned—which he strongly hoped he'd get to see again.

Though the central part of the chamber was virtually empty, all four corners were piled high with dusty artifacts— paintings, vessels, books, even solid gold coins. The untouched treasures glittered in the torchlight.

Emma took it upon herself to poke through one of the piles, intrigued by a painting that had caught her eye. She dusted off the simple, wood-framed painting of a woman from an unknown place and time. Emma instantly liked her. The woman's hair was a shock of red, infused with tiny twigs and delicate green leaves, and her skin looked very much like the bark of a birch tree. The woman's emerald eyes were forlorn, but radiated nobility. Had she been a lady, or a queen, perhaps? Had she visited the island or was her likeness taken as a means of remembrance? Emma pondered the sordid—hypothetical, of course—details surrounding the red-haired subject.

Rogerson spotted a second blazing cauldron at the back of the chamber and walked over to investigate. A modest feather mattress lay near it, surrounded by stacks of ancient books by unknown authors with titles citing unknown places. The books, Rogerson noted, were not covered in dust—nor the twenty wooden crates stacked at the foot of the mattress, each packed with glass bottles full of wine. Rogerson ran a finger across the logo imprinted on the top of one of the crates: *Marousel & Voort.* No vineyard he'd ever heard of. Hidden a bit further in the shadows were four more crates, imprinted by the *Pyysh & Shyyte Rum Company.* Rogerson decided that, perhaps, he should keep Dr. Marrow from investigating this side of the room.

Just then, Captain Rogerson caught sight of the Doctor in the opposite corner, ungracefully stuffing his pockets with gold coins instead of patching up his damaged crew.

"Joe! Shouldn't you be tending to the wounded?!" Marrow furrowed his brow.

"Damn it, Captain! I'm a doctor, not a doc—I'll go tend to the wounded." He hung his head in defeat and slowly walked over to the first cauldron, where Berta and The Swede were seated. The Swede silently nursed his numerous claw wounds. Marrow knelt beside him and opened his rucksack. Out came four bottles of whiskey, which he gently set down on the floor. He finally removed a tiny leather doctor's bag. Rogerson shook his head in disbelief.

"Remind me why I keep you around."

"Why, for my rogue-like charm and witty banter," Marrow grimaced as he extracted a jagged fingernail from The

Swede's right shoulder. Blood oozed from wound. "Shit. I don't think I brought enough gauze."

"Ah!" Wesley reached down into his own pack and pulled out several small tubes. He held them out to Marrow. "Here. This stuff is called Insta-Heal. It's a synthetic ointment. We carry them wherever we go! It accelerates blood cell reproduction to the wound and causes near-instantaneous clotting and skin mending. Truly amazing stuff!"

Sarah smiled as she lifted a tube to her cheek and waved her other hand over it with a flourish. "Bleeding, dying, outta luck? Insta-Heal will fix you up! A product of Moonshield Incorporated!"

The name caught Grimstead's attention from across the room. "Moonshield," he growled through grit teeth.

"Easy, pal, it was just the slogan," Wesley said as he handed the tubes to Dr. Marrow. "A little goes a long way! With Insta-Heal you'll be A-Okay!" He smiled and winked.

"Yeah, sure," Marrow grumbled. He squeezed a bit of the ointment onto the gash in The Swede's shoulder. The wound began to fizz, bubble and—much to everyone's amazement— heal. "I'll be damned—"

A man suddenly appeared at the chamber's entrance. He was covered from head to toe in gore and smiling broadly. Emma was the first to spot him, her gasp alerted the others to his presence.

"EVIL ASS-PICKLES!" Wesley screamed as he drew his laser pistol and shot the man through the chest. The laser not only sent the man flying several feet backwards down the corridor, but blasted a hole through his torso. There were murmurs and shrieks from the group. Grimstead snatched the weapon from Wesley's trembling hand.

"You *have* to stop doing that!"

"I-I'm sorry! M-my condition. I—"

"Killed the man who saved us!" Rogerson interjected. "He could have helped us! He could have taken us to wherever the hell it is we're trying to *get* to! And now he's dead! Now he's—"

"Standing right behind you!" Emma squeaked, pointing at the doorway.

FIFTEEN

THE MAN HAD returned and was standing among them, eyes alight with rage. Everyone watched in astonishment as the hole that had demolished most of his torso rapidly mended itself before their eyes. They were so amazed in fact, that it took them a few moments to notice that the man was holding Captain Rogerson several inches off the ground by his throat.

"Et uskalla iskeä minua! Olen säästänyt teille ja tämä on, miten voit kiittää minua?! (How dare you strike me! I have saved you and this is how you thank me?!)"

"Ystäväni... on... idiootti (My... friend... is... an... idiot)," Rogerson choked. The stranger pulled Rogerson close and glared at him with an intensity only seen in wild animals. He then let out a raucous laugh and set the Captain down.

"Ymmärrän hyökkäys! Haluaisin verrata itseäni verinen dragur! (I understand the attack! I would compare myself to the bloody dragur!) Ha ha ha!"

They all watched in stony silence as the warrior walked to the torrent of water pouring down from the ceiling and stepped in, straddling the opening in floor. The blood and bits of Night Stalker that clung to his body and hair were quickly stripped away. Once clean, the man stepped from the torrent and squeezed the excess from his long black hair, then stretched out his muscular upper body. He turned to face the explorers with a broad smile.

"Minua kutsutaan Vargas, poika Ragnar. (I am known as Vargas, son of Ragnar.)" He extended his arm toward Rogerson and the two grasped each other's forearms, as was the old Norse greeting. Rogerson thanked Vargas profusely for the aid and explained that he would act as translator for the group.

They spoke in Finnish for several minutes, as the rest looked on.

"Did you know the Captain spoke Finnish?" Grimstead whispered to Dr. Marrow, who shrugged.

"The Captain speaks a lot of different languages. He is worldly and all that bunk."

Rogerson turned to face the group. "Excellent news. First of all, we're safe here. Those beasts are as superstitious as they are vicious, and—"

"H-how on Earth did you survive the laser blast?!" Wesley interrupted. He couldn't contain his curiosity any longer. "I-I'm *so* sorry, by the way." He was twitching. Sarah stepped forward and made him sit down. Vargas stared at him with amusement while Rogerson quietly translated his query. The viking's voice boomed throughout the chamber as he gave a lengthy explanation. Rogerson did his best to keep up. His face morphed through a series of expressions, starting out intrigued, then excited, then surprised, concerned and finally pleased. The rest watched the two in eager anticipation.

"His name is Vargas, son of Ragnar," Rogerson began. "And, I'll be damned! He is the very same Vargas from the inscription on McParland's Varangian map! He said that Wesley seems to have harnessed the lightning of the mighty Thor himself, and if he had not eaten one of the legendary Apples of Idunna, he would have surely perished from the blast."

"Apples of Idunna?" Grimstead felt a surge of adrenaline. He knew the mythology well. "As in the Norse goddess?"

"One and the same." Rogerson nodded. "Our friend was

presented with one of the apples by the daughter of the island god, whom he believes was taught how to grow the sacred fruit by the goddess herself."

Vargas nodded, acknowledging the truth in Rogerson's translation. He glanced down and realized that a puddle of rainwater had collected beneath his feet. He gestured toward the fire and Rogerson followed him over to it. As he stood drying himself, Emma, Sarah and Berta couldn't help but notice how the firelight accentuated his muscular build. He happened to flex as he brushed some excess water from his biceps and Emma let out an audible sigh.

"Where exactly was this fruit benefactor found?" Grimstead asked, raising a questioning eyebrow at Emma. Her eyes were distant. She was still holding onto the painting she had found and gripped the frame so tightly, it was on the verge of cracking. Grimstead rolled his eyes.

"Within the tower of the island god, apparently. The god is named Ïsur." Rogerson answered, oblivious to the slack-jawed faces of his female comrades. "Vargas said he will take us in the morning. It's not far from here."

"To think, the legendary fountain of youth is... actually a *tree*..." Grimstead's voice trailed off as he became lost in thought.

Vargas spoke again, at length. Rogerson's face grew stern.

"When Vargas, his father Ragnar, and their crew were attacked by the Night Stalkers on their fateful journey, each man died horribly. During the battle, Vargas lost sight of his father and thought that he had been slain by those horrid creatures. So, he fought harder. The battle lasted for hours. The beasts slowly herded him up the side of this temple and to the doorway. There, he fought with so much intensity that he made a mountain of bodies, so high and deep that the moonlight could barely penetrate the temple's entrance. He then sat in this very room with only the light from that ceiling opening to see by. He sat and waited, while hundreds of Night Stalkers scurried and howled outside. Come morning, he pushed the bodies from the entrance and down the temple steps, only to find that the plaza was completely empty. Not a beast stirred, nor corpse rotted. The bodies of the dead had vanished. He felt a great swell of anger and dismay at not being able to build a pyre for his fallen father."

Emma had set the painting down and moved closer to the fire as Rogerson spoke. She noticed Vargas watching her and they exchanged a smile. "Should we tell him that his father went stark-mad and ran off, leaving his son to fend for himself?" She asked after a moment of silence. Grimstead and Rogerson both glared at her. "Perhaps not, then." She turned and smiled harder at the ancient viking.

Thanks to the Insta-Heal, Dr. Marrow was just about finished tending to the wounded. Rogerson motioned for him to hand over one of his bottles of whiskey.

"Marrow."

"But, Captain—" Rogerson's eyes widened with anger. "Fine, fine." He removed a bottle from his bag and tossed it over. Rogerson caught it, took a swig, then offered it to Vargas. He accepted the bottle graciously, took a hearty gulp and then violently spit it out. The liquid traveled a couple of feet across the room, directly hitting the flame of one of the lower torches and causing it to flare and singe a CC who happened to be standing nearby. He yelped and jumped out of the way. Everyone howled with laughter, save for Dr. Marrow and the singed crewman.

"Bloody waste," Marrow grumbled. Vargas took another mouthful and, this time, swallowed it. He slapped his leg and laughed.

"He isn't what I pictured at all," Emma quietly confessed to Sarah.

Sarah nodded. "Oh, I agree. He's not bad for a man his age." The two stared in equal admiration.

"I mean, from the account we'd read before coming

ashore, I had imagined him to be some hulking brute with green teeth and a mess for a beard. I certainly had not expected well..."

"Perfection in male form?" Sarah giggled.

"Exactly!" Emma blushed and they tried to contain their giddy laughter. Vargas spoke again. The room quieted down as Rogerson cleared his throat.

"After his encounter with the Night Stalkers, Vargas wandered west and came upon a graveyard of sorts, though it was not for the remains of people. This was a graveyard for the chariots of the sky gods. Just beyond that is the tower of the god he calls Ïsur. Vargas met this god and his children in a room of brilliant lights and images. Ïsur spoke of many things, things that Vargas couldn't begin to understand at the time. Ïsur's only daughter took a shine to Vargas and offered him a sacred apple as a means of protection, and to ensure that they would be together for eternity. This angered Ïsur because the fruit was meant for the gods alone, and our friend here was subject to horrendous torture. It was an experiment as much as it was a punishment, so the god could see what effects the apple had on his human form. Flesh was torn from his body and then grew anew. Limbs were severed and reattached simply by pressing the pieces together again. He was made to breathe poisonous concoctions that caused his lungs to choke and his skin burn with the heat of a hundred suns. Still, his body mended almost as quickly as it was damaged. But, the anger of Ïsur was indeed a terrible thing to endure."

Rogerson took a gulp of the whiskey and passed it to Grimstead. He took a sip and kept the bottle moving.

"Vargas recalls waking up in the center of the plaza, naked, and with no memory of being placed there. It was night and he was surrounded by those creatures. His clothing and sword had been neatly placed within arm's reach. Our friend did not waste a moment. He immediately began to butcher the Night Stalkers, stacking their bodies in small mounds. He then claimed this temple as his own. To this day, the bastards won't go near it, knowing that something far worse then themselves lives inside. Since then, he has made his way all over the island, discovering the many—and varied—civilizations and creatures that dwell within."

"There are other active civilizations here?" Grimstead's eyes grew wide.

"Vargas says many have perished as a result of warfare and the ravages of time, but a few do remain."

"Why doesn't he simply leave?" Emma wondered.

"Where could someone like him go?" Rogerson shrugged. "Centuries have lapsed, this is the only world that exists for him now. What modern place would have him?"

"He must be so lonely!" Sarah sighed. "Can we keep him?"

"Now, wait just a moment!" her husband objected.

"Yes, well—" Rogerson interjected, "Tonight let us rest and mend, for tomorrow we shall be standing at the threshold of a god!" He raised a triumphant fist into the air. A few lackluster *huzzahs* murmured through the ever-shrinking group. Grimstead was, again, lost deep in his thoughts. Rogerson landed a heavy hand on his back, which jolted him back into awareness. Everyone set about arranging themselves for the duration of the night. They huddled together in small groups on the floor near the cauldrons and tried to fall asleep. Berta and The Swede found a darkened corner where they curled up together. Vargas retired to his private corner of the chamber, and Rogerson followed so that the two could speak further.

Emma and Sarah lay side-by-side near the first cauldron, where they spent some time whispering and giggling before drifting off to sleep.

Grimstead sat alone, away from everyone else, his thoughts wandering as they did before. After about an hour, he got up and approached a stewing Wesley, who had quarantined himself in a corner near a large pile of plunder. He sat down next to him and pressed his aching back up against the cool, limestone wall. Wesley was feverishly chewing on the skin around his fingernails. His right hand had already been gnawed raw. Grimstead noticed an open tube of Insta-Heal on the floor beside him.

"Doctor."

"Professor."

"You looked vexed. Aside from nearly being mauled to death by a horde of twisted monsters, are you alright?"

"Well," Wesley lowered his voice to a whisper. "Not entirely. I tried to check in with my son Paul moments ago, but Connie cannot establish a connection with his com link. I think it may have something to do with the limestone we're surrounded by. Without satellites, Connie doesn't have that oomph I'm used to her having."

"I am certain the little master is safe as houses, Doctor." Grimstead placed his hand on Wesley's shoulder for reassurance. Wesley nodded and began to chew his nails once again. "May I impose on you for a moment? My curiosity is beyond measure. Could you tell me more about New Atlantis?"

"That's a real tall order, my friend," Wesley sounded put-upon. He was still a bit heated from Sarah's exclamation.

"Well, if it's not too much trouble, that is. I understand if you would rather be alone." Several moments of silence passed.

"New Atlantis is a hypocrisy. If one would juxtapose cutting-edge technology with third world squalor, it would only scratch the surface. The original settlers from the wastelands were the most fortunate. They were able to utilize it for what it was: a haven. However, as with any truly decent idea, once you add humans into the equation, it turns into rubbish. Look at religion, any religion, for example. Mortals trying to comprehend the words of gods? Impossible! So they elected few to 'translate' the god-texts and tailor them to their own designs. And the end result? Close-minded sheep, bloated braggarts and murderous fanatics as arrogant as they are ignorant!" His sudden outburst caused a few of the nearby CCs to stir in their sleep. Wesley paused to compose himself.

"My apologies. I digress. Please don't misunderstand me, Alexander, New Atlantis and the other megacities are by far a more agreeable choice than living in The Wastes. Even *with* The Laughing Man in the Devil Mask running around."

He started on his left thumb.

"The who?" Grimstead attempted to find a comfortable way to lean against the pile of treasure beside him.

"Oh, *right.* Sorry. I keep forgetting that you and I are from different eras. Where, or I should say *when,* I come from, only those in the deepest recesses of The Wastes haven't heard of the Laughing Man. He is, well, *they* are, in my opinion, a cell of urban terrorists. According to the most common folklore, the Laughing Man is either an immortal or some kind of demon. Maybe even a ghost. Personally, I think there is a cult of insane people with AK47s and explosives who all dress alike. Or maybe robots that have been manically programmed and then set loose upon the populace one at a time."

"*Row* bots?"

Wesley nodded. "Bipedal, humanoid automatons with artificial intelligence guided by programming and electric circuitry. You know, *robots.*" Grimstead politely nodded as if he understood Wesley's circular explanation. "No one can determine many facts about the phenomena as a result of the use of rather sophisticated explosives. It's kind of clever, if you think about it. Picture this, you're standing at an intersection in Chronos Dodecahedron, right? Maybe sipping a twenty-dollar latte, just minding your own business when all of a sudden, there's a... a man-demon standing there, dressed in black with a black hood and cloak! And if you happen to look closely, you'll see a red devil mask smiling in the hood's shadow. So, of course you immediately think, *Oh no!* but before you can even react or think a second thought, you can hear his bellowing laughter. Then the, whatever he is, pulls out a high-powered assault rifle and starts picking off people at random! *BOOM! BOOM! Rata-tat-a-tat-tat-tat-a!* All the while, he's still laughing. People start falling left and right. Most are stampeding each other to get away. The authorities arrive and begin to fire at him, The Laughing Man. He probably takes several hits without even losing his grip on his weapon. Hell, he's laughing even harder now. He lobs a few old-world grenades haphazardly, causing massive damage. Once the police surround him, he detonates a bomb that he's had strapped... somewhere... to himself and just like that, everyone is vapor. Nothing left. No fingerprints, no DNA, nothing. People mourn their losses. Funerals are held. Businesses are rebuilt, all under the probability that The Laughing Man is really dead. Then a month or so later, another one pops up somewhere else. And then the month after that. It never really seems to end."

"How utterly atrocious! And... sinister." Grimstead shook his head. "A question, if I may? What exactly is DNA?"

Wesley yawned and cracked his back.

"DNA? By your standing, it has yet to be discovered, so never mind that." He waved off the Professor's inquiry as one would a panhandler. "So, anyway, New Atlantis is a very interesting place to live. Dangerous, yes, but it beats getting eaten by someone's radioactive grandparent. Now if you'll excuse me, Professor, I'd like to get some rest." He turned his face to the pile of dusty treasure.

"Of course. Sleep well, Dr. Adams." Grimstead was a bit startled by Wesley's explanation of the city, however, he decided that it wasn't worth trying to decipher at this point. His weary mind had about as much information for the day as it could stand. He turned his attention to the rest of the chamber. The fires had dimmed, but were still burning. Nearly everyone had fallen asleep. The chamber seemed almost peaceful. Determined to capture at least an hour's worth of sleep, Grimstead rested his head on a nearby pile of palm-sized gold and silver coins and closed his eyes. His last waking thought was on the prospect of the new day. And the hope that most of them would survive it.

SIXTEEN

ALEXANDER GRIMSTEAD LOOKED down upon the damaged, lifeless body of his beloved Lilly as he held her. His own body was numb, save for the trembling in his legs. He could feel the trembling amplify, spreading out to the floor beneath him and the walls surrounding him. The underground temple of Goy Gothog was crumbling.

He knew this dream well. He had relived the wretched event in his sleep numerous times over the last year. This time, he felt as if he was an observer rather than a participant. He could see himself standing motionless in the subterranean temple. He knew that his heart ached to cradle Lilly in his arms and kiss what was left of her face, at the same time he prayed for a boulder to fall and crush his skull. But, as always, the massive, ebony hands of Algernon Colborne pulled him to safety while the ancient boulders fell.

"We has got to go, Alexander!" Algernon said, as he always did. Grimstead knew that it was useless to struggle against Black Hercules, so he surrendered. Algernon threw Grimstead over his shoulder as if he was a rag doll and ran from the collapsing temple. Just as he always did. Except that, tonight, Grimstead found himself standing on top of a dilapidated building. Instead of being carried out into the harsh light of day, he was standing high above a dead city. His clothes were tattered and slowly burning away in the light. He looked skyward and saw a sun that was not only thousands of times larger than Earth's but it was also spreading directly towards him. He felt his skin being slowly burned away, then mended and burned again. Panicked, he looked to the wasteland of a city below and recognized it as New Atlantis. It no longer felt like a dream. Grimstead could feel his own skin blistering and smell his hair singing against his scalp. The city below him showed no sign of life. He suddenly knew he was the last living creature on Earth. Possibly in the entire universe. Grimstead became keenly aware that he was soon to join the others in extinction. He closed his eyes, but could still see the outline of the fallen city and the undulating tendrils of the supernova. The wind roared in his ears. His skin continued to burn, but now it would not heal. This was it. With outstretched arms he smiled and was destroyed.

SEVENTEEN

GRIMSTEAD WOKE GENTLY. His eyes opened slowly, as if from a long blink. He was in the temple, his face pressed against a mass of ancient coins. He glanced around the chamber and saw that the others were still sleeping soundly. The room was silent, save for an errant snore. He noticed that the chamber's waterfall had ceased, meaning the rain had finally stopped, and the dim glow of dawn entered in its place. He attempted to move, but found that he was being weighed down by Wesley, slumbering deeply, his face pressed into the Professor's left arm. Wesley's mouth was wide open and a small puddle of drool had collected on the Professor's shirt. Grimstead slowly eased himself out from under the Doctor and stood. Wesley fell back onto the pile of coins with a thud and slept on, clutching at the coins beneath his face and giving them a gentle kiss. A jeweled crown slid down from the top of the pile and rested on his head. *Perfection*, Grimstead thought.

The muffled shriek of a Night Stalker suddenly reached his ears. It seemed a bit too close for comfort. Stepping softly around his sleeping cohorts, Grimstead made his way to the chamber entrance where he could clearly hear the inhuman cries coming from the plaza. He paused to unsheathe the machete that was harnessed to his left leg before stepping out into the corridor and slowly walking toward the sounds. As he approached the temple's entrance-way, he could see Vargas at the top of the steps, looming over the bone-filled plaza like a vengeful king. He stood motionless, with his left arm extended. The creatures murmured, but did not shriek. Grimstead paused just inside the entrance-way to observe. The viking raised his arm higher and revealed there was a Night Stalker in his grasp. Vargas held the creature over the steps by its throat, it squirmed and hissed, struggling desperately against his tightening grip. Vargas suddenly plunged his right hand into the creature's chest and ripped its beating heart from the tangle of meat and bone. He threw the lifeless body down the steps and held the heart high over his head. The Night Stalkers fell silent. Vargas brought the heart down to his mouth and bit into it, blood spraying across his face. The creatures began a nervous chattering noise. He smiled, his teeth a bright contrast against his blood-soaked skin. Vargas sensed Grimstead's presence behind him and turned to see the Professor shrinking back from the entrance. He extended his bloody hand.

"Niiden on opittava. (They must learn.)"

Vargas nodded. Reluctantly, Grimstead placed his hand into Vargas'. *Like a bear trap.* Vargas pulled the Professor to him and raised his hand high as if he were the winner of a boxing match. He then placed the remains of the heart into Grimstead's hand and the creatures immediately began to hiss and shriek in anger. He felt a throb of concern: he knew what the viking expected of him, but could he actually do it? With a trembling hand, he slowly brought the heart to his mouth. Every eye was upon him. Grimstead's mouth went dry, he now regretted leaving the tranquility of the inner chamber in order to quell his curiosity. Vargas sensed his hesitation and urged him on, his eyes wide and intense. He opened his mouth and bit down. Blood gushed down his throat and over his face. His stomach churned with nausea. He began to gag, but Vargas' menacing glare overpowered it. Grimstead forced his teeth deeper into the heart and then tore his head away, taking a chunk of the still-warm muscle tissue with it. He gulped it back into his mouth and chewed. The Night Stalkers howled in anger. Once he'd swallowed, Vargas again lifted his hand high in triumph. The viking let out a bellowing roar and Grimstead, much to his own surprise, joined in.

Vargas reached into the leather pouch on his belt and produced four egg-sized balls made of what seemed to be pitch and dried fur. He brought one up to the torch flame and it ignited with a brilliant flash. He then held the burning orb aloft with great flourish, making sure that it caught the attention of all in the plaza below, before throwing it with all his might. The ball sailed through the air and landed on the back pelt of one of the creatures, setting it alight. The plaza erupted in a panic as the creatures frantically scurried to escape the flames. Vargas quickly lit and threw a second ball of burning pitch, then a third. He placed the fourth and final ball into the torch flame and held it high as it burned. The plaza was now empty, save for a few disoriented creatures hurrying to find sanctuary. Vargas casually tossed the burning orb to the stone below with a smirk. Grimstead caught sight of the viking's charred fingers and watched in astonishment as the flesh mended itself within seconds. Vargas grabbed Grimstead by both arms and held him tight.

"Veli! (Brother!)" he shouted, "Veri veli! (Blood brother!)"

Alerted by the commotion, Captain Rogerson, Berta and three CCs came running down the corridor with guns at the ready. They burst through the temple entrance and were taken aback by the curious sight of the two grinning, bloodied men.

"What happened?! We heard shouting!" Rogerson exclaimed, trying to comprehend the scene before him. Vargas nodded and patted Rogerson on the shoulder as he pushed past the five and entered the temple without another word.

"This is totally FURBS," Berta said matter-of-factly. The others' faces turned from concern to confusion.

"FURBS?" Rogerson raised an eyebrow.

"Yeah. Fucked-up repugnant bull shit. FURBS." She

looked blankly at the Captain. He blinked a few times, trying to process the definition. He finally shuddered and approached the Professor, who was looking out over the plaza in a daze.

"Grimstead, old boy, what went on here?" The Professor slowly turned his gaze toward the Captain.

"I'm not... entirely certain," he replied, softly.

THE SUN LURCHED from the tree tops like a zombie from the grave. A sound, not unlike the bleating of an enormous goat, filled the air. Vargas, sporting a spare crimson tunic given to him by the Captain, stood at the entrance of the temple's central chamber and blew a large, hollowed-out animal horn. Once the group began to rouse, he disappeared through an unseen doorway at the rear of the chamber and returned a few minutes later with a wooden slab topped with an array of exotic-looking fruits, berries and nuts. He placed them down on the floor at the center of the room. The groggy explorers stared uncertainly at the spread.

"Ne ovat syötäviä (They are edible)," he assured the Captain with a laugh. Rogerson took hold of a roundish, dark purple orb that was roughly the size of his fist and bit into it. The flesh inside was translucent, but there were no seeds. The others looked on expectantly. He chewed thoughtfully for a few moments and swallowed.

"It's very sweet. I can't say I can describe the flavor exactly, but it's quite good." There was a collective sigh as the rest began to help themselves. Vargas grinned and patted the Captain's shoulder. He went into the back again and quickly returned with a second wooden slab, this one carrying a set of small, carved-wood bowls.

"Mead." He nodded to the Captain, who nodded back and accepted a bowl. Once everyone had food and drink, Vargas took his seat beside the Captain. "Nyt, puhutaanpa suunnitelmistamme (Now, let's talk about our plans)."

It was decided that Vargas would escort the group from here on. His knowledge of the island was now their greatest asset.

The group was on their way shortly after breakfast. Vargas took the lead and they began heading west through another stretch of dense forest. It wasn't long before the viking was tugging at his new shirt and scratching at his skin. He typically did not concern himself with covering his upper body, as the island's weather was generally warm, but he wanted to honor his new friend's generous gift. He looked genuinely uncomfortable.

"If hotness over there is having a wardrobe malfunction, I'd be happy to help him with it," Berta cooed. The Swede grumbled louder than he'd hoped. Berta rubbed his back in a patronizing fashion. "Don't you worry love mountain, *nobody* can drag me away from you. For long." The Swede turned his head and swore so intensely that a bird fainted from a branch above.

It wasn't long before the Tower of Ïsur loomed over the forest like a giant. The group paused on the crest of a tall hill where they could see the layout of the island for miles all around them. Vargas pointed toward a narrow roadway that cut through the greenery below, gesturing that they would be traveling on it as they made their way to the tower.

The road, though narrow, had once been expertly paved and maintained. All that remained of it now were stray cobble stones that randomly poked through the patches of overgrowth. As they walked, Vargas explained that the road had once connected two ancient kingdoms, and had fallen into disrepair because it was no longer being used. Many of the long, flat stones had been carved with glyphs which Grimstead tried to study as he walked. This resulted in him frequently stumbling on the vines and other debris in his path.

"Are you having a fit, Professor?" Emma teased after witnessing Grimstead flail as he struggled to keep his footing.

"Ha! I have yet to fully lose my balance. Have you noticed the road carvings, Emma? These glyphs are brand new to me. And some have been etched so deeply into the stone, that they haven't worn away in the slightest."

Now everyone, fascinated with the contents of the road, began walking slowly. Vargas soon found himself to be several yards away and let out a growl. "Viivyttelijät! Meidän täytyy kävellä vielä tunnin!"

"Vargas says we'll be at the tower in an hour's time. So we best hurry along."

Sunlight punctured the tree canopy in brilliant rays that created a dazzling show of shadow and light whenever there was a light breeze. Around them was silence, save for the birds warbling from unseen perches and occasionally floating by in a blaze of vibrant color. A rabble of enormous butterflies flew overhead and, to the group's delight, weren't blood-thirsty or poisonous.

A familiar hoot and howl sound started up in the treetops. The *Skidbladnir* crew froze and reached for their weapons.

"Guys?" Wesley asked nervously. "Is something wrong?"

"Capuchins!" Rogerson growled.

"Ah, hell, not *again*." Marrow spat.

A few of the primates dropped from the branches and hopped around them. But, surprisingly, they didn't attack. The Capuchins simply regarded the travelers with curiosity. A baby Capuchin jumped down from a nearby tree and on to Emma's shoulder. She gasped and braced herself, only to find that the little fellow only nestled himself into her shoulder.

"He is adorable!" she squealed. The others lowered their weapons, bewildered. The other Capuchins began playfully jumping around the group.

"Are you guys, like, afraid of monkeys?" Berta asked Rogerson, who remained with his rifle at the ready. "Do they not have monkeys in the 18-whatevers?"

"No, no," Grimstead replied as he fought to keep his

glasses from being stolen from his face. "When we first arrived on Antillia, we met with a rather—*rowdy*—group of these imps."

"Damned disease-ridden buggers!" Dr. Marrow shouted, attempting to shoo away the monkeys that were trying to rummage through his rucksack.

Vargas laughed aloud as two Capuchins sat contentedly on his shoulders while he fed them something from his pouch. He turned and kept walking and several of the Capuchins hurried to catch up with him.

Roughly twenty minutes later, Vargas stopped abruptly and turned to face the group—which, incidentally, now included a handful of monkeys. The path ahead appeared to lead directly into a patch of particularly thick foliage. The tower was extremely close now, they would be upon it within minutes. The viking called Rogerson and Grimstead forward, much to the Professor's surprise. He spoke to them in hushed tones, his face stern. Though Grimstead didn't know exactly what his new friend was saying, he understood that whatever lay before them was to be taken seriously. When Vargas finished speaking, Rogerson assured him with a nod and a smile. He then turned to Grimstead and grasped his shoulder.

"Brace yourself, old boy. We're about to experience something that few mortals in all of existence have ever laid eyes on."

The Captain then addressed the others, explaining that they were about to enter sacred ground. It was the final resting place of the sky gods' chariots, as well as several of the gods themselves.

"So be sure to conduct yourselves with the utmost reverence and respect," he commanded.

The Tower of Ïsur loomed in the middle of a sprawling moss-laden field littered with decaying aircraft. The landscape was unlike anything that the *Skidbladnir* crew had ever seen before. Both Grimstead's and Wesley's jaws dropped at the sight. The tower's silver-gray metallic walls—untouched by growth—shot a straight-and-true five hundred feet into the azure sky. The Sun reflected down its metal length in brilliant, shimmering rivulets.

Vargas spread his arms out wide. "Kävele varovasti. Maa on lumottu."

"Be mindful how you step." Rogerson kept his voice low and calm. "Our friend warns that this land is enchanted."

"BY THE SCIENCE GODS!" Wesley shouted.

"Uh, Wesley? Hon?" Sarah had a hunch that this might not go well. Deaf to Sarah's words, he hopped gingerly over the mossy ground towards a hunk of rusted metal that he recognized as a fighter plane. It rested in the shadow of a large, lenticular vessel.

"A P-51 Mustang! Ha! I used to read about these as a kid! Oh wow, everything here is straight out of my grandfather's history books! Flying saucers, Tomcats, Messerschmitts! This place is like an aeronautics museum! This. Is. *Fascinating*!" Wesley worked to pry open the Mustang's cockpit door, tugging furiously at the rusted metal and tossing pieces of rust and moss that fell into his hands. Vargas watched him in disbelief, muttering under his breath. The others approached the metal carcasses with caution. Beneath the thick mossy ground was a metal-like substance, closely resembling the tower itself. It appeared to span out from the tower for several hundred yards in each direction, like a sheet. It also made walking much more difficult; as soon as the moss was stepped on, it slid along the metallic surface.

"This... burial ground... seems to wrap around the tower," Grimstead noted. He carefully walked close to a few of the vessels, but did not dare to touch any. "Curious, though, these machines. Some seemed to have landed with nary a scratch, while others have plummeted directly into the ground."

"Wesley! *Wesley*! Get out of that cockpit!" Sarah shouted at her husband, who was now dangling from the waist up inside the plane's opening. Vargas slapped his forehead and grimaced. Wesley sheepishly withdrew and lowered himself to the ground. He pulled an old leather pilot's cap with goggles onto his head with a big grin. He left the straps unfastened and they hung down on either side of his face. He giddily shifted his head from side to side, making them dangle and bounce. Sarah grunted.

"We should check in with Paul, again. Let him know where we are." Wesley nodded with vigor, and the straps slapped him in the nose.

"I *love* this cap!" He pulled his communication device from his vest pocket. Connie's blue countenance immediately appeared. She cocked her eyebrow at the Doctor.

"You look like an idiot."

"Just patch me through to the boy, wiseass."

"I don't have enough signal power. Give me a sec." She momentarily disappeared into the device as she scanned for a power source. "Ok, I've found one. Take me to that ship over there." She gestured with her chin. Wesley and Sarah walked over to a saucer-shaped vessel that had been tipped to one side, but was otherwise in decent shape. Sarah took notice of a blue, British police call box that looked sorely out of place next to all the aircraft and shrugged. Connie scanned the ship over and located its central computer.

"Well, the ship's computer is definitely online and, quite frankly, she's a bit of a bitch," Connie reported. "The crabby-ass has been rotting here for at least a hundred years or so. Guess that'd make anyone a bit wackadoo."

"Will she let you boost your signal?"

"Yes. But she said I have to tell you how stupid you look in that cap."

"She did NOT!"

Vargas threw his hands into the air in disgust and spat out a string of words that needed no translation.

"Maybe she didn't, but you totally do." Her head flickered

and was replaced by a shimmering blue version of Paul's face.

"*Whaaaaaat?!*" he scowled. "Make it quick! My transmitter is on my wrist, a wrist that is currently attached to a hand that is trying to fix our only means of exit off this smelly island of smelly smells! And what the HECK is that thing on your head?"

"Easy, son. I just wanted to check in on you and see how you're making out."

"Hi, baby!" Sarah shouted over Wesley's shoulder. "Did you sleep OK? Do you have enough to eat?"

"Yes, Mom, I'm fine. Same as I was just a few short hours ago. Ugh!" Paul shook his head. "Anyway, things are coming along here. I've got the main system back online. I just need to get the nav system linked back up then run a few *hundred* diagnostics."

"Does that boy ever make sense?" Dr. Marrow grumbled.

"Good to hear!" Wesley said brightly. "Alright, son, Connie is going to send you our coordinates. When you get here, be careful. There are a lot of downed ships and planes and whatnot. We're about to head into the tower of an ancient god, so if things are going haywire when you arrive, just fly out as fast as you can. Our old-timey friends here have a steamer ship waiting off the east coast where you can go. They'll help."

"Ok, Dad. And I'll... ry... a..." Paul's face began to cut in and out of sight, his voice intercepted with static.

"What's happening, Connie?" Sarah asked, startled.

"This ship's computer is being a douche. She's trying to kick me off her signal."

"A man's h... by birds... *crazy!*" The transmission suddenly ended.

"Somebody with a foot please kick that stupid, fat cow of a ship for me!" Connie yelled. "No wonder you crashed here, with a big ass like that!"

"Enough, Connie," Wesley said, as he pondered that last transmission. He turned to the others. "Did anyone else hear that? What do you think he meant?"

"He sounded more excited than in a panic," Grimstead replied. "He has the *Explorer* for protection, as well. Try not to worry... too much."

"Agreed," Rogerson added. "The boy's resourceful. We should press on to the tower before Vargas completely gives up on us." He looked over at the viking, who was kneeling close to one of the downed vessels and whispering to himself.

The explorers followed Vargas toward the east side of the tower. Before them lay another score of air- and space- craft that had met their demise on the ground below. As they drew closer, the moss began to dissipate and the metallic sheet beneath them became more visible. Grimstead paused to kneel and placed his left hand to the smooth, cool ground.

"Metal earth?" he whispered.

Finally, the tower was immediately before them. Vargas approached its base with slow, purposeful steps. He silently raised a hand as signal for the group to be still. The explorers gathered and waited a few yards behind him, taking in the sight. The crew craned their necks to see to the tower's top. At closer inspection, the structure wasn't a straight rectangle of metal, rather, it tapered in slightly toward the apex which subtly jutted out on all sides.

"Looks like a giant, metal member." Marrow remarked.

"Member of what?" Emma asked. The group smirked in silence. Emma's eyes grew wide with understanding. "*Oh!*"

The fifty-story structure appeared to be untouched by age or the elements. Grimstead couldn't quite explain it, but he had a distinct feeling that this seemingly brand-new tower was older than the island itself. The group stood eagerly—but silently—waiting for some time. Vargas knew that the only way into the tower was to be *let* in, and it was only a matter of time before those who dwell inside would show themselves.

"Is something supposed to be happening?" Marrow grunted in a loud whisper. Emma whirled her head around to face him, his finger to her lips.

"*Shhhhhhhhhhh!* Don't be a big, metal member!"

It wasn't long before a faint *clunk* sound was heard and a rectangular outline materialized in the wall right in front of them. The outlined portion of the wall began to retract in a slow vertical motion, and it was soon clear that it was a doorway. As the wall ascended, it revealed two figures standing side by side. When the door finally reached its pinnacle, the pair—a male and a female—stepped forward into the daylight. Both were dressed entirely in black. The male, tall and lean, wore a high-necked jacket made from a thick fiber; a pattern of large, isosceles triangles was boldly stitched across the jacket. He also wore shiny, leather-like gloves and pants that tucked neatly into combat style boots. His female counterpart, elegant and reserved, wore a short, high-necked leather-like dress, printed with the same triangle pattern, and knee-high boots.

The CCs raised their weapons immediately. The two stepped out from the tower and the male turned his head sharply and glared at Vargas for a moment before looking upon the travelers with a kind smile. Both strangers were quite human in their appearance, their eyes being the primary exception. They each had vibrant, violet eyes, slightly larger than usual. They had pale skin and long black hair, the female's was done up in an elaborate knot above her head. Both looked to be in their mid-twenties. The male raised his right hand in greeting.

"Hello, travelers." His voice was deep, smooth and calm. "There is no cause for alarm. You may enter our home freely and of your own accord. We have been expecting you."

EIGHTEEN

TOWER OF ÏSUR
THE ISLAND OF ANTILLIA
1898

"PLEASE, LOWER YOUR weapons." The young man spoke slowly and purposefully. "You have no need for them here. My name is Orrin and beside me is my sister, Ïella." They each bowed in turn. The Captain stepped forward, exchanging a brief glance with Grimstead as he passed.

"I am Captain Robert Rogerson of the SS *Skidbladnir*. With me are my crew and our colleagues. Our guide, Vargas, brought us to you and we are grateful for your hospitality. We mean no harm. We are adventurers on a mission of... scientific curiosity."

The Captain cleared his throat and used the opportunity to steal a quick glance back at his companions. Grimstead and Emma nodded encouragingly, urging him on with wide eyes. He responded with a slight shrug. Orrin raised his pale hand and tilted his head knowingly.

"I am certain you are eager to continue your quest, but first you must meet our father, Ïsur. We can accommodate you all with a place to cleanse yourselves, a hot meal and fresh clothing in preparation of this encounter."

"He is the island god," Vargas said, his voice low. It didn't register with the group that they could suddenly understand their Finnish guide. Orrin and Ïella regarded each other silently and then she took a graceful step forward and stood demurely before Vargas. He smiled wide.

"Hello, Vargas Ragnarson." Ïella smiled, her voice like silk. The viking reached out to Ïella but Orrin pulled her away. Vargas swallowed a growl. He composed himself and looked upon the face of his beloved.

"Greetings, Ïella, my moon and stars," his voice softened. "It has been far too long since my eyes last drank in your beauty."

"He's spoken for?!" Berta hollered.

"He can speak English?!" Rogerson exclaimed. Orrin stepped out and placed himself between Vargas and Ïella.

"You know you are forbidden to enter, *savage*. Inside, sister." Vargas didn't take his eyes from his beloved.

"Vargas," she began. "I must—"

"Inside. Now."

Ïella turned on her heel and walked back through the doorway into the tower. "Please, friends, follow us." He smiled at the travelers and bowed, remaining at the entrance while they filed in. Rogerson approached Vargas, perplexed.

"You... speak... English? Why did you only speak to us in Finnish before?"

The viking smiled.

"One who has lived as many lifetimes as I learns a great many things about dealing with people. It is easier to learn a few *secrets* when those around you are led to believe that they are not understood. To be quite honest, it was nice to speak the old language with someone again. It was a comfort that I have not felt in ages. Friend Rogerson, I will remain here and wait for your return. When you have found whatever it is you are looking for, I will escort you back from whence you came."

They grasped forearms in farewell.

"Thank you, my friend." Rogerson tried to mask the unease he felt knowing that his immortal ally wasn't joining him.

Once everyone was inside, Orrin took a moment to glare once more at the viking before he turned and entered the tower. The passage sealed itself instantly, leaving Vargas alone among the avian fossils.

ÏELLA LED THE explorers down a stark, metallic corridor illuminated by a series of self-contained light sources that were embedded in the space where the floor and ceiling met the walls. The glow of the artificial light was a bit too harsh for the eyes of the *Skidbladnir*'s crew, and they stumbled along, squinting and shielding their eyes as they slowly made their way down the corridor. The Adamses, on the other hand, were unimpressed.

"What, no red carpet?" Berta guffawed.

"This is merely one of several airlock passages that lead from the outside environment to the inner hull of the ship," Ïella explained.

"Ship?" Grimstead asked, intrigued, but Ïella continued.

"Just beyond this door you will find what we call the Great Chamber. Its open design of passageways and observation platforms that served to create a sense of space and freedom within the confines of the vessel. The aesthetics, I hope, you will find pleasing. Beyond the Great Chamber are several other passageways, each leading to other portions of the ship. The one we are concerned with will lead to a lift which will then take us up the tower to the ship's control room. That is where you will find our father."

As Ïella approached the end of the corridor, the wall automatically began to retract upwards, revealing a bright and radiant room behind it. There was a collective gasp of awe from the small crowd.

The room overlooked a lush and exotic garden, encased under a glass dome. A giant terrarium. A winding, glass pathway circled in and around the garden dome and spiraled upward. The garden extended for several floors below where they now stood and ended at the level just above them.

There were murmurs of astonishment from the group. Orrin joined Ïella at the front and they stepped forward into the Great Chamber. Grimstead approached the dome without invitation and Emma immediately followed, pushing her way through the others like an excited child.

The pair peered down at the extraordinary display: plants and flowers of all shapes and sizes, and in every color imaginable. Some were not indigenous to the island—or to Earth. Within moments, the rest of the group pushed their way through the ingress and marveled at the terrarium's contents. The trees and plants swayed gently in the artificial breeze, brilliantly-plumed birds sang and flitted to and fro. Below, they glimpsed a small body of water glimmering in the artificial sunlight.

"Remarkable," Grimstead murmured.

"This garden houses a vast collection of flora and fauna," Ïella explained. "Including some species that have been reported as extinct. And a few that have never existed outside of that dome."

"A tree of life, for instance?" The words fell out of Grimstead's mouth before he realized what he was saying. The question caught Ïella completely off guard. She looked at her brother, who glared intensely at the Professor.

"Of *course* the savage told you about the tree," he snarled, fighting to compose himself. "Make no mistake, travelers, you are our guests and will be treated with the utmost courtesy. However, there are many areas in our home that are restricted. Disobedience will not be tolerated. This garden is off limits. Now, if you will please follow us down this corridor to the lift, our father eagerly awaits your arrival. We will see that all of your questions regarding Antillia are answered."

Stepping away from the dome, Emma caught sight of her reflection for the first time in days and was appalled.

"Perhaps we should, uh, freshen up, first?" she suggested, her lips curling in horror at the reflection of her own sweaty, dirty face and frizzy hair. Orrin was beside her instantly, and she started when she felt his sudden presence.

"Be assured, fair one, that your beauty cannot be soiled by exterior means. However, you will have the opportunity to bathe before your evening meal." Emma flushed, unable to find the words to reply. Orrin turned smartly and strode away, leading the others towards the lift. Emma, feeling a bit queasy, stayed put until Sarah grabbed her by the arm and pulled her along.

"He's what I'd call the dark, brooding hottie." Sarah winked.

"He is rather *intense* isn't he?" Emma bit her lower lip.

"Oh, my dear, I do think you've got a crush," Sarah snickered, causing Emma's cheeks to redden even more.

Orrin paused in front of a cylindrical glass tube which ran vertically through every level of the tower. Inside it was a large, almond-shaped capsule, also made of glass, that seemed to hover within the tube. As they approached, the front panel of the tube slid open, granting them access inside. Once everyone was within the capsule, Orrin said the word "Bridge," and the panel slid closed and the capsule rose smoothly. Within seconds, it stopped at the top level and the panel opened. The room before them was split into two tiers and glowed with artificial light. Both tiers were outfitted with multiple rows of brightly-lit control consoles, their surfaces a maze of buttons, dials and other contraptions. Numerous screens hung overhead, each displaying something different: the interior and exterior of the tower, as well as various areas of the island.

Despite the unusual-looking gadgetry, the tower's bridge

was recognizable as the vessel's control room. Captain Rogerson was particularly interested in finding out just what was on those screens. He was certain that he'd be able to pilot this thing.

Among the second tier of controls, a very tall man stood monitoring the screens. As soon as Grimstead caught sight of him, he became extremely alert, attempting to capture and file away every detail of this encounter in his mind. They were now in the presence of Ïsur, the so-called god of the Phantom Island of Antillia. The moment was tremendous. In theory, anyhow. The entire journey, the fate of this mission, was coming to a head. Ïsur was more burly than his son Orrin, and had long, milk-white hair that fell gently past his shoulders. His hands were clasped casually behind his back. The explorers silently filed out of the lift and stood among the consoles on the first tier. Rogerson cleared his throat and took a step to the front of the group.

"Father," Orrin spoke, "they have arrived." Slowly, the man turned to face the group. Ïsur was a handsome man, his reserved expression depicted strength and nobility. His eyes, a piercing sky-blue, were like his children's, only slightly larger. His face was smooth and pale, one could easily assume that he was about fifty human years of age, however, it was nearly impossible to gauge how old he actually was. He wore clothing similar to his son, but his color scheme was black and green. He looked upon the gathered group and bowed his head slightly.

"Good afternoon, my children. Welcome, honored guests. I am Ïsur. Welcome to my vessel and my home. I know you must have many questions, but I must insist that you all keep them until the banquet that is being prepared for you and our other guests. Please take this time to clean and rest yourselves."

The god snapped his fingers and a door slid open at the back of the chamber. A dozen automatons came rolling out in single file, pausing in a line directly in front of the group. The automatons were identical in their design, constructed almost entirely of silver chromium-plated metal. Each automaton had a cylindrical head—with two light bulbs protruding where the eyes would be and a small round speaker for a mouth—attached to a torso resembling an inverted triangle. The thinnest point of the torso was set into a giant ball bearing, below the bearing sat a wheel spoke affixed to a large rubber tire. A bundle of silver cables served as arms and a clamp-like claw with two pincers at the end as hands. Shiny as they were, the crudeness of the automaton's design was a stark contrast to the sophisticated elegance of the tower itself.

"Row bots." Grimstead looked to Wesley, who replied with a lackluster nod. A murmur of astonishment passed through the group, their eyes were wide as the automatons idled in front of them. Grimstead was flush with excitement. Marrow eagerly gulped from his flask. Wesley grimaced.

"I presume these fellows were made from recycled toasters?"

"I've seen better designs scribbled in baby diapers!" Berta chuckled.

Ïsur's face was expressionless. "We have assigned the assist-bots to assist each of you for the duration of your stay. You will be escorted to your sleeping quarters where they will launder your clothing while you bathe, and attend to anything else you may need. They will also escort you to the tower's dining hall when it is time for tonight's banquet. That is where you will meet with our other honored guests. I have some other matters that need my attention until then."

"Other guests?" Emma inquired.

"Yes," purred Orrin, who had maneuvered himself closer to her. "There were other explorers who arrived the day before last. An interesting lot, I must say." He smiled and leaned closer to her. "If you would do me the honor, I truly would like to personally accompany you to your quarters." He extended his elbow to her.

"That would be absolutely lovely." Emma beamed, her cheeks flushing. Sarah smiled and clicked her tongue. Rogerson rolled his eyes.

"*Hem!* Aren't you forgetting someone, *Miss* McParland?" Emma gazed up at her escort's violet eyes, transfixed. She fought to look away from him.

"Hmm? Am I?"

"A certain *doctor* of the *paternal* persuasion, perhaps?"

"Oh? Oh!" Emma snapped out of her daze and looked back at Rogerson. "My father, of course! You are quite correct. We promised to let him know when we arrived so that he could join us." She turned her attention back to Orrin. "Would you be a dear and summon him for me, Captain? Thank you, so much." She looped her arm through Orrin's once again and they walked back to the lift together.

Everyone stood watching after her, speechless. Except for Dr. Marrow, who enjoyed a hearty snicker.

"Unbelievable," Rogerson sighed. He turned to Ïella, who seemed to materialize beside him. "We have a colleague waiting offshore whom we must contact." He pulled the flare gun from his belt pouch. "Could you direct me to a place outside where I may use this?"

"A flare gun?" Ïsur's face allowed something of a smile. "How... *quaint.* Ïella, please take the Captain to the tower summit. As for the rest of you, the bots will escort you to your chambers now."

The assist-bots sprang into action, their bulb-eyes flashing. Each bot simultaneously reached a clamp-like hand out for a traveler and spoke in unison: "Follow—*pop*—me, please. *Squak.*"

"I would like to accompany you, Captain," Grimstead volunteered, moving his arm away from the bot in front of him. Ïsur raised an eyebrow at this, but said nothing. The bots ushered the others off the bridge.

"Let us go quickly, then." Ïella lead both men to a separate lift on the opposite side of the bridge. This one was solid and opaque, far less elegant than the glass lift. As the door slid shut, Grimstead shuddered, it felt rather akin to the closing of a coffin lid. When the bridge was empty once more, Ïsur turned his attention back to the screens.

Above the lift, a set of metal panels in the bridge ceiling retracted, opening like an iris. The lift instantly ascended through it and opened, revealing a rectangular rooftop roughly the size of a main street intersection, with the lift at the center. The three exited into the humid air. Upon realizing that he was several hundred feet above the ground, Grimstead was hit with a sudden wave of vertigo. He gingerly stepped back against the lift wall as he attempted to gain his bearings. From the tower's apex, they could see nearly every point on the island, including the coastline. Rogerson walked to the edge of the rooftop and carefully looked out over the metal railing that surrounded the perimeter.

"What a sight! Wouldn't you say, Professor?"

"Y-yes, quite... remarkable."

"What's the matter Grim, afraid of heights?" Rogerson stepped over and patted him on the back.

"Not. usually. I suppose the excursion has finally taken its toll on me."

"Is this tower located mid-island?" Rogerson asked Ïella. She nodded. He produced a gold-colored tube and slid it into the flare gun's chamber. "I'd ordered several crew members to help Dr. McParland keep a constant watch for a signal. I just hope they're able to see this from such a distance." He fired the flare into the sky and it detonated in a series of small explosions. He turned to Grimstead with a grin. "It's just like Morse code. A McParland tinker-special." He and Ïella gazed up at the flares. "You'd better be awake, old man," he muttered under his breath.

TWO HOURS LATER, Captain Rogerson, Professor Grimstead and Ïella were still waiting on the terrace, sweltering in the late afternoon Sun. Rogerson paced the length of the roof, occasionally scanning the horizon with his rifle scope. Grimstead sat slumped against the outer wall of the lift, idly clicking the electric torch that Sarah had given him. Ïella peered down to the length of the tower and smiled. Grimstead joined her and saw Vargas waving down below.

"You two have history, eh?" Ïella nodded solemnly and sighed.

"It is of no concern to you." She fought back any indication of emotion. Her violet eyes strained against the tears. Grimstead removed his right hand from the railing and waved.

"I apologize for my prying, Miss. It really isn't my place. I only see two souls drawn inexorably together, and yet held just out of reach. I have some experience with that, I'm afraid. Vargas told us about you. About what happened."

"Then you know the futility of this conversation," Ïella snapped. "Some things are not meant to be. Vargas is, and shall forever be, out of reach."

"I suppose even the idea of hope is something to be feared."

"I *hope* whomever it is we're waiting for arrives presently." Ïella replied as she gingerly removed herself from the ledge.

"What if he didn't get his flying contraption to work?" Grimstead yawned. Rogerson snapped his head towards the east and squinted. He shouldered his rifle and peered though. In the distance was a blurry, black dot. A smile crossed his lips.

"Sometimes, one just needs a bit of faith!"

The blurry dot steadily grew in size. Sure enough, it was the good Doctor in his auto-dirigible. As the contraption approached, they could hear the faint hissing sound of its steam-filled pipes, followed by the soft groan of its balloons expanding and contracting The hiss and groan repeated continuously, like a call and answer, growing louder as the minutes passed. Ïella placed her hand over her eyes and cocked her slender eyebrow at what she beheld.

"Is that... an elderly man flying some kind of antique automobile attached to a makeshift dirigible?"

"Aside from that being an antique, you are correct, Miss!" Grimstead jumped to attention with renewed vigor. "Dr. Douglas McParland is a renown scientist and inventor! He also teeters on the fine line between eccentric and remarkably mad."

"Logically, that *thing* shouldn't have been able to make it off the ground without crashing, let alone travel this far!" she laughed. "Astonishing!"

"Like the man said, the good Doctor is eccentric enough to bend the laws of logic!"

The auto-dirigible drew closer, seemingly picking up speed. It also seemed to be tilting to one side. Grimstead and Rogerson exchanged glances. "He can fly it, but can he *land* it?" Rogerson said, a hint of concern in his voice. The contraption sped toward the tower, though the automobile was tilted so that it was lying completely on its right side. The dirigible jolted upright abruptly and then the automobile was tilted on its left side. The contraption jolted back and forth several times attempting to level itself. Rogerson peered through his scope and saw Dr. McParland jerking levers and turning dials at random, as he most likely forgot which did what. The auto-dirigible began to rise and fall erratically before dropping out of the sky and into the trees several hundred yards from the tower.

"No! We have to get down there quickly!" Rogerson exclaimed. Moments later, the tree tops shook violently and the dirigible burst forth from the canopy like a shark breaching the ocean. It sped directly towards the tower at an alarming rate. Rogerson no longer needed his scope to see that McParland was frantically trying to keep the vehicle's wheels level with the top of the tower.

"He's moving too fast!" Grimstead cried, but his warning came a moment too late. The old man swooped in mere inches above his head before touching down on the rooftop with a thud. The Doctor immediately applied the vehicle's breaks, which sent him careening past the three to the opposite side of the tower. He finally came to a halt with the front wheels hovering over the tower railing. The three released a collective sigh.

"Woo hoo *hooo*! That was a close one, eh?" McParland cackled with delight as he removed the driving goggles from his eyes. "Let me just back away from this ledge here and I'll be right with you lads!" He threw the auto-dirigible into what he thought was reverse and promptly drove off the tower.

"DOC!" Grimstead and Rogerson ran to the tower's edge and reluctantly looked over. The auto-dirigible shot straight up into the air, startling the two so that they both fell backwards onto the roof. Dr. McParland deftly maneuvered himself back over the tower and landed safely.

"Silly me! Next time I'll try and remember physics before I land! Ha ha! Say, why are you lads on the floor?"

"Never mind that," Rogerson grumbled. He stood and dusted himself off before assisting the elderly doctor out of the machine.

"Alexander, my boy! I'm elated to see that you've survived the expedition so far! What do you think of the Dirigi-Stead?"

"I... the *what*, now?"

"Let's just get inside!" Rogerson barked.

They walked over to the lift where Ïella stood, waiting. She nodded her head in greeting. McParland rubbed his hands together eagerly as they stepped into the lift.

"Welcome to the Tower of Ïsur, Doctor. And to the Island of Antillia. Due to the amount of time we've spent in anticipation of your arrival, we don't have the luxury of getting you properly settled in. Instead, we will go straight to the dining hall where my father will tend to your every inquiry."

"Doctor," Grimstead began. "Allow me to introduce to you, er, Miss Ïella, daughter of Ïsur. He is the, ah, person in charge of this island. I'm sure you'll be astounded to learn that they are of an extraterrestrial origin!"

"A dining hall did you say?"

"Yes. It is equipped with a rather high-powered fabricator that is able to create whatever foodstuffs you may desire." Ïella replied.

"A fabricator!" McParland exclaimed as the platform lowered into the tower. "How delicious!"

THE LIFT OPENED onto one of the tower's central levels, where the dining hall was located. Ïella led the three men down a long corridor, similar to the one they passed through when they arrived. This corridor, however, was adorned with paintings and tapestries from various eras of mankind, several appearing to have been created by unearthly hands. Ïella walked quickly and remained silent as she lead them to a large, arched doorway. The door retracted as she approached, revealing a replica of a Victorian-era dining hall. The large room was lit by several extravagant crystal chandeliers The centerpiece of the room was a long, dark wood table, exquisitely set with fine china and glassware and an extraordinary spread of food and beverages. Seated around the table were all of Ïsur's dinner guests, freshly groomed and dressed in clean clothing. Everyone looked pleased, clearly enjoying this reward of luxury after a harrowing few days. A large mahogany chair at the head of the table stood empty, presumably where Ïsur would soon be seated. There were a few unfamiliar faces to the right of Ïsur's chair, and Grimstead took notice of four burly men, dressed head-to-toe in black, also standing near the head of the table.

"I feel it is best that we keep our fingers close to the trigger." whispered Grimstead. The Captain met his gaze and grunted in agreement. The Professor approached the table slowly.

These men were silent, motionless, presumably the bodyguards of the slender blond who sat in front them, picking at her food with a disgusted look on her face. He studied them, inspecting every inch of their buttoned-up leather trench coats and dark, metallic goggles with crimson lenses. There was something eerily familiar about them. focusing his sight on the fourth guard's right arm. There was a red and gold patch stitched onto the coat's sleeve. All of the guards' coats bore the same insignia: a circular shield with two swords that crossed in an X formation through an ebony obelisk. A crescent moon was set on either side of the shield and they were facing away from each other.

Moonshield!

He felt himself bristle. Behind the men a fireplace blazed —for show, only. One of the unknown gentlemen guests stood facing the fabricated flames.

"Father!" Emma cried, jumping up from her seat to embrace the old man. Orrin, who was seated next to Emma, also stood.

"Good evening everyone," Ïella addressed the room. "Please allow me to introduce three more of our honored guests for this evening, Dr. Douglas McParland, Captain Robert Rogerson and Professor Alexander Grimstead." Their introduction was met with smiles and nods from their colleagues around the room. Emma walked her father to the table and helped him into the empty chair to her left. Two bots rushed in to escort the Professor and the Captain to their seats, which were to the immediate left of Ïsur. The bots graciously pulled the chairs out for both men and then scooted away. As they were about to sit, the fellow by the mantle-place spun on his heel and smiled.

"*The* Professor Grimstead? Well, well, well!"

Grimstead suddenly felt as if he were falling. A fire ignited in the pit of his stomach and his head began to swim.

"Hello, Alexander. It's been a while."

Grimstead jumped to his feet, drew his revolver and aimed it at the man's forehead.

"Fowler!"

NINETEEN

THE CLIMATE OF the room changed drastically. Everyone was on their feet, weapons at the ready. All but Dr. Marrow, who remained seated, casually eating a turkey leg. Emma placed herself in front of her father, who was trying desperately to see what was going on. Ïella and Orrin locked eyes with one another, staring in silence.

Beads of sweat began to form on the furrowed brow of Eva Perle, the mysterious blond guest and second-in-command to Kristian Fowler. She sat with both fists clenched, her gaze locked onto Grimstead's hand. She was engaging every ounce of her telekinetic abilities to prevent his finger from squeezing the revolver's trigger. The room had gone silent, save for her barely audible straining. The Moonshield guards trained their Borchardt C-93 semi-automatic pistols at Grimstead, but he did not flinch. His finger trembled on the trigger. Rogerson had his rifle directed at the guards.

"His... will is too... strong," Eva muttered in a heavy German accent. She could feel her grip on Grimstead's finger slowly slipping. "Please... Herr Fowler... move." Fowler stepped closer to the table and smirked.

"Oh, it's alright, Eva dear. Old Alexander knows that if I am struck down, Andras, the Great Marquis of Hell, will take over my body and simply wipe him from existence," Fowler chuckled. Eva felt Grimstead's anger intensify.

"You are a third rate conjurer, Fowler," Grimstead snarled through grit teeth. "It is common knowledge that your pact with the Goetia is... a... crock... of *shit*."

Fowler laughed heartily. He shook his head and sighed.

"Alexander, Alexander. My conjuring is a crock, you say? Why don't you ask your dear, sweet wife how much of a farce it is. Oh, I am *terribly* sorry, old friend. You see, I just, this very moment, remembered how difficult that would be."

The revolver's hammer snapped back.

"Herr Fowler... please..."

Ïsur entered the dining hall from an unseen door and approached the head of the table. His eyes grew even wider as he took in the scene.

No.

Ïsur's voice thundered but his lips did not move. Ïsur cast his preternatural consciousness out like a web, ensnaring every mind in the room. The air lit up with a sort of electricity—hair stood on end, skin tingled, muscles throbbed, brains ached. When he spoke, his words pounded in their heads like a migraine.

Stand down, humans. I will brook no violence on my ship!

He held his arms aloft, eyes staring straight ahead. Their color had shifted and were now a deep cobalt blue. Not a single person in the room was able to even twitch.

Is this how your human race acts in the home of another? I have accepted each of you as a guest and I consider you under my care and protection while you remain. However, there are rules! If you cannot abide, you cannot stay.

He partially released the force-field, enough to allow all weapons to be lowered. Assist-bots wheeled themselves close behind each in attendance as silent enforcers. Heart pounding like a freight train, Grimstead stared down his enemy. Fowler returned the gaze, a cocky grin playing across his face. The Professor's cheeks blazed red and his breath was shallow. All eyes were, in fact, on him.

Be seated, please.

No one moved a muscle, anticipating that they might bear witness to the mental unraveling—and possible death—of Alexander Grimstead.

Sit!

A pressure, so solid that it may have crushed them had it continued, rested on everyone's head and shoulders. Reluctantly, they all took their seats. Some resumed eating. Fowler took his seat next to Eva, and the guards, known as Night Cloaks, returned to their rightful place behind them.

Grimstead could not bring himself to look up from the table. His heart still pounding, he sat hunched over his plate and took a few slow, deep breaths in an attempt to slow his heart rate and calm his racing mind. He felt his anger slowly congeal and release him, a sense of primal power sliding in its place. He forced a bite of food into his mouth and began to chew, envisioning that he was standing at the top of the Tower of Ïsur, with Fowler's heart in his hands and blood spilling across his face.

With one eye on Grimstead, Fowler leaned his head close to his companion's and whispered.

"You know, dear heart, the next time you would like to stop a madman from shooting me in my rather dashing face, I would suggest using your telekinesis on the weapon itself. I surmise it would cause you—and I—far less grief in the end."

"Or perhaps I shall let him pull the trigger," Eva muttered.

"Hmm?"

"Nothing, Herr Fowler. I shall bear that in mind for the next time. And I am certain there will be a next time."

A stony silence engulfed the room for the remainder of the meal. Grimstead was expressly focused on Fowler. Everything else remained in his periphery, swirling in an amalgamation of shapes and shadows. After what felt like an eternity, Ïsur raised his right hand, palm up, and a metallic orb roughly the size of a bowling ball descended from an opening in the ceiling and hovered several feet above the center of the table. The lights in the room began to dim and the orb emitted a soft glow. Below the orb, a brilliant image of the Planet Earth appeared, rotating in perfect three-dimensional clarity. Grimstead couldn't help but be intrigued by this display, though he continued to keep a wary eye on his nemesis. Rogerson, leaned over to him and spoke in a low voice.

"There's not a single rod or string holding that globe up, is there? Incredible."

"Nothing in this universe is what it seems."

Rogerson raised an inquisitive eyebrow. Across the room, another projection appeared and materialized into three large, triangular-shaped vessels, surrounded by dozens of smaller floating objects, slowly floating toward the planet, en masse. Dr. McParland gasped out loud.

"Honored guests," Ïsur began. "Now that I have your attention, allow me to share with you the origin of man."

TWENTY

THREE-DIMENSIONAL IMAGES, clear as day, appeared in front of, and around, those seated at the table. They were suddenly immersed in a lush, prehistoric jungle and about to bear witness to a rather lively demonstration. The room was deathly silent, save for the sounds of the jungle.

Five Velociraptors, in hunting formation, stalked slowly through the thick vegetation that now covered the dining hall walls and floor. The pack leader paused behind a bush and produced a clicking sound with its throat, three times in quick succession. This signaled the others to pair off and continue on to the left and the right. The pack leader remained in place, peering through the bushes at its prize, a lone Triceratops. The Velociraptors inherently knew that, in an open fight, the hunt always had the potential to turn sour, so they took advantage of the dense foliage. If the hunt was successful, their kill would satiate the small group for a while. Several answering clicks indicated that the others had reached their flanking positions. The leader clicked only once in response, which signaled that the attack had begun. One Velociraptor jumped over the bushes and shrieked, startling the Triceratops. As the beast recoiled, another Velociraptor sprang from the foliage and attacked its prey's blind side, digging its claws deep into the beast's flesh. The threatened Triceratops stomped the ground and forcefully bucked the Velociraptor off its back. The first

Velociraptor took this as its cue to pounce, seeking to gain the beast's full attention. Angered, the Triceratops attempted to gore its enemy, but as the animal made its move, the entire Velociraptor pack rushed in, clawing and biting the Triceratops in a frenzy. The Triceratops roared in frustration and pain as the flesh was torn from its body.

Not one of the dinosaurs took notice of the massive shadows that suddenly swept across the land like an eclipse, or what caused them. High above the Earth, three wedge-shaped space crafts, each the size of a small city, slowly crept across the sky with hundreds of smaller scout ships orbiting on reconnaissance.

"The Anunnaki," Ïsur began, "or what your human race has colloquially deemed *spacemen* or *extraterrestrials* first came to this planet during its late Cretaceous period, somewhere between one-hundred and sixty-six-and-a-half million years ago." A flurry of prehistoric images flashed before their eyes.

"The first humanoid beings to touch Earth's soil were representatives from three warring races: the Draconians, the Zeta Reticulians and my indigenous race, the Pleiadians. Also known as the Nordic Anunnaki. Together, we represented the most prolific of the myriad beings that exist beyond these stars. However, over time, we began warring with one another for control over interstellar trade routes and planetary resources. The fighting continued for many lifetimes. And, as with any great culture, all of our accomplishments were tainted by this war. Finally, a few noble and brave representatives proposed a truce, a groundwork for peace and a potentially unified league for exploration and colonization. We decided to meet on a neutral ground, far beyond the reaches of our respective territories. We chose Earth based on accounts of its abundance of rare minerals and natural resources. The planet was to play a pivotal role in the negotiations, serving as starting point for our collective colonies.

"So, we traveled from three separate solar systems to this

remote corner of the Universe in order to broker a peace treaty, and to finally put an end to thousands of years of pointless bloodshed. I was among the brave and hopeful pioneers who made the journey. Together, we were to cultivate this planet for the benefit of our fledgling trinity. Each race proudly prepared the most exceptional of our star ship fleets for the journey and commissioned our most brilliant scientists, engineers, and, of course, security personnel in the event that the treaty crumbled under the weight of political hypocrisy and guile. The simple fact that this virgin planet was ripe enough to satisfy the demands of each culture made negotiations expeditious and cursory. The treaty was signed, a pact made and our ships were set down to begin the cultivation of the Earth. However, our utopia was short-lived."

The holographic scene faded out and the images of two bi-pedal creatures appeared over the table.

"The Draconians, as you can see by example on the far left, share a marked resemblance to the dinosaurs that roamed the prehistoric Earth. So naturally, they felt an affinity to the lumbering beasts and attempted to utilize their might. They quickly learned creatures of that magnitude would prove difficult to tame. The small, gray-pallored specimen in the center is a Zeta Reticulian. They claim that their oversized craniums and brains are filled with superior knowledge. Well, the Zetas saw the beasts as a hindrance to progress and took it upon themselves to annihilate them. They secretly placed several ion cannons in strategic locations across the planet, then detonated all at once. The result was an extinction-level event. The power of the multiple ion blasts was equivalent to striking the Earth with a massive meteor. The land was blanketed with thick ash, and the Earth's yellow Sun was shrouded in a veil of death, not to be seen for a very long time.

"The truce was shattered. The Draconians and the Zetas once again began their tired dance of war, and death. It was our people who stepped in as the voice of reason. Our powers of mediation fell embarrassingly short, however, and we had to invoke cataclysmic threats to quell the violence, counter-intuitive as that may sound. The Zetas thought it was best to leave this system, but vowed to return. The Draconians, on the other hand, chose to stay on Earth and bide their time as it were. Curiously, they decided to burrow their flagships—and themselves—deep into the ground. They have thrived as a subterranean culture ever since. Apparently, they are waiting for an appointed time, known only to those within their race, when they may rise up and take what they feel they are entitled to. We Nords chose to seek solitude in order to continue on with our own peaceful existence here, so we utilized our shift-ship technology to travel through the fourth dimension and into late the Paleocene Epoch. As you can imagine, we were quite surprised to find that not only had some of the sauropods survived, but they had evolved into an innumerable amount of creatures that were thriving across the globe. Of course, the mammals and the hominids were among these creatures." The projected images slowly faded out, leaving the majority of dinner guests staring blankly up above the table.

"I assume that some of you may have questions." Ïsur prompted.

"The, ah, fourth dimension?" Captain Rogerson broke the heavy silence.

Wesley waved his hand in the air like an eager schoolboy. "Ooh! Ooh! I know this! May I explain?" Ïsur nodded. Wesley proudly stood and began to speak. "Ok, so we all know about the three dimensions, right? Right. So, like, fourth dimensional space, or Spacetime, is all about vectors and coordinate geometry. Spacetime is a fourth dimensional continuum where gravity is curved, or folded, if you will." He plucked a cloth napkin from the table and held it up for all to see. He then folded it in half. "The entire fabric of the Universe can be folded, allowing one to travel to and from the Earth from, say, a galaxy away with relative ease. Then there's superspace and supersymmetry and all kinds of neat things! And in the fourth dimension, it's all happening at once. At this very moment, we are having this discussion, being born and drawing our last breath. Everything is *always* happening!" He beamed with pride, panting and holding up the unfolded napkin with fervor. The room was silent. With a smile, Sarah patted him on the shoulder as he sat back down.

Dr. McParland cleared his throat. "Yes, alright. So, that explains how you came to reside here from, wherever you came from, but explain how you were able to jump from eon to eon."

"Through the same process," Orrin replied. "Instead of moving the distance of space around us, we moved the distance of time. Our shift-ships—like the one in which you are now—are propelled by something called a tesseract engine, which allows the ship to, you might say, slide through Spacetime and sail upon a chronological current."

"That explains why this island, or ship, as it were, is documented only sporadically through the ages," Grimstead said.

"Sure, you call *his* a ship, but *mine* is a boat," Rogerson grumbled.

"Very astute, Professor," Ïsur smiled, his lips parting momentarily to flash extraordinarily white teeth.

Fowler mocked a soft clapping, to his own amusement. Ïsur gestured and a new series of images began to form above them and the room fell silent once more. A small ape hovered and rotated, with strands of DNA swirling around it.

"That's DNA!" Wesley whispered harshly to Grimstead.

"Now, let us further examine the circumstances that brought mankind, as we know it, into existence." The ape began to morph into specimens of successively larger apes, until it finally resembled something almost human.

"Hominids came a long way from trembling in the treetops," Ïsur said. "From early on in our encounters with them—primarily as a means of work force—they had an exceptional aptitude for proactive problem solving. The species only needed a little *nudge* to hasten the leap from ape to man. Our scientists manipulated the genetic codes of the hominids, rewrote them, molding them into a creature capable of reason and comprehension. Given time, this manipulation would have happened naturally. However, our eager scientists were not willing to wait millennia; many grew restless and were quite overzealous in the potential that the hominids promised. So, we nudged. Cro Magnon. Neanderthal. Each step brought us closer to finding the correct evolutionary algorithm. And once we did, our experiment in civilization blossomed. Areas fertile and rich with resources became the cradles of life and prosperity.

Over time, great cities—including Sumeria and Babylon—were constructed under our guidance and instruction. As mankind became more self-sufficient, more self-aware, the Anunnaki—which now included several other species—stayed less at a distance than before. We began to regard them like progeny rather than a race of laborers. Unfortunately, as a result, many of us were then burdened with an almost *parental* sense of responsibility over them, and our relationship with mankind began to change. It is also worth mentioning that as mankind increased its own collective awareness and reasoning skills, it began to regard us as gods. It built temples, created mythologies and looked to us for a source of understanding and, at times, blame."

The orb lit up once again, this time projecting two, multicolored helix-structures. "Now these images demonstrate examples of both human and Anunnaki DNA," Ïsur continued. The Anunnaki DNA appeared to be much more complex than its counterpart, thicker and perhaps sturdier. The holograms rotated slowly in space, before breaking apart and combining into an imbalanced amalgamation of both.

"We Pleiadians, and, in truth, all Anunnaki, though more

powerful than our wards, share many of the same personality foibles. Many of us became power hungry and enjoyed being viewed as gods. Our technology was magic to the eyes of early man. Our occasional and varied appearances were perceived as either a gift from the heavens or punishment. Opposing ethical views caused a rift among our people, and we eventually separated into two factions: those who would teach and those who would dominate. And, then there was the inevitable reality of Anunnaki-human hybrid beings, as a result of inter-species breeding. These hybrids were often born possessing fantastic preternatural gifts, such as the ability to emit different energies from their bodies or spontaneously regenerate cellular matter. Others had extraordinary strength, the ability to take flight or many other fascinating abilities. While we never determined exactly *why* the coupling of such robust genetic material always resulted in beings of incredible ability, we did discover a slight quirk within the hominid genome. It seemed that the potential for these remarkable traits lay dormant within *every* human, either as a result of our varied genetic manipulations, or the simple fact that we are all made from cosmic particles. Though these traits of potential were impressive, many Nords wanted to utilize the species for more menial tasks, and control would prove difficult. We found a way to essentially block the gift-giving genome and, over time, evolution phased it out almost completely. There are a few who still carry the gene, however, and even fewer that are active. Be that as it may, with this new species under our charge, we finally had a workforce capable of reasoning and obedience.

"There were exceptions, however. The most powerful of the Anunnaki-human hybrids were rather well-known by mankind, though not all of them were a positive presence in the world. These so-called Children of the Gods became legends in the mythology of man. I assume you know of Heracles, Jesus the Nazarene, Cú Chulainn and the pharaohs of Egypt? They are but a few of these god-like beings. There were indeed many, many more."

"Mankind flourished in the Era of the Sky Gods, as it has been called. Celestial knowledge and technology were at its fingertips. Astronomy, complex architecture, arts and sciences became commonly known and widely practiced during this era in each of the thriving metropolises. At this time in man's history, it seemed that our initial agenda of exploration and cultivation gave way to playing gods. Those of us who had no intention of being worshiped took to the shadows and attempted to sway mankind away from their so-called divine rulers. Regretfully, the pendulum of influence swung from enlightenment to dark age in the power struggle. As time went on, mankind was also beset by the return of the Draconians, who had spent so long inside the earth, their offspring believed that they were indigenous to this planet and, therefore, had the right to rule. These Draconians were far more cunning than their ancestors, and took to the pulling of strings instead of the swinging of swords. They had rooted themselves deeply into the soil of society and could manipulate it in secret. It seemed that the world was once more caught in the throes of upheaval."

The image reverted back to that of a spinning globe.

"As a result, mankind became the spoils of warring gods. In an effort to try and put an end to these wars—and gain control for themselves—some of the more opportunistic members of your species attempted to utilize technologies they didn't fully understand. A nuclear device in the hands of children. This ended in the complete destruction of two cities by the Dead Sea: Sodom and Gomorrah. I recall the day they were turned to ash, and I recall my realization that the age of the sky gods desperately needed to end."

Ïsur stood for a moment in silent reflection. Eva Perle banged her fists on the table.

"You speak such blasphemy! You've taken the deeds of God Himself and twisted them so!"

Ïsur smiled. "You have not understood me, Miss Perle, and I am quite surprised to hear that *you* regard the truth of mankind as blasphemy. You are, after all, a star child with gifts far beyond your peers. There are no gods—not in the capacity you believe them to be. Your religious texts speak of *our* time on this planet, though the truth is veiled by allegory, metaphor and symbolism as created by the mind of mankind. It is the work of human brains attempting to describe what they could not truly comprehend. Beings descended from the sky in chariots, using magic and arcane knowledge. It is how your people made sense of things they never saw before. In essence we were the catalyst of your creation, yes, but we were not omniscient and surely not infallible."

He slowly raised his upturned palm towards the ceiling, the light show spreading outwards to the walls and ceiling once again.

"This is where *my* story truly begins."

An image of a bloodied, seemingly skinless man appeared. He wore nothing but a battered loincloth and a vibrant headdress made of feathers and small bird skulls. He sat on a pile of mutilated corpses and smiled a wicked, jagged-toothed smile.

"I was charged with keeping the balance in the world. Those who became too power-crazed would receive a visit from me. For instance, in Central Mexico, the Aztec worshiped a hybrid entity whom they named Xipetotec the Flayed God. His moral corruption was absolute and thousands of gruesome deaths were caused in his name. I confronted him on the steps of his own temple and demanded that he remove himself from power. He laughed as if he'd lost his mind and then attacked. The battle was fierce, but the outcome was never in question.

"I could not go it alone, however. Deities, hybrids, humans with technology far beyond their control eventually joined the struggle. Over time, it all became too much for me alone. Battles waged across and above the earth. Those who were not destroyed either took their leave of this planet or went into hiding in order to plot and scheme some greater destruction. Most vowed to return when, and if, mankind had matured and was ready for the next evolutionary step. The age of the gods had come to an end. Mankind was left to their own means of understanding the world. The new age that resulted was a dark one indeed. During this transition, myself and several others were tasked to remain here as mankind's sentinels, to a degree. And so it has been, ever since. With my shift-ship, I have dedicated the remainder of my existence to the tenuous balance throughout time. My son Orrin sees the Earth as a prison, with me as its warden. I neither agree or disagree with that assessment. However, I do hope that one day my children will rise to the occasion and take my place, so that I may take a well deserved rest."

The projection orb rose back into the ceiling.

"Questions?"

Dr. McParland and Dr. Adams raised their hands simultaneously.

"You mean to say that we humans are a biological mish-mash of simian and extraterrestrial gobbledygook?" McParland asked.

"I would not state it so bluntly, Doctor. Given an exorbitant amount of time, it would have happened naturally with a few more evolutionary trials and errors. We simply *forced* the issue from time-to-time with genetic prompts and manipulations. There were great strides forward simply because one of your ancestors learned how to make fire, which we had nothing to do with."

"I have a question," Grimstead turned to Fowler.

"But *I* was next." Wesley squeaked.

"How did you come to know of the island? How did you manage to not only locate it, but find it before we did?"

"Old friend," Fowler smiled. "I belong to a vast and highly resourceful global organization that boasts a staggering amount of gifted individuals. You have a floating hunk of metal refuse, and the blatherings of a thick-witted old man."

"Hello!" Dr. McParland waved.

"Frankly, I'm amazed you've made it here at all!" Fowler laughed. Emma leaped up from her chair, shaking her fist.

"Mind how you speak, filth!" she shouted.

"Oh, my! Such a lioness!" He feigned fright.

"May I *please* ask my question?!" Wesley shouted. "BEE-TITS! LEACHEROUS FART GOBLINS!" Everyone turned to stare. Sarah placed her hand over her eyes. "I-I'm sorry," he stammered, "I just get fl-flustered when there's so much yelling."

"What is your question, Dr. Adams?" Ïsur nodded.

"Yes. My question. Is South America the only place Antillia has appeared throughout the ages, or is this only a port of sorts?"

"*That* is your question?" Fowler scoffed. "What does that matter?"

"Right here, you little bitch." Berta flipped him off and sneered.

"Actually, I think it is a fair question," Eva stated. "The presence of this place would be interpreted in drastically varied ways by each culture."

"Yes, exactly! Thank you, ma'am!" Wesley smiled. Fowler swirled his index finger in the air and mimicked flatulence with his tongue.

"My ship traveled a great deal during the Great Sky War. My people and I went wherever we were needed. In times of peace, it remained here, shifting between the veil of time. And yes, this island bears many names from many tongues around the world."

"Why *here*? Why *now*?" Grimstead inquired. "Of all the places you could be at any given moment, why did you choose this area? Of all the ages you could occupy your time in, why now? There are other beings outside of this tower whom I'm sure could benefit by gaining access, so why only grant us entry? It all seems too convenient, sir. What game are you playing at?" Ïsur looked upon Grimstead with stern eyes for a brief second, then smiled warmly. The doorway behind him opened. He silently walked to it and then turned back to face the group.

"Enjoy the remainder of your meals. Once you have finished, my assist-bots will escort each of you back to your quarters, where I request you secure your weapons. You will not be tolerated to carry them, nor will you have any need of them. Rest, and enjoy yourselves. I bid you good night."

The door closed after he exited, and the guests were left with quite a chunk of information to process.

"Nice going, Beef McQueef," Berta chuffed at Grimstead. "Way to piss off the alien."

TWENTY ONE

LIGHTNING DARTED FROM black cloud to black cloud, arcing in brilliant angles. The rain fell like daggers as Grimstead ran toward the Adventure Guild's New York chapter house, then bound the stairs two by two. With no Kunal to greet him, he threw open the door as thunder shook the ground. The foyer was dark. Grimstead closed the door and charged into the main hall, where the old fireplace tried its best to illuminate the tall shadows. Two men and a woman stood there, between the chairs he knew so well. They spoke in hushed tones.

"Catherine!" Grimstead's voice scattered in the void of the large room. "Catty, come see your brother!" His feet were like marble slabs in mud as they plodded against the wooden floor. Something felt wrong. He could sense the absence. Catherine was not among those by the fire.

"Alexander. I am truly sorry." Grimstead immediately recognized the burly man as Captain Connor Stout. A knot the size of a cannonball formed inside his stomach. Time has not served the proud sailor well. His once fierce eyes were little more than embers now, and the creases of a hard-fought life on his face were deepened with sorrow.

"Sorry? For what, Stout?!" Grimstead clutched the Captain's pea coat lapels and lifted him to his toes. "Where is my sister?!" A shrill cry punched Grimstead in the chest. Over

Stout's shoulder was Alexander's brother, Otto, Otto's wife, Marjorie, and an infant—wrapped in a coarse gray blanket and resting in Otto's arms. "Otto? What is happening here?" The question came as a sharp whisper as the air in his lungs escaped. He threw Stout into Mr. Ammon's chair.

"Alexander..." Otto rocked the baby to settle its cries. "Brother... Catherine..." he struggled for the words. "Catherine has... passed." He bowed his head. Grimstead's legs gave out and he fell into his grandfather's old chair. His mouth moved silently, searching for strength.

"H-how?"

"By bringing the little one into this world," Stout wiped his eyes on his sleeve. "There were... complications. Once we knew she was with child, we set a course back here. But we were too far and too slow. My crew and I were not prepared for a birth, especially a difficult one." Grimstead smashed his fist into the arm of the chair.

"You let her die! How could you?!" The infant began to cry again and Marjorie kissed its little head as Otto swayed.

"What could he do, brother?" Otto asked. "What could anyone have done?" Stout rose from the chair with his jaw and his fists clenched. The stories of Stout's prowess in battle and his fits of maddening rage were legendary. The embers in his eyes burned as an inferno now. If Grimstead were of a clearer mind, he may have regretted his outburst.

"I loved your sister like no other before her! I can think upon no happier a time than that spent with her. Do not take my grief nor my respect for your family lightly, sir. Would that I could strike a deal with Satan himself to get her back. My life for hers. Without hesitation or regret. I'm dead without her either way. I hope you *never* have to feel what I do this day. So I ask you once more, do not take me lightly, sir."

Grimstead hung his head low. If only he went with her that day. If only he had the courage. Stout set his hand on Grimstead's shoulder. A sign of peace. A sign of brotherhood.

Grimstead rose from the chair unsure if his legs would hold and returned the gesture.

"I apologize, Captain. It was wrong of me to speak to you in such a manner."

"I understand. It is with a heavy heart that I share this news with you. It is also with a heavy heart that I give my only son to you."

"What?! Why?"

"My ship is no place for an infant. My life is a garden where healthy crops cannot grow. This is why we set sail back to New York—so Catherine could raise our child in the sanctity of family. Now that she is no longer among us I ask, no, *beg* that you honor her memory by raising that boy as though he were your own. I am prepared to donate all of my earnings to the child's well being."

"A baby? I—"

"Brother," Otto interrupted. "I would like to take care of Catty's child. As you know, Marjorie and I are unable to sire our own, and I believe this could be the dark blessing we need to make our family whole. My banking business is more than successful and we've such a big house. The child will want for nothing! Connor could keep his earnings and you can stay in that... whatever it is you've joined. We cannot trade one globe-trotting parent for another, now can we? This child will have the stability and love it deserves. What say the two of you?"

"Are you sure, Otto?" Grimstead watched Marjorie hold the baby boy's hand and kiss it several times, tears welling up in her eyes.

"Oh, yes," Marjorie whispered. "This little one is a blessing. Aren't you? Yes you are, little boy!"

"Then it is settled." Stout smiled weakly. "Otto, don't you think you should introduce Uncle Alexander to his nephew?"

"Oh, of course, of course!" Otto placed the infant into Grimstead's arms. "Meet Alexander Benjamin Stout."

Grimstead looked down into Catherine's eyes and smiled.

The boy cooed and reached up to pull at Grimstead's lips.

"Hello, handsome." Tears fell to the child's forehead, Grimstead could not help himself.

SOMETHING WET AND rough lashed out against Grimstead's face like sandpaper, waking him. It happened again and then again.

"Ungh. What the—?" His eyelids broke apart and a massive orange face greeted him. The tiger's tongue shot out from its mouth and dragged itself from Grimstead's chin to his eyebrow, knocking his head hard into the tree trunk that he had been sleeping against.

"Alright, Kero, alright. I am awake." Grimstead used both hands to scratch the beast behind its ears. Kero's purr rumbled in Grimstead's chest, as he brought his big tiger head in for a head bump.

"I'm impressed, Alexander," Scott chuckled. "Kero rarely shows that level of affection to anyone. This is high praise, my friend."

"Jealous of the cat's wandering tongue, Scott?" Kristian Fowler said with a sneer.

"Stow it, Fowler—lest I give Kero the order to pay *you* a visit!" Scott pulled on tiger pelt gloves and boots, fighting garb that he had fashioned himself from a great man-eater named Flayer. Scott had defeated the cat in single combat many years ago, and kept his enemy's remains as a trophy. The gloves covered his arms to the elbow. and the boots to the knee. Flayer's retractable claws and pads were left intact, which enabled Scott to stalk the jungles in perfect silence, and he could slay his foes with a single swipe. All it took was a simple flex of the fingers or toes to trigger the claws. Scott had also fashioned tiger skin pants from Flayer's hide, and a fur cloak with a fanged hood for inclement weather. Most days, Scott went topless and displayed his scar-tissue stripes with pride.

"Remind me why we're in the godforsaken Philippines, having a midday nap in the middle of a filthy jungle?" Fowler straightened his black pinstripe suit.

"Once *again*—we have come here to hunt and destroy a creature that has been terrorizing the nearby villages. I believe they called it an *aswang*. And since this is your first official field mission for The Order, I suggest you try not to screw it up."

"What the devil is an aswang? Peculiar name—*ass wang*."

"It is considered a ghoul in these parts," Grimstead said, scratching Kero underneath his chin. The mighty cat laid on its stomach and rested his big head on Grimstead's lap. Scott stared in utter disbelief. "It is like a vampire after a fashion," Grimstead continued. "Only, instead of fangs, the aswang uses an elongated proboscis to suck fetuses from the wombs of sleeping women, or to eat the livers and hearts of small children. From what we have learned from the villagers, we may be dealing with a particular type of aswang, the manananggal, which means self-segmenting flying fetus fiend and viscera sucker."

"Self-segmenting?" Scott frowned. "I'm not sure I follow."

"You had me at *flying fetus fiend*." Lilly Chambers cringed as she rolled up her shirt sleeves.

"Yes, well, the manananggal is known to detach its upper body from its lower at the hip, allowing it to soar into the night on retractable bat-like wings. I haven't the slightest clue why it would do such a thing. Perhaps this is the only means of activating its wings? It only hunts at night, which as you know, is why we took a bit of a midday nap. By the time we reach the beast, it should already be hunting, which suits my plan swimmingly. Oh, I might add that it often takes the form of an elderly woman."

"Charming." Fowler rolled his eyes. Lilly moved toward the brush and seemed to speak to the ground. Fowler watched with curiosity.

"Kero. Up. We've work to do." Scott snapped his fingers.

Kero sighed heavily and ignored him completely. "Kero!" With great reluctance, the tiger rose and padded to his brother. The cat turned to Fowler and sniffed at his shoes before letting out a low growl.

"Filthy beast," Fowler muttered. Scott loudly cleared his throat.

"Need I remind you, *Herr* Fowler, that I am the Mission Leader on this expedition, which technically makes Kero here my second-in-command. And need I also remind you that this mission will either cement your membership in the Lucifuge or revoke it."

Fowler shrugged. "Fine, fine. I simply feel at odds with taking orders from a half-naked man dressed like a tiger."

"Having Scott and Kero here as leads is the perfect choice, Kristian," Grimstead stated. "We are in a jungle. The jungle is their domain."

"It is far more than that, Professor," Scott nodded." The jungle is in our blood, and we have a bond greater than most humans. I was found by Kero, as an infant, hidden in the brush of the African jungle. My dear mother, along with my father and siblings, had been plucked from the marketplace by painted men in blood-dyed robes and forced to march the jungle by knife-point. She did not discard me, rather, she *saved me* from the clutches of the Diamond Spider Cult. Kero immediately took a liking to me and presented me to his mother, Padmini, who tried to convince her precocious cub to kill me at first. But somehow, once the tigress looked into my eyes, it was like we had an unspoken conversation. It was like she knew my plight and she felt compassion for me. From that day on, Padmini treated me as her own cub, raising me to be strong, quick, fierce and loyal. Kero, ever at my side, was, *is* and ever shall be my brother.

"About thirteen years after that day, I was discovered by Lord Nelson Barton, the infamous hunter. Thrilled at the idea of a 'jungle boy,' Barton had designs on bringing me back to

England and exploiting me as some sort of living novelty. I was tricked into following him back to his camp, but Kero sensed danger and followed me there. He even fought against Lord Barton's cohorts to save me, even disemboweling one of his men before my brother was shot in the left shoulder. Regardless, Kero was able to kill two more men before I was secured on the ship. They shot at him as he chased the ship out of port. I was brought to Barton's estate in London and was subjected to the ways of civilized men for four long years. It was absolute torture. Barton hired tutors to teach me math, science, philosophy, social etiquette and other assorted nonsense. The only lessons I truly enjoyed were fencing and military history. Fortunately for me, I excelled in each and every subject, despite being bored and miserable. Barton once confessed that he viewed me as a protégé, yet he was also compelled to strut me out like a trophy dog at social events.

"Despite the Lord's best efforts, the heartbeat of the jungle within me remained strong as it had ever been. The longer I was away from my home, the more I yearned for it. I knew that I needed to return there. My chance came during a horse riding lesson, when I managed to break away from my instructor and rode like the devil to the docks where I commandeered a schooner named the *Dirty Bastard*. Much to my dismay, Barton wasn't keen on the prospect of losing his protégé. Once news of my escape reached him, he immediately set sail with fifteen hunters hand-picked for their accuracy, cunning, and cruelty.

"When I finally returned to the jungle, I immediately made my way home, and thankfully, I was recognized by my family. The joy of our reunion was short lived, however, because once Lord Barton and his men arrived, they took to the jungle and began slaughtering, without reservation, any living creature that happened upon them. I clearly recall how red the ground became. The Lord's message was clear: Surrender or bear witness to further atrocity. Kero and I sent a message of our own in the form of mutilated hunters. Each morning, we left one mangled corpse outside of Lord Barton's tent. Fear made the seasoned hunters panic. Panic made them sloppy. Each were killed in brutal and creative manners, until only Barton was left."

Scott paused. There were several moments of heavy silence. Fowler seemed to be intently studying something near the ground.

"Whatever became of Barton?" Grimstead ventured.

"He went stark raving mad!" Scott let out a laugh. "We last saw him run screaming into the jungle." He smiled and gave Kero a firm scratch behind the ears. He never told anyone the part where he and Kero ate him alive.

"Well, enough about us. Tell me, Herr Fowler, why is it that you choose to wear a suit on a jungle expedition." Scott smirked. "I would imagine that you must be uncomfortable, no?"

"Oh, not as uncomfortable as being poorly dressed, *Herr* Scott. What do you think, Miss Chambers?" Fowler swatted at a mosquito.

"I think you boys talk too much," she chided, not allowing them to see her smile. Before her stood a five-year-old girl with a gaping hole in her chest. She held an infant who was gaunt and bloodied. Lilly winked and the girl giggled.

"What do you see? Is that our guide?" Grimstead stepped closer, squinting at the vacant air in front of his teammate. Lilly nodded. "What does it say?"

"*She* says we should get a move on. Also, that Kristian should stop making that horrid noise with his face." Lilly stood and winked at the little girl, who giggled even louder.

"Oh, ho! A thousand apologies," Fowler bowed dramatically. "I would so regret driving off our dear, sweet, *dead* children guides. I wouldn't want to sabotage our delightful romp through this tepid jungle in order to slay some winged monstrosity. Furthest thing from my mind."

Grimstead stood and brushed off his khaki pants and green cotton shirt. His leather boots were by far the wiser choice to Fowler's dress shoes.

"Come now, Kristian, surely you aren't afraid of a giddy little old lady that just so happens to be a carnivorous beast, are you?" Fowler shook his head. "And surely our plan to destroy it would crumble without your participation." Grimstead smirked and patted Fowler on the shoulder.

"Quite right, my friend. Quite right. In fact, you have just reminded me of an intricate piece of the puzzle. The mission hinges on these, quite frankly." Fowler reached into his jacket's inner pocket and pulled out four paper squares adorned with an intricate design. He handed one to each of his companions and slid the last back into the pocket. Lilly and Scott studied the symbol with curiosity.

"A seal, Kristian?"

"Yes, Alexander, a seal. And quite the powerful one at that."

"What is a seal?" Scott turned the paper this way and that, trying to make sense of the lines and letters.

"What you have in your hands is a sigil, or a seal, as you've heard. This one in particular, is the magical conjuration and containment of Duke Astaroth."

"The demon?" Grimstead studied it closer. Scott, on the other hand, threw it to the ground as if it burned.

"The same. And pick that back up, jungle boy." Fowler pointed. "You've no idea how difficult it was to obtain the gift that sigil grants us."

"For instance?" Lilly folded her arms.

"For *instance*, the entity that symbol represents is immeasurably powerful and can give men the benefits of invisibility."

"Preposterous," Lilly scoffed. Fowler bit his lip in frustration

"You speak to the unseen dead and *I'm* the preposterous

one? Have a care, friends. This paper holds the will of Astaroth and will cloak us from the monster's senses."

"Then let us trust in Kristian and finish this mission," Grimstead said with a nod. Fowler smiled.. Grimstead turned his attention to Lilly. "Where to?"

DUSK SET IN. The ghost girl pointed to a ten-acre islet out in the middle of a stagnant river, roughly twenty yards from where they stood.

"She says we're here," Lilly whispered. At the center of the islet stood a massive, dead tree with hundreds of skeletal branches reaching every which way. A ramshackle hut rested against the tree, dark and lifeless, and barely seeming to stay erect under its poor design. A small cauldron hung over a circle of ashes doused long ago. Nothing moved in or around the hut as they drew near to the river. Grimstead studied it, turning over thoughts in his head. *Perhaps they were too late?* It didn't take long for him to decide that the abandoned hut was a front: a trap disguised to either display normalcy or perhaps something far more nefarious. A trap to lure in tired wanderers.

"Should we swim across?" Lilly asked.

"This river looks deep," Scott replied after a moment of consideration. "And it's likely to be inhabited by who-knows-what."

Fowler grunted. "Absolutely not. This suit does not touch filth water." Lilly looked to the ghost-girl who pointed down the riverbank to a small raft that had been crudely fashioned from wooden planks and tethered by vines.

"We take that."

"Absolutely not. This suit does not touch filth *wood*," Fowler protested. Kero dipped his paw into the water and splashed him. The group stood in amused shock. Fowler stood in muted rage. He knew better than to make a disciplinary move against the jungle cat. He may have been soaking wet, but he was no fool.

"Enough!" Scott kept his voice low. "We do not want to give the hag any indication that we are near."

"The sigils will conceal us until we strike. In the meantime, try to keep your lowly fleabag under control. I known my tailor in Munich would just love to get his hands on tiger pelt." Scott smiled and shook his head.

"You are welcome to try. Kero's never had a German before." Scott strode over to the raft and pushed it to the water's edge. He then looked around for a means of propulsion.

"Does anyone see a long branch or piece of driftwood that we could use as an oar? Or anything that could be fashioned into a paddle?" The three combed the surrounding riverbank to no avail.

"Nothing." Grimstead called back to him. Scott jumped up suddenly and retreated into the jungle for what seemed like mere seconds, then exploded from the brush carrying a length of vine coiled around his right shoulder. Without a word, he leaped across the thirty-foot gap as silently as a falling leaf. He immediately shrugged off the vine and tossed one end to Grimstead, who caught it and tied it around his hips before sitting in the middle of the raft. Lilly climbed on behind him and wrapped her legs and arms around him. Grimstead gripped the planks to steady himself and keep the raft from capsizing. As Lilly pressed in against him, he found that he was suddenly distracted by her presence. He thought of how Lilly's cheek felt against his back and the warmth of her legs and arms around him. Even in this tepid jungle her embrace was welcome. Grimstead suddenly wanted nothing more than to hold Lilly's hands and kiss them as gently as one would rosary beads.

"Scoot up, Alexander. I have no room to sit behind Lilly," Fowler instructed. Lilly smiled and pressed her cheek more firmly against Grimstead's back.

"That's the idea, Kristian," she said. "Get in front and

make sure that Alexander doesn't get pulled into the water."
Fowler grunted and reluctantly did as he was instructed.
Mostly because Lilly had done the instructing.

"Wouldn't want that now, would we?" he muttered.

"Here, Kristian, take this." Grimstead removed his satchel
and handed it over. "It contains the items you need for the rest
of the plan.

"Danke." Fowler slung the bag across his torso. The
cacophony of insects and night birds stopped rather abruptly.
Scott dropped to his stomach and became still. The others held
their breath and tried not to move. A high-pitched squealing
sound emanated from the hut—much like the sound of an old,
wooden floor or a rusted door hinge. *It's vaguely human*,
Grimstead thought. The source of the sound rose higher and
higher up the tree, until a figure with bat-like wings burst
through the branches and into the sky.

The manananggal was on the hunt.

Scott allowed several minutes to pass before he stood up.
Surely, the creature would have attacked if it had sensed the
interlopers. Somehow, they had gone unseen. Scott didn't want
to admit to Fowler that he was right about the sigils, he'd be
impossible to live with. He took hold of the vine and swiftly
pulled his cohorts across the muddy river.

"Alright, Professor," he said in a loud whisper. "Let's go
over the plan one last time."

MARIÁ AQUINO PLACED her infant daughter into her
modest wooden crib with great trepidation. Everyone in her
village knew that to leave a baby unattended was to invite
death itself to your door. The manananggal never missed a
poorly-guarded meal. Mariá had heard the stories of the flying
witch since she was a child and never doubted their validity—
even if she had never seen it for herself. The elders had said that
the manananggal was lying dormant in her nest of bones and

decay, but you never knew when it would rise again. As she grew older, Mariá had wondered if the elders' stories were nothing more than a way to frighten children into behaving, a cruel trick that the adults played on their children. But now that she was a parent herself, the legends were never far from her mind. Especially now the children from neighboring villages—and hers—were being found mutilated in their beds, or vanishing entirely. A cold realization swept across every parent's mind. The elders were right.

Mariá gazed up at the large, black American man who sat in the corner of the room on a chair that barely held his muscular frame. He had simply *arrived* that day, with a promise to rid them of the creature. But why had he chosen this house? And who was he to take on such magic? He had knocked on her door that morning and assured her that no harm would befall her baby that night. Mariá had never heard of The Order of The Lucifuge, or this strange yet brave man, who went by the name Black Hercules.

She kissed her daughter on the forehead then looked again to the stranger in the corner. His smile was warm, and vaguely comforting despite her pounding heart. Mariá opened her mouth to speak, but the visitor placed a finger to his lips as if to say, *there's nothing left to do but wait.* There was a strong chance that this monster would chose another hunting ground, as it never showed much of a pattern, but Mariá felt the throb of inevitability in her veins. Call it intuition, but she knew the manananggal was coming. Mariá then left the room without a word, shutting the door behind her.

Algernon Colborne, the Black Hercules, rubbed the paper square with the sigil of Astaroth between his fingers. He never liked the supernatural. As a younger man, living and working on plantations, he witnessed many secret voodoo rituals. He often wondered, *how could this possibly make life better in a way that a good old fashion whuppin' couldn't?* He was a fixer, and his hands were his tools. How he got the gift of immeasurable strength and unbreakable skin, he couldn't say, but he was damn sure he wouldn't squander it. That gift proved useful no matter what calamity reared its punchable head.

But he never could stomach magic.

The full Moon's light poured into the room like a stroke from a wide paintbrush, and was momentarily blotted as a dark shadow swooped past the window. If the creature had chosen another village, it would have been greeted by another member of The Order, but Algernon felt lucky that it had chosen his. If there was one thing that could drive him into a blind rage, it was the harming of little ones. He slid the paper into his pants pocket and listened. He heard a low creaking sound; it started slow, like a conversation, then quickly intensifying as the window opened with a *thunk-thunk-thunk*. Long, cadaverous fingers sprawled under the bottom pane and pushed it the rest of the way open. The manananggal's head rose over the windowsill like the Moon over the horizon, and two pale eyes scanned the small bedroom in twitchy movements. It looked directly at Algernon, yet made no indication that it saw him sitting there.

Sonuva gun.

The manananggal slid itself into the room and straddled the crib with its hands, its shriveled, veined breasts swayed as it lowered itself down closer to Mariá daughter. The manananggal's mouth opened up wide, and a barbed, tube-like tongue slithered out from between jagged teeth. The tongue struck like a cobra, but was caught before it reached the infant. The creature shrieked as Algernon pulled it away from the crib, its wings flapping wildly as it tried escape. The manananggal railed its claws against Algernon's face and chest with less effect than a summer breeze. It was the first time the monster had ever known fear. Algernon pulled it close and smiled.

"Lady, don't you know that lil' ones need they sleep?" He landed a haymaker into the creature's face, sending its jagged teeth raining to the floor like coins and the creature itself through the roof. It instinctively spread its wings and caught air. The manananggal floundered, fighting to stay conscious long enough to fly back the way it came. Algernon watched as its form grew smaller and smiled. He was pleased that the infant was not only safe, but still sleeping soundly. He touched her gently on the cheek. "You grow up strong, lil' one. You grow up good." He looked out the window and wished he had a way to tell his comrades that the she-devil was heading back their way.

"HERE! I FOUND a lantern!" Grimstead said, lifting the rusted case up from a cobweb-coated wooden crate. He quickly wiped the cobwebs off with his hands, sloshed kerosene into the fount, removed the glass cover and lit the cotton wick with a match. The manananggal's hut was small and thickly cluttered with a variety of items—clothing, tools, exploration gear, personal effects—all left behind by the doomed souls who had happened upon it. A single mattress was tucked into the far right corner of the room, but it looked as though it hadn't been used in quite some time. Scott sniffed the air and took in the earthy scent.

"I see no legs, no lower body," he said. The ghost girl tugged at Lilly's sleeve and the movement was seen by all. "Zounds!" Scott exclaimed. The girl pointed to a crooked panel in the wall next to the bed.

"Scott," Lilly smiled, "would you be so kind as to move that panel?"

"As you wish." Scott tossed the wood aside with ease, revealing a hole that led directly into the trunk of the tree. It also revealed the lower half of a torso standing within. From the hips to the ankles, the torso resembled the naked body of an elderly woman, but its feet were like those of an owl's.

"By the jungle gods!" Scott jumped back in shock and disgust.

"Fascinating," Grimstead whispered. "Scott, I need you to take hold of it and bring it out to Fowler."

"Can't you?"

"Your strength far exceeds mine and we cannot risk making a mess of things."

"Seems as though that is already the case." Scott crept closer to the creature with his hands extended in front of him as if he was trying to catch a mouse. He looked back over his shoulder anxiously, but Grimstead and Lilly waved him on. The manananggal's legs jumped up suddenly, kicking Scott in the sternum with such force that he went crashing through the front of the hut. The torso scurried up the wall of the hut, using its talons to dig into the wood. It lunged at Grimstead, who ducked the attack. The torso spun around quickly and kneed him in the gut. He sailed like a rag doll through the opening in the wall and into the hollow tree trunk. The impact caused numerous ancient bones to come raining down upon him. As he looked up, Grimstead saw what could easily have been a thousand bones—of all shapes and sizes—dangling from strings that ran the entire length of the hollow tree. Up above the bones, the trunk opened out into the pale night sky, and for a moment, Grimstead nearly categorized the sight as serene.

The manananggal torso darted towards Lilly, who had her machete at the ready, and jumped up to swipe at her with its talons. Lilly side-stepped the attack and swung down hard into the creature's right ankle. The blade nearly lopped the foot clean off, but the wound immediately began to mend itself. Scott pounced on the creature, digging his own claws into both of the manananggal's thighs. He landed with his full weight on the torso and drove it to the floor. His face, regretfully, was mashed into its ass.

"Scott?!" Lilly cried.

"I know! I know! My face is against its horrid ass!" Scott struggled to subdue the flailing and kicking. "Less gawk and more help would be greatly appreciated!" Grimstead rushed over and helped him to his feet. Scott refused to loosen his grip, even to move his face into a more favorable position.

"If I let up, the chase begins once again."

"That is exceptionally honorable of you," Grimstead said as he guided Scott outside to where Fowler had nearly completed a circle of salt three feet wide. He paused to take notice of the evening's catch. Kero lowered his body and raised his hindquarters, ready to pounce if need be.

"Your face is practically buried in that thing's ass," Fowler sneered.

"Shut up, Fowler!" Scott growled as he stepped into the incomplete circle's opening. "Finish it! Hurry!"

"You sure you'd like me to rush? It seems the two of you are getting along so well."

"*Fowler!*" Scott roared. Fowler shook his head and poured the last bit of salt from the burlap pouch he held. Scott set the torso down and back-flipped out of the circle. He landed and dragged his face against the dead grass and spit and cursed and wiped his mouth raw. "I'll never drive this smell from my nose!"

Grimstead quickly drew his revolver and pointed it over the tree tops.

"What is it?" Lilly asked. She pulled her pistol out and scanned the sky.

"You hear that?"

"What?"

"I hear it," Scott said, extending his claws. "Creaking."

"Better get a move on, Kristian." Grimstead cocked the hammer back. "We are going to have company." Fowler reached into his satchel and pulled out another, smaller pouch. He quickly opened it and began to mumble a chant as he created an outer circle beyond the perimeter of salt.

"What is that you're pouring now?" Lilly shook her left arm out to get the blood flowing better after griping her machete so tightly. She was ready to shoot, chop and insult whatever came her way.

"This... is pulverized iron ore," he replied between the chants. "The metal has... magical properties to ward off supernatural... influence. Salt contains, iron keeps away."

"It will essentially keep the manananggal from its lower half," Grimstead explained. "Once daylight comes, even if the top hides itself away, the lower half will burn, causing the top to ignite as well."

"Fancy that!" Lilly said, genuinely impressed. "Where did you learn such a thing?"

"Folklore, mostly."

"That fills me with such confidence," Scott sighed. Grimstead aimed his sights up to a dark shape in the sky that was closing in on them with great speed.

A shape with bat-like wings.

"Fowler, look out!" Scott dove directly into the manananggal's path of attack. The creature swooped so quickly that Grimstead couldn't follow its movement for a clear shot. The creature and Scott went careening into the hut, shattering it into splinters.

"Why Scott, I didn't know you cared." Fowler muttered to himself as he closed the circle. The manananggal emerged from the detritus and frantically flew around the circle, but could not enter. It shrieked with frustration. Scott was nowhere to be seen in the rubble. The creature swooped down into the dead branches of the tree and perched on its clawed hands. It began to sway to and fro, making a deep, creaking sound. The river water began to churn, growing more violent as the manananggal swayed faster and faster.

"The devil is it doing?" Lilly asked.

"Looks like a summoning to me," Fowler replied. He slid his pant leg up and removed a small revolver from his sock.

"You brought *that* to a monster hunt?" Lilly scoffed. "You'd be better off throwing pebbles at a dragon!"

"These bullets are coated in silver and have been blessed

by priests. If anyone has pebbles, my dear, it's you."

Kero turned to the water and roared. Four massive saltwater crocodiles burst from the churning waves and rushed the circles.

"She's controlling them!" Fowler yelled. "Do not let them break the circles!" Kero leaped onto the back of a crocodile, sinking his fangs into the beast's skull. The crocodile rolled and thrashed but it could not shake the powerful tiger. Kero flexed his mighty jaw, puncturing the beast's brain with his sharp fangs.

"Good kitten!" Fowler cheered. He turned to face the manananggal, still deep in her trance, and saw another dark shape positioning itself above her.

Scott dropped onto the manananggal and dug all eighteen claws between the creature's shoulder blades and the small of its back. The manananggal lashed out, but Scott shredded his hands across the creature's back and into its arms, holding them still. The manananggal released its hold of the branch and together they tumbled through the air with bloody claws and flailing wings. Grimstead turned his eyes back to the ground and shot a crocodile in the head.

"Hey!" the crocodile shouted.

I don't recall that *happening, Grims*tead thought. *I shot it and it died.*

He stepped away from the action, which carried on in his absence and rubbed his chin in confusion. *We fought the manananggal tirelessly until daybreak, when it burst into brilliant flames, then exploded. I would have recalled shooting a talking crocodile.* Grimstead turned and looked over at two spectral figures in the jungle, standing perfectly still. They were beautiful in their bluish-white radiance. Grimstead knew straight away who they were and what was transpiring.

"A dream, then," he said without meaning to sound disappointed. A young female stepped forward and laughed.

Catherine. Slightly older than that fateful night at the

university. Her youthful vigor had been replaced with stoic grace. And a wickedly mischievous grin.

"Of course it's a dream, you dolt! Since when do crocodiles yell?"

"Of course." He pursed his lips. "I suppose it was too much to hope that I was somehow transported to the exact moment where I knew I wanted nothing more than to bind my soul to Lilly."

"In a way, you have been, my love," the second figure stepped forward. Lilly. She pointed to the ruckus that played out silently behind Grimstead. He looked from her spectral luminescence to her physical representation that struck at the monster with her machete.

The peculiar dream-time scene sped up before Grimstead's eyes until the Sun dragged itself from the grave. The manananggal shrieked without sound as it clawed the burning sky. Scott shouted, but not a sound crossed his lips. Grimstead could only hear the sound of his breathing.

"Hurry, you don't want to miss this, dear brother." Catherine smiled and urged him forward. Grimstead walked to his place beside the Lilly of the past and watched as both halves of the manananggal cracked like sun-baked mud, beams of light bursting forth from the fissures in its skin. The creature finally exploded in an intense wave of light and energy that knocked everyone to the dirt. Blue rivulets of energy, dappled with searing white orbs, traveled up, around and through the hollow tree like a snake, finally shooting straight up into the sky. Tiny green leaves immediately budded on the tree's rejuvenated branches and the trunk became whole. The ghost girl disintegrated into hundreds of beads of sparkling golden light and danced away. The manananggal's young victims were finally at peace. Relieved, Lilly turned and embraced Grimstead. Her pure joy washed over and through him, warming him stronger than the rays of the Sun ever could.

That was the moment he knew he wanted to be the only

name on her lips. Such bitter-sweet nectar flows from the flower of youth and desire. Drink once upon its petals and forever know the thirst of its absence.

"I am sorry, Lilly," he whispered, a tear cascading down his cheek. "So very sorry, Catty," The spectral Lilly looked upon him with a radiant smile.

"Sorry for what?"

"If I had only gone with Catherine on Stout's ship, she may yet have lived. And had I gone, I would not have met you and condemn you to die by my failure!" His tears shimmered against the dazzling light of the souls. "Do you not see my foolish hand in all this?"

"Maybe, maybe not." Catherine sat cross-legged on the ground next to her brother. "Your guilt is holding you from moments of beauty, like this one. Let it go. Let *us* go."

"You didn't have to die!" Grimstead sat up. Lilly pressed his hand to her cheek and kissed it.

"Didn't we?"

TWENTY TWO

TOWER OF ÏSUR
THE ISLAND OF ANTILLIA
THE SECOND DAY

"THE TIME IS SIX A.M. TIME TO RISE AND GREET THE WORLD!" A chipper male voice jolted Grimstead from sleep. Its owner was nowhere to be found in his spartan sleeping quarters, which contained only a queen-sized bed and pale gray nightstand.

"H-Hello?" Grimstead bolted upright and rubbed is eyes. He wore muted blue cotton pajama bottoms without a top. He groped the nightstand for his glasses.

"GOOD MORNING, SIR. YOUR HEART RATE FLUXUATED ERRATICALLY THROUGHOUT THE NIGHT. I TRUST YOU ARE NOT UNWELL?"

"Are you... in this room?"

"ON THE CONTRARY, SIR, I *AM* THE ROOM. A CYBER CONCIERGE, IF YOU WILL."

"I... see."

"WERE YOU UNCOMFORTABLE, SIR?"

"No... just... dreams."

"UNDERSTOOD. WOULD SIR LIKE TO HEAR THE DAY'S ITINERARY?"

"Alright." Grimstead threw the covers off, swung his legs

off the bed and stretched.

"EXCELLENT, SIR. ONCE SIR HAS SHOWERED AND DRESSED, AN ASSIST-BOT, THAT WAITS JUST OUTSIDE, WILL ESCORT YOU TO THE COMMISSARY WHERE A DELECTIBLE FAMILY-STYLE BREAKFAST AWAITS. THEN, YOU WILL BE TREATED TO A TOUR OF OUR SHIP. I AM TOLD IT IS NOT THE LEAST BIT BORING."

"A shower. By the gods, how that sounds inviting. But—"

"YES, SIR?"

"I do not see a bathroom door."

"OF COURSE."

A panel near the corner of the room slid open. Grimstead padded to the ingress and peeked in. The bathroom was just as plain as the room, only a toilet, sink and a glass shower stall lay beyond the door.

"I am unaccustomed to such sparse décor," Grimstead admitted as he entered the bathroom and removed his pajama bottoms. "Where I come from, people tend to occupy every single space with clutter."

"THE ROOM IS FULLY FURNISHED, SIR. ONE HAS BUT TO REQUEST AN ITEM, AND IT WILL DESCEND, RISE, OR SLIDE FROM ITS RECESSED COMPARTMENT."

Grimstead entered the shower and inspected it with curiosity.

"IS THERE A PROBLEM, SIR?"

"Well... how does one *partake* in a shower in this stall? There are no spouts, spigots, chains or anything resembling a functioning mechanism. I don't even see where it would come *out* from!"

"JUST SAY WATER."

"Water? What abou—?" Thirty streams of hot water abruptly doused Grimstead from various angles. The age-old debate of whether to protect the face or the genitals first entered his head. Even with his martial arts training, he could not deflect the torrents fast enough. "Stop! Make it stop! Muh —" A blast struck him in his open mouth.

"I AM QUITE IN AWE, SIR. I HAVE BEEN TOLD ON SEVERAL OCCASIONS THAT THE FOOD HERE IS SUBLIME, AND ITS AMENITIES THE ENVY OF THE COSMOS."

"For the love of *guh—stuh—*"

"I'VE OFTEN THOUGHT ABOUT THE IMPLICATIONS OF THE CORPORIAL AND HOW TITILLATING IT MUST BE TO FEEL...WELL, ANYTHING, REALLY. I THINK I WOULD LIKE TO KNOW WHAT HAVING A NOSE IS LIKE."

Grimstead squatted into a ball and cursed his luck that of all the rooms on the ship, his was the one in love with the sound of its own voice.

THE TOWER'S COMMISSARY was a cavernous and sterile-looking room, akin to those found in military facilities, with row after row of long, metal tables and benches to either side. It could easily accommodate several hundred people.

Grimstead entered and approached the table where Captain Rogerson, Emma, Dr. McParland and the Adamses were already seated. On every table were several large trays, each containing a variety of breakfast foods, as well as plates and cutlery. A raucous noise erupted from the CCs table, and there was little doubt that Berta was behind it. Several tables over, Fowler and his company glared.

"Grab yourself a plate and load up, Alexander. Everything is delicious!" Wesley spat pancake crumbs onto the table as he spoke. Grimstead scooped scrambled eggs and diced fruit onto his plate and sat next to Wesley.

"If you'll excuse me," Rogerson stood and threw his napkin onto the table. His companions watched with curiosity as he maneuvered his way over to Fowler's table. The Captain forced his way onto the bench to Fowler's right and threw his arm around his shoulders. The Night Cloaks rose in unison, but Fowler gestured for them to sit.

"Just what in the hell do you think you're—" Fowler felt a sharp pain between his ribs. Rogerson smiled and moved his head closer.

"That pain you're feeling?" he whispered. "That's a dagger made from the tooth of a tiger shark by a great Polynesian warrior chief. He fashioned it with a small, curved bone handle to be clutched between the index and middle finger. Small as it is, this dagger is astoundingly sharp and strong. It is my last resort weapon, and at times, my assassin's blade. No one knows of it until it's too late. I have but to cough and it will slid right in. And, by this angle, deflate your lung. I could then remove with ease and shove it into your neck. You would be dead before your pretty companion could raise an eyebrow. The chief claimed to have defeated the shark with his bare hands, but you know how men talk."

"You're absolutely mad!" Fowler exclaimed. The Night Cloaks jumped to their feet once more. Rogerson sat up and looked Fowler in the eyes.

"Tell your men to sit and enjoy their meals. You play along and we'll get along fine."

"Herr Fowler, should I dispatch this American *scheiss*?" Eva set her water glass down.

"No, let him speak."

"I knew you and I would be fast friends."

"What do you want?"

"I wanted to tell you that I am on to you."

"What?"

"I know the things you've done. I know that you are a horrible smear dressed as a man. But I *know* you. You are a weak-kneed braggart who hides behind people far above your station. You are nothing. And I would like nothing more than to tear you limb from limb for the atrocities you've heaped upon Alexander. I would like to take my time with you, and ensure that each and every breath is agony for you. But alas, our gracious host has forbidden acts of violence. So, I may have to simply opt for a quick kill."

"You strike me down and my men will strike *you* down!"

"Fair enough. Then mine strike yours and Ïsur strikes them and so on. The point remains that *you* die first."

"When I die, a great demon will take control of my body and wreak havoc against those who stood against me. Your little dagger would do nothing to stop him." Rogerson laughed and slapped Fowler on the back.

"You miss the point, magician. No matter what occurred, you would still be dead. Keep that in mind." Rogerson pulled Fowler close once more. His voice lowered to a rumble. "Just give me a reason." He slid the dagger back into his boot and returned to his friends. He poured a cup of coffee and smiled.

"What was that about?" Grimstead asked, suspicious.

"Oh, just trying to be a friendly neighbor. And failing miserably."

"TO OUR LEFT is the zoological preserve, host to thousands of Planet Earth's sentient creatures." The thirty-seat hover trolley glided along the thoroughfare of the ship's entertainment level. The mannequin-esque robot driver—and tour guide—wore a blue jumpsuit with gold shoulder brushes. His mouth fell open and closed as he spoke, like a ventriloquist's dummy.

The group peered through the glass walls of the preserve and saw numerous rows of stasis tanks.

"That doesn't look like any nature reserve or zoo I've ever seen," Wesley commented. He sat in the row just behind the driver along with Grimstead, Sarah, and Dr. McParland. Behind them sat Rogerson and a snoring Dr. Marrow. Then

Fowler and Eva, then the Night Cloaks. The CCs filled up two more rows, and Berta and The Swede had a row of their own. Emma and Orrin shared the very last row. She found that she cared very little for the tour's content, save that it provided her the opportunity to be near him.

"*Pre*serve, sir." The driver's head spun one-hundred-eighty degrees to face his passengers, while his body drove on. "We have amassed quite the catalog of species from this and other planets for research and preservation in the event of a cataclysm. *Escape extinction!* is our motto, here. Perhaps once the tour is over you would like to see for yourself?"

"Yes. Per... haps." Wesley said, unnerved. He fought to contain a verbal assault outburst.

"Splendid!" The driver's head spun back to its natural position. Emma placed her hand on Orrin's. She anticipated him to recoil, but to her delight, he did not.

"This must be a terrible bore to you."

"Not at all, Miss McParland." He smiled. "To see the wonders of my father's ship through the eyes of newcomers is a thrill."

"Call me Emma, please. I would like to think we are beyond such formalities."

"Emma it is. Though if I am being honest, *Emma*, I am not here for the tour." His smile widened. Blood rushed to Emma's cheeks, betraying her hope of looking composed.

"Is that why you haven't taken your eyes off me?"

"Oh, you've noticed. I—apologize." Orrin quickly removed his hand, but Emma replaced it just as fast.

"I didn't say that I minded, did I?"

The driver chirped on.

"To the right is one of our many cocktail lounges, where an unlimited drink menu is at your disposal." Dr. Marrow leaped up from his seat and nearly fell out of the trolley.

"Where are you going?" Rogerson barked.

"This is my stop, Captain!" He saluted, then spun on his

heel to the door. Eva scoffed at the insubordination.

"You should control your people, *Captain.*" She nearly laughed. Rogerson turned in his seat to face her and Fowler.

"The way this one controls you, ma'am?" He jutted his thumb to Fowler. "He's beneath you, you realize." Eva sneered but stayed her tongue. Fowler had instructed not to engage the enemy unless absolutely necessary. "Nothing to add? Shame."

"If we can *puh-lease* keep the jibber-jabber to a minimum while the tour is underway, it would be greatly appreciated!" The driver chimed as his head spun around once more. "Now, as I was saying, this level has several movie theaters, restaurants, galleries, a gym and even Simulated Reality Fabricators! Yes, indeed! We have everything we need to ensure a lengthy space-time voyage isn't so boring that you would submit to base desires for cannibalism and cantaloupe sodomy!"

"W-what was it you just mentioned?" Dr. McParland asked.

"Cantaloupe sodomy!"

"No, no. Before that."

"Cannibalism."

"Slightly before that."

"The word *for.*"

"No, you automated nincompoop! The *simulated* whatsis!"

"Ah! Yes, the Simulated Reality Fabricators, SRFs for short. They are singular chambers that utilize special technology to recreate just about anything you can imagine! Reenact your favorite war crimes! Lounge at the beach! Use an aphrodisiac and go buck-wild in the produce section of your favorite grocery store! It simulates life so life doesn't simulate suck! Be the hero of your own adventure, or, I don't know, read a book. Whatever floats your boat!"

"Ship!" Rogerson and Grimstead exclaimed.

"Those two are so gay for each other," Berta mumbled.

"Driver," Fowler interrupted. "If I wanted to recreate a medieval dungeon with a woman chained to a stone altar, the room would oblige?" Grimstead stood and prepared to lunge. Rogerson grabbed his arm and pulled him back to his seat.

"Now, now, let's not ruffle each other's feathers, lads." Rogerson turned to Fowler who, up until that point, looked confident. "I see that pain you've had earlier has subsided. It would be a pity if it were to return, no?"

Fowler's cocky smile faded. He wanted to keep Grimstead frustrated.

Bite your tongue, bide your time. Keep his mind befuddled with grief and anger. Even the best laid plans can be thwarted when some damn American stabs you to death with a shark tooth. Another opportunity will present itself.

Eva leaned close, her lips brushing Fowler's right ear.

"Why do you brook such insolence? The Red Right Hand of The Moonshield Society should never stand for this affront! This entire lot should be put to death. Just say the word and I will make it so," she growled. Fowler looked her in the eye and glared. It was all the answer she needed.

"I would throw my hands up in abdication, if my hands were designed to move from the steering wheel!" The driver yelled. "I am trying to conduct a tour, and you all seem so easily distracted by your drama! It's a short tour, people! Just one level and you can piss off to do whatever kind of crap you do! Master Orrin, what say you?" The group turned to face the empty back row where Orrin and Emma once sat. "Great, just great! Even my master has abandoned me!"

"I have a question." Sarah raised her hand. The eyes of the driver locked onto her.

"Is it tour related?"

"Yes, actually."

"Splendid! What is your question, human I do not hate?"

"You've said this level was designed to give the ship's crew a place to unwind—to escape, if you will."

"Yes?"

"How many people could this level entertain at any given

time?"

"Thousands."

"Where are they now?"

"I don't understand."

"Yes you do. This ship held thousands of people inside it, yes?"

"Several thousands, to be vaguely precise. This ship was one of many civil ships designed to be its own habitat. People could spend lifetimes on this ship if they chose."

"What happened to them?"

"I am not, uh, programmed to say, ma'am."

"Furthermore," Dr. McParland interjected, "why are we only seeing just one level of the ship besides the bridge and our living quarters? I want to see some science!"

"For once, I agree with the doddering simpleton," Fowler chimed.

"Thank you!" Dr. McParland nodded.

"We came here for knowledge, hidden truths, secrets that could damn or save us all. We haven't come all this way for these, these *distractions*!" Fowler stood and the trolley stopped. "This as been an abysmal waste of time. Thank you for a lovely ride down a hallway." He and his underlings stepped off and began walking back the way they came. Rogerson, Grimstead, and the rest followed. The driver spun is head one last time and shouted,"If a bunch of strangers came to your houses, would *you* let them rummage through your underwear drawer?!"

The driver was alone, just a machine fused to another machine—with opinions and little else to justify his existence. "I hate this job."

"HELP YOURSELF TO a seat." Orrin guided Emma down an aisle of a dimly-lit theater. At the front of the room was a movie screen.

"Which is most advantageous?"

"I prefer the center... here." He took her hand and led her toward a pair of center seats. "Take this one, it's my favorite." Emma sat and Orrin plopped down next to her.

"You seem so excited and so comfortable all at once."

"Cinema is one of my great passions. I am something of a connoisseur."

"Cin-em-a," Emma repeated.

"Yes, moving pictures."

"Like the moving pictures that showed at the Berlin Wintergarten Theater? I've heard stories, but never had the privilege to attend."

"This is far beyond whatever you could imagine, sweet Emma. Oh! And there's more!" He snapped his fingers and a assist-bot, dressed as a bellhop, rolled down the aisle to greet them with a tray of assorted candies, a tub of popcorn and two large soda cups. Orrin passed the items to Emma and stuffed a handful of buttered popcorn into his mouth. "I've taken the liberty of compiling a few movies from the twentieth and twenty-first centuries for us to view. That is, if you were so inclined to spend several hours in blissful escapism."

"I have nothing else planned." Emma sipped from her straw and choked on the fizzy liquid.

"I should have warned you about the carbonation in the drinks. I apologize!"

"Wh... what... *is*... this?" Emma stammered between fits of respiratory failure.

"It's a lemon-lime soda."

"Well, it's quite tasty, albeit extremely sweet" She regained composure and took another sip. "You've mentioned escapism. What is it you want to escape?" Orrin shoved another fistful of popcorn into his mouth.

"This... ship," he replied as he chewed. "Wondrous as it may seem to a newcomer, try spending a few hundred years here. It begins to feel like a prison."

"Why not come away with us?"

"I wish it were that simple. My service to my father is more important than the petty whims of a wandering mind and the toils of boredom. Besides, one such as I would not so easily traipse around the earth, as it is today, without causing a stir. So for now, I will content myself to escape by watching movies with a beautiful woman by my side."

Emma smiled coyly. "You flatter me, sir. Tell me, what marvel of a *moo-vee* will I behold first?"

"Ah, yes! I have tried to narrow down a few choice selections that adequately represent each genre that I think you will find satisfactory. For our period piece, I have *The Last of The Mohicans*, starring Daniel Day Lewis."

"Ugh. I've read the book."

"You'll find it strays from the original text. It is a stunning movie, I assure you. Then, for our action segment, we'll see *Enter The Dragon*, starring Bruce Lee, Jim Kelly and Shih Kien as the nefarious Mr. Han!" Orrin clenched his fist and imitated a Bruce Lee's trademark shout. Emma broke into a fit of giggles.

"What? What did I do?"

"It's so nice to see you so animated and honest. I find comfort in those who are passionate about what they enjoy. I suppose I've developed that from watching my father work. He too, is a passionate soul. You know, Orrin, we have just so recently met, but it is like I've known you for ages."

"I share that sentiment."

They gazed at one another for several seconds of awkward silence. Orrin broke it with a clap, which signaled the lights to dim and the projector to start.

"Also, on the agenda are Stanley Kubrick's *The Shining*, the original *Godzilla*, *Abbot and Costello Meet Frankenstein*, *Blade Runner* and possibly a Tarantino film... or six. Let's enjoy ourselves, shall we?" He leaned in toward Emma and she rested her head on his shoulder.

"Let's."

As the opening scene appeared on the screen, Emma raised her head up off his shoulder with wide eyes and mouth agape. The camera's bird's-eye view swept across verdant mountains and wooded vistas to the achingly beautiful score. Orrin looked upon his companion with the same veneration. For once in her life, Emma was speechless.

"AFTER THE INITIAL battles ended and the majority of Anunnaki had either fled or were dismantled, I spent a great deal of time patrolling the earth, keeping a keen eye on those of us who stayed." Ïsur poured a burgundy liquid from a squat decanter into four glasses. "It was a daunting task. However, if I had not remained, I would never have had the privilege of meeting the mother of my children, my one true love." Ïsur placed the glasses on a wooden tray and brought them over to Professor Grimstead, Dr. Adams, Captain Rogerson and Dr. McParland, all comfortably seated in dark leather chairs positioned beside a lit fireplace.

The room around them was large, but dimly lit and crammed floor-to-ceiling with various trophies, plaques, taxidermied beasts and artifacts. In fact, it was an exact replica of nearly every Adventure Guild great hall across the globe. The room even smelled of the same musky mixture of whiskey and stale cigars. All present, save Wesley Adams, were among the select few people in the world that have intimate knowledge of the Adventure Guild. Members came from all walks of life around the globe, and all pledged to dedicate their lives to the pursuit of adventure and glory.

"Your wife is no longer with us?" Grimstead ventured. Ïsur started, as if he had been struck. The Professor immediately regretted his inquiry. "I apologize, Ïsur. I spoke out of turn."

The Pleiadian handed each man a full glass, but remained silent. His expression grew sullen as he thought of his dear wife. They each took a sip of the beverage and nodded in approval.

"Think nothing of it, Alexander," Ïsur finally replied. "I see my beloved Agéta whenever I look upon my beautiful children." He spent another moment in silent reverie, a thin smile finally crossing his face. "Now, what do you all think of the wine? It is vintage 1945, from my personal vineyard on level 3B in the North-West wing of the ship. It is one of few things that are not fabricated by molecular re-assignment. I take great pride in my wine, though so few get to taste it."

"Such an earthly endeavor, wine making," Rogerson mused after taking two big gulps. "Bloody good, though! And from the future no less!"

"Or from the past," Wesley quipped. "To perspective!" He and the Captain raised a glass in salute.

"It is not so earthly an undertaking, Captain, considering that the very knowledge of the art was brought from the stars," Ïsur pointed out. He held up the decanter. "There is enough for another glass each. Would anyone care for more?" Everyone accepted, and held their glasses in salute before partaking.

Dr. McParland gulped down the contents of his glass then threw it into the fireplace. It shattered and caused the flames to swell.

"Mazeltov! Now, tell us about this room! How the deuce are we sitting in an Adventure Guild bragging hall?" Ïsur straightened up from his already impeccable posture.

"We are sitting in one of the Simulated Reality Fabricators that you learned about on your tour. By utilizing a blend of transported matter, replicated matter, tractor beams, and shaped force fields, I am able to mimic just about anything I so desire. By tapping into my particular mental abilities, I gleaned that you would be more at ease speaking with me in a familiar setting. The images have, essentially, been taken from your minds and are being projected, if you will, onto the force fields. And that is what produces the objects you see and feel. Scents are released into the room to heighten the level of realism.

Allow me to demonstrate. Processor, initiate simulation 1967."

An audible computerized flourish signaled that the order was acknowledged and the room abruptly changed scenery from a cluttered Victorian chamber to a psychedelic European nightclub full of dancing, scantily clad people gyrating under the swirling, rainbow-colored lights. The leather chairs that the four had been sitting on became bean bags. The air was heavy with acrid marijuana smoke and their ears assaulted with a cacophony of strange sounds. Ïsur chuckled at the dumbfounded looks on the faces of his guests.

"Processor, initiate Kyoto."

They suddenly found themselves outdoors in a tidy, rectangular space. Each man was now sitting on large rock surrounded by white sand. Circles within circles had been meticulously drawn into the sand. A light rain fell, making the air cool and crisp and they could smell the fragrance of cherry blossoms.

"Processor, initiate Battle of Clontarf."

The stones beneath them morphed into piles of human bodies and the peaceful garden became a cold, sandy beach. Swords and axes clashed all around them, as the Irish of Leinster and the Vikings of Dublin fought to the death. Wesley shrieked and all took to cover. Except Dr. McParland, who simply clapped his hands in delight, like a child on Christmas morning.

"Processor, initiate Adventure Guild."

The warriors disappeared and the room returned to the way it had been. Grimstead and Rogerson stepped out from behind the leather chairs. Wesley slowly dragged himself out from underneath his.

"Im-impressive, sir," he stuttered. "Vuh-very convincing."

Ïsur smiled. "Actually, this room is a very eloquent representation of human theology, and to a degree, philosophy. Things you *believe* to be true aren't always what they seem. As you may find within any mythology or religious faith, nothing is wholly true nor entirely false. Gods do not exist, at least not literally. In actuality, they are only beings far more evolved than indigenous man. Science is magic to the ignorant. The stories and myths of man were simply a recounting of actual events, but through the eyes of babes. Everything you know is simply truth falsely told."

"What of the paranormal?" Grimstead asked. "There are things I have witnessed first-hand that cannot be explained away as spacemen. What about, say, demons?" He thought of Fowler's infamous boast. Ïsur looked him straight in the eyes.

"Do you believe in ghosts, Alexander?" The Professor nodded. "And what do you suppose a ghost truly is?"

"I believe a ghost is residual energy. Energy from a person who has departed its mortal shell."

"And what of those who were never human? Beings whose energies are something quite different." Grimstead furrowed his brow.

"Demons, Alexander. Angels *and* demons, to be fair. There are many powerful energies in this Universe—most are quite ancient. There are benevolent ones, naturally, but there are others who are very, very angry. Neither should be taken lightly. Also bear in mind there are beings far older than my kind, and they are both great and terrible in their enmity. There in the dark expanse, they wait, voiceless and without clemency. They are predators that know only of hunger, and the aching desire to snuff out the Sun. What I have told you is but a glimpse into truths so complex they could shatter the mind." Ïsur placed a gentle hand upon Grimstead's shoulder and telepathically espied a vision of tentacles and torment—blood, agony, and the abyss. "Though, perhaps you are more acquainted than I thought. Ïsur finished his wine and tossed the glass into the fireplace.

"Huzzah!" McParland shouted. Wesley threw his, but it smashed against the brick mantle.

"Buh-ball-licker!" he stammered, while his cohorts

laughed heartily.

"I invite you all to utilize the fabricators," Ïsur nodded and spread his hands. "They are quite remarkable. And perhaps they can assist you with your aim, Dr. Adams." They all laughed harder.

"Har har," Wesley grimaced. "Everyone's a comedian."

TWENTY THREE

TOWER OF ÏSUR
THE ISLAND OF ANTILLIA
THE THIRD DAY

PAUL STRETCHED. HE had spent all day rewiring the *Explorer*'s mainframe and his stomach growled. The main cabin of the vessel was just an open space that lead to the storage compartment in back. The panel on the wall by the cockpit door sported a ridiculous amount of buttons. Paul tapped one near the bottom and a long, thin container rose from the floor. It contained enough food-paste packets to keep a family of four comfortably alive for six months.

Three weeks, if one of those family members was Berta.

"Let's see, let's see. What do I want? Beef and garden cheese blend? Fettuccine ala dolphin?" Paul took a quick look around the cabin and remembered no one was there to judge. "Ice cream it is!" He took two packets from the container and walked back to the panel. *Boop.* The container sank back into the floor. *Boop.* A starboard side ceiling panel descended, revealing two cots in bunk formation. Paul scrambled up the ladder to his cot on the top. It only took him thirty seconds to suck down the ice cream and he contorted as brain freeze set in.

"NNNnnnnnyyAAArgh!" He clamped his hands to his

face until the rush melted away. He tossed the empty packets to the floor and pulled three comic books out from under his mattress: *Wasteland Blues*, *The Raging Cock*, and *Captain Commander*. One of the comics followed a small group of survivors trying to stay alive in an unforgiving American wasteland full of marauders, cannibals and assorted psychopaths. Another was a superhero yarn about a rooster-themed vigilante who *'Clucked for justice!'* The third was about a heroic space captain who always managed to escape certain doom at the last minute, while reciting terrible one-liners to buxom beauties.

Captain Commander #14: Captain Commander vs the Zombots from Alpha Cryptauri X.

Maybe that one.

"*Comic books, little bub?*" A voice from the bottom bunk asked. "*Ain't you a little old for that?*" Paul swung his head over the side and saw an ethereal, yet scruffy, surfer-looking fellow thumbing through *Chastity Inferno*—one of Berta's romance novels.

"What would you prefer, Dwayne? That I pummel my frontal lobe with the dreck you're holding? Comic books are, and always will be, high literature." Dwayne stood next to the cot and rested his chin on Paul's mattress.

"*Whatever you say, little bub. Hey, I gotta question.*"

"Okay?"

"*You could have been done repairing this clunker, like, a day ago, right?*"

"Maybe."

"*Maybe nothing, little bub! You know I know you know I know that you didn't need to undo the mainframe to rewire it. You're stalling, little bub!*" Dwayne winked.

"So...?"

"*So! Like, what's the raisin? There gots to, has to, be a raisin why you want to be alone.*"

"What do you want me to say? That my parents irritate

the Bea Arthur out of me? That Berta makes me feel about as useful as a suppository?"

"*Don't take Saint Bea's name in vain, little bub!*" Dwayne frowned.

"Oh, stuff it. You're just a figment of my imagination. A mental projection of the trauma I endured by seeing you die in front of me!"

An image flashed into Paul's mind: lifeless bodies strewn across the city street like rag dolls. The Laughing Man in The Devil Mask chuckling maniacally as he threw grenade after grenade. Where's Berta? Mom and Dad are trying their best to get Paul to safety, but they are just scientists. They stumble and crawl like all the rest. The Laughing Man sets the sights of his machine gun at Paul. The police are close now, Paul can hear the sirens. Too far. Too late. A man jumps in the way and takes six large bullets to the torso. Six bullets meant for Paul. Blood and meat hit the child like a morbid food fight. "*Run, little... bub... Dwayne made a good'n.*" His eyes go dark, and Paul can taste copper on his lips. Hands now. Mom's. Dad's. Pulling him down and behind an Attitude Adjustment Booth as more bullets tear into the night. Paul doesn't mean to swallow Dwayne's blood.

"*Or maybe, I'm a guh-guh-guh-guh-ghost!*" Dwayne chuckled.

"Unlikely."

"*Maybe you're just asleeping, little bub.*"

For a moment, Paul was blind. He sat up and *Captain Commando #14* slid down his face. The overhead spot light felt warm. A small comfort considering the sound of Berta's earthquake snoring. He turned to face the cabin and watched his parents sleep on the port-side bunks. How was such a thing possible? Berta sounded like fifteen gorillas trying to simultaneously squeeze themselves into toilet bowl. Miraculously, she rolled to her side and the snoring stopped.

He heard the scratching of a thousand hands on the

Explorer's hull, the chilling moans of the doornails trying to find a way in. There were so many of them—all eager to tear the *Explorer's* crew limb from limb. Devil's Landing was a dead zone. That is to say, a zone where the dead walked and searched for flesh to eat. Because the city was also an island, the dead had nowhere to go.

Paul had asked his father why they needed to explore the dead city, but the answer was always just,' *The boss wants what the boss wants'.* The boss in this case being Moonshield Pharmaceuticals. Paul had his theories on Moonshield, but they were difficult to recall with the orchestra of rot performing their greatest hits just outside the reinforced hull of the *Explorer.* Despite his better judgment, Paul climbed down the ladder and approached the cockpit door. His small hand hovered over the button for a small eternity before he finally pressed it. The sound was instantly much louder. Every hair on his body did jumping jacks. Paul stepped into the co-pilot seat positioned behind and slightly above the pilot's. For once in his verbose life, he was without words.

The streets were filled with the dead. And the dead were hungry.

High up as he was, fingers splatted and smeared the windows. Paul looked over the sea of doornails and felt something he'd never felt before: pity. Those poor bastards probably never knew what hit them. One day it was panic, the next terror, then finally... this. Paul pressed his face to the glass, which caused a small frenzy. Barely human voices sang to him in a cacophony of moans and gore-choked shrieks. Their great numbers caused the cockpit to sway slightly. Paul curled up in the co-pilot's seat and was lulled to sleep by the undead lullaby.

"*Wake up, little bub.*"

Paul bolted upright and looked around the cabin and saw he was alone. No Dwayne, no Berta, no carnivorous New Yorkers. Just the faint late-morning sounds of the jungle and a tummy ache.

"Note to self, no more ice cream dinners."

"NO, I'M NOT saying I don't love my son, it's just that —could you refill this? Thanks—just that he's a bit of a prick. Being the mother of a child genius isn't easy, you know." Sarah rattled the ice in her empty mint julep glass. She reclined on a levitating chaise lounge, dressed in a complimentary white cotton robe. Immediately, the human-looking android servant before her stopped massaging her feet and stood. "Mm! No, no, not you. You keep on a-rubbin'." The android complied, kneeling to continue the foot rub while another servant, a female, approached with a silver tray in her left hand, topped with five drinks. The spa androids moved just like humans, spoke just like humans, but their look was decidedly plastic. They felt real enough, though, as Sarah, Emma and Berta could attest. Emma and Berta were laying face-down on levitating massage tables while warm, scented oils were rubbed into the bare skin of their necks, shoulders and backs by male spa droids —two for Emma, four for Berta. The female droid placed a full drink in Sarah's hand then approached Ïella, seated at a small table nearby and receiving a manicure. The ship's spa was one of Ïella's favorite places. The spa droids tended to her every need without hesitation or judgment. It was the only place she could truly let her hair down. The room was decorated in soft hues of white and blue that never seemed to steady, creating a sense of lulling fluidity. In the center of the room was a heated mineral pool that reflected shimmering waves upon the high, vaulted ceiling.

"Mistress Ïella?" The female droid approached her and offered the tray. Ïella took a mint julep and waved the droid to her guests. "Of course, Mistress." The droid bowed. Berta grabbed a glass, chugged it, then grabbed another.

"I don't usually drink this carpet-muncher crap, but it seems to do the trick. Hey, Ïella!"

"Yes, Miss Thompson?"

"Who's Miss Thompson?" Emma muttered, her face pressed into the table's head padding.

"I'm Miss Thompson, Barbie," Berta chuffed.

"You're no Miss, miss!" Emma giggled. Her buzz was kicking in.

"Psssh! Whatever you say, giggles. Have another drink."

"Yesh, please." Her face melted deeper into the padding. The service droid placed the last mint julep into Emma's reaching hand. Emma managed to maneuver the straw into the headrest's opening and sipped long and slow.

"You were asking a question, Miss Thompson?"

"Yeah, I was wondering if these massages came with a complimentary happy-ending."

"I'm not sure I follow?" Iella sipped her drink.

"You know, *full release.*"

"Emma's right, you're no miss," Sarah laughed. Berta blindly tossed her empty glass at Sarah and it smashed her foot masseuse in the head.

"You're one to talk, sister!" Berta chuckled. "Way I heard it, you were a regular knobologist before you met Wesley."

"A *what*-ologist?" Emma inquired. "I never know what you people are saying!"

"A knobologist," Berta began. "Someone who's had plenty of practice making men religious. You know, *Oh god oh god oh god!*"

"What does that have to do with doorknobs?"

"A knob is—I can't believe I have to explain this— another word for a dingus."

"A ding—? Oh, for god's sake, Berta. I give up!"

"Knob: noun. The dangling squishies between a man's legs. Synonyms: wang, doodle, wangdoodle, one-eyed monster, mule, pecker, hammer, ween. See also: schmeckle, dong, dork, dick, meat rocket, bone, sauseech, tube steak, tuna slapper, love truncheon, schlong, politicians, the 'ol worm, snakey meatsocks, baloney pony, cock, lizard, chub, the main vein. And my personal favorite, Rumple Foreskin."

Ïella couldn't hold back a loud laugh despite herself. The other ladies soon joined in.

"When was the last time you laughed like that?" Sarah asked, wiping a tear from her eyes. "You don't seem like you get many light moments. You know, with your father being a—what did he call it? A god warden, or time lord, or whatever."

"Not for some time. Not since..." Ïella's voice trailed off. Her thoughts flew back to several months prior, the last time she had been in Vargas' temple. He always made her smile and laugh, Her thoughts shifted to the sensation of the two of them locked in a sweaty, fevered passion. The keening wails of the savages in the plaza were drowned out by her own voracious screams as the lovers ravaged each other. Vargas had smelled like the earth, Ïella recalled. She had lied about her excursion that day, and if her father or brother found out about the secret rendezvous, there would be hell to pay. But, an hour with her beloved was worth suffering through ten hells.

"Whoa, is she someplace sexy in her head or what?" Berta chuckled. Ïella snapped back with a blush. "Yer thinking of that manly man man with the big sword, aren't you? What was his name? Varney?"

"Vargas!" Emma, Sarah and Ïella corrected in unison.

"Well, excuse me all to shit! I was too busy looking at his pecks to catch his name."

"He is a hunk." Sarah raised her glass to toast. "You're a lucky gal!"

"Am I? Being forbidden to see the light of my soul seems quite the opposite." The spa entrance opened and Eva Perle entered with meek hesitation. Everyone turned to look at the newcomer. "Miss Perle. Please, join us." Ïella waved her over.

"Are you mad? She's with the *enemy!*" Emma said just loud enough for Ïella to hear.

"She is no enemy of mine. In fact, she is just as much my

guest as you are and deserving of equal hospitality." Eva slowly rounded the pool and walked to the ladies. She was dressed in her black uniform, but without the leather trench coat. She looked quite uncomfortable in the steamy room.

"I do hope I am not interrupting." She smiled politely. Her demeanor struck Emma as irritatingly genuine.

"Of course not," Ïella assured her. "Please, let one of my servants fetch you a robe and a drink."

"Nein, thank you, mistress Ïella. The air is too perfect to be covered. However, a drink would be lovely." Eva pulled her turtleneck over her head, then unhooked her lace bra.

"Look at those perky sweater puppies," Berta stammered. "Like two perfect dollops of whipped cream." Eva then unhooked her belt and unbuttoned her pants, sliding them down to reveal two milk-white legs.

"Gods, even her *bush* is adorable," Berta whispered in reverence.

"I apologize, does this make any of you uncomfortable?" Eva asked.

"That depends," Berta grunted. "How do you feel about happy endings?"

A chaise lounge swooped across the pool and halted inches from Eva's legs. She reached out with her mind and lifted her clothes. In several fluid motions they were folded and set down neatly. Eva then reclined on the lounge and accepted the waiting drink. The women stared like children at a magic show.

"What is... *that*... like?" Emma asked, now sitting on the massage table, her towel draped over her. Eva drew a slow breath in through her nose.

"I cannot describe it so easily, I'm afraid. Imagine hundreds of invisible strands of energy flowing out from the mind. Always moving, always connecting themselves to whatever I come across. Once that connection is made, I feel the object as if it were in my hand. When my gift first appeared, I could not control the connecting strands and they would latch to everything all at once. It was a sensory overload, not to mention a mess. My parents locked me away in the attic when I was still a child. I was inhuman, an outcast, a *thing* no one spoke about. If anyone did inquire, they would say I was off to a boarding school in Vienna. Food would be delivered by a dumbwaiter that my father had installed and it was the same for my waste. Once a week, Heinrick, my father's manservant came to wash me. Among other nefarious proclivities.

"My parents were far too proud and popular to acknowledge that their own flesh and blood was different. They didn't see this power of mine as a gift, but as a curse. This was punishment for some undetermined inequity, and to my father, I no longer existed. For two years this continued. But in my solitude, I decided to hone my power. I took control. I taught myself to manipulate those strings, and eventually, I was able to control them so adeptly I could carry a mouse by its tail. Or, lift Heinrick off his feet by the throat until he died. That same day, I descended the attic stairs and sent the strings to seek out my parents. As I suspected, they were asleep in bed. I connected to a box of matches and sent them dancing to the wall sconces, lighting the room silently. I caught my parents in a web of those same strings and they rose like marionettes. For two years I had scripted the words I would say to them as I strangled the life from them. Two years of torment endured only because I was different. Two years and I wanted nothing more than to ask them why... w*hy, poppa? I am not a monster! Am I not your little Eva?*

"I became one, however. I forced my father to strangle the only woman that mattered to him. I then shattered his arms and legs so that he was rendered cripple. I sealed him in the attic along with my mother's corpse. My theory was that he would either succumb to starvation as she putrefied next to him or he'd be forced to eat her. His whimpering ceased after a week." Eva fully reclined and stretched her toes. "I wish I hadn't left my cigarettes in my coat."

"Ho. Lee. Shit!" Berta exclaimed. "Express train to Buzzkillington, lady!"

"Is that how you wound up with that scoundrel, Fowler? He sought you out to be his lackey?" Emma tied her robe closed and sat on the table with her legs dangling. Eva sighed heavily and dragged her finger across her bottom lip.

"Herr Fowler is no scoundrel, little girl. He is a visionary. And I am blessed to be his lackey, as you say. He rose so quickly through the tiers of the—of *our*—organization, that I knew greatness would come to any who followed him. I sought him out. He saw my abilities as a blessing and not a curse. He made me feel... loved."

"You are fascinating," Sarah said. "You would make a brilliant case study—"

"The last study I was a part of ended in mutilation. It was the authorities who took me and locked me in an asylum. Apparently, society frowns on revenge. But it was just another prison to which I had the key." Eva stood and walked to the pool. She turned cool eyes to Emma and smiled. "And since we are all such good friends, I'll let you in on a secret, little girl. No one speaks ill of Herr Fowler without some tragedy befalling them." Emma jumped to her feet with raised fists.

"Was that a threat?!"

"No, schatz, just friendly word of advice." She lifted off the floor like a specter, then dove into the steam-covered water with an elegant *splash*. The ladies looked at each other in confusion.

"What just happened?" Sarah shook her head.

"What happened is I think I'm in love." Berta fanned herself with her large right hand.

"I thought you were in love with The Swede."

"He is such a nice man," Emma added. She realized her hands were still tightly clenched and shook them open.

"Hey, I got a *lot* of love to give, you feel me?"

"Yes, ma'am, I am feeling you currently," her robo-masseuse nodded.

"Not you, spanky." Berta's eyes were crotch level with the automaton. "Say, you ever get freaky with one of these things?"

"Is sex all you think about, Miss Thompson?" Ïella handed her empty glass to a servant and shooed it with a wave.

"No. Yes."

"Ïella only wants Vargas and who could blame her?" Sarah smiled. "And Emma has Orrin following after her like a goofy puppy. No offense, Ïella."

"None taken. You are correct, Dr. Adams. My brother is quite smitten with Miss McParland. I hoped that his affection would change his mind toward Vargas. But my brother is too proud."

Emma blushed and felt a stir in places she dare not talk about. She also couldn't admit that she felt the same way for Ïella's brother. Truth was, she longed to see him, to hear his voice.

"I have an idea!" Sarah jumped from her seat and pointed at Emma. "You distract Orrin while the rest of us *pretend* to go on a walk while Ïella has a romantic encounter!"

"No, really, that would be far too—" Ïella began.

"GREAT!" Berta exclaimed. "We all go to the exit, then, when Mr. Big Brother shows up, Emma can distract him with a little coochie-snappin'!"

"Um... I don't know what that means." Emma's brow furrowed.

"That's pretty much what I just said, Berta."

"Well, it's a *collective* idea."

"No, it isn't." Sarah shook her head. Eva rose from the pool and hovered. The water no longer cascaded off her body, but instead floated away then dropped slowly back into the pool. She set herself down next to her clothes and was perfectly dry.

"What about you, toots? You in?" Eva reclined on her

chair once more, lifting her glass with her mind.

"Nien, I think I will stay here and have these affronts to god pamper me awhile longer. For what it's worth, I think it is a novel idea. There is no greater travesty than a woman's empty —"

"Coochie!"

"Arms, Frau Thompson. Empty arms. But might I make a suggestion?"

The ladies nodded. "Do not wait for him to come to you, schatz. Make the first move and see the distraction sweep across his eyes like a blizzard."

"You know, for a murdering psycho-babe, you're alright." Berta smiled. Eva held her drink up in salute. Ïella clasped her hands in nervous excitement at the prospect of embracing her true love, even for a moment.

"Ship," Ïella spoke. A flourish of beeps acknowledged her. "Where is my brother currently?"

"THE BRIDGE."

"And my father?"

"UNKNOWN."

"Of course."

"That going to be a problem?" Sarah asked.

"Only one way to find out." Emma winked.

"Agreed! Let us dress and set the plan to motion." Ïella could barely contain herself. Her purple eyes were wide and eager as the four women gathered their things and headed out. Once Eva was alone, she sighed and drained the contents of her glass. A male figure appeared from the bar across the room and made his way over. The droids closed in to address his needs, but were shooed. Eva smiled.

"Herr Fowler," she cooed.

"Eva, my dear. You look simply ravishing, I must say. Clothes are simply a sin for a figure such as yours." He slid his hand into his jacket and produced Eva's silver cigarette case with the Moonshield sigil engraved upon it. He slid a cigarette out and placed it between her lips. He muttered a few words then snapped his fingers. The tip of the cigarette flared then smoldered. Eva sucked the smoke in deep, then let it snake its way from her mouth.

"This is a non-smoking section of the ship." One of the male droids quickly moved closer with an accusatory finger. "Put that out at once—" His head caved in with a sound not unlike a crushed can. Sparks arced from the exposed circuits as he fell.

"Put that on my bill." Eva smiled.

"Have you learned anything of use?"

"Yes, these drinks are watered down." Eva lashed a telekinetic tendril at the bartender and smashed its head into the counter.

"You have a way with people, you know," Fowler laughed, then kissed her.

THE ELEVATOR DOOR opened. Emma saw Orrin at the monitors and stepped onto the bridge. He turned and smiled with surprise. "What brings you up here at this hour, Emma?" She made her way to him without a word, then kissed him on the lips. Nothing more needed to be said.

"BY ODIN'S BEARD! Ïella?" Vargas sprang up from the hood of the flying saucer that served as his temporary lodging. They ran into each other's arms and kissed passionately. Sarah and Berta stayed by the tower entrance, to give the lovers privacy.

"Time cannot claim me, my moon and stars. But the distance between us is worse than any hell."

"We haven't much time, my heart," Ïella said between kisses. Vargas pulled her to the saucer, then up the entrance stairs. The hatch closed with a sharp hiss.

"If this saucer's a-rockin', don't come a-knockin'," Berta laughed. "I gotta hand it to you, Redhead Redemption, this was an excellent idea."

"Why, thank you, Berta. That's nice of you to say."

"Sure, but—"

"But?"

"You and me are stuck out here while everyone else is getting laid!"

TWENTY FOUR

TOWER OF ÏSUR
THE ISLAND OF ANTILLIA
THE FOURTH DAY

A VELOCIRAPTOR CREPT through the dense jungle brush looking for the beast that had slain its pack. This monster struck with the same precision and ferocity of the big hunters of the Cretaceous. And it was cunning. The dinosaur paused and sniffed the air. The monster was near. A slender rifle barrel extended from the flora, unnoticed, and rested barely an inch from the Velociraptor's head. The dinosaur never heard the rifle's report, nor felt the bullet pierce its brain. Rogerson stepped from the brush and chambered another round.

"Not so clever, girl." The felled Velociraptor transformed into bright blue grid, then dissipated. The entire jungle followed suit, leaving Rogerson standing alone on a platform in a massive, dome-like room. An array of wide moving disks held orbit near the platform.

"WILL THAT BE ALL TODAY, SIR?" The room spoke with a soft female voice.

"Actually, I was hoping for something a bit more challenging. Big game hunting. Really goddamned big, to be precise."

"UNDERSTOOD, SIR. I BELIEVE I HAVE JUST THE PROGRAM."

The platforms moved into various positions and the vector grid rose from the floor. The jungle smoothly came back to life like a ripple moving across a pond. Rogerson was once again in the Cretaceous Period. The ground shook violently. *Thoom. Thoom. Thoom.* Rogerson pressed himself against a moss-covered tree and cocked his replicated rifle. *THOOM. THOOM. THOOM.* The shock wave nearly shook him off his feet. A Tyrannosaurus Rex stormed through the brush and roared so loud Rogerson winced.

"Now we're in business!"

IN ANOTHER SIMULATED Reality Fabricator, Grimstead panted and wiped the sweat from his eyes. He stood among the twisted, twitching corpses of three Kristian Fowlers dressed in red robes. Grimstead shook his hands to get the blood flowing back to his bludgeon-happy fists. The room was assembled to look like a dungeon. Grimstead had decided to take the real Fowler's idea as a morbid form of inspiration. There wasn't a beautiful woman chained to the stone altar, though. Grimstead couldn't bring the illusion *that* close to home.

"Again," he uttered with a heavy breath.

"SIR, MAY I SUGGEST YOU STOP AND HYDRATE YOURSELF? YOUR BIO-SCANS ARE INDICATING THAT YOU ARE NEARING PEAK PERFORMANCE."

"Again. Five instead of three. And make a few wear a black suit with a red tie."

"VERY WELL, SIR." Five familiar forms materialized and stood leering at the Professor. "SHOULD I REMOVE THE LAST THREE YOU'VE DEFEATED, SIR?"

"Leave them." Grimstead dropped into a fighting stance.

"VERY WELL, SIR."

The Fowlers attacked. Grimstead dipped below a right roundhouse punch and drove his right elbow into the simulation's ribs, then jammed his thumbs into its eye sockets. The faux-Fowler howled in pain. Grimstead moved him around like a macabre marionette before shoving him over the body of one of the fallen doppelgangers. Grimstead then jumped onto that Fowler's chest like a trampoline, and sprang with a leaping punch, shattered the jaw of a third Fowler. Grimstead's attacks were ferocious and primal. A fourth Fowler struck him in the mouth. The simulated fist felt real enough, as did the taste of the non-simulated blood on his tongue. Grimstead spat a thin stream of it to the floor and smiled. *A little pain to clear the mind,* he thought. He attacked once more.

If the Fowlers were cattle, Grimstead was the meat grinder.

Five more bodies were added to the killing floor. Grimstead stood victorious and slightly battered. His opponents were black belts in karate, but only karate. Grimstead's training was much more varied and iron-handed. As good a feeling it was, slaughtering his enemy with his bare hands, it did nothing to quell the burning in his heart.

"SHALL WE CALL IT A DAY, SIR?"

"These... simulations... are they governed by parameters?"

"OF COURSE, SIR. SEVERAL SAFETY PROTOCALS, TO BE EXACT."

"So they hold back?"

"IN A WAY, YES. THEY CANNOT KILL OR MAIM. THEY MAY STRIKE, BUT IT IS QUITE RESERVED, SIR."

"Disable it."

"PARDON, SIR?"

"The safety protocol—deactivate it."

"IMPOSSIBLE. ONLY LORD ÏSUR MAY OVERRIDE THE PROGRAMMING."

"So be it. Another round, then."

"ANOTHER FIVE, SIR?"

"Twenty."

"ARE YOU CERTAIN?"

"Twenty! Now!"

"VERY WELL, SIR." Twenty Fowlers appeared in suits and robes and surrounded Grimstead.

"One more thing." Grimstead stretched his neck.

"SIR?"

"Keep them coming."

THE REAL KRISTIAN Fowler and two Night Cloaks barged onto Ïsur's bridge as if it were theirs. Ïella and her father stood at the monitor console, watching footage from thousands of cameras that were hidden throughout the island and ship. Each display floated in a grid-pattern above the console, rotating continuously through each camera feed. Inactivity remained tiny, while the displays registering notable activity swelled in size for immediate viewing. Ïsur could control each camera by just looking at them. Ïella turned to face Fowler, but Ïsur did not—he simply enlarged the bridge's camera, making Fowler's angered face prominent.

"What is your game?" Fowler said accusingly

"Kristian Fowler, if you would just—" Ïella raised her hand to quell her guest, but was interrupted.

"I am not speaking to *you*, girl," Fowler sneered.

"I beg your pardon? I will not be spoken to in such a manner by anyone! Let alone a mortal speck of a man! In my own home!" Ïella clenched and unclenched her fists, blue bio-energy radiated and then arced between her fingers as she splayed them. The Night Cloaks moved between their master and certain death. Ïsur placed a gentle hand on his daughter's shoulder and smiled reassuringly.

"Beloved daughter. Stand down. I will not tolerate violence from any aboard my ship."

"But, father—this insult!" Ïella protested. Ïsur tightened his grip ever so slightly.

"Leave us. Allow me to personally address our guest's grievance."

Ïella bowed her head in obedience and took her leave. Once again, she was just Ïsur's erratic, half-human child, governed by emotion and callow desire. She could not understand why her father didn't acknowledge the accomplished woman she had become. Her dreams were nothing more than a pin prick in the immensity of Ïsur's grand designs.

"What troubles you, honored guest?" Ïsur's voice was pleasant, but he loomed over them.

"I am under the impression that I am not honored *anything* in your eyes!" Fowler pointed an accusatory finger. "It is evident that you do not want me, or my party, on your ship to learn what you have to teach, to make this forsaken trip worth a damn!"

"What draws you to such conclusions, Herr Fowler? Have I not granted you access to my home? Allowed you to partake in my food and my lodgings? Did I not share my knowledge with you?"

"Only in part. But I seek more!"

"Then seek it elsewhere, if you are so inclined." Ïsur folded is arms across his chest. "I will not stop you from leaving."

"You talk of balance, yet I see you dote upon those peons as if they were invited. Were they?"

"I do not know what you mean."

"Don't play coy with me, sir!" Fowler clenched his jaw. "What do you tell *them* but keep from *me*? What right do they have to learn your secrets that I do not? You claim this vessel can travel through time and space—so I can only surmise that you have seen the future! What does it hold for me? What can you tell me about the fate of the Moonshield Society? Surely you know the answers! Why keep them to yourself? I am beginning to think your boasts of omnipotence are little more than smoke and mirrors!" Ïsur turned to the surveillance grid and folded his hands behind his back.

"I have witnessed the events that brought you all to my door and those that are crafted hence. To divulge what is to come will illicit calamity. My role on Planet Earth is not to force the hand of fate, but to gently guide it from time to time. If I told you of your fate, would life not become pedantic and stale? Would you not try to alter fate to better suit your desires?"

"Of course I would."

"Even if those actions would meet with ruin?"

"As long as the Society prevails, then yes."

"That is why I do not speak of futures, Herr Fowler. As for my so-called prejudiced hosting, observe this screen here, and see why I have little desire to cater to your whims. This is but a simple representation of what your so-called *designs* have wrought." Ïsur blinked, causing a single screen from the console to enlarge and prominently display itself. Fowler looked to the screen with a mix of awe and concern. Grimstead moved across the screen like a man possessed, striking down opponent after opponent without the faintest misstep. Bodies were bludgeoned and broken and strewn across the floor like a gruesome ticker tape parade. He had witnessed his old friend's prowess many times.

"What has this to do with me?" Fowler feigned disinterest, but his eyes were fixed.

"Look," Ïsur pinched his index finger to his thumb, then slowly spread them apart, triggering the screen to widen. The view of the chamber pulled back slightly and Fowler could see just how many bodies littered the ground. He also got a better look at who Grimstead's opponents were. The camera zoomed closer to Grimstead's face and Fowler could see the blood lust in his eyes. Fowler's hands began to tremble slightly. Ïsur turned to his guest.

"Now do you understand?"

EMMA AND SARAH sat together in an empty bar on the entertainment level. Both were perched in concave, white swivel chairs next to a high counter top. They sat in silence while Sarah tugged, looped and twirled Emma's golden locks into a braid. Beside her was a margarita, which, as far she was concerned, was what they used to drink in *antiquity.*

"Paul is alright?" Emma asked between sips of sweet red wine. Behind the counter a slab of sleek, black metal stretched along the entire length of the wall, displaying a three-dimensional menu of countless libations, bottles, jugs and carafes of all shapes and sizes. A swipe of the hand move these images in a scrolling motion, granting access to the vast inventory. Once selected, the bottle, and an appropriate glass, would rise up from the section of the bar directly in front of the patron.

"He's fine. He says he's almost finished with the repairs, but I think he's been done for a while. He's probably just enjoying some quiet time."

"Why don't you use your motherly powers and simply order him here?"

"Honestly?" Sarah blushed. "I'm enjoying this time away from him as well. Is that terrible?"

"It *is* good to get away, sometimes, I suppose." Emma shrugged and raised the glass to her mouth.

"You're talking about Hunky the Space Boy, aren't you?" Sarah snickered. Now it was Emma's turn to blush.

"Whatever *could* you mean?"

"You two have been nearly inseparable since minute-one. Everybody sees the way you both carry on. Don't deny it. I'm a doctor that specializes in human conduct, and sister, you've got a one-way ticket to Hunksville."

"Sometimes, I really have no idea what you are saying."

"Pssh! Act coy all you want. The fact of the matter is—"
The doorway slid open and Orrin walked in with a gentle
smile. "Speak of the man in the devil mask," Sarah finished
under her breath.

"Apologies, but may I request a moment of your time,
Emma?"

"As you can see, I am in the middle of something." Emma
straightened her posture and tried not to let on that she would
very much like to run into Orrin's arms.

"To the contrary, my young bestie, you *are* ready to go!"
Sarah beamed, as she tied off Emma's braid and spun her
around to face Orrin. Emma's hair was now a beautiful golden
rope descending her back.

"Isn't it rude to leave proper company so abruptly," Emma
protested.

"I should go and see where my special-needs husband's
got off to anyway. And I'll remind you to not offend me by
calling me names like *proper*. We're besties. Besties don't do
that." Sarah winked and finished her margarita in a single swig.
As Emma stood, Orrin bowed and extended his hand.

"Care for a walk?"

"On one condition."

"Yes?"

"I lead."

VARGAS SAT ON the wing of an aged, though
completely intact, Lockheed Model 10 Electra. He took a large
gulp from the whiskey bottle Dr. Marrow had handed to him
—much to the viking's surprise—just before entering the
tower. His mind drifted to his old friend Amelia, and how she
had landed there in 1937. *She was a brave soul and noble
warrior*, he recalled. They had many adventures together on
Antillia. She had died—in her sleep, aged ninety years—as a
queen of one of the island's northern kingdoms and rich

beyond measure. Her only regret was not being able to see her husband one last time.

"May the gods smile upon you, little sister," he whispered and raised the bottle. His attention snapped toward the tree line several yards away. There, seemingly out of thin air, stood forty large men in bulky black clothing, which Vargas thought resembled the body armor of the Knights of Wessex.

The viking calmly slid down from his perch and sauntered towards the newcomers, the bottle in his left hand and his right hand resting on the pommel of his sheathed sword. Vargas smiled when he noticed the men tense at his approach. Some reached for their handguns, removing them from their holsters as a precautionary measure. Vargas chuckled.

"Ho, lads! I mean you no harm." He halted and addressed the group with only ten yards between them. "I am Vargas, son of Ragnar. And whom might you be?" His question was met with silence. "I see. Would any of you chatty bastards care for a swig?" He sloshed the contents of the bottle. A particularly tall man stepped forward. Vargas noticed that this man alone displayed a skull pin on the lapel of his overcoat. He wore the same goggles as his comrades, but no face-mask. Instead, he sported a thick handlebar mustache that curved low on his face and then back up, nearly brushing his goggles.

"Sir, we have no desire in your company, nor the contents of your bottle." The man spoke with a thick Scottish accent.

"Are you sure? It's quite good! You must be someone of great import to brandish such an intimidating pin and mustache, sir." Vargas smirked. "What is your name?"

"My name is of no concern."

"I only ask because I offered up my name as a courtesy, and, lest I am mistaken, social protocol mandates that you do the same. Am I mistaken? I understand that there must be some trepidation in engaging in social platitudes with a man who has a sword and a bottle of strong drink, but I can assure you that my boredom and desperate need to behead something will be sated with a simple act of common courtesy." All forty men stared at the lone warrior in disbelief. The mustached man twitched his nose as he processed this random event.

"My name is McKean. These are my men. We are waiting for our superiors to exit that tower and escort them off this accursed island. That is all I will say. Good day to you." McKean saluted and stepped back toward his regiment. Vargas returned the salute and poured some whiskey into his mouth.

"Good day indeed, McKean." Vargas walked back over to the Electra, and took his seat once more.

"Some people," Vargas said aloud to himself, "have no upbringing."

TWENTY FIVE

TOWER OF ÏSUR
THE ISLAND OF ANTILLIA
THE FIFTH DAY

KRISTIAN FOWLER AND Eva Perle met on one of the glass walkways overlooking the garden. They approached one another casually, glancing around to make sure that they were truly alone.

"It's as if he knows what we will do before *we* do," Fowler said, his voice low. They walked slowly, side-by-side. "He has seen the future and is pushing us—*grooming* us—toward something. He has a plan and I would like to know what it is."

"Herr Fowler, let us leave this place. We are not welcome and you have said yourself that we are purposely shunned by those blasphemous space creatures."

"We cannot leave until we have learned something, *found* something, *stolen* something that could make this trip worth while! I'll not disappoint the Society," he whispered urgently. "We've been in this, this *ship* for days now, we've taken all of those useless tours, and we have been treated like absolute simpletons by our gracious hosts. And to what end? We haven't learned a single secret that could benefit the Society. And now,

Alexander and his merry band of fanny bandits have somehow managed to gain the spaceman's affection." He stopped walking, grasped her arm and squeezed. "What we *need* is the very thing we cannot get to freely. The armory! If we could but glance at the inside of that area, get our hands on something, *anything,* that could aid us in bringing this world to heel—" Eva yanked her arm from Fowler's grip and resumed walking.

"I would like to obtain the tesseract engine." She peered down through the glass dome. "Imagine what we could accomplish with the ability to travel through time. We could rewrite history as we see fit."

"I feel there's only enough room for one daring act of thievery on this trip, my pet." He flashed her a cunning smile, which was not returned. Eva was not keen on having her idea dismissed with such cavalier, but she would never let it show. She was, after all, a professional.

"I believe I can enter the room. If I were left with no distractions, I could manipulate the door."

"Perfect. Access the armory, grab what you can and then head out to the tree line just beyond the ship's entrance. McKean and his men have set up camp there, they'll see you safely back to our vessel on the west side of the island. Meanwhile, I will create an appropriate distraction."

"You... you won't be with me?" Panic swept across Eva's face. Fowler took both her hands in his and pulled her close. He softly kissed her forehead, then smiled his infamous crooked smile.

"You need a distraction, my dear. And I have someone who is in need of a good and proper murdering." Eva looked into the garden and tried to hold back tears.

"Please, Herr Fowler, reconsider leaving. I am... with child..." Fowler smiled wickedly, then knelt before her. He took hold of her hips and moved his mouth close to her womb.

"You are the great serpent. The fire giant. The bane of man. Yours will be a wicked reign, my child," he whispered, then lovingly kissed Eva's stomach. He rose and kissed her on the mouth. "Now we have more reason to bring home something shiny and doom-filled. Ïsur fancies himself a playwright of the highest order. Let us find out what will happen when the actors stray from the script."

HAND IN HAND, Emma and Orrin approached the garden's sealed entrance on the tower's subterranean level. As they approached, his mind and body churned. Admittance to the garden by anyone other than its caretakers was forbidden, and even when Orrin or his sister did enter, their time was closely monitored by their father. If he was caught granting access to a human, there would be consequences.

On the other hand, he'd found himself completely taken by this young Earthling, from the moment he'd first seen her. And if she was interested in the garden, then well...

He paused before they reached the door.

"Emma, why did you take us here?"

She blushed. "I would like us to be away from prying eyes. For days now I've longed to express my... feelings for you. We've grown so close, so quickly. And, I know our fathers would not approve. But in that garden, we could be ourselves."

Orrin looked into her eyes and felt his heart swell. He placed his right palm onto the bio-scanner and the door opened. The warm, fragrant air reached them, and Emma sighed. Orrin felt a pang of guilt and concern as they stepped in. His concerns soon melted away as he watched Emma delight in the garden's splendor. He laughed as she began to dance like a little girl in an enchanted grove, spinning and jumping amid the vibrant, sweet-smelling flora. It amazed him how they'd become inseparable when they had been but strangers just days before.

Emma turned to him. "I would very much like to see the Tree of Life."

His smile quickly faded. "That is forbidden, you know that."

Emma pulled him close and kissed him. She kept her face close to his.

"I only want to look upon it! Just a peek! To see with my own eyes the very object that so many, for so long, have surrendered their lives for. It's my father's obsession. Please, Orrin, I only want to know that his life's work, and our journey here, hasn't been for naught." He pulled away from her, a look of hurt on his face.

"Even if the tree did not exist, I should hope that you wouldn't find your journey, or your time spent with me, wasted." Emma's eyes did not leave his, and they stood in silence for several moments. "Come then, I will show you." He led her down a luscious path bordered with exotic flowers, some long extinct and some yet to be discovered. The lovers soon arrived at a small, verdant grove with a single tree at the center. Emma gasped at the sight of it—the tree was like nothing she had ever seen before. Thick and knobby, with long twisting boughs reaching out in every direction. The tree cast a deep golden aura and the air around it seemed to hum. As they drew closer, Emma saw radiant golden orbs hidden among the tree's broad, emerald green leaves.

"Oh, thank you my dearest," she whispered. "It is simply beyond compare!"

"Well, compared to you," Orrin whispered, his voice husky, "it is nothing." Her whole body throbbed with excitement. She reached for Orrin and pulled him down to sit with her against the trunk of the tree. They began kissing passionately, the whole of their essence clouded within a golden haze. Clothing was shed like snake skin. Nothing else existed outside of that encased Eden. Nothing else mattered.

FOWLER QUIETLY ENTERED the crew sleeping

quarters, a futuristic-looking barracks, with shiny metallic bunk beds, showers, and latrines all occupying the same general area. He looked over at the bunks, where his guards should have been waiting on their next order. Instead, he spotted them sitting, shirtless, at a metal card table in the center of the room. Around the table also sat Berta, Dr. Marrow and two CCs. They were engaged in a seemingly one-sided game of strip poker. Fuming, Fowler carefully approached the table through the darkened room, stepping over numerous empty whiskey bottles, stamped out cigars and discarded articles of clothing. He finally stood in a silent rage behind his semi-clad insubordinate men.

"Sucks that us *hired* help have to sleep in these stupid post-modern barracks, while everyone else gets, well, whatever everyone else got," Berta complained as she shuffled the deck of cards. "Speaking of insult, who's in? I refuse to believe I haven't lost a single hand or peeled off a single piece of clothing because of luck. I damn sure know it wasn't skill. What gives? You two boys in black lost your shirts and boots early on, the tampon boys here are practically naked and ol' Marrow's down to his tighty whiteys! And I've still got *aaall* these clothes to take off!"

"Gotta be the luck of the draw, Berta," Marrow grinned as he lit a cigar. "Right, boys?" The others murmured their agreement, not wanting to admit they had been throwing each hand to keep the burly gal covered up.

Fowler cleared his throat and everyone jumped.

"How is it that I leave two of my highly-trained mercenary bodyguards alone for *one hour* and return to find them drunk, half-naked and fraternizing with the enemy?!"

The two guards quickly stood to attention. One began to sway a bit, his balance compromised. Fowler placed a hand on his shoulder to steady him.

"You two are Night Cloaks! Moonshield's crimson blades! I am... *very* put out! Get dressed, come with me and be grateful that our host has banned violence!" Fowler stormed out of the room with his shamed lackeys scrambling behind him. The others turned back to their game without skipping a beat.

"Did you hear me, jackasses, who's in?" Berta boomed. "You all have plenty of clothes left and mamma wants to see some danglers!"

EMMA'S HEAD ROSE and fell on Orrin's chest as they embraced beneath the Tree of Life. Orrin stared at the golden orbs that hung overhead and frowned. Emma kissed his chest and neck, but the frown remained.

"What could possibly trouble you at a time like this?" Orrin sighed and kissed the top of her head.

"I have been terrible to my sister. And to that outsider whom she loves. Our father forbade us from attaching ourselves to mortals, *'the fragile and finite'*, as he calls them. It is as though he sometimes forgets that my sister and I are half human."

"Your mother was a mortal woman?" Emma was genuinely surprised.

"They met over a century ago. They spent many happy years together."

"What... happened to her?"

"The very thing that happens to each of you. Old age claimed her, despite my father's constant pleas that she partake of the fruit above us. She refused him time and again, saying that she did not want to be *'robbed of the human experience'*. My mother could not be swayed. She knew immortality was not for everyone. To my father's dismay, she grew old and passed away in his never-changing arms. He was never the same after that day. I suppose he discouraged us from coexisting with mortals for that very reason."

"That shouldn't be his decision to make."

"His only intention was to protect us. Immortality takes

lifetimes to get used to." A thin smile crossed his lips. Emma kissed them.

"A comedian." She smiled. "I could lay like this forever."

"As could I," he sighed. "We must never take moments like this for granted. Time is fleeting." Emma kissed him once more.

"It doesn't have to be."

TWENTY SIX

GRIMSTEAD STOOD IN one of the tower's many artifact chambers alongside Wesley and Sarah. Together, they perused the museum-like displays of art, technology, and other representations of Planet Earth that Ïsur had collected over eons. Each exhibit was set up to show progression from oldest to newest, for succinct comparison. The three kept up a lively discussion as they strolled through the rooms, Grimstead finding himself in continuous awe of the twentieth century and beyond.

"It's remarkable how, over centuries, Humankind has pursued advancement in so many new and exciting ways, and yet, its interests always boil down to the same creature comforts, if you will."

Sarah smiled, but before she could comment, noticed that Wesley was speaking into his shirt pocket. "Pardon me a moment, Professor." She crossed the room and tapped her husband on the shoulder. "What are the two of you conspiring about?" Wesley immediately tried to look nonchalant.

"Hm? Oh, *nothing*," he replied loudly, then pulled his wife in close. "I've had Connie record, scan and process everything that we've come across," he whispered, looking around to make sure no one was listening. "We have an abundance of alien tech schematics now. I'm not really sure just what we can do with it all yet, but, it couldn't hurt to have it."

He paused to glance around the room again. "I don't know if we're being listened to. I certainly wouldn't want to upset any, shall we say, persons of a melt-your-face-with-a-thought variety." He winked.

Sarah sighed. "Whatever you say, dear." She returned to the Professor, who was engrossed in the *Marvels of Modern Broadcasting!* display. It featured a series of devices used for broadcasting television programs throughout the ages, from the Baird *Televisor* of the 1920s to the floating 3D holographic models of the early 2100s. Each played an infinite loop of clips from programs that were popular in each corresponding era.

"You look concerned, Professor. I'm sure this is all very peculiar for you, witnessing things that were invented long after your time. The world was very different in the 1800s. It must be a strange dose of culture shock." Sarah wasn't sure if her words were comforting or condescending. Grimstead's eyes never moved from the illuminated screens.

"After the past few weeks I've had, I doubt I'll ever be surprised again." He smiled. "Actually, it rather makes sense that we would progress to mass-produced, scripted farce. What perplexes me, however, is how the content of these broadcasts have... degraded... into mindless exhibitionism. Take the following specimens from the United States as an example." He pointed to a black and white set. "Here we have an American family going through their daily lives. They seem a decent lot, though they named their child after a semi-aquatic rodent. Now look at this color unit from the 1970s. It is showing the tale of a man who is pretending to be a foppish dandy in order to live in the same quarters with two women. But he makes no effort to attempt to court either one. And look how tight and scant their clothes are! Rather inconvenient." Grimstead next pointed to an HDTV from the twenty-first century. "I've also been trying to assess the antics of this rotund jabber-mouthed cretin for quite some time I'm afraid, and I'm *still* not entirely certain of what a Honey Boo-Boo is. If this is entertainment, then my outlook for America is grim!"

The tirade caused Sarah to burst out laughing and it wasn't long before Grimstead joined in. They laughed heartily for a good few moments. *It feels good to laugh*, he thought. It had been far too long since he had been able to open himself up to something lighthearted.

"No worries, Professor, the apocalypse pretty much wiped the slate of prime-time television clean." Sarah smiled. "There are several pre-war examples of technology and society that survived, but not a great deal of it was useful. New Atlantis has a myriad of televised broadcasts that, to be honest, haven't really evolved much out of the exhibitionism you've mentioned."

"So there *is* no hope after all," he chuckled.

The museum's main entrance opened and Kristian Fowler entered with his mostly sober underlings in tow.

"There you are, Alexander! I should have know I'd find you among the relics." The three approached Grimstead and Sarah. Fowler paused at the broadcast exhibit and marveled for a moment. "Oh, look, a program about *ghost* hunting. Perhaps one day they'll find our shades in some ramshackle hotel room, eh?"

"What do you want, Fowler?" Grimstead growled, stepping between Sarah and his enemy.

"I would simply like to have a conversation with my old friend Alex. In private. Would you mind asking this vision of beauty and her bumbling husband to leave us be? I'll send my two visions of stupidity out with them."

"Why would two men who are actively seeking to kill each other engage in formal conversation?" Fowler smiled and lifted his head wistfully.

"As my dear Gran Gran used to say, *'Homicide sollte nie auf Höflichkeit verletzen'*"

"Which means?"

"Homicide should never infringe on civility."

"German is such a comforting language." Grimstead nodded to Wesley and Sarah, indicating that it was alright for them to leave.

"Isn't it though?" Fowler replied, shooing his Night Cloaks.

"You sure about this, Professor?" Wesley eyed Fowler suspiciously.

"I am, Doctor, thank you both." Grimstead offered a deep nod before turning his attention back to Fowler with a false smile. "Now that we are civil, what do you want?"

"Why would that affluent white gentleman adopt two colored children?" Fowler wondered aloud, his attention drawn to a television set from the 1980s. "Perhaps he means to bugger them?"

"Fowler."

"Hm? Oh, I do apologize. These programs are addictive. Shall we move on to another display? Perhaps there is an exhibit of faulty Scottish dungeon architecture." Grimstead clenched his fists.

"I'll have you know that it has been absolutely infuriating to me that I haven't been allowed to kill you," he muttered. Fowler responded with an exaggerated pout and several patronizing tongue clicks.

"Do you recall how I caused the demise of the only beautiful thing you've ever had?" Grimstead could feel the blood rushing to his temples. His chest began to ache.

"*Do* you?"

"I. Do."

"I figured as much. *Weeell*, I would like to apologize for the misunderstanding. I remember back to when I was a member of The Order. Before I was so abruptly removed."

"We removed you of rank because you were a damned traitor! You fed the Moonshield Society explicitly vital and confidential information! And what of this *misunderstanding*? I do not recall misunderstanding your betrayal or my vow to end you, make no mistake."

"As I said, I remember being at those meetings, listening to you all blather on and on, and all the while I was being swept away with the idea of drawing an ancient squid-monster into that scrumptious Lilly of yours. She was so pure and beautiful. Oh, how I wanted so badly to do it. Every time my eyes fell upon her, I wanted more and more to defile her. I became obsessed. Day and night I thought of nothing but her perfect breasts and how wonderfully they would cradle the Eye of Goy Gothog." Fowler closed his eyes in reverie, an obnoxious smile spreading across his face. Grimstead remained absolutely still. "As for that misunderstanding I mentioned? Well, I was led to believe, and I *did* truly believe, that the essence of the deity would be absorbed into Lilly—in spirit only. I had no intention of anything more. I wanted to corrupt her mind and soul with an ancient evil, then corrupt her body with my own. It simply never occurred to me that Goy Gothog would need to practically obliterate her in order to attain proper absorption. Really, who could see *that* coming?" He chuckled as if he'd just heard a naughty joke.

Grimstead felt himself plunge into shock, his fingers went numb, his ears started ringing.

"*That*? That is your fabled misunderstanding?!" He heard his own voice, but could not feel his lips moving. "THAT?!"

"Well, in part," Fowler spoke calmly. "The true misconception is with whom you lay blame. I merely gave her limitless power. It wasn't I who pulled the trigger that ended her life. That was your precious Hargraves' doing." Fowler strode toward the museum's entrance. The door retracted and he paused at the threshold. "Think on it, old friend."

"Why... why would you say such things? Haven't you done enough?" Grimstead's voice was barely audible in the large room.

"You've read Sun Tsu, old boy." Fowler winked. "And you, of all people, should know that I'm a *perfect* bastard."

ÏSUR STOOD AT the monitor console and watched the drama unfold before him. He felt a swell of guilt mingle with the sense of purpose he held in his heart. He thought of his wife and children. He thought of poor Alexander Grimstead and the others, and the imperceptible strings that bound them.

It was not pleasing, nor rewarding, to play god. Ïsur hung his head.

"For balance to be maintained, no act is too monstrous."

TWENTY SEVEN

THAT NIGHT, GRIMSTEAD did not dream of his beloved. He instead dreamed that he was pushing his thumbs so deep into Kristian Fowler's eye sockets that they reached his brain. Then he located Gran Gran Fowler and repeated the process.

TWENTY EIGHT

TOWER OF ÏSUR
THE ISLAND OF ANTILLIA
THE SIXTH DAY

"**I BELIEVE THAT** we should take our leave soon," Captain Rogerson confided to the Professor over re-fabricated eggs and sausage in the commissary. He kept his voice low even though they were the only two present at breakfast. "It is now our sixth morning here and we've little more than tales to bring back with us. I see you've got your revolver on you. Good." He patted his rifle. "I'm relieved that I'm not the only one who feels something looming, and with those Moonshield imbeciles lurking about, who knows what could happen."

"Agreed."

Grimstead, still perturbed by his little chat with Fowler, had barely touched the food he'd taken. "Have you heard from Douglas? Wasn't he supposed to meet us for breakfast?"

"I suspect he's spent the morning with Ïsur, testing the man's tolerance for inane banter, no doubt." Rogerson finished his cup of coffee and belched louder than he anticipated.

"Well done."

"Thank you. Shall we see about saving Ïsur from our mad

scientist?"

"We can certainly try." Grimstead wiped his mouth on a napkin then rose from his chair. They strolled out onto the ship's promenade. "I only hope Douglas doesn't give us too much grief about—"

Ïella rounded the corner ahead of them with great speed, an expression of dread twisting her face. Her eyes widened when she saw the pair.

"You must come with me! Quickly! There is trouble on the bridge!"

The three ran to the glass lift and jumped inside. Before they had fully ascended into the room, Grimstead saw Fowler confronting Ïsur.

"Dammit!" he reached for his pistol. As soon as the lift doors opened, Rogerson and Grimstead sprang out ahead of Ïella, weapons at the ready. Fowler was standing mere inches from the ancient alien, shouting, and with arms outstretched. Ïsur was seated, a blank expression across his face. All present knew Ïsur could swat Fowler like a fly if that was his desire, but none could fathom why he allowed his rant to continue unabated. Emma, Orrin, Dr. McParland and the Adamses were also present, standing to the right of the control display, frozen in shock. Fowler's two Night Cloaks raised their Borchardt C-93 semi-automatic pistols at the sight of the Captain and the Professor. Ïsur raised a hand, causing Fowler to flinch.

"No. Weapons." They complied hesitantly.

"What are you attempting to do here, idiot?" Grimstead demanded.

"I am trying to find out why our host has allowed that decrepit madman over there—" He gestured with his eyes toward Dr. McParland.

"Hello!" McParland shouted and waved.

Fowler grimaced. "Why he has extended an invitation for *him* to stay here indefinitely but has not offered the same to the members of my expedition."

"You're staying?" Rogerson interjected. "But why, Douglas?"

"*So* much to learn, Robert! Lord Ïsur has made it abundantly clear that though my quest for immortality was validated, I am forbidden to partake in the fruit—and at my age, I do not anticipate living long enough to visit again. And I've many, many questions. I am fulfilled on so many levels, you see. My dream, my life's work have come to fruition. Everything I've ever done has lead me to this point. So I'll stay and learn all I may while I may."

Rogerson turned to Emma. "You're alright with this?"

"What say do I have in the matter?" Her face twinged with sadness and anger. "You know my father."

"Hello?! Remember *my* say in the matter?" Fowler shouted. "He stays, I leave. Where is your precious balance, Ïsur, old scratch?"

"Certain events must come to pass in order for particular outcomes to manifest," the alien stated, his expression unchanging. Grimstead's brow furrowed. That statement sounded terribly familiar. "Free will is only so free," he continued. "Besides, Fowler, we both know that you are not here for knowledge." Fowler's eyes grew wide. He opened his mouth to protest but a loud, computerized voice interrupted the debacle.

"ATTENTION. ALARM. A BREECH HAS OCCURRED ON LEVEL 2-E. SEND SECURITY PERSONEL IMMEDIATELY."

"Eva," Fowler said under his breath. "It's about damned time."

The voice continued to loop its warning.

"2-E!" Orrin cried. "The Armory!"

Ïsur's expression still did not change. He pressed a button on the console in front of him, activating the security camera display. Everyone looked and there was a collective gasp. Inside the armory, Eva Perle and two Night Cloaks were frantically grabbing weapons off racks and stuffing them into large sea bags. Rifles, pistols, unidentified ordinance—anything that managed to fit. Eva paused at a small display case containing four vials of viscous, colored liquid—amber, green, red and black—and stuffed them into her bag as well. Several assist-bots wheeled in, clamps open and ready to strike, but were greeted by a hail of bullets. Eva lashed at them with her mind, shattering and scattering every last bot in a flurry of invisible energy. Then she and the Night Cloaks fled with the overstuffed bags. Each time they were confronted with a secured door, Eva's impressive telekinetic powers tore it down. Fowler smiled. *Mission almost accomplished.* He only had to ensure the distraction continued.

"Isur! Why are you just sitting there?! By the time we reach them, they'll be outside!" Rogerson exclaimed. "At least let me contact my crew?" Isur remained still and silent. Orrin rushed over to the Captain, took him by the arm and led him over to another console, where he pressed a green button.

"Speak," Orrin commanded, his voice bellowing throughout the ship.

"This is Captain Rogerson speaking. All hands, arm yourselves and meet me outside on the double! Keep your eyes peeled for a spooky blond and her goons in black. If you see them, *stop them!*" He nodded and Orrin pressed the green button once more. Without another word, Rogerson drew his rifle and marched past the others into the lift, then disappeared down into the ship.

"Sh-should we go with him?" Wesley asked nervously. Grimstead shook his head, his eyes still on Fowler.

"I think it would be better that you stay, Doctor."

"There is no balance here! Only chaos!" Fowler laughed maniacally, throwing his hands up into the air. "This must be rectified! If I cannot stay..." He whirled around, quickly drawing his semi-automatic pistol and fired three rounds into Dr. McParland's chest. "...then *no one* stays!"

McParland hit the floor hard.

"POPPA!" Emma screamed, dropping to her knees to cradle him. Grimstead lunged at Fowler, sinking an elbow deep into his chest and pinning him to one of the consoles. Fowler pressed the muzzle against Grimstead's temple and clenched his jaw in an angry smile. Ïsur raised his right hand causing the pistol to spring from Fowler's grip and dismantle in mid air.

"Bloody showoff!" Fowler grunted, and shoved Grimstead off.

Emma looked down at her father; blood poured from each of his wounds, surging forth with every beat of his weakening heart.

"Poppa! No, Poppa, please! Don't die!" she sobbed. The Doctor gently grasped her arm and looked up into his daughter's eyes.

"...proud. So proud..." He smiled, despite the blood pooling in his mouth. "Will... try... very hard... to haunt you."

And then, Douglas McParland, inventor, mad scientist, loving father, was no more. Emma held him tight and wept. Orrin fell to his knees, embracing them both, and wept along with her.

Ïsur slowly stood.

"Alexander Grimstead. I hereby lift the ban. You may engage in violence whenever you deem fit."

Without hesitation, Grimstead drew his revolver and planted a single bullet into the brain pan of each present Night Cloak, then trained his sights on the self-proclaimed perfect bastard.

Finally.

"Come on, then," Fowler taunted, stretching his neck. He sneered and rolled up his sleeves, revealing his infamous tattooed skin. Grimstead felt his blood lust intensify with every beat of his own heart. He tossed the revolver to the floor and moved himself into a ready stance.

"As you wish."

WHEN ROGERSON REACHED the ship's airlock shaft, he was relieved to find Berta, The Swede, Dr. Marrow and the CCs waiting for him. There was no time for briefing, the crew dutifully followed their captain through the corridor and back into the humid jungle air. As the exterior door of the ship rose open, it revealed the broad, grinning face of their viking companion. As promised, he had waited there for the group's return. He was not alone, though. Thirty well-armored Night Cloaks, each brandishing a semi-automatic pistol and saber, stood stoic several yards behind him.

"Hail, Rogerson!" Vargas shouted.

"Vargas, my friend!" The Captain smiled and they embraced forearms. "What is all this?" He gestured at the ominous group.

"Ah." He drew close. "That yellow-haired witch ordered McKean and his brutes to stand guard and thwart any means of pursuit. They were forty strong at the start, but she took ten along with her as she fled to the west. I would have intervened, however, those who remained chose to stand with me here, silent as the grave. They have not made any attempt to attack."

"Who the blazes is McKean?" Marrow grumbled.

"They *are* the enemy," Rogerson informed the viking. Vargas stepped back and unsheathed his sword.

"Is that so?" His face split into a smile. "I was hoping you'd say that!" He turned and charged. The Night Cloaks responded by unleashing a hail of bullets on the group.

"Take cover!" Rogerson ordered, as he ran from the Tower and jumped behind one of the nearest downed aircraft. His crew followed suit, barely having time to fortify themselves before bullets began to rain against the hulls. Vargas fell to his knees, his body riddled with bullet holes.

McKean approached the bleeding viking and pressed a gun to his forehead.

"Surrender, or I will end this savage's life!" Vargas grabbed his attacker's chest plate and pulled him onto his sword with a grunt.

"Savage? I offer you drink and you name me savage?" Blood gushed from McKean's mouth as Vargas pulled him close. "That mustache looks terrible on you. I've been wanting to tell you that." He pulled the blade from the body and charged again. His bullet wounds were already healed and he was quite eager to spread the hurt around. He ran straight into a throng of Night Cloaks and dispatched them one by one.

"Pin them down!" Rogerson commanded from behind a circular-shaped vessel. The CCs—half hiding behind a B-52 Bomber and the other half behind a mangled private jet—were firing a constant volley at the Night Cloaks. Their bullets, however, were proving to be ineffective against the Cloak's seemingly impenetrable body armor.

Berta fired her Light Bringer into the crowd, hitting one of the guards dead-on. Not only did the laser pack enough power to punch through his armor, but he also caught fire.

"Hell yeah! Critical shot!" She pumped her fist into the air. "Bring it on, bitches!"

Marrow pulled a bottle of whiskey and gauze from his satchel.

"My last goddamn bottle!" He took two mouthfuls then shoved the gauze onto the bottle's neck. He mumbled angrily as he fumbled for his matches. The gauze was lit. He lobbed it overhead with a silent apology to Bacchus, the god of drink. The bottle exploded in the moist mossy ground and barely caused a flinch. "I give up."

The Night Cloaks drew their sabers and charged. Together, they rushed towards the *Skidbladnir* crew with a roar. Rogerson jumped up and rallied his own men for their fight.

"Hold! Hoooold! Ready yourselves!"

"We're boned," Berta said, flatly. The Swede stepped forward and threw his bearded ax toward the charging fighters, hitting one with so much force that he was sent crashing backward through the air—and into several others. The downed Night Cloaks immediately cast off their dead comrade and scrambled to their feet.

"Ah, to hell with it," Rogerson sighed He raised his rifle into the air. "Charge!"

Just then, they all heard the sound of a voice bellowing from the distance. Everyone paused mid-fight to listen as it drew closer. Two Thunderbirds burst forth from the trees, with a young man standing on their backs, one foot on each. He was topless, and wore a red sash around his head, which flapped wildly in the breeze. The newcomers galloped swiftly toward the Captain. Directly toward him, in fact.

"YyyyyyAAAAH!" The half-naked lad cried, yanking back with full-force on the four leather belts that he had fashioned as reigns. Rogerson leaped out of the way, rolling as he hit the ground. The birds came to a squawking halt.

"Wh-who the devil are you?!"

"Crimson Crewman Finnbar Stratton, reporting for duty, sir!"

GRIMSTEAD LUNGED AT Fowler like a wolf to its prey, striking him on the right side of his face. The blow caught Fowler entirely by surprise, and he fell back against the console. Grimstead followed quickly with a roundhouse kick that caught his adversary in the ribs. Fowler dropped to the floor, coughing.

"A... lucky... shot," he gasped, slumping into the console. He flashed a blood-tinged smile. Grimstead moved again into a ready stance. Unnoticed by the old rivals, Ïsur silently moved nearer to the others on the lower level of the bridge and pressed a button on one of the consoles. Eight assist-bots came rushing onto the bridge in single file.

"Initiate protocol six-three-one." The robots immediately

seized Ïella and Orrin—one bot on each limb—and ushered them to the door.

"What is the meaning of this, father?!" Ïella shouted.

"Emma! My love!" Orrin cried, struggling to free himself from the bots' iron-like grip. The four bots responded by lifting him several inches off the ground.

"My children, I must protect you. My legacy." Ïsur turned to address the others. "Be advised, I will activate the tesseract engine immanently. We will be leaving this era. If you wish to remain in the year 1898, I suggest that you leave my island with haste."

"Whaa?!" Wesley cried, exchanging a look of panic with his wife. "H-how long do we have?"

Sarah gasped, clutching her husband's arm. "Paul!"

"Use the lift behind you in order to access the roof. Your means of escape will be waiting there."

"How LONG?!" Wesley shouted. Ïsur turned back to his control panel in silence.

"Take Emma and Sarah to the dirigible-car. Warn the others!" Grimstead roared from above.

"What about my father?!"

"His body will be attended to," Ïsur nodded. "He spent his entire life in search of my home—it is only fitting that he is interred here." Sarah gently pulled Emma away from her father's body.

"Come on, sweetie, we have to go," she whispered. Emma nodded solemnly as she slowly stood, and they ran to the rooftop lift.

Wesley spun on his heels when he noticed Grimstead was not following.

"What about you?"

Alexander turned to meet his friend's gaze. He looked almost jovial.

"Leave me, I've got what I want right here!" he growled, just before Fowler tackled him to the ground. Fowler sat on his chest and punched him several times in the face.

"I love you, too, Alex!" he cooed.

Wesley hesitated at the door of the lift. He really wanted to leap to Grimstead's side, but he knew he had little time to spare. He reluctantly jabbed the up button with his thumb and hoped for the best.

Grimstead arched his back and threw Fowler off him, then jumped to his feet.

"Get up, filth."

Chuckling, Fowler stood up slowly and took a wide fighting stance.

"Careful now, you may hurt my feelings."

The two circled one another for what seemed like eons; they tried desperately to make contact. A flurry of attacks erupted from both men, their nearly-matched skills canceling the other's out with every move. When it came to technique, the men could practically mirror one another, but Fowler had never prided himself on his commitment to the art of fighting. He had never been Master Ng's prized pupil. That *superfluous* title belonged to Grimstead alone. Fowler, on the other hand… if he could exploit something or some*one* to gain an edge, he would. If he could cheat his way to victory, even better.

Fowler knew it was only a matter of time before Grimstead's superior skill would overwhelm him. There was always a chance, however, and he enjoyed the thrill of possibility.

Fowler threw a right roundhouse kick at Grimstead's face, and as he moved to block it, Fowler used the momentary distraction to slip his left hand down behind his back to the knife sheathed inside his trousers. Then, using the centrifugal force of Grimstead's block to spin his blade hand, he slashed him across the stomach. Grimstead stumbled backwards in shock. His adrenaline levels were soaring and he had barely felt the blade's touch. He looked down to access the damage: the cut had not been deep, but resulted in a thin, crimson line forming across his vest. He touched his fingertips to the wound and watched in disbelief and shame as they grew bloody. He felt like a fool. He heard Fowler step closer, the tip of the blade coming into view. Grimstead stared at it, feeling as if he were trapped in a bad dream. The curved blade began to sway back and forth in front of his eyes, taunting him. He suddenly made the connection. This was the same knife that had ended Lilly's life. He stood, eyes fixed on the blade, as if he were hypnotized, and let out a sharp breath. Fowler grinned manically, dancing the blade in elegant loops.

"Remember me?" he trilled, then lunged.

ORRIN CONTINUED TO fight against his robot captors as they transported him to a yet unknown location. Apparently, Ïella had been ushered off to an entirely different location, which angered him further.

"Release me this instant!" he roared. They turned down yet another corridor.

"*BZZT*. Negative, master." The bot latched to Orrin's left arm stated in a static-laden voice. "Protocol—*bzzt*—six-three-one."

"So I heard. What is protocol six-three-one, exactly?"

"The overseer indicated that—initiate quote—*My son will comprehend—BZZT—when he sees it*. Terminate quote." They rounded another corner and the bots abruptly released Orrin in front of a massive door. One of them shoved a green, canvas rucksack into his hands. As they rolled away, Orrin looked at the door and laughed.

He understood completely.

THE BATTLE OUTSIDE of Ïsur's tower continued to rage. It was one of flashing blades, pistols, gouging fingers, fists and talons. Thanks to Finnbar Stratton's tamed Thunderbirds

—whom he had affectionately named Goldie and Rosie—the *Skidbladnir* crew gained an unexpected advantage over their enemy. The birds galloped through the battleground at Finn's direction, savagely tearing into, and through, the armor of every Night Cloak in their path. The Swede and Berta each lifted a Night Cloak high above their heads and, on the count of three, threw them up into each other. The men collided and then landed with a thud.

"Romance!" Berta laughed.

Captain Rogerson was putting his seemingly endless warfare repertoire to good use, felling foe after foe with his rifle and large Bowie knife with great enthusiasm. This was a dance he knew all the steps to. A Night Cloak aimed his gun at Rogerson and squeezed the trigger.

"Captain!" A CC dove into the line of fire, taking the bullet to his chest.

"Damn it!" Rogerson shouted. That made four CCs lost in this battle alone. He quickly fired his rifle, hitting his would-be assailant square between the goggle lenses. As the Night Cloak fell, a cold realization swept over the Captain; that for all of their efforts, he and his comrades were still greatly outnumbered, and it was likely that they would succumb after all. Rogerson smiled and chambered another round.

A spray of rapid gun fire erupted from above, striking down a score of Night Cloaks.

"Hit the deck!" Rogerson screamed as he threw himself to the ground. The remaining crew members followed suit, except for Finnbar, who halted the girls and braced for impact. The Captain looked up and saw a large, shimmering object hovering over the battlefield like a guardian angel. Beneath its hull were twin machine guns, each rotating in a separate direction and dispensing fifty-caliber rounds with extreme precision. It was the newly-repaired Adams exploration vessel, with Paul at the helm.

Three of the surviving Night Cloaks broke from the

carnage and fled. Vargas caught sight of their escape and ran after them with super-human speed. He raced up the wing of a nearby jet, then leaped up and out and landed on the first Night Cloak in the pack, smashing him to the ground. The viking immediately jumped up and spun so that his sword plunged directly into the torso of the second Night Cloak. The final Night Cloak stopped and stood his ground. He aimed a trembling pistol at Vargas' head. He squeezed the trigger, but the gun was empty. Vargas turned to him and motioned that he reload.

"I offer you this courtesy so that you may meet your gods as a warrior and not a shivering kitten." Vargas grinned as he pulled his sword from the second Night Cloak's still-twitching body. "It is an empty gesture, as you cannot harm me. You will see that your weapon is as impotent as your heart. I, on the other hand, will not cease until this blade is bathed in your blood. I will not yield until you and your doomed brethren are no more than a stain on an empty battlefield. I am a nightmare, you see. A nightmare dressed as a man. Since your first breath of life, you were destined to quiver on this blade. So please, fill your useless weapon, raise your useless hand and squeeze your useless finger. Then make peace with whatever lie you subscribe to." He rolled his shoulders and cracked his neck while he waited. The Night Cloak managed to reload despite his trembling fingers. He again aimed at Vargas, then abruptly tore away his face guard, placed the barrel into his own mouth and pulled the trigger. Vargas spat upon his body.

"Go, then. As a kitten."

GRIMSTEAD SHIFTED HIS body at precisely the last moment, allowing the knife to pass his face. He quickly smashed his forearms into both sides of Fowler's left arm: right at the wrist, left at the elbow. The knife clattered to the floor. The impact had ripped Fowler's elbow from the joint.

Grimstead rallied himself instantly, pummeling fist after fist into his opponent's face and chest. With each successive blow, the memories of that tragic day grew more intense. His whole body was alight with anger and grief, every fiber of his being became intent on shattering every bone in this man's body. All reason had left him, he struck Fowler again and again with the ferocity of a wild animal. He grabbed Fowler by the head and drove a knee into his face, then his other knee, then, finally, a crushing left elbow down on the back of his head.

Fowler flopped down to his hands and knees. Blood poured from his mouth and nose, his eyes swelling shut. He coughed and sent a meaty pulp splattering across the floor. Then he raised his battered head and smiled.

"This... won't bring her back... you know," he said through shattered teeth. "And I'm quite sure that I needed whatever it was I just spat out." Grimstead knelt before his old friend and looked him directly in the eye. Without a word, he placed his hands upon his throat and squeezed until the light from his bulging eyes faded. Fowler's cocky smile remained.

"I know it won't," he whispered. "It doesn't have to." Grimstead slowly rose to his feet and stared at Kristian Fowler's corpse for just a moment before walking to the lift. He hesitated, then quickly ran back to the lifeless body, grasped Fowler's head between his hands and twisted until he heard a sharp crack. "Just in case."

THE EXPLORER HOVERED above the carnage, having successfully assisted in disposing of every last Night Cloak. Berta waved.

"You're late you little prick!" The PA system popped and squealed to life.

"Sorry for the delay, everybody. Traffic was hell." A wave of intense energy suddenly rippled across the sky, causing the entire island to tremble. "Uh, th-that wasn't me!"

Up on the tower's terrace, Sarah and Emma sat in the dirigible as Wesley attempted to bring the engine to life when they felt the disturbance. He hopped out of the vehicle, peered over the side of the tower and spotted his son.

"Sweet Monkey Bourbon! It's Paul!"

"Ohmigosh!" Sarah squealed, jumping out and running over see for herself. Wesley pulled Connie's device from his breast pocket.

"Connie! Patch me into the *Explorer's* PA!"

"Sure thing, boss. Whenever you're ready."

"Gah! P-Paul, this is your father. Land the *Explorer* and let those people on! That energy surge we just felt must be Ïsur revving the tesseract engine! If we're not off this island fast, we'll be stuck in who-the-hell-knows when!"

"Tesseract engine?! Are you freaking kidding me?! How did—"

"Paul! Now!"

"FINE."

Paul landed the craft and opened the bay doors at the rear before popping open the cockpit hatch. He stood on the seat and pointed towards the stern.

"Everyone, that way! Hurry!"

Berta, The Swede, and the six remaining CCs ran towards the vessel as another wave of energy shook the island. Finnbar, Rosie and Goldie intercepted Captain Rogerson as he made his way over to the bay.

"Sir! Who's what is revving?"

"No time for explanations, son, get on board! And take those birds with you. They saved our skins, and I haven't the fortitude to tell them to git."

"You hear that, girls? You get to keep me!" Finnbar grinned. The Thunderbirds clacked their massive beaks as though they shared their master's elation.

Rogerson paused and scanned the battlefield. "Where the devil is Marrow, dammit!" A small pile of bodies to his left began to move. A hand sprang up from between the legs of a fallen Night Cloak. "Swede! Over there!" Rogerson ordered. The Swede ran over and tossed the bodies aside, uncovering a relatively unscathed Dr. Marrow. He rose to his feet and wiped his bloody hands off on his slacks. Then he looked up at Paul and laughed.

"Well what do you know! The little turd made it after all!" Paul responded by flipping him the bird.

Berta made her way into the cockpit and plucked Paul out of the pilot's seat.

"I'm the only one who can fly this clunky bitch the way we need. Back seat, runt." To Berta's surprise, Paul complied without any fuss.

Wesley's voice blared through the PA again. "Do I need to explain again why we have to HURRY THE HELL UP?!"

Rogerson turned to Vargas and they clasped forearms. "Can I convince you to come with us, my friend?"

"As long as my heart remains in that tower, so shall I," he replied. "You have proven yourself a mighty warrior, worthy of Asgard. Farewell, Robert Rogerson."

"Farewell, Vargas Ragnarson. We owe you our lives."

Wesley attempted to fire up the auto-dirigible once more. The engine sputtered and clanged before finally steadying. Sarah placed her hand on her husband's.

"If we leave the island, we'll be stuck in the nineteenth century, you know that." Wesley lifted her hand to his mouth and kissed it.

"If we stay, who knows where or when we'll end up? It isn't like we can get back to our era now. We've been evicted! But imagine what we could do in *this* era with the technology we have? We could do very well for ourselves."

"Or be burned at the stake for witchcraft," Sarah laughed.

"Wrong century, love." Wesley reached into his utility belt pocket, brought out the leather aviator's cap and pulled it tight onto his head.

"I know, hun. I was just—oh, not *that* hat again!" Wesley winked at her and flipped the auto-dirigible into gear.

The vessel rose to the top of the tower.

"We got no more room, Wes!" Berta shouted over the PA. Wesley waved her on.

"Go, we'll be fine in this!" The *Explorer* turned and shot off toward the east. Wesley pulled a lever that switched the steering column from drive to float. "Eh, *maybe* we'll be fine in this. Ready, steady, *go!*" As the vehicle began to rise, a familiar voice called out.

"Emma! Wait!"

"Orrin?!" she gasped, jumping to her feet. "I... I thought I would never see you again!" He ran with astonishing speed across the terrace and leaped up onto the runner on car's left side. Clinging to the side, he leaned in and quickly kissed his paramour before thrusting a green rucksack into her hands.

"You left this in the garden." He smiled before jumping down from the car and running back to the lift. Crestfallen, Emma watched him pause by the lift entrance to look at her one last time before vanishing back into the ship. She clutched the rucksack wistfully.

"But, I didn't," she whispered, puzzled. The vehicle rose higher, then suddenly descended to the tower again.

"What's wrong? Is something wrong?" Sarah panicked.

"Look!" Wesley pointed to the lift. There stood Alexander Grimstead, bloodied and bruised.

"Alexander!" Emma cried.

"Well, I'll be damned." Sarah smiled. He hobbled his way over to the auto-dirigible and smiled up at his friends.

"Permission to come aboard?"

"Granted!" Emma exclaimed, placing the rucksack on the floor and extending both hands to her friend. "You certainly look like someone who needs a lift back ho—" Her eyes widened in shock.

"What is—?" He reached up for her, and a searing pain

exploded across his back. Emma screamed, grabbing onto Grimstead's arms as his body fell. Behind him stood Fowler, his bloodied head lolling to the side. He made a gurgled noise that sounded eerily like a laugh. Summoning what strength he had, Grimstead tried to engage his foe, but was pulled into the back seat by Emma and Sarah. The curved knife was deeply embedded in his back.

"You were warned, were you not?" gurgled Fowler's flopping head. His eyes glowed a preternatural red. Another wave of energy shook the island, this time with greater force than before. Fowler lurched forward.

"SHIT TACOS!" Wesley grabbed his Light Bringer and shattered Fowler's head with a blast. Blood gushed like a geyser from his neck while his body fell to the ground in a twitching heap.

Sarah yanked the knife from Grimstead's back and attempted to apply pressure. Emma cradled his head, as tears streamed down her cheeks.

"You... finally... shot the right person... Doctor." Grimstead smiled weakly.

"Hardy har har," Wesley replied. He holstered his weapon and sat back down behind the steering column. Finally, the auto-dirigible rose swiftly and set off toward the coast. The waves of energy steadily increased in power and frequency.

"He going to be OK?!" Wesley shouted.

"I can't stop the bleeding!" Sarah shouted back. "The wound is too deep!"

Emma held him tighter. "What about that ointment we used in the temple?"

"We don't have our gear! Even with it, the wound's too deep!" Tears began to well in Sarah's eyes. "I don't know if I can help him."

"No! *No!* I lost my father today! I refuse to lose my friend, too!"

"I'm sorry, Emma. I truly am," Sarah replied softly. Wesley

opened the steam vents to full throttle and they soared through the rippling sky.

"This isn't fast enough!" he shouted. The island, now several hundred feet below them, began to warp and distort before their eyes. The tesseract engine had begun its time-altering cycle. "We're not going to make it!"

In the distance, they spotted the exploration vessel heading back towards them at an incredible speed. It arched and rose up slowly underneath the auto-dirigible before making contact. Two metal arms came out of the top of the hull and clasped onto the car's side runners. At the helm, Berta pushed the throttle and the two vehicles swiftly flew away from the island as it shimmered in and out of sight.

"You came back for us!" Wesley cheered through Connie's communications system.

"You keep signing the checks, I'll keep saving your ass!" Berta laughed.

In the back of the car, Emma shook the Professor each time his eyes closed.

"Stay with me, Alexander!" she pleaded, "We're almost to the ship!" Grimstead gently touched his fingers to Emma's cheek, leaving two small streaks of blood. As he smiled, blood trickled from his mouth.

"It's alright. Alright. I am... at peace. Lilly...is..." Emma felt his breathing stop. His hand slowly dropped from her face. She held him close and rocked him.

"No. No, no, no, no."

As the SS *Skidbladnir* drew closer, the Island of Antillia vanished in a brilliant wave of light and vibration that shook the escaping vehicles violently. The jolts caused Emma's rucksack to slide out from under Sarah's leg.

Emma had an epiphany.

"Sarah! Hand me that bag!"

TWENTY NINE

UNIVERSITY OF CAMBRIDGE
CAMBRIDGE, ENGLAND
JUNE, 1899

EMMA MCPARLAND SQUINTED as she stepped out from the Cambridge University Library and into the midday Sun. She paused to reach into her satchel and retrieved a pair of tinted spectacles that her father had fashioned for her several years prior. She smiled as she made her way down to the waterfront, knowing that her father had taken the very same steps less than a year before. She wore a white linen shirt and khaki slacks to keep herself cool, and her hair was tucked up and completely covered by a long, cobalt blue scarf. In the distance, Emma spotted her destination. A small café, named *Jitters and Bitters*, tucked in between two larger establishments. She approached one of the café's two outdoor tables, where a man in a light gray suit and matching fedora sat with his back to her, reading a newspaper and drinking a cup of coffee. Emma plopped herself down directly across from him and snatched his cup from the saucer. She gulped down its remaining contents before slamming it back down. The man bent the top of the paper down slightly, uncovering his eyes.

"I thought we've come all this way to make good on a past theft, not partake in another," he chided. "You could have just as easily ordered one for yourself, you know."

Emma rolled her eyes. "Don't be cute, Alexander. I don't have the patience for it today."

Grimstead folded the paper in half and looked at his friend with affection. "I take it things didn't go well?"

"Go well? They threatened to have me arrested! I tried to explain to them that my father had little intention on keeping the maps indefinitely, but they wouldn't hear it. Their police arrived and I had to force the issue. Six against one. Terrible odds. For them."

"You seem no worse for the wear. I'm certain you managed to handle yourself."

"Naturally." Emma smirked. "I'm sure they won't be too quick to admit that they were bested by a woman. I doubt they'll be in pursuit. I must say that I've never felt so capable in my life. The strength, the clarity, the abilities that the golden fruit have granted me—I'm not certain I will ever get used to it."

"I suspect we now have the time to try." Grimstead turned to gaze at the throng of people—merchants and travelers—bustling about. Emma fidgeted with the empty coffee cup. They sat silently for several minutes.

"Alexander, about what happened. I know we've never really... *discussed* it. It's been quite some time now, but it's been weighing on my mind. I... I simply did what I thought was the right thing to do." She frowned. Grimstead could see the guilt in her eyes even through the tinted lenses. He reached across the table and touched her hand.

"I know."

She breathed a small sigh of relief and squeezed his hand in return.

"I'm curious, though. How did you even know that Orrin had hidden the golden apples in your bag?"

"Well, he had said that I left *my* rucksack in the garden, when we were, um, there." She blushed. Grimstead gave her a knowing smirk and they laughed softly. "I knew I hadn't brought it with us into the garden, so how could I have possibly left it? It wasn't until your last breath that I made the connection. It was selfish of me, I know. I just couldn't stand the thought of losing you after losing my father. I reached into the bag and pulled out the fruit and squeezed some of the juice into your mouth. You stirred almost immediately. It was amazing, that the juice alone was enough to bring you back from the dead. I forced the rest of the fruit down your throat and within minutes, it was... it was as if none of it happened. The bleeding stopped, the wound healed, even the cuts and bruises that you sustained during your fight—it was all healed before my eyes! It left you... nearly perfect."

"*Nearly?*"

"No sense in further inflating your rather tremendous ego." She stuck her tongue out at him.

"Then, of course, I realized there was one more apple left. And, naturally, I ate it, wanting to remain a stunning vision forever." She dramatically removed her tinted spectacles and mimed running her hand through her golden locks.

"A stunning vision indeed." Grimstead laughed, mock-bowing in reverence.

"Indeed, indeed! Now here we are, back where it all started—more or less. Strange when you think of it, the things we have learned. Do you get the feeling that it was all somehow —"

"Orchestrated?" Grimstead nodded. "As we have witnessed, the Anunnaki—*'those who from the heavens came'*—work in mysterious ways. Who could truly know what Ïsur had planned? At the very least, you and I now possess the longevity and the stamina, if you will, to find out."

Emma smiled to herself. "Immortality takes lifetimes to get used to."

"I'm sorry?"

"Ah, never mind. I just reminded myself of something." She stood and returned her spectacles to her face. "Come, my friend! There is a wedding today and I'll not miss it!"

Grimstead rose, the two linked arms and disappeared into the crowded streets.

ANGELO LAVEGLIA STOOD between The Swede and Berta wearing the blackest suit he could find. He fidgeted anxiously on the makeshift ceremonial platform that had been hastily built on the main deck of the SS *Skidbladnir*. He wasn't particularly keen on public speaking, but he was doing this as a favor to the Captain. To his left, The Swede was beaming, proudly wearing a crisp, blue uniform shirt. His was hair slicked down with a heavy coat of pomade. To Laveglia's right was Berta, looking very much the same as she always did, except now she was wearing a rather ill-fitting white gown. On the deck, the entire crew had turned out to witness the impeding nuptials. The ceremony was already ten minutes behind schedule and the natives were growing restless. Mr. Laveglia took a deep breath and then raised his hand to silence them. The crew immediately stood at attention.

"We are gathered here today for a reason you all know, so I'll just get to it." Laughter bubbled through the crowd. "Do you, The Swede, take this... *this* to be your bride? To have and to hold, etcetera etcetera until she most likely kills you in a drunken fist fight?"

"I do." The Swede looked into Berta's big green eyes and they smiled at each other. Mr. Laveglia then turned to Berta.

"Um, your breast is, um, popping out, there." He tried to point nonchalantly. Berta ungracefully hoisted her errant breast up with one hand and stuffed it back into the dress as best she could. She nodded at Laveglia. "OK! Do you, Berta, take The Swede here to be your husband and all those things I said to him just before?"

"You bet your narrow ass I do!"

"Then by the power vested in me by the good Captain Rogerson, I now pronounce you man and wife! You may kiss the—*er*—each other."

The happy couple embraced and shared their first wedded kiss to a roar of cheers. Finnbar Stratton, proudly wearing a blue shirt, whooped and cheered with Goldie and Rosie beside him. Both Thunderbirds were sporting blue bandannas around their necks. Paul Adams, wearing a dark blue suit, sat on Goldie's back like a child at the petting zoo. For once, he looked like a happy little boy.

Finnbar turned to Dr. Marrow with a laugh, "Strangest goddamned thing, this life."

"Wouldn't have it any other way, boy. Trust me on that." Marrow smiled as he took a hit from his flask. He passed it to Finnbar who happily obliged.

"What about me?" Paul extended his hand. "I save your skins and I don't get a swig?"

"Alright, alright. Stratton, toss the flask to the cherub, willya?" Finnbar obliged. Paul gulped a mouthful down and fell off Goldie's back, clutching his throat. Marrow just smiled in wicked satisfaction.

Wesley and Sarah Adams, accompanied by Professor Grimstead, Emma and Captain Rogerson stood at the back of the crowd, applauding enthusiastically. With a loud whoosh, a squadron of Adams-modified McParland auto-dirigibles—a sleeker, rocket-powered fleet—flew overhead and dropped confetti onto the revelers.

"A fantastic upgrade on the Grim-Zeppelin's design, Dr. Adams!" Emma beamed. "My father would be extremely proud."

"That's not really what they're called, is it?" Grimstead grimaced.

"Thank you, my dear. The Douglas McParland-Adams, or

McAdams, airship fleet will be the pride and joy of the American military, just you wait and see!" Wesley said, clicking his heels and saluting. "The Adams family is on their way to becoming the world's foremost, and dare I say, *richest*, science heroes the world will ever know!"

"As long as you remain on *our* side, Doctor." Grimstead added. "Your family is an integral part of our plan to bring down the Moonshield Society, and maintain balance."

"Rest assured, Alex, we're in it for the long haul."

"Speaking of plans," Rogerson interjected. "We need to focus our attention to our next task: Fowler's blond mistress. We need to find her and bring her down before she or any of her ilk get a chance to use whatever they escaped Antillia with. With that kind of power, who knows what she would be capable of?"

Grimstead nodded in agreement. "Our next order of business is figuring out *how* to track her down before she does something devastating."

"I'm pretty sure I can finagle something," Connie said as she approached the group. During her time on board the ship, Connie learned to replicate Ïsur's advanced holographic projection technology and used it to provide herself with a body. The computer was no longer just a shimmering blue head; she was now able to fully interact with the rest of the world. Connie appeared to her cohorts in full, life-like color. In homage to her former self she chose to outfit her new body in a long, shimmering blue dress.

"But enough biz-talk about the *end* times, Professor. This is a time for celebration!" Connie exclaimed. She then looked at the two at the altar and shivered. "Buh! Can you imagine the magnitude of ugly that'll be the result of those two procreating?"

"I thought you said this *wasn't* the time for apocalyptic discussion," Wesley joked.

"One catastrophe at a time, friends," Rogerson added.

"Agreed," Grimstead laughed. "On to the next adventure."

EPILOUGUE

"All the pieces are in motion, once more."

"Excellent. Everything went according to plan?"

"There were... complications."

"Variables are to be expected. Nothing too drastic, I hope?"

"That remains to be seen. Regardless, the climacteric gambit has begun. That is the priority."

"Agreed. I only hope the pieces become greater than the game."

"Time will tell. You and I know better than any."

"Indeed. Once again, I commend you on a job well done."

"Thank you."

"I will contact you soon. Be well, Lord Ïsur."

"Until next time, Hargraves."

END TRANSMISSION.

ABOUT THE AUTHOR

© Angel Sarcoma, Sarcoma Studios 2014

Peter Hammarberg resides in the New England region of Earth with his wife, Christina, and a cat named Freya. He's been called "The Patron Saint of Bourbon and Hearty Laughter," and a "Magnificent Bastard" by genuine Coney Island sideshow performers. His other published works include *The Mermaid of Maxport: A Bedtime Story for Not-So-Grownups and the Malcontent.*

His mother still swears that he was a normal pregnancy.

website: hammermountainarts.com
facebook: facebook.com/HammerMountainArts
twitter: @p_hammarberg